Excerpts from the Prayer Journals of the
Women of David

Ronda Scott Sherrill

Preface

For some years I had heard teaching and preaching to the effect that Michal was condemned eternally for despising the Holy Spirit as David danced before the Ark of the Covenant, before the Lord. Since I had been reading through the Bible each year (and still do so), I had several other pieces of Michal's life for a context into which to place her anger at David's dancing. Therefore, I did not interpret her anger as being against the Holy Spirit. I believed in defending her against what I consider an unjust charge and too-harsh judgment. I began writing her story in 1999. Using an analytical concordance, I found cross-references that revealed even more of her life and increased my empathy for her and all she had been through. It was my hope, endeavor, and prayer as I wrote that, even using my imagination to fill in what
Scripture does not reveal, my story would line up with the Bible, including nothing contradicting what had been revealed.

After I completed her story, I started working on the stories of the other two wives about which Scripture reveals more than their national origin and the son each one bore to David. So the original intention expanded to include Abigail and Bathsheba. Again, I used the analytical concordance to cross-reference each revealed fact of these two women's lives, and again I found more than I had in reading through the Bible each year.

Even though imagination is employed and extra characters were invented, the basic story line and major characters and places are as the Bible reveals, upon digging with a concordance.

The reader may disagree with the way these characters are fleshed out, at some particular point in the story that resulted from the combination of my research and imagination. That is all right. If your observation does not contradict what my cross-referencing turned up, I may well say only, "You may be right," and I may well have thought of your same objections. Today writing the stories I might change a few details here and there. The main point is to consider that these were real people and that the Bible reveals bits about them that can be a springboard for "putting ourselves into their shoes". It is never wrong to extend to them the same mercy the Lord extends to us and enjoins us to extend to those around us.

Personally, I hope to meet Michal in heaven and visit with her.

Also, Abigail and Bathsheba.

We shall see.

Excerpts from Michal's Prayer Journal
Part I: Michal and David

*   In my opinion, Dad never should have been made king. He was a fine man, before, none finer, when he was a private citizen. And he was a brave soldier. He was never made to be under all the pressure of having the whole army under him. At first, I was so proud of him. He was so tall and handsome. But it was more than that. He never wanted to be king. He ran from it. It was thrust on him. Modest, he was. And noble! Who else could have been so lenient toward those who opposed him? Yes, all was looking up, in the beginning. You, Lord, were pleased with him, the people were pleased with him. But Dad just crumbled when desertions threatened to outnumber soldiers staying for the battle, and Samuel kept not arriving to sacrifice for the Lord's blessing on the army. Where is the man who could have stood there, waiting, day after day, while the enemy army grew and his shrank? Before, it served him well when he took charge, but when he overstepped his bounds, all the

trouble began for him. My Dad, my hero, disintegrated bit by bit before my eyes. No one could stop the descent once it started, not even Mama.

*	Lord, I am so weary of war. Our enemies have provoked and harrassed us all my life, it seems; and first Dad, then Jonathan, had to go to war, over and over. Now with Dad being king, Jonathan is already pushed up higher in rank and leading a battalion into battle--at his young age. I miss him. He is such a dear brother. He always was. He knew when I needed to talk--or needed a joke to lighten my mind. I fight fear for him and Dad all the time. What would I do, Lord, if I could not pray for them? Will our enemies always lord it over us? What would it take for us to be free again? I used to be able to wander the hills, when I was not a princess. It helped. The sky, the wind, the birds, the wildflowers. Greeting the children, going to market for Mama. Now, I must not wander, must stay with the maids, hairdressers, and music tutors. Merab is in her element as a princess. Not me.

*	Lord, there is something worse than seeing Dad and Jonathan marching off to battle, and that is seeing Dad berzerk. His eyes, once so tender, now so wild, they scare me. He scares me. When did I lose the Dad I always knew? He is scared; he never was scared before. And Mama--she is consumed with worry over him. She's changed completely. Our family, our country, everywhere I turn, everything's falling apart. I hate it. I want to run and sing and feel the fresh air and have nothing to weigh me down. I want life to be simple, as when I was a child. It helps some when I make music, but it pains my poor, long-suffering teacher to listen to

my efforts. I am grateful when my teacher leaves and I can play for myself.

*   Lord, you are still here. An amazing development. The best-looking boy (man?) I ever saw has come to play harp for Dad when Dad's at his worst. He's been a shepherd and has learned his music with sheep to hear, not a teacher. And his music carried me where I am no longer free to go.   I hear in the harp, as he plays, everything I felt when I could wander the hills, free. Almost, I can forget that everything has fallen to pieces around me, when he plays on his harp. Oh, if I could only make my harp sound as he can make his sound.

And then there's Dad. He comes back to himself, starts to act whole again, for a while. I can actually see him unstiffen, his eyes turn upon us instead of in on his inner torment, when David has played that music, like none ever written by man before. Is my Dad being made whole again, as he was?

*   Lord, the days are taking on a sweetness. My heart is lighter than in ages. David plays for Dad and lifts off the madness, over and over. Oh, if only it did not return. David and Jonathan often go out together when Dad has peace and can spare David. Jonathan sees as I do, as we always have. We see David the same.

When Jonathan and David have been outdoors, they come back in such high spirits, smiles come upon every person they pass. Then David comes to play for Dad again and all the freshness and beauty of your creation is translated into that enthralling sound, the harp of David. David's music is born of the outdoors, where he has spent his life with the sheep. He even looks like the outdoors.

He speaks to the servants with respect. He speaks to Dad with respect. He bears himself with an inner assurance. He sings some with his harp. He sings of you, Lord. He knows you; it shows in all he does and says, even in his appearance.

Oh, what good is it to know my heart is being drawn to him, when I am daughter of the king, and my heart will have no say in my destiny?   But that is what is happening.

*   It is so quiet and lonely. David is back to his father's sheep, and Dad and Jonathan are back to battle. Servants bring reports. Tensions are mounting. No one has struck yet, just a standoff, while a giant champion of the Philistines challenges any soldier of ours to meet him one on one. None of ours will come forth. Who can blame them? Who would go to a sure death, and bring a sure defeat upon our people? They say he is half again as big as any normal man, and his weapons likewise oversized. No one has a chance against such odds. Of course our soldiers are paralyzed in fear.

Lord, only you can deliver our people. Which is worse, to wait here with time almost suspended, or to wait on the battlefield, slinking in shame from the impossible challenge?

*   Lord, I do not believe my own ears. The giant is dead. One man, and you with him, went forth. He even chose to place greater odds against himself, disdaining to wear armor or carry arms, only a slingshot. A slingshot! To bring down a fully armed giant! It had to be the power of God. Your anointing, Lord. Who was the man? The messenger had not heard yet. If only it could have been

Dad, yet my heart is sure it was not. Maybe in the old days, he could have. Not any more. Was it Jonathan?

*   Another messenger arrived. The battle is raging. Our army's total paralysis is turned to total fury and force. Goliath is dead; hope is alive. Lord, protect our men and boys. Deliver our people from bondage to the enemy. Set us free. Let it be, Lord. Your people were made to serve you, Lord, not a foreign power. ...And Lord, spare Dad and Jonathan.   ...I'm going back to the wall to wait with Mama and Merab, and the servants.

*   Lord, a wonder beyond imagining. It was David, David who slew the giant. David, the sweet singer who can capture in his song the wonder of your vast creation, David who alone can restore some peace and good sense to my tortured father, this same David to whom my heart is pledged beyond recall--he it is who was there only to bring food to his older brothers, yet took up his shepherd's slingshot and went in your power and conquered the unconquerable champion of our enemies, the giant on whom they cast all their hopes for our final and total subjection. I knew that he knew you, Lord, but, oh, the extent of what it means to know you, that I did not realize. If David can do this, go from watching sheep to the greatest battle feat of all time, nothing is impossible to one who abides in you. Oh, glory, glory.

*   A great victory is won. Everyone is home. Dad has asked David's father to release him to live here all the time. I can barely think of it. David here, all the time. Maybe a princess could never marry a shepherd, but a

mighty warrior. Surely! Oh, what am I thinking? I must be realistic.

After dinner, Jonathan asked me to walk in the garden. We walked past the ears of servants, and all his talk was of David. He and David cut a blood covenant! They are brothers forever. They exchanged weapons and clothing and heart and soul. Jonathan would even rather David be king in his place, one day, so full is he of the praise of David's valor, wisdom, and depth of character. "He's a man of substance, Michal. He's anointed by God," Jonathan said, "I would gladly give my right to the throne to one more worthy than I."

Lord, only you and I and Jonathan heard what was said. But the covenant they made will be known by all the world one day. I am sure of this. Yet I dream, I who do not care for being a princess, dream of being married to a man sure to be a king. Oh, but it is the man I wish to marry. What do I care whether he is shepherd or king? He is David.

*   Dad has been giving orders and David has done everything well. There have been more battles, all going well for Israel, David leading a whole battalion. Dad is pleased with him. The servants and people on the street have been talking of David, David, David. Crowds have been filling the streets. Today was the celebration of these battles won, the parade, and all-around day of jubilee. I started today in highest spirits, not alone, that is sure. All our people were exultant. With joy I heard the singing women praising my father, their king. Then, with increasing shock, I heard them sing greater praises to David, who carried the victory. A chill went through me. I have seen my father's eyes these last months. They are

an open window to a mind that is all wrong. Can he handle the people's hearts putting David first? Oh, what is to come next? Lord, protect us all, especially Dad and David. Inside, my joy turned to a frozen landscape of fear. On the outside, I kept up the smile and the appearance of joy.

Surely, when David plays his harp, it will be as before when he played and brought a right spirit again to Dad. David has brought good to Dad in private, and now this huge victory for the record of his reign. Let this be enough. Let this good overpower even whatever power takes hold of Dad's mind, even as a slingshot overpowered a fully armed giant.

*   Jonathan again has come to walk with me in the garden where we can be alone. Dad has hurled his javelin to kill David, not once, but twice, and David has avoided, but narrowly. Dad is a sure shot, at least in his right mind, and as he used to be. I think he would have killed David without your anointing upon David's life. But, Lord, where can it go from here? And how did it get here? How can Dad turn upon one who brought him so much good, nothing but good. David has done nothing to bring this wrath up in Dad. It is all wrong. What more could go wrong? Oh, Lord, protect David, and, Lord, restore his right mind to my father.

*   David is gone again to war with the Philistines. There is no one to play the soul-changing music. Meals with Dad are horrible. He is absent from us, as we have always known him. More and more he seems a madman. I watch the change in Mama, too, and feel almost an

orphan. Merab shows fear in her eyes, but we do not talk. Only Jonathan and I, when he is here, can speak openly.

*   Oh, God, my heart is breaking. It is too much. David is back, but only for a moment. Dad has sent him to kill a quota of Philistines to win the hand of Merab in marriage. Why Merab? She has never thought of David! What does she know of music--or anything of his soul? She only wants to marry a prince and live with luxury. It is I who have David in my heart. I shall surely spill my heart to Jonathan. He is all I have of family now. I shall never marry if I cannot marry David. No royal edict can overrule my heart's loyalty. Merab to marry David! Horrible! God, have you left me, and forgotten me, letting my heart be trampled until it can never be whole again? Come and make things right.

*   The wedding date is set. David is back. I see now that Dad thought he would never return, never fulfill the impossible quota of enemies slain. But he has. His whole life is a wonder. And all that is to be given in marriage to the wrong woman. Where can I run to hide from the sight?

*   God, the most amazing thing has happened. Mama came to my bed in the night to comfort me. How did she know? She said she has seen it in my eyes. Have I been so transparent? Who else has seen? Has David? Oh, what must he think of me? But Mama was so sweet. She wept. I know it was for Dad and the change in him. But it was also for me, oh, for all that could have been--should have been--and can never be. We wept together. She has gone. I must see if I can get any sleep tonight.

*   Oh, Lord, another wonder. Merab came, after Mama, to weep with me. She, too, has seen it in my eyes. She does care for me as a sister, as different as we are, but she is helpless before a king's pronouncement. She asked me to forgive her. It is not Merab I have to forgive, but Dad. And she is in the same position. And Mama is, too. Merab said, "Oh, Michal, I do not want David. He is so intense, he scares me." But, Lord, that is what I love in him. Everyone is miserable. I do not know that any of us is sleeping tonight. The whole world has gone mad, it seems.

*   Lord, you are still here. Suddenly Merab is being married to another. Dad is breaking his promise to David. My father has turned faithless. Lord, I see that he has gone from you, and you have gone from him. You have revoked his calling to be king. It is only a matter of time. But how long will this drag on? How low will he go? And what is to happen with David? God, help us all.

*   Merab came to my bedroom in the night again, crying, but fiercely rubbing the tears off her cheeks with her fists. I just listened, gave her hugs, and waited till she seemed spent. His name is Adriel. At last I told her gently, "At least, his name means 'honor of God'. He can't be all bad, and maybe he will be good to you. Oh, I do hope so, Merab. And you know he is well off; Dad picked him." She laughed. She is moving miles from here, to Issachar, where his inheritance is. We know nothing of that tribe. One whole life is dropping off her and another one will greet her, in only days. Life is so full of surprises. She was not crying by the time she left

my bedroom to go see Mama. Go with her, Lord. Who knows whether we shall ever meet again?

*   Time is passing. Life goes on. More of the same. They go off to battle; they come home. I thank you each time that they come back alive. My own life seems at a standstill. I wait upon your plan, Lord. Grant me trust. And patience.

*   Lord, I am too stunned to feel the joy that I would be feeling now, otherwise. Now Dad has made another promise to David. For a dowry of 100 foreskins of dead Philistines, David can become the king's son-in-law yet-- by marrying ME! Jonathan put the idea to Dad, I know it. Is it possible? Is Dad only scheming to turn ME to another marriage at the last moment, too? What is real here? And David is gone again. Oh, keep him safe. One hundred of the enemy to slay. One man.

What does it all mean to David? Does he want me, or only to be son-in-law to the king? I know. I know David. He wants your will.   Oh, so do I. I cannot think any more. Your will alone. That is all.

*   David is back with not one hundred, but TWO hundred Philistine foreskins, and only his chosen band of men went into enemy territory with him. Oh, I shudder to think of the danger he was in. But you have kept him once again, Lord, and brought him to be my husband. My husband. What music to say those words.

Jonathan talked with him and then with me again in the garden. David is joyful and exultant and eager, Jonathan said. Eager, for me. Oh, after all these months of ups and downs, I must be faster to soak in all the rapture that is mine: the marriage I have wanted is the one that I will have. I would that I had more time to revel in anticipation, but my father is moving fast. The wedding is upon me, that I never thought could ever be. I cried for joy before Jonathan. I know he is carrying to David a report of talking with me, and I thought, "Now David will know what a silly girl his wife is." Then Jonathan told me David cried for joy, too. Oh, we are one in our souls. I knew it all along. I feel my soul will burst. It is an overflowing torrent of joy when dreams and truth unite.

*   Earlier today, I looked at pretty clothes longer than I ever have before, wondering what David would like me to wear, choosing and rejecting one after another of the garments the giggling servant girls have brought for my decision. I have endured too many hairdo's fussed over by hairdressers harder to please than I am. Finally, after the servants left me to go to bed, I could express myself before you, Lord. I have danced and leaped and sung and shouted for joy, and I have fallen motionless upon my bed between times. I have sobbed for joy, I have laughed and laughed, and I have smiled into the dark, wide-awake with excitement. I have fallen on my knees to thank you a thousand times over for your wonder-working. For surely this cannot have happened other than by your working another wonder. Shall the bride sleep any the night before her wedding? I fear you will have to work another wonder, Lord.

*   Lord, you know you have been in my heart and thoughts all along, but this past week has not allowed me to draw aside with my pen and scroll. It has been too full. But I shall surely burst if I do not let out here with you

some of the fullness overflowing my heart. You are so wise. You made Eve for Adam, and me for David. Nothing could be more right. David is playing softly upon his harp now so that I might have this time I need. By the time I have done, he will probably have another psalm composed, himself.

All week, afternoons and into the evenings, we have been in the whirl, the crowds, dancing, eating, drinking, laughing, and David going amongst them in perfect ease. Is there anyone in the kingdom who does not love David? If so, that one stayed home. Such a time of joy and a wonderful break from daily duties--and war. David brings comfort to those who have lost sons and husbands, fathers and brothers, in the recent battles. He takes a moment for each and enters into their situations--loss or grief or, for some, pride in some battle feat of some young Samuel or Josiah, or some more homespun story of local events. It is real, he is genuine, he does care for our people. Sometimes I mingle in the crowds with him, other times draw aside to watch him and visit with Mama and Merab and a few old girlfriends from old days.

Merab is doing all right with Adriel. I am so glad of that. And she looks good in maternity clothes. It is so good to see her again, for this once at least. Adriel stands by, beaming in the background, proud and protective of Merab and her condition. I see in her a gain in depth. She has her prince, and his provision is all the luxury she wanted. And I, who never wanted a prince, have my prince.

For now, I am not thinking of the increasing darkness of Dad's countenance as he broods, set aside from the people. Were ever two men in such contrast?

Finally, when I think I have no more energy for this social scene and long for our time alone, at the end of the evening, David and I are at last free of the last servant. My energy returns; his has never been depleted. And we have our life together--all I could ever have dreamed of and so much more. We have everything to discover of each other's soul, mind, feelings, memories, body. And we are one in every way, just every single way.

We are allowed our mornings too, the servants waiting until we call. David is awake long before I am. Incredible energy level! I awaken slowly to his soft harp melodies after his quiet time. David is teaching me on my harp, how to evoke from it some of what he evokes from the strings of his harp. But we both know I will never come near to his skill--oh, it's much more than mere skill. It's the depth of his soul. But my soul responds to his as he plays and sings. My union with David is deepening along with my love for you, Lord. I worship you, and I really am nearer to expressing what I want to when I take up my harp. And have more within me to express, from being near David. And I am content with that.

I am content with everything. The week of wedding festivities is almost over, and only you know what my father's orders to David will be. But I set my will to keep this far from touching our present rapture. It would be wrong of me to have a worry when everything is so right. I do, we both do, give you the glory for all your good gifts. I will trust you with the days to come for us. I will. I promise.

*   Lord, I praise you for "ordinary" days, if ever days are ordinary in such extraordinary times as these. David has duties with the army, drilling and training, duties with

the king, playing his harp when Dad is upset, which is becoming more and more the ordinary event for him. Most days we are able to have the noon meal together. Some afternoons we have time for a ride out on horses. Oh, I love that. Or a walk in the garden. Of course, David still goes out with Jonathan, too. We have the evening meal with the king and the family, and whatever guests are there with the king. Later we have our own evening time, our nights alone, and late breakfast together.

Besides Dad's increasing madness, there are rumors of the enemy building up again for battle. David and I are able to speak of the concerns of our hearts, but we are not overwhelmed by them. We choose to be overwhelmed with our love, while we can. And always, behind it all, the horrible and the precious, the fearsome and the glorious, we worship you, Lord. We are singing together the psalms of David's own composing, my harp a weak accompaniment to his--my harp, and my heart. We pray together without the music as well as in it. The spiritual ecstasy and the physical ecstasy that we experience together--what can I say? Life is full of eternity.

*   The moment I have willed never to come is upon us. David marches with the army to war tomorrow morning. Of course, Dad and Jonathan are off as well. I once thought I knew fear for my own, when they went to war. But how can I cope with the wrenching away of my own flesh and soul, my own sweet husband, my beloved David...   God sustain us, protect him to come home whole, and God hasten the day when this war is over for good.

*   In the night David was entirely with me. This morning he was entirely with his army and his duties. I understand, even admire, but I am so alone. If ever I thought I was alone before, I was mistaken. This is so much deeper. Then I began to wonder. Is there within me a child of his, of ours, to mitigate my aloneness in some way? It would be like you, Lord, to leave me with a tangible comfort, although your Spirit is all but tangible in me, many times. I weep and I wonder, as I watch the army from the wall, David on his horse a tiny speck before his men. Mama and I cling for a moment to each other and then watch again till all are out of sight. I remonstrate with myself, all absorbed in David marching away, our first separation, when Mama has experienced this so many times. I know now more what she has endured. But the worst of it is that her husband has been destroyed before her eyes, while he is still with her physically. I must not even think of David ever going mad, being absent in his essence while present only in body. Oh, my poor Mama. I must be with her more, now that we have only each other, of our family, left, as long as this war is on.

*   Once more messengers bring reports. David's battalion is victorious, every time. Not so with the others. Sometimes they win, sometimes they are defeated. David is a master military strategist, the messengers report, and all his men would go anywhere he ordered them, do anything. Morale is high, where David is. Ah yes, I know, I know.

But what of Dad? The messengers have almost nothing to say of him. What of Jonathan? Dad and Jonathan are still alive, but the news is all of David.

*   Lord, it is a comfort to know David is so loved by his men, and so wise in battle strategy, and our army is growing stronger.   But at the same time, are these accomplishments of David's driving my father farther into his insane jealousy? Lord, this is it! It is insecurity. My Dad, who was never meant to be a king at all, is insecure. Every downfall of his, every sin, I must call it, is rooted in insecurity. Lord, what harm is brought into so many lives by one man's insecurity! Protect me from ever indulging thoughts of insecurity. I set my will to run from them, should they arise. My position is secure in you, Lord. This is the same assurance in which David walks. May it ever be so.

*   Lord, another realization. If David is leading so many battle victories, it means he is placing himself directly in the path of the enemy--and of potential death at their hands. Lord, bring him home whole to me. Now that I have known our union, how could I live without him?--here I am, just after realizing my position is secure in you, asking how could I live without him. Stabilize my poor woman's changeable feelings, please, Lord. It is such a trial to wait on a war.

*   A break in the war, for the seasons. They are home again, my three men, all alive and well. What a reunion, mine all joy, Mama's so troubled. David is full of praise, and more of his blessed psalms, giving you glory for the defeat of the enemy. He believes the Philistines cannot hold out much longer. They are as good as defeated, only they have not admitted it. They are regrouping. One

more campaign, another season, David says, and we will be free of Philistine domination.

He will have training of the troops each day, after a time of respite; and meantime, we have the most time we have ever had to ourselves, since Dad is not calling him to play on his harp for him. We do not speak much of the future. It is too uncertain. But I do know that David would like a son. I wonder, Why is there no son on the way?

David and Jonathan, too, have more time together than ever before. They enjoy archery practise and the outdoors together. They are as close as born brothers. Sometimes Jonathan has his dinner with us. We are not speaking much of Dad. He is the source of so much of the uncertainty. Just the mention of him brings tension into the air around us. We avoid the subject. Same with Mama; was ever a woman in more pain? We are as orphans.

* Lord, today David rushed in from his meeting with Jonathan, and, staring intently at me, then grabbing me in a crushing hug to his chest, desperately croaked out, "Michal," as if on the verge of breaking down. "David! What is it?" I asked. But he only held me close, breathing hard as from running. Finally, I wrapped my arms around him, too, and we stood there a long moment. Then he stood back. "Michal," he spoke with low but intense tones, "Jonathan just told me the king has ordered him, and also some servants, to kill me." I clasped on to him in horror. He drew me near again, and spoke into my hair over my ear. "Jonathan believes I must go into hiding for a day while he seeks time to try to reason with Saul. Reason!" he hissed. "There is no reasoning with

that man." He shook his head as if to clear his thoughts, shuddering. "Michal, listen carefully. I must be gone for a day. Regardless of what happens, I will come back to let you know. You know that I love you." I could barely speak. "I know, and I, you." "Yes," he said, "My precious wife. I could have been given no better." Then, springing into action, "Help me throw some things together. I'll be sleeping out tonight." A moment later, and he was gone, with a last, long kiss, and a wrenching away.

*   Who will come for me first, Jonathan or David, to let me know what happens? I pray for your wisdom for Jonathan, your power on behalf of David, the innocent, your healing in my father, the crazed and tormented one, the destroyed one, scarcely an empty shell of the man he was before he was a king, the man I cannot forget, but mourn as if a death has occurred. Indeed, it has.

Oh, David, where are you tonight? Where can you go if...   I set my will not to finish the awful thought, and I went to my harp and played softly, slowly. I vowed, "I will not sleep until I hear."

*   Jonathan found me, sleeping fitfully on the floor beside my harp. He had no time to wait. "Michal, I talked to Dad. I spoke softly, listing all the good David has done for him, and for all Israel, always bringing it back to Dad and what David's deeds have meant to his kingdom and his reign--the giant slain, the battles won, the strengthening of our army and the weakening of the Philistine army, all the times Daved risked his life, faithful in Dad's service. At first, I was not sure he could even hear through what goes on inside his own head, but

then he almost went limp. Michal, he gave me his word," Jonathan repeated each word separately, as in a pronouncement, "he gave me his word, swearing as the Lord lives, that David will not be slain."

Now it was my turn to go limp. Jonathan clasped me and held me up, holding me close as he finished, "Michal, I will report to David by daybreak. I must go try to rest some, myself. You must rest, too. Goodbye, sweet sister. Oh, how hard this is for you."

"For you, too, Jonathan," I said, "You love him, too--both of them."

"Yes," he answered. And he was gone.

*	Once again, David is home. Dad is calling him to play the harp in the throne room, or wherever he is, different places. In appearance, it is as old times, but the appearance has not brought assurance to my heart. But David is near, and if anything, our prayers and our love--everything between us, is more intense than ever, having as a background the terrible uncertainty of David's position. I am reminded again, Lord, of that insight of months ago, that our position in life is safe in your hands. Let the peace of that knowledge penetrate. Increase my trust, I pray. Let me absorb enough for me and David both. He sings now of great need for you, and the triumph over enemies only you can give to him. He is still strong, but he is being tried.

*	The home interval has been terminated again by war. David, the faithful, has gone to battle heading his troops for King Saul and for Israel. This time he said to me before he left, "Michal, something is about to be decided. The Philistines, the war, your father, all is coming to a

head. Whatever happens, know that I love you. In other times, we could have...” His thought was not finished. He had to go. Each time seems harder.

Philistine women, too, send their husbands, sons, fathers and brothers off to war. But they have only deaf and dumb gods of stone to ignore them. What would I do without you to be my strength, precious Lord....

*   A mighty victory has been won, led by David. So many Philistines have been slaughtered; are they ready to call themselves defeated? Surely it must be near.

David has come home. He plays for Dad, the evil spirit so strong David feels no lifting as he plays. Lord, help us all.

*   Today, Lord, David barely dodged another javelin thrown by Dad at him as he played his harp. The javelin had such force behind it that it remained in the wall after David ran out; Jonathan saw it. Dad sent messengers to the front of our house shortly after David came running in. I told him he had to leave and go away or he would be killed by tomorrow. There were no guards behind the house yet then, but there would have been soon had he delayed. I could hardly bear to let him go, but his life must be spared. You have a destiny upon him, Lord, and being killed by my father is not part of it.

We made a rope of bedclothes and fastened it to a door inside and he climbed down. I watched him run, after we had waved a last kiss to each other. When will I see him again? Oh, Lord, how long?

After he had left, I quickly arranged an image in the bed and a pillow of goats’ hair and covered it all to appear as if David were asleep there.

When the messengers came from the king, it was not hard for me to act distressed. I cried, I folded my body in two and wrung my hands, and told how sick and feverish he was, that I was afraid he had a deadly fever. They fled in fear.

When they left, I collapsed beside the bed, my arm on my supposed husband, and cried myself to sleep, sitting there, crying to you, Lord, for David, wherever he is, to be safe, alive, for all this madness to be over forever.

* I had slept only a short time when more messengers than before arrived in a storm of noise, stomping and shouting orders, taking up the bed and declaring that King Saul will kill the sick David in his bed. Two of the guards took my arms and dragged me along as well. I was brought before the throne of King Saul. I will never say Dad again. No Dad can keep that name and do what he has done to his children. He may be my king, but he is not my father. He showed no knowledge of me as his child. He raged at me. I was trembling all over, so afraid he would kill me, since he wanted to kill David and was thwarted. My body jerked so that I sank to the floor at his feet. He raged on. "Why have you deceived me so?" he shouted in a voice not his own. "Why have you sent away my enemy and allowed him to escape?" His enemy! How dare he! But this madman would dare anything, even to kill me. Lord, I lied for my life, not to my Dad. I have no father. To this crazy king with whom our country is cursed. I cried out, "He told me he would kill me if I tried to stop him." How preposterous! I said what I thought in my distraught state that I had to say, anything to get away from that man.

I was not allowed to return to David's and my house. My king sent away all my familiar and trusted servants. I was in an isolated room under guard. Food was brought in. Mama was not to come to see me. But before these things were all settled, she slipped through and brought my harp, pen, ink, and scrolls, and--a wonder and a blessing--a copy of the Books of Moses. She stayed long enough to say that she would always pray for me, whether she ever saw my face again or not. She reminded me that my name means "Who is like God?" and enjoined me to keep that question before me through whatever comes. One last hug, and she was gone. Will I ever see her again?

I am sure that the king never meant for me to hear a word of David, but I overheard the guards saying that David was with Samuel at Naioth in Ramah. Dear, wise, good, old Samuel. Months into our marriage David had confided in me that Samuel had come in secret to his father Jesse's house to anoint the next king since King Saul had lost the kingdom for his posterity in his gross act of disobedience in performing the priest's function. David, baby of the family, like me, only with seven older brothers, had not even been invited to the feast for the great prophet, but had been left with the sheep as always. Jesse told David later that Samuel had waited upon the Lord over each son, starting with the oldest, and had grown more serious as the Lord said No to each one. Finally, he asked if these were all the sons, and Jesse sent a servant to call David from the sheep, while the banquet food waited. He'd had no time even to clean up. As David came to him, Samuel had heard immediately from the Lord that David was the chosen son. The older brothers had been harder than ever on David after that, even though David took no different actions, but went back to herding sheep--until being called to play harp, and then, of course, Goliath. So now, it was to Samuel, who knew of David's intended position before God and all Israel, that David turned in his affliction. Samuel would know what to do. This is some comfort to me in these days.

Lord, forgive me, but I also long for the most tangible comfort I can think of, since David cannot contact me. Let me bear his son, Lord; let me have this much of David.

*   Lord, so many of your answers to my prayers now have been No. Why does this one have to be No, also? Oh, I am not the one to question the Almighty. But, Lord, this is very, very hard. But, as David would do, I praise you for what I do have, Lord, my harp, my memories, my position, wife of David, even if not mother of his child. I must find a cause to praise you, Lord, I must not let myself be destroyed. I must be strong for David, pray for him, more than for myself, and believe that one day it will be made right, somewhere, someday, somehow. And, Lord, one thing more. I ask to hear the news of David.

*   Lord, I stand in awe of you. Let me never whimper doubt again. I heard news--that King Saul sent messengers to take David, and they fell amongst the prophets and they, too, came under the Holy Spirit's power and prophesied, instead of proceeding on with their orders from their lesser king. You are King of kings. Your will for David will prevail.

*   Lord, again! It all happened as the last time! Saul's servants all prophesying again.

*   Lord, yet again! And this time King Saul himself went after David, and fell under the power of your Holy Spirit and was unable even to get to David, much less to take him.

David is safe in you, Lord, until he comes into your plan for him.

How long, oh Lord?

But I wait in hope, not in despair. Even as far gone as King Saul is, you spoke through him that day. Nothing is beyond you to accomplish, Lord. Shall my king be restored to my father?

*   Lord, though King Saul tried to be sure my guards were loyal to him alone, they all love Jonathan, and let him through to speak with me, even withdrawing a bit from us, as he did. Jonathan had gotten a trusted messenger through to David and arranged a secret meeting. David told Jonathan he is still hoping that King Saul will turn from his murderous intent, it is so hard to believe he can stay in a plan so insane. David cried out to Jonathan, "What have I done, that King Saul would want to kill me?" Jonathan told David that he is sure King Saul would not keep any plan from his own son. But David thinks the king has caught on by now that he has special favor in Jonathan's eyes, so that Saul won't tell Jonathan any more. David is sure that his life is in danger. His plan is that he will absent himself from dinner at the new moon, something he has never done before, so Jonathan can observe and report back to David the king's reaction. Jonathan is to tell the king that David went to Bethlehem

at the request of his family to have new moon time with them.

Jonathan said, "Michal, I reminded David of his covenant with me so that when all his enemies are defeated, he will be kind to my descendants, leaving me a line to carry on my name, for I know that King Saul is on the way out, and David will be next king, not me." I said, "Oh, Jonathan, how is all this to come about? What awful times we live in."

"Michal, I will come to you to let you know what is happening, every time I have the chance, but as to how long I will be able, I cannot say. Now, I will meet David the third day at the stone Ezel and tell him all I know."

Neither of us dared to say more of what could be the fate of any of us and what events could happen to prevent Jonathan getting through to me. A person can take in only so much at a time. And everything is so uncertain. How we need your help, Lord.

* Jonathan just came and left quickly, was here just long enough to let me know that now the king's anger has extended to him. It started at the second night of new moon dinners, with Dad raging at Jonathan for preferring David to Jonathan's own welfare. He shouted, "Don't you know you won't ever be king if David lives?" Then when Jonathan defended David as innocent before the king, our father threw his javelin at his own son. Jonathan fled then, in the middle of the meal, came here, and tomorrow morning will urge David into exile for his life's sake. How I long to go with Jonathan and into exile with David. It cannot be. I am under heavy guard. Now I have fears for my dear brother as well as for David, and

for myself, and for when I shall ever be with my husband again, where I belong.

Lord, I remember setting my will to trust you. I will require your grace and strength to keep that vow. You know I am not able on my own. Lord, may my own harp, as I play and sing to you, lift my soul to you as my father once was lifted out of his madness when David played to you.

*   Lord, after some weeks with no news, my guard is being changed over, this group leaving to go with the king to track David and some 400 followers he's training to be his own army. This is what I picked up from the talk as the new guards came on. David's parents he placed in asylum in Moab. That's where I should be, too, not here with his enemy. He's been moving around, evidently feeling unsafe in any nearby country as well as in ours, but now is reported hiding in the cave of Adullam in Judah. Meanwhile King Saul ordered the slaughter of all the priests of Nob simply because Ahimelech in innocence gave David food and Goliath's sword weeks ago when David first left. Not only have Merab, Jonathan and I no father, but Israel has no king. This sickening act of treachery against your priests, Lord, cannot be lifted off him by any harp's playing. We are all bereft. What loss, what destruction. What a broken kingdom David shall inherit one day when your plan is brought to pass, in some way I cannot now foresee. But I fear we have more horrors to pass through on the way, inescapably. Eighty-five priests dead for no reason, slaughtered in cold blood, defenseless. Only one escaped to David's protection. I staggered at the news as if in physical illness. How many more must die before we have our rightful king? I say

rightful king, but I know you were meant to be our king, and all this is why. Only you are capable of governing your people, Lord. You're the true king. Among men, David is your choice now. Let it be. Soon.

*	Lord, as the guard changed this evening, I overheard that David and his army (about 600 men now) fought the Philistines and saved the city of Keilah, and now King Saul is heading out with his army to Keilah to take David. Lord, protect David.

*	Lord, again I hear through the guards that King Saul is still after David, only he is moving around the forests, the hill of Hachilah, plains of Maon--all that area, and the Ziphites are aiding Saul. Lord, may King Saul never find David.

*	Weeks, months, are going by and my life is nothing but waiting. I wait to hear what is happening out there. Nothing is happening around me, only sameness, my harp, my pen, my only company. And you, Lord.

*	Lord, King Saul and his army are returning from pursuing David because the Philistines are invading again. If David were still with our king, where he wanted to be, the Philistine threat would be over by now. Oh, foolish king, giving over your throne to fears that are unfounded.

*	The guards are saying that the battle is over and King Saul is coming back here--no clue as to whether the battle was a defeat or a victory.

*   All these months of nothing happening and I thought I could not bear it. But there is always something worse that can happen. Now I am numb. But before I could put pen to scroll, I have endured the greatest anguish yet. I am ordered to be ready to leave tomorrow morning to be married to another--all part of this madman's revenge against David. I am not to be allowed to wait for David. This destroyed king must destroy all around him. He thinks if he cannot kill David outright, he can make him want to die--violating our marriage and the bond you put together, Lord.

I repeat what I said before I knew I would ever be allowed to marry David: no royal edict can command or change my loyalty. I am David's wife. No thought can be more repugnant to me than being forced to marry another.

Lord, I repeat, too, my prayer. Let me hear news of David.

Oh, Lord, protect and comfort me. I would rather this king had ordered my death. But you have ordained the harder task. Give me grace to trust in you, in all this chaos to trust that you are still there.

And go with David.

And   thank   you   for   the   time   we   had.

Excerpts from Michal's Prayer Journal
Part II: Michal and Paltiel

*   *His name is Paltiel,* I kept telling myself, as we jolted along, on the way here to Gallim, in Benjamin, where I would be living with him. *Paltiel means, "God delivers."* How opposite, it seems to me, is deliverance from what I am being taken to.   Not deliverance, but the worst bondage. *I am already married,* I told myself, *I cannot be married. But yes, dear soul, if the king says so, anything can be.* Then I tried again, to encourage myself as I had tried to encourage Merab with the meaning of Adriel's name, *His name is Paltiel, "God delivers."* Oh, God, can there be a deliverance for me in this travesty? My heart is forever loyal to my husband, David.

Riding along, I brought up the memories--painfully precious ones of our marriage; monotonous ones of my months, stretching into more than a year, of isolation, by order of King Saul; horrible ones of the announcement of the king's intent for me, the physical agony, the alien sounds I heard coming from deep within me, that I never heard before, the lifelessness that overtook my whole body, the most hopeless and helpless feelings of all my life, worse than the worst I had experienced in seeing my father destroyed by madness, in hearing David was to marry Merab, then later in sending David, my husband, off to battle so many times, and finally to exile. Always, I found hope in you, Lord. I am not able to hope, now. I have not the energy. Like a dripping of a leak from rain, a voice in my head repeated, "His name is Paltiel, 'God delivers'," and I found what small comfort I could in the sound itself, since meaning escaped me.

I had not slept or eaten much and my body ached from the jolting of the beast under me. It seemed such a long trip.

At last we were there--here!--and a man, a large man, surely Paltiel himself, came forward. What I could see of his face as he saw me showed a sudden horror. I was vaguely aware of being lifted and laid into a bed.

When I awoke this morning, the sun was well toward the noon hour. A servant girl was spreading a meal on the small table near my bed. The room was lovely. The food smelled so inviting. I think the aroma is what awakened me. The servant bowed, murmuring that the food was mine to enjoy, and left. I was relieved to find that I was alone, and even more relieved to find my harp, pen and ink, scrolls, and the books of Moses nearby. I ate, and have been writing and shall write as long as I can.

Lord, I am like one of the flowers I have seen after too long without rain, out in the heat and sun, bent over, crumpled and crisp, instead of juicy with life, all but dead. Is there to be a rain for me? This food, my own dearest possessions close by, this lovely room, being left alone, perhaps these are the first mercy drops. Send a shower, Lord. I am dying.

I look around the room. There is light coming in from several windows. On the window sills are blooming plants, some of which send out a fragrance I am noticing for the first time since my meal is eaten. I hear some children playing in the street below, calling to one another and laughing. How long has it been since I heard children laughing--any laughter at all?

The bedcovers are the most luxurious fabrics and scented with wildflower scents, lovely colors, some pale, some purple with red cord trim. Perhaps I shall lie down again and pull them up around my face and rest.

*　　Lord, what a shock! I awoke to the sound of a man's voice, speaking softly my name. "Michal." I gasped with a shriek of fright, and I jerked away, turning my back to him as I did so, and pulling the covers around me, wrapping them with my arms folded in front of me. I could sense him rising to his feet from where he had been kneeling beside my bed. He spoke so softly and gently to me, and slowly, with a sweetness I could not push away, "Michal.....you have been through so much; I will give you time. Whatever you want, only let the servants know, and you shall have it. You have been brought here to be my wife, but I will not try to touch you before it is time. Let it never be said of Palti that he is a harsh husband. I am here to do the loving thing by you. I am your servant."

There was grief and pain in that voice, not only sweetness. He suffered. I could not think, then, whether his suffering was for me or for himself, but it was unmistakeably a suffering that laced his gracious speech.

I sensed, more than heard, first his hand raised over me as if to stroke my head, then being drawn back, and finally, his soft footsteps going out.

I slept again.

*　　This morning there were fresh flowers in a vase on the small table, along with some fresh rolls and fruit and cheese. A cruse of water stood beside. I started with a long drink, and ate with hungry haste, noticing that the dawn was still in progress. I tiptoed to the window to watch my first dawn in many months. I don't know how

long I stood there, just breathing deeply, looking, and listening to the birds' dawn chorus. Lord, you are here, too.

I freshened myself with the water bowl and cloths that were placed on another table in the room, watching for servants to come, but I was mercifully still alone.

I picked up my harp and played some psalms, starting with plaintive psalms of pleading for your presence, and finally, even some psalms of praise for your creation. But I did not sing. I played slowly, not trying to arouse my heart.

A servant girl brought lunch, and, seeing me up and hearing the end of a psalm, smiled shyly at me. "I am Anna, your handmaid," she said in musical tones, with almost laughter just under the surface sound. "Shall I brush your hair--such beautiful hair. I can wait until you have eaten, if you wish."

"Thank you, Anna, yes, come back in a few minutes."

She gave a quick bow and left. As if she knew when I was finished with lunch, she appeared and gently brushed my hair, with no talk, but a melody hummed lightly. It was refreshing.

"May I sit outdoors?" I asked on an impulse, as she finished, and followed her as she led me out to some stairs to the roof. On the roof, she indicated a divan, "Master Palti placed this here for you." Anna whispered, and left.

I reclined and dozed in the sunlight. When I came back in, I went for my pen. Lord, the shower I prayed for...thank you, Lord. I have some juice of life in these wilted leaves now. No blooming, oh no; that is a long way off. But I thank you for this much.

*   In the evening, Paltiel came in. His steps were long and slow. He pulled up a chair beside my own. I had found a chair placed in the room for me, just in front of a curtain in one corner forming a dressing area. This chair was where I had played my harp, and the harp sat beside me now. I was glad I had finished and set it down before he came in. It is for me alone, now that David...

I looked down, but not before I saw a slight smile on his gentle face, and noticed his eyes approving the advance in me since he saw me the evening before. He knows a wilted plant from one after rain. But I am not ready for his approval.

"Is there anything you need?" he asked.

"No, thank you. It is all so lovely." I stopped. "Thank you for the roof chair." It came out of me, unbidden. I looked down at my hands, where my fingers were knotting up a handkerchief.

He laughed, a very small laugh for such a big man. I wonder what his work is. "The view is good from the roof in all directions," he said. "Sunrises and sunsets are my favorite times to be there."

He was quiet. What a lot of patience this man has. Finally, "Would you like to go up to see the sunset?"

"No," I cried with alarm.

"Maybe someday," he spoke slowly, "before too long. You have been alone so long, it must be hard to come out."

Again a silence, but no tension in him. All the tension was in me. *I already have a husband,* I was saying in my head. *And you are not the one.*

He was there so long that I glanced up at him. He was leaned over, his elbows on his knees, his hands whittling silently on a small soft stick, as he studied it intently. His eyebrows were bushy. His hair, dark like his eyebrows, was unruly with curls. He was a Benjamite, like us. Why am I thinking of his tribe, now? Is there any comfort in his being a Benjamite? It did seem less alien than, say, Merab's marrying into Issachar.

I sighed and he looked up in time to catch my eyes, and smiled, this time hugely. "Your eyes are so big," he said. I looked down. More softly, "So big, and so full of pain."

I sat without speaking. This man certainly did not have David's intensity. I could not have stood it if he had.

I began to wish he would leave. I felt weary again.

He rose and reached his hand to touch the top of my head. I flinched and he paused there in the air over my head. It was an eternal moment, till I had to look up at him. And I had to keep looking into those eyes, another long moment. Eyes full of love and tenderness--and still, pain. I sighed, and he said, "Good night," and left.

Lord, his name is Paltiel, "God delivers," the litany recurred as if on its own.

*   This morning, I hear you, Lord, for the first time in I don't know how long. I am thinking again, for the first time since the sentence of the king that I regarded as my doom. Lord, my father--my king--allowed himself to be destroyed, and as he went down, it seemed he had determined to take others down with him--me, David, Mama, Merab and Jonathan, on and on. I once vowed not to entertain feelings of insecurity. That is not what I am doing now, is it? Yes, in a way it is. I am insecure in this new position. But, Lord, it IS my position now. It may have started all wrong. I was not free ever for another

marriage. But this is where I am. My life is here now, regardless of where I wish it to be. Lord, I have considered myself destroyed. But perhaps, if I refuse to destroy another with me, I myself will not be destroyed, after all. You did not make Paltiel to be destroyed, any more than you made me to be destroyed--or any of us.

God, this is another task I cannot do, that you have called me to. Empower me, teach me, lead me--but, Lord, please, only one small, small step at a time.

*   This morning, after your words to me, Lord, and after watching some sunrise and bathing behind the screen, I changed into a new garment hung on the screen for me, one that I might have chosen for myself--a marvel. I ate the simple breakfast, read from Moses' writings, and played on my harp, ending with singing one of the psalms, before laying down the harp to write again. I am so frightened of this new position I am in, to be wife to another man, so against my own will. But I do not forget your words to me early today. After lunch, I will sit a bit in the sun, or better yet, walk around the roof and take in the view from all directions. I will read some more in Moses. And, Lord, I hear from you what I am to do to make a start with Paltiel. I will ask him if we may watch the sunset on the roof.

*   Before I sleep, I must unburden my heart of all these feelings that have swept over me this evening. When Paltiel came in after my quiet supper, we were both silent until I brought up enough courage to do your bidding. Lord, I managed only a small voice and said only, "The sunset, I--" He rose and gestured me to ascend the steps ahead of him. There were two chairs there and the divan.

We sat in the two chairs, facing slightly, but not directly, toward each other, so that we could each face west easily. The sunset had to have been one of your most spectacular, Lord. Such colors, fading into one another gradually as the dusk approached. We watched in silence for a long time.

It was almost startling when he spoke. "How many eyes in Israel tonight are also watching this splendor?" he mused. Paltiel has some poet in him, Lord. Then more startling was his next statement, a question. "Would you like to hear something of why you are brought here?" I did not trust my voice. I nodded and he went on, facing the declining sunset.

"I am a trader in fabrics. I was detained in King Saul's--your father's--palace." (Later, I will tell him how my father abdicated his father position, but surely he knows something of that, just by my being here.) He went on, "Your father was remodelling the west wing." (I remember when the guards spoke of that.) "The decorators took quite some time to finalize the fabric order, perhaps because your father changed his mind several times in the process." (Yes, he did that a lot, about so many things.) "As I was detained, messengers came to inform me that my new wife had died in early childbirth."

I gasped, this last statement so startled me.

He turned to me. "I left immediately for home, of course. Your father was furious over his plans being delayed, and sent to order me back to the palace until the fabric order was all in. His decorators had informed him of my loss, and he added to the order that he would provide a new wife for me. I finished the work and returned here to line up the delivery of the fabrics. You were delivered here just a few days later."

He watched me and I looked at him. We share a similar pain, then. I looked away at the western sky as dusk deepened.

"So you see it is not time for this marriage for me, either," he finished.

"Thank you for telling me," I finally said. "I will pray for you and your loss, too."

"Yes, we shall pray for each other," he all but whispered, rising, and motioning me ahead of him as we descended the stairs. And at the door of my room, "Good night," was all he said before walking away.

Lord, by this evening's revelation, you have lifted many loads off me. He needs time, just as I do. He does not want me, did not ask for me, any more than I wanted or asked to be here. It is something we both must do. It is the life we have been given. Because of a king's commands, yes, of course; but ultimately because in your sovereignty you have willed it, or at least allowed it, to come to us. Lord God Almighty, ease the pains of our two hearts in a corresponding time frame. May we each be part of the other's healing and not part of any destroying--there is enough of that without it happening under this one roof we both must call home. He and I have each had all the destroying influence we can cope with already. May we each be your agent in the other's life, for good.

Lord, I know you will fulfill your plan for David. But I have not the energy--the heart--to keep up prayers for him, too; I see my work laid out for me in my new home. May your peace make all sleep sweet in this house tonight.

*   Now it is one week since the revelation from Paltiel--he wants me to call him Palti--since Palti told me of his pain. We have sat on the roof for sunset each evening, and even dawn the last couple of days. And we have begun to talk, hesitantly at first, now more fluently allowing some thoughts and memories to be revealed to each other that we might learn to know the one we shall wed in due time. I will not speak of David, but of our life before there was a king in Israel, of my Dad, Mama, Merab and Jonathan, and some of what I have observed about an earthly kingship.

Palti has told me of his boyhood family. I may meet his relatives when I am ready. His father, mother, brothers and a sister live a few miles away. Maybe next new moon, we can meet. And he has described some of his work, dealing with weavers, camel train drivers, and his wealthy customers. He has many skills; I can pick up on them as he talks of the people problems, the accounting, the bargaining he must do. He has two assistants in the business, and of course, the servants here, to manage as well.

I am thinking of how I may assist him when the time is ripe for more participation. Meanwhile, Anna and I are becoming friends, while I do not forget that I am her mistress. I have met the cook, Jozie, and the laundress, Rahab, the gardener, Uzziel, and Malchijah, the stockman for Palti's animals.

And I have met some of the children of the neighborhood, whose laughter I heard that first morning. I enjoy chatting with them, hearing of their games and pets. At times what they say is so funny, I heard myself laugh again. It is good to laugh. Lord, I would like to raise a child one day.

While Palti is out on business each day, I am reading in Moses' books, disciplining myself to read all, but often finding myself back to Joseph's story. He was in a strange land and a strange position, and his faithfulness to his duties made a home for his people, eventually. You blessed him, Lord, for his obedience. May I be obedient. And may I recognize your blessings when they come. And your plan. You have one for me as you did for Joseph--and for the good of more people than just one.

And there is my harp. Now when Anna hums, sometimes it is one of the melodies she has heard me play. I do not stop now when she comes to tidy the room. Sometimes I have gone to the garden with her to pick the flowers to arrange in vases in my room and the other rooms, including the dining room where I have dined with Palti now, twice. The table is so large for two. We can talk better on the roof.

*   Lord, it has been a month now since Palti and I began to know one another. It seems longer, so much of this new life has become customary now. Palti and I eat each evening meal together. He is a dear, good man, very patient still, though I had begun to sense that he loves me and would be ready for our wedding before I. He has the man's need for a woman. I would not want to have a husband who could do without me, of course! But I thought I was not ready yet.

He has been sitting nearer as we sit on the roof. He has walked with me around the roof and the garden and put his arm about my waist, as he showed me the landmarks we can see from the roof, and the various flowers and vegetables he has had planted in his garden. I have felt him restraining himself that I might be ready before he should come nearer. And I have been grateful to him.

Yesterday he came home, early and unannounced, from his work. As I played my harp, I sensed his presence in the doorway and stopped. I had not played for him yet. He said, "You don't need to stop. I enjoy your music." I looked into his eyes, and all was trust between us. He sat on my bed, and I played softly. Then I began to pour myself out into a new composition that came, slowly at first, then gradually faster and louder the more I played. He arose early on in the melody and did some of the men's dance steps around the room, faster as I played for him. We each fed on the other's expression until he fell back on the bed, and I dropped the harp beside my chair. He lay there a moment, catching his breath, then arose and came to me and held out his hand. I reached mine out, and clasped his, and all our pain was gone, in longing for each other. We held and kissed, and we knew the time was ripe. It was our wedding.

*   Lord, a bond is made between us that cannot be broken. Palti is my husband. His husbandry is steady, strong but quiet, forceful but sensitive. In our world there is no war, for King Saul is mostly involved in taking his chosen 3,000 soldiers after David. There have been some battles with Philistines, but Palti has not been called. He has been to war in the past, and I thank you that he was spared. And that I have not had to send him to war. May the full army of Israel never be called out again, and may every home in Israel be as whole as this one. I never could have believed how my life would go. I am grateful.

The morning after we were wed, Palti sent Malchijah with instructions to his business assistants and stayed with me. After a late breakfast in my bedroom, we moved all my things to his big bedroom, as lovely and as light as the guest bedroom where I had been living since my arrival some two months ago.   Only two months? It seems an age in many ways.

We cannot look enough, touch enough, each other. His face, his hair, his bushy eyebrows, his hands, his eyes, all of him, is so dear to me. And he can say such things to me, that I am warmed all over, and finally, as he goes into exaggeration, I push him in jest, and he pulls me, and we laugh until we cry, for the joy of being set free from our old lives and pains, and into this new union.

*   Samuel has died. All Israel is in mourning. An era has passed, Lord. The prophet who spoke to the nation for you when we had no king but you, Lord, and who then anointed both Saul and later David when you took your Spirit from Saul--the prophet who loved and warned all Israel and never wavered from speaking your word has gone to his reward, in a ripe old age. Lord, will we ever see the likes of him again? Palti and I are fasting and praying for our nation, now a kingdom, and in great need. How glad I am not to be facing alone this loss I feel for our land and people. You have allowed me a strong man of God to lean upon in whatever grief I yet will face, just as now.

*   Lord, your timing is so perfect. A month into our marriage, I asked Palti if I might go to market each day for our household groceries and other needs. At first he protested that we had a servant to do that. But when he

saw my face, he realized I had a need. He heard me tell of how I loved going to market as a girl, and granted me this wish. Lord, he is as understanding of me as Jonathan ever was.

The second day at market I overheard two girls saying that David had taken two wives. I froze and held my breath. Of course! He would have heard the news of King Saul's action against us. "David, we had to go on with life, didn't we?--though our king would have had us destroyed. But TWO!!!?" Well, he is to be king, and this is what kings do. How it would have pained me if I had heard this news before I had a husband, or if my husband had been less a match for me than Palti is. My pain in the hearing is fully cushioned by the knowledge that I am treasured as Palti's wife, and that I treasure Palti and this life here. The two girls realized I had heard. People do know who I am around here. I had spoken with these girls once or twice. I went to them. "It is all right," I said. They said, "I'm so sorry," and their eyes teared up. "It is all right," I repeated. They seemed relieved. I went on, "I am Palti's wife now, but I am always interested in the fate of Israel, and you may tell me what you hear with no fear that it will harm me now that I am one of you here in Gallim." They perceived my intent, that I am no daughter of the king, but a local housewife, not to be regarded with any awe or distance, or relating to the past. I reached out to embrace and we had a three-way hug, and I learned their names, Rebecca and Elizabeth. They are friends, younger than I and still unmarried. I would see them at market off and on.

Thank you, Lord, for friends, for news, for healing, for keeping the news from me till now that I am able to hear.

*   It is just not possible that a year has gone by now for me and Palti, but it has.   Yes, Paltiel means "God delivers." Your rains, Lord, have come upon this once-dying plant and I am blooming in many ways. Since Palti has allowed me to go to market, I have become acquainted with many vendors. I love visiting with all of them, and now they know me as Palti's wife, greet me with smiles and small talk, and some quality produce, or fish, chicken or mutton, set aside for me. I am slowly becoming privy to some of the events of their lives, and ask after their families each time.

The servants now come to me instead of to Palti for instructions, all but his stockman. I have not learned that. I have met Palti's family, and am aunt to his nieces and nephews.   We exchange visits for new moons and birthdays and holy days. His mother is so happy to see Palti happily married. She has become like a second mother to me, and for this, too, I thank you, Lord. We have been to feasts, festivals, and synagogue each Sabbath.

Palti and I pray daily together. His relationship to you is close. He speaks so simply, as a child with a father. And he is so thankful for small blessings. He is thankful for me in his life. And I now sing too, when I play my harp for him.

By now I should also be blossoming out in another way, Lord, and I wonder, "Why is there no son on the way?" Palti has not said much, but he wants a son. I know it. He is so good with the neighbor children. Sometimes in an evening time, he plays catch with them. And our nieces and nephews love him, climb all over him when we have our visits.

Lord, may I not question your withholding of one blessing when I have so many surrounding me. I had thought to be destroyed. And here I am, blooming where I was transplanted.

*   Two years married now. Our anniversary was just yesterday, and today a man knocked on the door. Anna came running for me. As I approached the door, I studied the face, trying to remember. Then, "Adriel!" I exclaimed, and quickly, "Merab?!!!" His face told me all. "Oh, Adriel," I sobbed and clutched his arms with my hands. I looked into his grief-stricken eyes as tears rolled down his cheeks. He glanced down and I followed his glance. There at his legs, clutching tightly were three little boys. I knelt and hugged them, crying as I had not in months or years. All three I wrapped in my arms at Adriel's knees. The boys were wide-eyed but unresponsive. It was too soon for them, after losing their mother. And then, I was crying so.

A maid-servant came up on Adriel's right carrying a baby. Another came up on his left, carrying another baby. I gasped and took one on each arm and went to sit in a nearby chair, still crying. No words had been spoken yet.

Adriel wrenched out his news. "Merab never recovered after the birth of the twins. She died last month. She asked me to bring the boys to you, Michal. She wanted you to raise them. I tried to keep them, hired another maid besides their nursemaid, but they need a mother."

"Oh, yes, Adriel, yes. I will ask Palti, of course, but I know what his answer will be. Oh, not one son, but five."

"This is Samuel," Adriel laid his hand on the biggest boy's head, "He is just six. This is Abiathar, four and a half." (Merab has named them after dear Samuel, and after the one surviving priest of our father's slaughter of the priests of Nob.) "This is Jonathan. He's two. And the twins are Adriel and Paltiel. They are just three months old."

I heard a sound crooning out of my inmost soul, a long soprano moan that went on and on, as I took in all that was happening here, my sister, dead, her little sons all to be raised, dear Adriel so bereft.

"Where is Palti? Oh, Lord, let him come home early," I prayed.

After asking all the attendants in and seating them, I knew some planning had to be done. I sent Anna to the market to ask after a nursemaid. We would need one very soon. Of course, the one who travelled with them could stay over until they all had to return.

When Anna came back from market, she and Rahab began making extra beds for our guests. Jozie went to market for more meat and produce, sent Uzziel to pick some vegetables from the garden, and went to work with all haste. By the time Palti came home, all the boys but Samuel were napping in little beds made on the floor in the extra room, and beds were ready for Adriel in the guest bedroom, which had been my room when I first came, and beds for his servants in the barn.

As soon as Palti came home and heard the news, he first of all held Adriel, and wept with him, his heart no doubt remembering his own loss a few years ago. After the dinner, he and Adriel walked and talked in the garden.

I was busy with the boys, learning from the nursemaid and other servants what they were used to. I asked many questions, for I knew I would need all I could learn from them.

Samuel informed me, "Mama went to heaven," and Abiathar, Abe for short, seconded his big brother's declaration, "Yeah, she kissed us all and told us to mind Aunt Michal, and be good boys, and pray every night. Then she went to sleep, to heaven." Samuel studied my face and added, "You look like Mama, only not as pretty." I laughed in my tears. This would be an adventure, for sure. Five boys. I had asked, "Why is there no son on the way?", and it is clear now; it's because there were five on the way to me, me and Palti. And one named after him.

The babies, the maids said, were good babies, and not too fussy in the night. They showed me the garments for each boy. They handed me each twin after he had nursed, and I rocked them each, sang to them, and put them to bed. Then it was time for baths and bedtime for the older three boys. We put them all into a tub at once, and such a splashing after they recovered from an initial shyness over all the new surroundings. Each spurred the others on. I could see that their closeness would aid their adjustment here. But there would be some rough days after the familiar faces left for their home in faraway Issachar.

Lord, I have stayed up to record this incredible day's events and changes. I am very tired, but I needed to let this all out. I thank you for this new position, mother of five sons, and I pray your comfort to Adriel as he goes through his grief and builds another life for himself. Comfort all my family too as they receive the news of Merab. This is my prayer, and it is Palti's prayer. He said that he knows it is you who have brought us these five motherless boys to raise. He said he is ready. Oh, he is a good man. As he sleeps, I look over at his tousled curly head on the pillow beside mine. I tiptoe around for one last look at three tousled little heads and two tiny ones with wisps of black hair coming on. I touch and bless each beloved head, Palti's first and last. God, you are good.

*   Palti has put his assistants in charge of his business for a week, in order to be here for the end of Adriel's visit and our first days as parents of the boys. He said they will need to get to know him as much as possible before their father has to leave them, and that I need his support as I begin to mother five at once. He is making a swing in the tree in the garden, himself. Jozie is to do the marketing for now, and purchase, along with extra groceries, a wooden toy for each of the three older boys. Rahab has extra laundry to do. Malchijah is to begin looking for a pony that the boys can learn to ride. Uzziel is to till up another section in the garden for Samuel to have his own plot for growing whatever he wishes. Samuel is already making friends with Uzziel, and helping carry water for the plants, chattering about the plants he grew with his Mama. Uzziel never saw a boy so young know so much about plants.

As I read to them from Genesis, all about creation, Samuel and Abe nestled on each side of me--the sweetest feeling, surprising me with their attentiveness, while Jonathan listened as he played with some wood chips he had brought in his bag from home, making towers on the floor nearby. Palti came in and waited till I finished reading and called the boys to go see the donkeys with their father and Malchijah, who would help them take a ride on one. Their joyous departure left me some time with the babies.

We have decided to have no nicknames for the babies. That was Merab's wish, and it helps us to distinguish little Paltiel from big Palti. The twins are identical, but Adriel wears a blue ribbon on his wrist, and Paltiel a red one, so they can be told apart until they grow some differences. I reflected: Adriel, "honor of God", wearing blue for loyalty, and Paltiel, "God delivers", wearing red for the blood of the sacrifices. Merab surely thought of this, too. *Oh, Merab, I must tell Adriel before he leaves how glad I am that, if you had to die young, at least you had those years with him. I know they were good years for you.*

The big table that so oversized me and Palti sitting alone at it will be comfortably filled as the boys grow. Now Adriel sits with us and the three older boys, but he soon must leave.

Lord, as I am suddenly in a new position, not only mother now, finally, but mother of five growing boys, all at once, I have an overwhelming sense of need that is altogether new in my experience. I need wisdom to know how to shape the character of each boy, that he might be a Godly man--in whatever influence my part as mother includes. Palti, I know, will do the father part, and do it well, and also seek your wisdom. Lord, help me to be a good mother to Merab's boys, now mine. Bless Palti as father, and Adriel as he leaves and goes back to an empty house. Fill it for him, Lord, as you have filled ours.

*   Yesterday was our third anniversary and today is the first anniversary of the arrival of our five sons. I need to reflect on the past year. There have, of course, been ups and downs with them, most of all the first few weeks and then again these last few after they returned from a month

with Adriel and his new wife, Hadassah. It was so quiet around here without them. We missed them terribly, but, too, we needed the time to ourselves.

Palti and I have had our adjustments as well as the boys. At first, I was so thrilled and also overwhelmed, starting with five at once, that I let the care of the boys consume too much of me. I was forgetting Palti, to a degree, and my life was becoming unbalanced. We had a long talk, and planned some changes in scheduling. I delegated more to the servants and we even hired another, Rachel, to help tend the boys. I still spend time reading to them, playing my harp and teaching them to sing some psalms, tucking them into bed most nights, along with Palti. He likes to bless them each at bedtimes, and he usually does early evening rough play with them climbing all over him and shrieking, and he is working with them and the animals as he can spare the time, which is at least once a week for each of the three older boys.

As for the boys themselves, let me summarize. It does me good to put it into words. How precious to me is each one.

Samuel and Abe are most responsive to the stories from Moses. Jonathan listens as he builds with his blocks, but they have comments, questions and observations, such as, "Did it hurt Adam when God took his rib out?" and "Joseph's brothers didn't get spankings when they were mean to Joseph so they could learn to treat him right the way you make us treat each other right!" They make me laugh--and think.

Samuel is the horticulturist, diligent to keep weeds out of his growing garden plot, and to try new plants, and keeping Uzziel on his toes to answer all his questions. He prefers being outdoors, and is the most involved, so far, in the training with the animals, having questions for Malchijah, too.

Abe is more an indoor boy, and the most musical. As he grows older, I will teach him to play the harp, and even now he sings as he goes about his chores and play.

Jonathan is the builder. He builds out of anything and everything and wants to take things apart. As he grows older, we want him to have time in a local carpenter's shop where his questions have better chance of being answered adequately.

The twins, Adriel and Paltiel, are still pretty small for discerning individuality. They are both walking and running about and providing laughs for all the rest of us. They have jolly dispositions and have never been fussy or cranky.

The older boys are good with the twins and each other, but, as they see, we require them to get along and to help one another as well as helping us, as they are able, according to their age. So far, it has seemed that most of the time when one boy needs extra attention or discipline for a while, the others are in a stable time and can be on their own or with Rachel while we concentrate on the one in need.

The boys play tag and hide-and-seek and other games with the neighbor children often in the afternoons. The little neighbor girls are all fascinated with the twins and play at mothering them. All the servants adore the boys. I would not be able to handle all that is involved in raising five without their help, as many women must. But then, most women do have them one at a time, not five. I am organized to the extra responsibilities enough to do the marketing once again, and enjoy visiting, as I always have.

Palti's business is flourishing, as it surely must with his hard work and people skills. I am glad most of his trips are not overnight.

As for the news, it is more of the same, King Saul pursuing David and then relenting for a time, David having chances to kill him and not taking advantage but still leaving it to you, Lord, to judge between them. David is still in exile, the Philistines still rising up to attack and falling back to regroup, neither side having decisive victory. David keeps his two wives with him, as all his men have families with them, now. Strange how remote David now seems. There is so much to claim my immediate attention.

Life is very full, very rich, very good. So very different from anything I could ever have foreseen. Accept my gratitude, Lord, for your abundance in my behalf--in our behalf. And please, continue to give wisdom to raise these boys. I will never feel I have enough understanding on my own.

*   Lord, your time is coming to pass, for fulfillment of your destiny for David, and for Israel. The news has come of a decisive battle. My father, King Saul, and my brother Jonathan are among the many of Israel slain by the Philistines at Mt. Gilboa, also two half-brothers I never knew, from other wives I hardly heard of. In one way, it has been so long expected, it is less a shock than it might be. Then, too, my long years since last seeing my childhood family have taken the edge off this loss. But, oh, Jonathan, what could your life have been, in better times?

Evidently King Saul never recovered from his madness or came back into your favor, Lord. At least Mama did not have to live to see this. They say she died before the battle. And at least Jonathan was able to marry and have a son to carry on his name. I am the only one left living now of my family. It seems all a dream in a way, that we lived those years, first common people, then in the palace--like someone else's story. Mine went another way, a better way. I prefer to be common people over the life in a palace. I am in my right place.

They say that David paid highest tribute to Saul and Jonathan, and required mourning for them, and execution for a messenger who had a part in killing Saul and had thought that David would reward him. Now David has been crowned king by Judah, and has set up a throne in Hebron, but a strong military movement has arisen to put yet another son of King Saul on the throne of Benjamin and of all Israel but Judah. Why, I do not know. It is useless and will only lead to bloodshed, brother against brother. Are we not all Israelites, regardless of tribe?

Shall I have to send Paltiel off to battle against our own people, just because a few wish to fight for the house of Saul? Underneath, surely everyone knows the Spirit of the Lord left Saul long ago and David is the rightful king of all our people. It has been so long already. Why make the dispute go on longer?

*   Yes, Palti is called to war. Benjamin and all Israel against David and Judah. Bizarre. We are all such helpless pawns in the hands of our kings and rulers. Supposedly "our" king is Ishbosheth, who has not distinguished himself as having the qualifications of a king and is sure to be defeated after needless loss of life, possibly even Palti's life. Lord, keep him, bring him home. Bring this war to a quick end, that the killing of

brother by brother will stop, and peace come to all the homes of Israel.

*   The boys and I all miss Palti. I keep my spirits up for them, but after they are in bed, I cry out to you, Lord, end this evil civil conflict. Bring Palti and all the other husbands and fathers home. It is as if my father's madness has passed to his general, and Abner continues the destruction. Let it be stopped.

*   Palti is home, safe, alive, and well, only his mind needs a healing from all he has seen. Worse, he says, than war against your enemies, is war against your own people. He weeps when we are alone, but in the days, with the boys around, he is himself. He will recover.

Best of all, he says that Abner has turned on Ishbosheth, over some trivial matter, and will side with David to bring all Israel and Benjamin under David's kingship. Finally! Then we shall have the peace I have prayed for, all my life. Maybe our boys will not have to go to war at all.

*   Palti and I have just had our seventh anniversary and have had the boys for five years now. At the milestone of anniversary time, I always like to reflect.

Samuel is now eleven, and almost as tall as I am. He has been in synagogue school the past three years and is a bright enough scholar, but his primary interests are with the plants, and the animals. His father, Adriel, will leave him part of the family land, although Adriel and Hadassah have sons now, too, who will take part of the inheritance. Samuel will be able to manage a farm of his own, at any rate.

Abe is nine and has had only a year of school, but has attracted the notice of the rabbi, for his intelligence. He has made progress too, on the harp, and even composes pieces on his own. With his music and his scholarship, what can he do, Lord, with a father of Issachar and a mother of Benjamin? He ought to be a priest. Can he be a tutor? He likes teaching the twins.

Jonathan, now past 7, is developing athletically as well as in his carpentry. He makes toys of wood, and he is learning archery and is a sure shot. He may be headed for a military career, as his namesake, my brother. He and some of the neighbor boys play at battles. He is the general.

The twins are now five. How I have loved watching their little limbs grow from babyhood on into strong young boys. Growth is a wonder.

Adriel seems to be taking up with the animals more than Samuel. He spends as much time with Malchijah as with anyone, and has a touch that the animals respond to. He is the one most likely to have us all laughing at the dinner table. He was the one who first drew a laugh out of Palti when he came home from the civil war.

Paltiel is very much taken with Palti, more so than any of the other boys. He takes having Palti's name very seriously. Palti has taken him a couple of times when camel trains are being loaded with fabrics. He causes no problem, sticks close and wants to see and hear all that Palti does and says. He is the son Palti always dreamed of, following in his footsteps, looking to him as the wisest man who ever lived, and wanting to learn his trade.

Palti is, of course, not a perfect man. No man is. But whatever his imperfections, he suits me. And I suit him. When I think of my dread as I came here, I can still feel as I felt then, and understand why. But I understand so much more now why you allow things that seem too hard at the time. In the end, you are the all-wise One. And you bless us when we give up our way to yours.

*   Good news for all Israel. Abner has been to meet with David to begin negotiations to bring all the tribes under David's kingship, as you intended from long ago, Lord. A unified nation again, a sane king, oh a bright future is surely unfolding.

Thank you, Lord, for blessings abroad and at home.

NOTE

THIS WAS THE END OF MICHAL'S LIFE WITH PALTIEL AND THE FIVE SONS OF ADRIEL AND MERAB THAT WERE GIVEN THEM TO RAISE. SHE MADE HER NEXT ENTRIES INTO HER JOURNAL IN ANOTHER PLACE AND POSITION. AT DAVID'S FIRST MEETING WITH ABNER, HE REQUIRED THAT ABNER BRING MICHAL TO HIM BEFORE ANY   FURTHER   NEGOTIATIONS.

Excerpts from Michal's Prayer Journal
Part III: David Again

*   Lord, here in David's palace, I take up pen and scroll again, seeking life. It was agony when I was taken from David, but being taken from Palti and the boys so far surpasses that other agony that there are no words for it. Then I said I was dying. Now I am dead. It is not showers that could help now. There is no help. How many times have I relived the moments of horror that seemed as if they would never end, and ended all too soon.

Anna called me to the door with a face blanched white with fear. Once again, as when Adriel came, I saw a man's face that I had known so many years before. It took me a moment to recognize him. It was Abner, general of my father's army, who had been to dine with us in the palace on numerous occasions, so long ago. Behind him stood some twenty men on horseback, filling the street. The neighbor children gathered around them in curiosity. It was late afternoon, their usual play time.

Abner spoke in tones of command. "Michal, by order of King David, you have two hours to gather your things. I am to return the king's wife to him immediately. My men will require a dinner before we ride."

"The king's wife!" My mind could not take it in. He has wives. I am Palti's wife.

Abner was issuing commands again. "Prepare at once to leave for Hebron. You are ordered to the throne of David. We leave as soon as we have eaten."

Anna and I wept as she packed my things. I could not help. I could not stand or move. Jozie wept as she went to market, came back, and cooked. the boys and Rachel wept, and as the boys gathered from their various activities, they clustered around me. I drew them near on Palti's and my bed, and we held onto each other, crying as I stroked their heads and kissed their cheeks and foreheads. Uzziel and Malchijah joined us and wept just inside the door of the bedroom.

But Abner ordered Malchijah to feed and water the horses of his men, and he went off, shaking with his sobs. The soldiers came back after leaving their horses, and filled the courtyard and entry, talking, talking, an invasion of our home.

When Palti came home, he came and scooped me into his arms, crying with me. We held each other the whole time Abner and the soldiers ate. None of us could eat. Palti was pale with shock, then red with rage and grief, convulsed with sobs.

As the horses were brought out for the soldiers and one for me, Palti chose another for himself. He held me until the soldiers pulled me away and mounted me on my horse. Palti mounted his and rode alongside us for miles, wailing and crying out for mercy, for his wife to be left with him, until finally Abner ordered him to go back. There was no use, nothing to be done. I can still hear his horrible crying out to me as we rode off and left him in the road. It will be with me forever.

I could not see for my tears. I do not know how I stayed on the horse, except that as I swayed and nearly fell, two soldiers came to ride flanking me.

When we stopped late that night, the soldiers made a fire and slept. I could not sleep for crying and for fear. Finally I realized the soldiers would not dare to harm me, since I was, to them, "the king's wife." I cried myself to an exhausted semi-sleep and awoke crying out in terror from a nightmare and saw that the nightmare was reality.

Dawn was breaking and the soldiers were putting out the fire and preparing to mount the horses again. I was lifted onto the horse once more.

After a long ride, at the palace, Abner gave the word to the first guard we met and it spread rapidly. As we approached the main door, servants came and escorted me to a suite of rooms where a bath, a meal, and a bed awaited me. Two maidservants bathed me, perfumed me, clothed me, and, as I refused to eat, helped me into bed and left. But I felt no mercy in their ministrations, nor in the aloneness that enveloped me after they had gone. I only felt dead inside. I see no hope, and dread equally to be alone and to have anyone, most of all David, to come near me. But it has to come.

At least, I am treated with enough dignity that my things are all here with me. I am writing, Lord, as a cry, as the only thing I can do. I can only stare at my harp. There is no music any more.

Lord, what are you asking of me now? What position can I have here? I cannot think.

Perhaps I shall sleep some more. Perhaps I shall never really sleep, or really be awake, again.

* Lord, tonight, as I write, the banquet is going on, Abner and his twenty chosen soldiers being honored at a feast at King David's table. I am confined to this luxurious suite, attended by many servants, but still confined, until I come around to David's demand, to be his wife. He has not seen yet that this can never be, for me.

He had me brought to his own bedroom and left there alone with him this afternoon. In spite of the efforts of many servants in make-up and hairdo, I know that I appeared not as he expected to see me. I have no life in me.

"Michal, look at me. Look at me, I said. I command you to look at me." Finally I looked up for the first time. He looked older, stronger, more mature, but the light I had once known in him was dimmed. He sighed. "Michal, I offer you the throne beside mine. You are my queen."

"No, David, you have wives, I don't know how many now." I did not say, "And I have a husband." He did.

"And you have a husband." He sounded disgusted.

"And five sons."

"Yes, I heard about Merab." He rose and strode around the room, as of old times, too intense to sit for long. "But Michal, our marriage, surely you remember, surely it does not count for nothing, just because King Saul ordered you to go to another. You gave me your heart. I know it. You know it. It was for forever."

"David, you have wives. Why do you need another wife? How many does it take?"

"Does your father have so much power? You gave over your love for me because he ordered it?"

"David, no, because the Lord allowed my life to be placed with another." I paused, and went on. "My father destroyed many lives, as his was destroyed. I vowed not to do the same. I vowed to build lives, for myself and those in the world I was sent to."

"Then you can do it again. Only, it should be easier, knowing the love we shared. I have not forgotten, if you have." He came nearer to me, reaching out to touch me. I shuddered all over my body. I drew back from him. When he gave up and kept his distance, I could speak.

"David, you have taken wives. You have given to many what you offer to me. You have known many as you knew me. You have sons by two wives and other wives pregnant. I will not be part of a harem. I know the commandments. I have done all I can do in the way of changing husbands."

"I see it is no use talking to you now. But we shall talk again. Michal, you will love me again. You loved me too much once, not to need me again. After you have been alone long enough, you will be glad of my offer."

With that, he called a servant to take me back to my rooms.

Lord, this time I know it is not you asking me to take this position of one, only one, of David's wives. The God who said "Thou shalt not commit adultery" never asked anyone to submit to polygamy. You never change. This time it is only an earthly king's order, not my heavenly King's.

So, Lord, what am I to do in this place, a prisoner? Ah, yes, of course, prayer. Prayer for Palti and the boys. Oh, they will need it. And, even, prayer for David. He will need it. We need a sane king. If he will not be sane in the matter of women, I can pray that he is in every other way. For the sake of our people.

I will pray, and only pray, until you tell me what else I may do with myself and my time and energy. I am not old yet, only I feel old tonight. But having an assignment is the start of a resurrection. I do not feel dead.

*   Oh, Lord. Oh, Palti, my dearest and most precious husband. This is too cruel to be real, but all too real, just

the same. I would give anything if it would take us back to where we were and our life could go on as it was. Oh, what do the boys do without me? To lose another mother? It is too cruel for them, for each of us. Palti has lost a wife before, too. His mother lost a daughter-in-law before. So much damage into so many lives, all because a king has so much power. David cannot see he is more cruel to me than my father was. And, as before, the destruction spreads to so many people.

Oh, my Lord, I say that the assignment to pray for these great needs has been a resurrection for me, my life being returned, just in having some purpose in this new imposed life. But the life returning has brought such pain with it, for all that is lost, and lost to so many. How shall I bear the pain? How shall Palti? I remember when he said that we would pray for each other. We were in pain then. But our union was being formed, and then was born, and grew. This pain now, having our lives torn asunder after they were grown together, is there anything to be compared to it? Oh, Palti, I know that you pray for me. Know that I pray for you, and for the boys. Oh, you must keep them and continue as much as you can the lives on which they were embarked. Oh, all of you, love each other for me and know that my heart is there with you, and not here where I am, in body only.

Oh, Lord, help us all, or there is no help for us.

*   It was two weeks that David waited until bidding me come to him again. During this time, I heard the servants speak of Abner's efforts to bring all Saul's army over to David. I am sure David has been busy in the negotiations. Then I heard that as Abner left David, he was murdered by Joab and Abishai, David's nephews and army generals,

not knowing Abner came for peace, and wanting revenge for Abner's killing of their brother Asahel. David declared his innocence and called the people to mourn the death of Abner, asking you, Lord, to avenge Abner's death, and putting a curse upon Joab's family. David can be so wise in some areas, as we need a king to be. The Israelites will appreciate David's mourning for Abner.

But he is so foolish in making all these marriages. Another son has been born now to David. He already has Amnon, born of Ahinoam (he's about two now), and Chileab, born of Abigail (he's about 1 1/2) and now Absalom has been born to Maacah, the daughter of Talmai, king of Geshur (a political marriage, probably). David is setting each wife up in her own house for her and her children. Another wife, Haggith, is expecting, also. How can he think I want to be a queen for such a king, doing in this matter of marriages as the kings in other nations who have not the word of the Lord, as we have?

But he does.

Again today he summoned me; this time a night meeting was arranged. Last time he wanted my consent in time to sit in the throne beside his for the dinner with Abner, hence, the afternoon meeting. This time, he surely thought the night had advantages for his cause, which I would not be able to resist.

Oh, I do not want to remember all that happened. But, Lord, I tried to warn him of all the trouble that is ahead for him with all these wives having sons who will want to be king, and their mothers wanting to be the queen mother. He kept trying to bring me back to my once-felt love for him.

He tried again to come near me. Again, my whole body was so repulsed that I was practically in convulsions before he backed away. When I could speak, I said, "David, I am disgusted by your spreading your fountain among so many. It was not meant to be thus."

At this point, he summoned a servant to return me to my room, telling me before the servant came that he would not be dictated to by me. He was the king.

Oh, I pray he is done with bidding me to come to him, done with trying to wear me down, done with trying to revive what is dead in me. What can he want of me, when he finds it so easy to add wives? Why cannot one of them be his queen? Is he only trying to nullify the power Saul once used against him and me?--to prove he has more power than Saul? Is he only trying to create another tie between the tribe of Judah and the tribes of Benjamin and Israel who wanted a son of Saul for their king?--giving them a daughter of Saul for their queen? Using me for politics as he is using other wives?

God help him, and stop him from adding still more wives. It is demeaning to his character, destructive to his inner man.

*   Lord, I ask for your presence to come to Palti. Encourage him, be very near to him, and show him what to do with the boys. Oh, the boys. Comfort them, too, Lord; oh, take the pain and grief off their young hearts. Let them not turn on you, Lord. Give them hope, that they may find reasons to be glad over the blessings their lives have known, and not to be damaged in their spirits by this blow--the older ones having been old enough to remember their mother and her death, and the younger ones being too young to cope with losing the only mother they can remember having. Lord, they are so dear to me, and I know they are even more precious to you. And

Palti, so good and kind, so gentle and caring, to be dealt such a blow. There was no warning, not even a hint or suspicion in either of us, that such a thing could happen. We had a life, he had a wife, and suddenly it was all taken away. It is worse than a death because he knows I still live, but locked away. Oh, Lord, let him know, assure him strongly in his inmost being, that I can never be wife to any other but him, now. Give him that peace. Let him rest, knowing I will be all right within, even if a prisoner without. My soul belongs to you, Lord, and my earthly allegiance to Palti. Let him know, as he knew me those years we had, with calm surety. Oh, Palti, I love you, and the Lord loves you. Make it as right as you can for yourself and for each of the boys. Be strong for them. They need you so, more than ever.

* Lord, they say that David has taken still another wife. Lord, work in him to stop this self-destruction. When I think of all the blessing that you meant marriage to be to a man and a woman, and know that David can never know this blessing, adding women as he adds battle victories--I hurt for him. How shallow, how trivial each of his marriages must be, the more of them he has. What a loss in his life and in each of the wives' lives as well. Lord, stop him before it goes any further. It has already gone so far that trouble of all sorts is sure to be ahead for him. Oh, let him see this as he sees so much in other areas of his life--in not taking revenge on my father, Saul, for one thing.

* Lord, once again David has shown wisdom and mercy. The two men who killed Ishbosheth and brought his head to David, expecting a reward, he had executed.

And he buried Ishbosheth's head in Abner's sepulchre here in Hebron. This, of course, will help to bring the tribes of Israel to rally around David as king. And it is already beginning. Israel is proclaiming the triumphs that David brought to the nation when he served my father, King Saul. He doesn't need Saul's daughter as queen. I am not a necessary aid to uniting our nation.

*   Lord, I don't know how many times this makes now, but once again David requested me to an audience with him. He wanted to know whether I had changed my mind since he is about to gain all the tribes and be king over a united Israel. He cannot believe I would choose to be alone rather than accept him as husband again and be queen over all his kingdom. He feels he has all to offer me.

"David, what I would want you to offer me, you have offered to so many, I would not have it. And what a marriage has to offer, I have had those past years. You can never know it, having so many wives. And, David, neither can any of them. Each of your present wives could have had a faithful husband in her own land or tribe. Maybe having a king to share with other women as husband is enough for some of them. It is not, for me. And if you think you need a daughter of Saul to unite Israel with Judah, no, that is happening already. You don't need me for that."

He called a servant to take me back to my rooms and told me I will be his wife in name if not in fact, and no one else's wife ever again.

"I know that, David. I ask you to seek what contentment you can find in the marriages you already have. I pray for our nation, for your kingship, and for wisdom in every area of your life."

"That is not all you were brought here for," he said as the servant arrived for me. "There is still some time before I am crowned king of all the nation. Think about it, Michal."

*   Well, Lord, it is about time for the anointing and crowning of David as king over all Israel. He took another wife. In all, in his seven years of reigning in Hebron over only the tribe of Judah, he took four more wives in addition to the two he took while on the run. He has had six sons in all here, one by each of these wives. Of course, there have been daughters, too. No one reports on their births or names, only the sons.

Late this afternoon, on the eve of his anointing by the tribe of Benjamin and the other 10 tribes of Israel, he had me summoned to his room again.

"Michal, I am to be crowned tomorrow. This evening you will spend here. We shall have a late dinner together. Please, just sit and make yourself comfortable. I will play for you on the harp."

David took up his harp across the room from me, and ignored me and everything but his own music. He is capable of great concentration, as well as musicianship. He wished me to see all that now, and to remember.

He started with the songs of the outdoors and your creation, Lord, that he played long ago for my father during his mad fits, and calmed his spirit. He played them for a long time, never stopping between, but for a musical pause. He played the psalms he had composed after we had been married, the ones crying out to you in agony over my father's turning on him, the ones crying for your hand upon him in battle, the ones praising your holy Name. As of old, he never tired, but played on and on. Then he began to play the ones he composed to celebrate our love and marriage, songs only he and I ever heard, or ever would hear.

After what seemed hours, he stopped. He did not look up, but hung over his harp.

From almost the beginning, I had wept, not with my voice, only with streams of tears running down my cheeks as I sat motionless, hearing, remembering, sorrowing.

As he hung over his harp, gradually my tears subsided. He looked up at me across the room. "You have not forgotten, you see, Michal."

I waited. He waited. I wanted to be able to speak steadily. Finally, I could. "David, I never said I had forgotten. David, there is much, so much, in you that is good, and wise, and I can see that you have kept much of it, and your love for the Lord, too. But I cannot live as one of many wives. You have spread yourself too thin to know what marriage can be. You have exposed yourself to too many women."

"Michal, they don't matter the way you do. You were first. You are too young a woman to live celibate, and that is what you are facing. I don't think you can keep it up. You have needs. I will not take a No answer until you have more years to try this loneliness you seem to think you want. Here, let us eat dinner together, as we used to do. Forget the other wives, and just enjoy being here with me. Remember the music. Do not forget all the times we made music together, and all we had together."

I sighed. I did not say just then that there is no forgetting the other wives. We had to eat this dinner. The king said so.

During the dinner, the times when the servants retreated from their serving and left us for the next course, David talked. He told me of his love for Jonathan--such a friendship, of his years of running, of gathering his army, his fears, his triumphs, the battles against Philistines, and later, against Benjamin and Israel, stories of his brothers and sisters and their children during the years we were separated, of Abner and Ishbosheth.

I had not spoken till then, only listened. He was not bragging, taking no glory to himself, giving you glory, Lord. "David, I admire and respect your wisdom in the matter of restraining yourself when given opportunity to kill my father, in mourning for him and Jonathan, in mourning for Abner and Ishbosheth. There is much that is noble and wise in you, and you shall be a great king, as you continue to turn to the Lord for your wisdom and give him the glory for your victories and achievements."

I paused, and he kept listening.

"But David, you have not acted wisely in regard to women and there is no way I can forget the other wives. They are there, you keep adding to them. They keep bearing your children. They cannot be ignored. I choose to live alone."

Again, he called a servant to take me to my rooms.

"You will be sorry, Michal."

I just looked at him and felt sorry for him, much more than for myself.

*   After David's anointing and crowning, he assembled a mighty army to take Jerusalem, the city of the Jebusites, who had never been driven out. The servants brought reports of the progress of the assault, until the city was finally the city of David.

Again, I was summoned to him, to hear of the triumph and the plans for fortifying the city and for his palace there. This time, Lord, after these last few years of being summoned to him at milestones of his life, I wonder, Does he have a form of love for me that he does not have for the other wives? Such a complex man, who can know but you, Lord? Publicly, I am "David's wife", and probably my being sent for from time to time is seen by the servants as having marriage relations, since he sends for other wives from time to time as well. He cannot see why I am not eager to be his wife, since I once loved him, and he is now king, and to many, obviously, a desirable man. But it is the opposite with me. I am more disgusted with him with each wife added and each child born from all of them. He still seems sure one more triumph will find me eager to be his wife again. He also seems sure that I cannot be satisfied always with a life alone, that there is nothing for me, living as I do under his control, apart from being wed to him again.

It almost seems as if he adds another wife after every meeting I have with him. If it were not so disgusting, it would be pitiful.

*   Lord, I am thinking of Palti and the boys so strongly tonight. Mostly I have prayed for you to strengthen each of the boys that they may grow into the way of life that you destined when you knit each one together inside Merab's womb. But today I want to pray that you prune out of each one those faults of character that go along with their strengths. For Samuel, Lord, enable him to care about people as much as he cares about plants and animals. For Abe, Lord, give him the practical knowledge of everyday things as well as his head

knowledge and musical skills. Tie him down to earth, as well as he can soar on thoughts and melodies. For Jonathan, let him not develop a violent side if he does go into military leadership, but let him find more satisfaction in building than in destroying; and, whatever warfare he may have to do, let it be for your cause, Lord, alone. For Adriel, let his humorous way of looking at things never become a trivializing of life, but an enhancement of the lives of those he touches. For Paltiel, Lord, I pray that his adoration of Palti does not lead him to expect perfection, or be disappointed when he sees imperfection. May he develop a balanced love for Palti, not an idealized one.

For them all, Lord, send loving and faithful wives, when it is time. And, Lord, the time is nearer than I think. Years are going by. Samuel should be 16 now, almost a man, Abe 14, Johathan 12, and the twins already 10. I cannot picture them that old.

For precious Palti, Lord, I have steadily prayed you to meet every need, but now I even pray that he may marry again, if he wishes and if there is a woman who would be good for him. I know I shall never see him again. I shall never hear any news of him or the boys, even. Thank you for the years we had, a balanced life, a common people's life, with no cruelty in it. Bless him every way. He has been such a blessing, to me, and to the boys, and to others in his association. I will always love him.

*	Lord, you are answering every prayer for David as king, except for him to have wisdom regarding women. Now he has not only added still more wives, but he has set up a harem. There will be young women who will spend one night with David and never see him again, or have anything like a normal life, ever after. There will be

preposterous numbers of king's sons, and those living mostly fatherless lives. No man can keep up with that many households. He keeps his devotion to you, it appears, in every way, but in that. I guess there is some area in most lives where we will not submit to you. I don't know, but I do know about your will for marriage.

Anyhow, he wants to bring the ark to Jerusalem. This is surely your will, for the ark to be in the center of the nation once again. He tried once and it was carried on a cart instead of on men's shoulders, as your law says. A man died for that. Now the ark is coming to Jerusalem in the method you have decreed for its transport. The people are built up for a celebration. Would that they loved your law as much as they love celebrating. But it really is a special day, and the ark a vital part of our heritage. Probably I can just never feel festive about anything any more.

*   Lord, I have to ask your forgiveness for my angry outburst. When I saw David in the linen garment dancing and leaping before the ark in genuine joy and celebration, his boisterous movements exposed his nakedness, I could not help the disgust that rose up in me over his exposing his body to so many wives and concubines already and now to all those singing women, too. When he called me in to exult over the ark being in Jerusalem and to try me again, if I was not ready to come to him willingly now, I poured out all the anger and hurt I have felt for all he has done to destroy in my life and for all, as I see it, he has done to destroy in many women's lives. I told him he was disgusting to display himself publicly. He threw angry words back at me. Now that he has finally seen my opinion of him for what it is, he has rejected me. He will

never see me again, I shall die childless, he says. It is meant to be a punishment. It is a relief. I am so glad to be done wth being called before him and pressured to be his queen.

Now I can live out my days in prayer, or whatever task you set before me in my limited scope of influence, in my prison.

I stand before no man as judge over me, only you, Lord. And the same is true of David. Only you, Lord, can judge the good and the evil in him, in me, in anyone.

*   Now that I know I will not be summoned again by King David, a peace is settling into my spirit. I have picked up my harp for the first time since years ago, when it was packed among my things in Palti's house as Abner waited to bring me to David. There is still no music in me, but I am strumming it, trying to toughen my finger tips again, for the day when a song comes into my soul. I make sure no servants are nearby first, before I let a sound go forth.

If I pray that the boys and Palti find what they can thank you for, then I must thank you for what good I find around me. Thank you for my harp still being here, the pen and ink and scrolls upon which I pour out some of what is inside me, and the books of Moses.

The servants are really the only people in my life. I am getting to know them, and now I shall make more of an effort. It is a relief that they no longer act as if I am David's wife. Maybe they can see me for a person, as they see how I treat them and how I live this life alone. They have a heart. They will care for a woman made lonely by the forces of her time, not by her own choice. But surely there would never be one to whom I might speak of Palti and the boys and the life we built when we had the chance. Only you, Lord.

*   The servants say David has begun the preparations to build a temple for you, Lord, where all the people can gather to worship, local people any day and people from every corner of the nation on holy days. This is good. But he is not to be allowed to build it, the prophet spoke to him from you, for he has been a man of blood. Lord, perhaps there is a tie-in between the thousands of men he has killed and the numerous wives and concubines he has collected. As he saw so many men dead and bloody, surely a man alive would have less and less meaning to him, and somehow a woman, too, would come to mean less.

Oh, what would have happened if my father had never broken our marriage apart? Would David have been a different man, or would he have taken his pattern from all the kings of the nations around, just the same?

Well, at least he has it in his heart to build you a house, though as you spoke to him, and he spoke to the people, you never asked for a house. Still, we can come together there and center our hearts on prayer to you. It is a good thing.

Oh, who will be king after David, to build the temple? What shall befall all of us and Israel between now and then?

*   David is leading the army into battle to retrieve cities the Philistines took in years past, and success crowns every effort he puts himself to. It is good. Our nation is being blessed. More nearby nations are being made to

pay tribute to us. God, grant that Israel is blessed in spirit as well as in wealth.

*   Lord, you have given me back a song for my heart and my hands to bring out on my harp, a song for each time I come to my harp. It comes from working in the garden, helping bring to life flowers and vegetables, hearing the bird songs as I work, smelling the breezes. It comes from my memories, mostly of Palti and the boys. It comes from your law, the story of Joseph sold into slavery by his brothers and ultimately saving their lives by his obedience through suffering--other stories, too: Moses bringing the children of Israel through the Red Sea and Miriam rejoicing, Joshua bringing the children of Israel through Jordan into the Promised Land. It comes from the lives of the palace servants and their families, as I have come to know them through the years in Hebron and Jerusalem. It comes from all the richness of life. The fresh song comes and refreshes my spirit, time after time.

Not only do I have the garden, my memories, the books of Moses, the servants' confidences, to occupy my time and my prayers, but also I am learning to sew, and sewing especially baby garments for the babies of the servants. They bring their babies to me to hold.

The years are going by. Holding the babies of the servants, I imagine the babies being born now to my five boys. It is my taste of being a grandmother. Though my body was ever barren, you gave me a way to be a mother. Though I am spending these last years of my life without a husband, you gave me those years with Palti, to know all that a husband's love can mean. Though I have spent most of my life in a palace, you gave me years to know life among the common people. For all these blessings, I am grateful.

*   The servants say that Mephibosheth, my brother Jonathan's son, dines at King David's table now, and his small son Micha. Did my brother's son name his son after me? Did my brother Jonathan speak of his sister Michal, and our brother-sister love, to his son in ways to make him remember and honor the memory by naming his son Micha?

By honoring Mephibosheth and his household, David is honoring his covenant that he cut with Jonathan, so long ago. Mephibosheth is crippled since the day that Jonathan died and his nurse rushed to take Mephibosheth from the palace, that a remnant of the line of Saul might live, as Saul's house lost the kingship to David. David is restoring my father's lands to Mephibosheth and to Ziba, the servant of my father, because of his covenant with Jonathan, too. David is honorable in so many ways. He just never listened or changed his ways with women. His many sons of his wives (not the sons of the concubines) are growing into positions of leadership in David's administration. And David finds favor among the people for his wise decisions in cases of justice.

There is still war. Ammon insulted David's emissaries and then called in Syria to their aid as David sent Joab and the army against them. I wonder whether any of my five, especially Jonathan, are involved in the battles. Lord, let there be peace for Israel, yet. And protect the sons of Israel who have to do battle.

*   Lord, what has happened now is not anything I foresaw happening, but it only follows from David's

going after women. He has now had one of his chosen 30, Uriah the Hittite, murdered to cover up that the warrior's wife is pregnant with David's child, not his own. First he tried to get Uriah to go home, calling him from the battlefront "for a report." (David has never needed a report brought from afar; before this, he was always at the battle himself.) But Uriah was so devoted to his men on the field, he would not take marital privileges denied to the other soldiers. David had misread Uriah's character (no doubt basing his estimation of Uriah on his own appetites). Uriah surely never suspected the treachery that ended his life, treachery by the man to whom he had devoted himself for many years, ever since David was on the run, all through Hebron and these several years in Jerusalem. ...It only follows that unlimited acquisition of women would lead to this.

Nathan the prophet, they say, spoke for you, Lord, to David, in certain and specific terms spelling out what his sin has been with Uriah and Bathsheba. David repented and sought your face. He now awaits your verdict upon the son that Bathsheba bore, whether the child will live or die. Lord, let this be the time you reach David's heart to give up multiplying marriages. It is too late to stop what will happen with all these sons, and that is the curse that Nathan pronounced upon David's house from you, that the sword would never leave David's house. But perhaps it is still not too late for David to settle down to love one woman alone. Which one, no one knows but you, Lord.

*   Their child did die. The servants were astonished at David's acceptance of the death, the way he had mourned and fasted as the child lay ill. They say he said he cannot bring the child back, but he will go to the child.

And I will go to Mama, Jonathan, and Merab one day, Lord. My father, I do not know about, whether he called on you at the end or not. All the reports I have heard reveal him still a madman to the end. Only you know, Lord.

But Palti will be there one day.

And David seeks you, does not run from you in his guilt, but to you. This is good. We need a godly king.

* Two big events for Israel: Nathan has called David and Bathsheba's second son, just born, Jedidiah, "beloved of the Lord", indicating his prophetic pronouncement of your acceptance of David's repentance, Lord, though David and Bathsheba are calling the child Solomon, "peace." You have made peace with them, Lord. You are gracious.

The second big event: Joab and the forces of Israel took the capital city of Ammon, Rabbah, and Joab sent word to David to come and strike the final blow if he wants the credit, or Joab will name the city after himself. David has gone to receive the crown of Ammon. Maybe peace can come now to Israel.

* Lord, these last few years, it almost appears to me that David has found in Bathsheba what he has been searching for in all the women. They have had another son, Nathan, no doubt named after the prophet. This tells me they have submitted to your judgment as pronounced by Nathan, as harsh as the honesty was with which he confronted the sin that started their marriage. Nathan means "giver." The prophet was the giver of your word to them. Do they mean this Nathan to give your words, too? And another son they have had and named him

Shobab, "returning."   Oh, I wonder what returning Bathsheba had in mind as she named him, or was the name David's idea? And then there was still another son, Shammuah, "famous." No other wife has borne him so many sons. She must be a special woman. Lord, you do work in mysterious ways. Such an ending to come of such a beginning. Mighty God, merciful God, you are altogether good.

*   Lord, the sword in the house of David has been lifted, as the prophet foretold. We were all stunned at the first reports that all the king's sons had been killed by Absalom, but then David's nephew Jonadab, Absalom's close friend, assured David that only Amnon, David's firstborn, has been killed. Absalom has obviously plotted this murder for two years, ever since Amnon raped Absalom's sister Tamar.

Now Absalom has fled from his father's wrath to his maternal grandparents in the kingdom of Geshur. All the other sons of David's wives are weeping together with David, to mourn the death of Amnon. Probably, too, they are in fear at being so close to being wiped out, each and every one, potentially. But Absalom's target was only Amnon, for the love that Absalom bore to his sister Tamar, and her hurt and shame after Amnon's assault and his rejection as soon as he was done with her.

Lord, comfort the people. Absalom is so good-looking, such a charming personality, that the people will probably mourn his exile far more than they mourn the death of Amnon. Amnon made no friends by his actions against Tamar. Public sentiment will be with Absalom, despite the fact that he did commit murder. His motives will be seen as justifiable. Perhaps if David had punished

Amnon according to his wrong, this might never have happened.

What wisdom can be enough in a father to deal with sons of different mothers?

*   I hear through the talk among the servants that Joab has gone to bring Absalom home after three years in exile. Absalom's wife went with him and they had two more sons and a daughter over there, in addition to the son they had when they went. They named the daughter Tamar, after his sister, showing the depth of his feelings for her. David had not planned to send for Absalom, but Joab saw his grieving for him, and put up a wise woman to weave a story for David to pronounce judgment on, about an exiled son; David applied his own judgment in the case to Absalom.

But then when Absalom got back to Jerusalem, David refused to see him, ordered him to his own house. All the servants are murmuring that this will fire up Absalom against his father even more than the long exile did. They whisper that Absalom is winning people over to him by cancelling their debts and making promises of what he would do if he were king. As third-born, he is next in line, with Amnon dead, after Abigail's son Chileab. But no one is supporting Chileab for king. So Absalom has a sort of claim on the throne. But how much better to win his father's endorsement.

*   Lord, it took a fire set by Absalom's servants in Joab's barley field, but finally Joab spoke to David and David has sent for Absalom to come to him, has received his homage, and given him the kingly, fatherly, kiss of restoration. It took five years since the murder, three in

Geshur and two here. A lot can happen in five years. David may be too late for Absalom.

*   Lord, I am packed and awaiting the order to evacuate the palace. This could come at any moment. Absalom has marshalled his support and had himself declared next king in Hebron, and is marching to Jerusalem to take over the palace. David is leaving only ten concubines to keep house and is taking the rest of his household. It is the first time since David was established as king in Jerusalem that I have left this palace. We do not know our fate. Lord, help us all. Oh, let the country not fall into chaos. Grant your plan to be accomplished for the transfer of power to the one you have in mind for the throne after David. He is getting old now, has had a hard life as a fighting man, and now this blow may take years off his life. It is hard to have an ungrateful son, who cares for his personal interests more than he cares for his own father. Strengthen David for what he must endure. And give your wisdom.

*   Father, here in Gilead, in tents with campfires amongst them, I am among the huge household of David who await the outcome of the battle raging in the forests of Ephraim. We crossed Jordan in the night and all were over by sunrise the day after our departure from Jerusalem. Ah, Jerusalem, the city set on a hill, what a sight to look back upon. But now it is a city of woe. Reports came back that Absalom went in to David's ten concubines left behind, in tents on the roof of the palace, sending a message to all the nation of Absalom's defiance of David. And Ahithophel, once David's counsellor, who defected to Absalom, committed suicide when his counsel

was overthrown by David's true friend Hushai, who returned to Jerusalem on just that mission by order of David. So we have the advantage of this retreat across Jordan and this difficult battleground. Many soldiers stayed true to David. But we do not know how the battle will go.

Meanwhile I am helping to care for the children, and praying, and as I can, gazing upon the vast sky and this countryside. In the midst of all the confusion of last night, fleeing and crossing Jordan, children and babies crying, everyone so exhausted, but not allowed to stop moving, I prayed for your will. And I know that Absalom is not it. Who is to be next king, I do not know, Lord, but I join many in Israel who surely pray for you to bring it to pass, and swiftly.

There is much to do in this refugee camp. The children of the servants for whom I have sewed garments, whom I have held as babies and toddlers, I now help to console in the tumult, with the parents, as best we can. I packed only my harp, books, pen and ink, and scrolls, wrapped in a few garments. I'll not leave these behind for Absalom's crew to destroy.

Lord, bring peace and stop the slaughter of brother by brother once again, please.

*　　　Absalom is dead. David is grieving rather than rejoicing that the rebellion is put down. Give him wisdom, Lord. Absalom had to die.

*　　　Joab finally persuaded David to rally and thank his men before they all fled his cause, seeing the way he treats victory as defeat! Plans are being laid to have David escorted to Jerusalem again in triumph. When

things are in order, we depart to retrace our journey, in victory this time, not in flight and fear. We wait for the organization of our return trip, so relieved this war is over and we are safe, there is much a different mood among us now.

However, the casualties reported are enormous in number of dead Israelites. God, I grieve for all the losses of all the families. But I do pray that my five were not among them. Palti would be too old now to be called out. But all five of the boys may have been not far from me, fighting in these woods, for Absalom's cause, through no choice of their own, only politics.

*   Well, here we are back in Jerusalem, but not safe completely yet. A rebellion led by Sheba has broken out because the men of Judah left out the tribes of Israel, they say, when David was escorted back. It is just that many of Judah who supported Absalom are now making sure that their support is speedy and seen by all. David had already forgiven Amasa for heading Absalom's army, and had made him head over David's army in place of Joab, but Joab slew him anyhow and remained in his position as always. Before the army could destroy Sheba's city, his head was thrown over the wall to Joab, and the army is back in Jerusalem and the rebellion squelched, with minimal loss of lives. Thank you, Lord.

Now, Lord, may we live in peace? Will our country now be free of civil conflict? Oh, grant it, Lord.

*   My Lord and my God. The worst blow of all my life. Oh, my sons, my sons, all five dead at once. It is more than I can bear. My mind is bursting, my heart is bursting, with the pain. Their wives all widows, their

children all fatherless, these daughters-in-law and grand-children I never knew but in my prayers and my imagination. How bizarre, how beyond imagining, that this could ever be. My five innocents given up for my father's cruelty in slaying the Gibeonites, all because Joshua, so long ago, made a covenant with them, based on the deceit of the men of Gibeon, pretending to be from a far country but actually in our midst. As King, my father wanted the land cleared of ungodly foreign influence and slaughtered many of Gibeon. All these years afterward, and centuries after Joshua's unwise covenant--made without consulting you, Lord, or you would have told him not to be deceived--here and now, the three years of famine we have been having, you revealed to David, were caused by the broken covenant with Gibeon. To make atonement for their losses (that the drought be stopped), David agreed to the Gibeonites' demand that the sons of Saul be given over to them to be hanged and displayed. David spared Mephibosheth and Micha because of his covenant with my brother, but he ordered delivered to the men of Gibeon my father's concubine Rizpah's two sons and my five. Rizpah went berzerk (of course her sons were her whole life), and stayed by the corpses of her two sons day and night to keep off vultures and varmints. David heard and ordered all seven bodies, and the bones of my father and brother taken to the tomb of Kish, my grandfather.

Oh, how the mighty are fallen! A reaping of the seeds sown by my father's madness. Oh, we are wiped out.

All but Mephibosheth and Micha.

Oh, Palti, the Lord comfort you in this loss, as well. He is all we have, in the end.

Oh, my sons, all gone at once, so cruelly taken. My precious ones.

Lord, I am ready to go to meet them. I am not long for this earth. Guide me through to you.

*   The grandchildren of the servants I knew when I first came to Hebron are brought to me, to gather in my arms and bless. You send them, Lord, to stand in the place of my grandchildren. I thank you for the love that has grown up in me for them, and in them for me, as I have prayed for their families all these years. This is a great comfort from your hand to me in my old age. I pray you to comfort Palti with the grandchildren born to us through our five sons. I try to picture Palti grown older and holding the little ones in his lap, as he held our sons.

David, too, has come into old age. He tried to go forth with his army again. He waxed faint, and the men finally sent him home. They recognize his fighting days are over. He has been a good king. But the record is almost closed.

*   Lord, singing with my harp when I am alone, I often return to a psalm that comforts me in my decline, as death approaches, when I shall go to those I love who went before me. I sing "... What shall I render to the Lord for all his benefits toward me? I will take the cup of salvation, and call upon the name of the Lord. I will pay my vows unto the Lord now in the presence of all his people. Precious in the sight of the Lord is the death of his saints. O Lord, truly I am thy servant..."

I thank you, Lord, for your benefits toward me. I have known your love and the love of mother, father (long ago), sister, brother, husband, sons, and my friends, the servants. I am warmed by all the memories that are good. I am kept by your promise: my death shall be precious in your sight.

*   Another rebellion for David to endure as he lies dying.   Adonijah, fourth-born, next after Absalom, decided he would be king, making himself a feast to which he invited all David's sons but Solomon, and also invited were some who sided with Adonijah, including David's long-time general and nephew, Joab, and the priest Abiathar, so long with David.   Others stayed faithful to David, including Nathan the prophet, who warned David what was happening so that David took all the necessary steps to establish Solomon on his throne, as he had promised Bathsheba. What a tumultuous day!

Now that Solomon is safely on the throne to carry on the kingdom as David wished, he is finally at peace to face his own death.

*   I am dying as David the king is dying. They have tried to keep him from chilling by having a Shunammite maiden to sleep beside him. Even in his dying, they think of a new woman for him.   The place belongs to Bathsheba. Instead Bathsheba had to suffer the shame of the presence of the young beauty as she came to solicit the king for her son's and her lives when Adonijah took the throne. Bathsheba and David, both old and wrinkled now, have been through so much together, she would have been a greater comfort to him in his dying than a lovely young stranger.

Lord, in many ways, David has had a hard life. He suffered much, and in his affliction he turned to you. He repented and turned to you when he sinned. He praised you extravagantly. He leaves an orderly kingdom, nations all around subdued. He leaves the psalms we and those after us can always sing to express every emotion of the human heart, and bring it all before your eternal throne, our perfect King, whose power is always used for good. He goes to you. I go to you.

Into your hands I commit my spirit. I see a great light. I   am   almost   home.

Excerpts from Abigail's Prayer Journal
Part I: Abigail and Nabal

Dear Lord, I wish Father had given me this journal years ago, when I was keeping the sheep, when Mother was still with us. I wish I had written down all she told me, and all that my mind turned over, the long days watching sheep. In one sense, I am sure all that is a part of me forever, but I would like to have it down in writing and be able to read it over, particularly now that I am about to become a wife. So much I would ask Mother if she were here. She and Father loved and enjoyed one another, that I remember, but as a background. I was too young to observe for learning for myself how to be a wife. Now my great question is that: how am I to be a wife? What do I need to know, and do, and expect?

If he is like Father, I guess I'll know how to please him. But Father is exceptional. What other father would treat me like the son he never had? Not that he forgot to give me what girls want, oh, no; that he did--and more. Not one of my girl friends has learned, as he taught me, to work in her father's business! I know sheep, every aspect of the business.

Anyway, I have also had to run our home since Mother died, as well as helping Father, evenings, on his records. So I am not afraid of managing servants and household procedures. That I know how to do. But, Lord, I am afraid of being with a man alone. Take my mother's place and teach me, Lord. I have only five weeks more to be a girl and to wonder what it will be like to be a woman, with a husband.

Nabal. Why did his parents name him THAT? Surely he cannot be a fool! Of course, Nabal also means "projecting", and he must be good at that, to have turned the stock his father gave him into such prosperity as he has.....

NABAL. NABAL. NABAL. **NABAL.** Who are you?

Father has known Nabal's father for years. They have met at market and synagogue, after playing together as boys at synagogue school. Father wanted to be sure I had a good match, that I need never lack any of what he has provided all my life so far. So I have no fears on that account. I shall be provided for. But what will he be LIKE? To live with... Father likes his father, but will I like him?

Lord, I'm grateful my dear Mary will go with me. Just to see a familiar face may make all the difference when everything seems too strange and new and overwhelming.

Today, our two fathers sign the contract, and father receives the dowry gifts. Father says he will never feel adequately compensated for the loss of my help in his household and business. I will plan to come over once a week to give whatever assistance I can to him, if it is all right with Nabal.

Today, when they come with the gifts, I have a plan for gaining a look at Nabal's father. I have NEVER spied, but I have to have some idea of what he looks like before he comes to take me away. I hope he is tall. I'll know in two hours! In only five weeks, I'll begin to know what he is like on the inside, at the feasting; and after the feast--oh, my stomach rolls at the thought--I will know what he is like with me.

Lord, how can I feast for days? Today, I cannot even eat until I see his father so I have a clue what Nabal looks like. Please quiet my heart, my mind, my queasiness, as I rest, if I can, before they come.

Lord, he is tall. At least, his father is. I liked the sound of his voice, too. Father never saw me, and I stayed only a minute. Oh, I am glad he is tall. I wanted a tall husband. And his voice sounds almost like singing. I mean, if his voice is like his father's. I hope I can eat some at supper. My stomach is growling.

Tomorrow will be fun, celebrating my fifteenth birthday with my girlfriends. All of them will be married, too, by this time next year. It will never be the same again with all of us. So we must have a special time to remember from now on, and laugh a lot. It wonder if any of them is as nervous as I am about being married, or are they able to talk with their mothers and have some questions answered. Of course, even with questions answered, there is still the great unknown factor: what will he be like? You could be expecting one kind of man and end up with someone totally unlike your expectations.

Well, for now, I will forget all thought of the future and just enjoy this party and the memories I share with these girls, and private memories of my own, with my own family, and sheep, and my favorite places to take the sheep.

Lord, please let my birthday be a treasure chest of happiness from beginning to end. And please, let Mariah and Lydia get through the whole party without an argument. I cannot abide the thought of them spoiling my day with their personality clashes. I know! They both love flowers. I'll put them to making us all garlands for our hair, and then Keturah and Miriam can think up games for us, and Hannah and Esther can play their instruments until we are ready for the games and refreshments, and I'll just fly around to make sure everyone is having a good time. And now, I need to stop by the kitchen to see that Beulah and Dinah have everything on hand for the refreshments for us girls--and later, for the grandparents and all the aunts and uncles and cousins coming for dinner.

Lord, thank You for meeting every need of my fifteen years so far, even with losing my mother three and a half years ago. I must trust you with my future, too, though it is so hard just now. You can help me do that, too. Trust, I mean. Help me trust You.

Lord, I cannot sleep, it has been such a full day. Full of blessings, oh, thank You. I just have to record my thoughts before I can let go and sleep--not that anyone will ever want to know what an insignificant young girl of Israel is thinking of as she turns fifteen, but maybe when I am old, I will go back and read and remember. Maybe, if I have a daughter, she will want to know what her mother was thinking when she was just about to marry. This time next year, I could have a child. Oh, I can hardly believe it.

Well, anyway, back to now.

Thank You, Lord, for the stroke of genius that put Mariah and Lydia to working with the flower garlands. Lydia arrived with her arms full of flowers she'd grown in her own flower gardens, and Mariah ran to her oh-ing and ah-ing, so they were as happy as newborn lambs as they trooped out to gather wildflowers to add to the garden ones. And we every one ended up looking like a beauty, if I do say it myself, by the time they had us all garlanded. Hannah and Esther never missed a beat of their music while Mariah and Lydia put their garlands on their heads, though they quit playing their instruments soon after, so we could play games.

Keturah went back to the game she thought up when we were little, called Binkums, and some other games we've liked to play through the years, and one new one, and then, even looking like young ladies as we garlanded beauties did, we acted like infants again and frolicked and laughed all around the house, courtyard and gardens, until we had the servants, every one of them, laughing with us. We hadn't called Kettie and Miriam Binkums and Minkums for a good two years, but we revived their old nicknames. Kettie is such a clown, outran us all in the games, and then suggested we all ride the horses before we had our refreshments. It was perfect weather for it, too.

After all that activity, we were hungry for the scrumptious delicacies that Beulah and Dinah had ready for us, and Kettie called for a Cooks' Parade so we could thank them, and then Lydia and Mariah brought out two extra flower garlands and crowned them. They were embarrassed, but pleased. It was so like Lydia to think of them.

Once we had satisfied our hunger, we went into my bedroom and fixed each other's hair in various ways and fell to talking, first mostly nonsense, then about our soon-coming weddings. Esther, being the youngest and not yet betrothed, asked to play a birthday tune she had composed for me, which was so hauntingly lovely it brought tears to my eyes and Hannah's, too; and then, Esther packed up her pipe and music, and with a round of hugs for each of us, left early. She said she wanted to play with her little brothers and sisters, but I know she felt a bit left out of the talk. I told her she'd be betrothed before she knows it, and, blushing, she said, Yes, her Mama and Papa know how she wants babies of her own and are in talks already for a bridegroom. "You'll probably be the youngest bride of us all!" I told her as she left.

It was as I thought, though the other girls have mothers to talk to, they every one wonder if they are ready for all that marriage means, and nervous about how they will be treated. Mariah hopes Jedidiah won't expect her to do what her folks never expected her to do, or she'd "just die." Lydia was biting her lips not to light into Mariah for her giddiness and helplessness, but she only said she hoped Ethan would LET her do all she wants to do and not expect her to sit on a cushion being a decoration for his house. But, she said she trusted her folks to know what she needed. And, she's glad she won't have to move far from them, as Mariah will.

Kettie, being engaged to Lydia's older brother, is the least nervous of us about what he'll be like, and thrilled to think of being Lydia's sister-in-law. She said Lydia's kept her posted on Simon, and she thinks he'll be fun. Then she added, "Anyhow, Lydia and I together can keep him in line, so he's probably more nervous about me than I am about him!" She put a hand on each side of her face, pulled her eyes and nose all out of shape, stuck out her tongue, walked like an ape, and had us all helpless with laughing.

Though I laughed with the rest of them, I hadn't missed the revelation her words brought. It was a new thought for me--the bridegroom being nervous. Is Nabal nervous, wondering what his Abigail will be like?

Miriam talked the least, but then that's just her way. Kettie's brother Jonah is a lot like Kettie and will be good for Miriam, make her laugh when she gets so serious. Kettie's already told him to call Miriam "Minkums" instead of "Sweetheart" or "Darling". Miriam said, "Thanks a lot, Kettie! You'll have him thinking he's getting a goofus instead of a girl for his wife. Just give me a nickname to use on HIM when he tries calling me Minkums." Kettie will, too.

Dearest Hannah was last to leave. She and Esther had played together so beautifully when they all first came, all the good, old, familiar tunes and then some they'd made up on their own. And then, after everyone else was gone, Hannah brought her harp up to my room, and played improvisations while we talked. I don't know how she can do that, but she listens to me, and the music even seems to help us think and express our feelings to each other. She can even look into my eyes as we talk, her fingers knowing where to touch the strings all on their own, after all her years of practicing. It's just now and then that her fingers will lift off the strings and pause as she brings forth a thought from her heart and mind. How like a sister she is to me. Lord, let nothing ever part us.

Hannah and Reuben will be married just a few months after Nabal and I, and will not live too far from Maon. Since we both ride, there should be no problem with our seeing each other often. We can raise our children up as friends, and even gather all us girls and our children together now and then, except perhaps for Mariah; but even she will be home to Maon sometimes, to see her folks.

Hannah said You have shown her, Lord, that Reuben is your perfect plan for her life, and will be not just a lawfully wedded husband, but a real soul-mate to her. I am so glad for her. If any girl deserves a soul-mate in her husband, it is Hannah. She is so in tune with You, Lord. Why have I not heard from You what Nabal will be like? Why can I not trust Father the way Lydia trusts her parents to make the match she needs? Maybe it is that Mother's insights are no longer here with us to balance his. There is more to think about than that I be provided for, materially. Bless Father, I know he's doing the best he knows.

Hannah prayed with me before she left, that my marriage be as blessed as any that ever were, as blessed as she believes hers and Reuben's will be. And we prayed for the other girls, the bridegrooms, the families of all of us, the town, and even our nation and our king, King Saul, and the one who shall succeed him, David, though he is now only a fugitive from Saul's anger.

Only Hannah, of all my friends, would have prayed this far-reaching prayer with me. I love all the girls. But Hannah is a sister-soulmate, one of my life's greatest blessings.

Before she left, Hannah gave me a big, long hug, and with tears in her eyes promised, "Abbie, we're friends forever." (She's the only one besides Father that ever has called me "Abbie", and it's therefore special to hear her say it.) After our hug, we looked into each other's eyes as I affirmed, "Yes, Hannah, we're friends forever." She looked down, picked up her harp, pressed a parchment into my hand, and fled.

I opened the parchment and read this poem she had written for me on my fifteenth birthday:

To Abigail

A garden called Womanhood,
with gate nearby,
and we outside,
breathing hints in the sweet aromas
from unknown flowers,
catching notes of new melodies
throbbing upon our heartstrings:
joys we may not foretell,
pain, too, we may not bear well,
deep, quiet pools,
thundering waterfalls,
gently rushing streams
full of life and sparkle,
joining other streams,
the flow never stopping,
drawn ever onward
to the ocean of Eternity
where our Lord awaits you and me,
arms of love outstretched.
    All is well.
        All is well.
            All is well.

I shall carry this poem with me always, and this journal, and Hannah in my heart, and You, Lord. Good night. Your own Abbie-pet--as Father calls me, when he's feeling most tender, as tonight when he told me Goodnight.

I'm ready to sleep now. Mary will let me sleep in, tomorrow morning.

        All is well.

This morning before I do anything else, I want to write also about the dinner with the relatives that followed the girls' celebration of the afternoon.

The first to arrive were Grandpa Thaddeus and Grandma Jael. He patted me on the head and rushed on to talk to Father. He's never forgiven me for being a girl instead of oldest son of his oldest son. He isn't mean, just rather abstracted. Grandma Jael inspected me from head to toe, checking, I know, to see whether I looked girlish enough. She's always been afraid I would grow unfeminine with Father's training me in his business. Evidently, I passed her inspection then, but when they left at the end of the evening, she told me "Now, dear, when you go to Nabal, best you remember all your Mother taught you, and forget all your Father taught you, if he is my own son. It's one thing to tend sheep, but quite another to enter the man's world of record-keeping. Men don't like women who take over their domain."

"Yes, Grandma Jael," I murmured and bowed my head to her wishes before giving her a hug. "I do love being a girl, you know."

She eyed me a long moment. "Yes, you do. It's a wonder, but I am glad. Sarah would be proud today if she'd lived, God rest her soul."

It was not the only time I teared up that evening, remembering Mother. And Grandma Jael hugged me. "I know you'll be a good wife, as she was," she said, as if to convince herself more than me.

Well, to go back to the beginning, things happened fast, once all the boy cousins converged, about the same time. It is all action when these boys get together. They remembered their manners enough to greet me, but that was about it. Before it was time to eat, they'd been out in the street playing kickball with the neighbor boys; and dinner was delayed while they all washed up from their running.

Meanwhile I had welcomed the little girl cousins to the courtyard and let them take turns wearing my flower garland from the party with my girlfriends. Only Jemimah, at 7, is old enough to have some idea that her cousin Abigail is about to be married. She was rather in awe of me and stuck close all evening. Her sister Jerusha and my other cousin, Cora, are both 4, and then there's Eve, who is 5, and Rebecca, who is just a year and a half. Jerusha and Cora were more interested in climbing the olive trees in the garden than in picking the flowers, as Jemimah and Eve wanted to do. Rebecca toddled along with us, humming a melody of her own inventing as she tucked her head to one side and concentrated on staying upright. All of us girl cousins were fascinated with her petite beauty and her changeover from baby ways to toddling. Any time she lifted her arms and asked, "Carry me?", she had a bigger girl to oblige her.

We were called to dinner before the flower pickers had all the blossoms they wanted, but they admired the effect as I put their treasures into a vase of water and set it on the table.

Before we ate, I had my first chance to greet Grandma Susanna and Grandpa Esau. Grandma Susanna thinks I can do no wrong. "Oh, Abigail, you look more like your mother every day, if anything even more beautiful than Sarah was. She should have lived to see your marriage. But the Lord had other plans." We shared a sweet-sad embrace and wiped the tears from our eyes together, as Father called the dinner to begin, first making a toast to me and then praying a blessing on my birthday and upcoming marriage.

The meal was delicious, and was also vacated as soon as permitted by all the boys, in a mass. They returned to the street with shouting and a bit of shoving, but no anger.

My favorite aunt, Aunt Martha, wife of Mother's just-older brother Joel, with whom Mother was very close as they grew up, came out to the garden to visit with me before any of the others. She and Mother had become very close, as Uncle Joel and Mother had been for years, in the years between their marriage and Mother's death. Aunt Martha would be like a second mother to me if they came more often. They came more when Mother was alive than since she's been gone.

Aunt Martha said, "Abigail, are you ready for marriage, any questions or qualms?", with such a sweet and interested looking into my eyes, I was ready to talk before she added her invitation, "I'll be glad to try to answer anything you can think of..."

I was glad the little girls were all absorbed in mothering little Rebecca, so that we had some privacy, though I knew it would not last long, with so many relatives here.

"Anything you can tell me about the first night, I'd be grateful." I thought that would cover the main things.

She looked thoughtful a moment, as if remembering. "Well," she breathed, "One thing I found out later was that Joel was as nervous as I was. I think if I'd realized that before, I'd have been less nervous myself, and thinking more of putting him at ease. It never occurred to me that he would be nervous, being several years older than I was, but his years hadn't included being around any girls other than his sisters and cousins, which is not the same thing at all as a sweetheart. At least that's what we all think before we are married. But there are more similarities than you might think. Of course, you've not had a brother and your boy cousins are all younger than you, but Abigail, you have a talent for setting people at ease, because you think of their needs. That's the main thing, I think. If you'll think of his needs, you'll win him over to think of yours, too, pretty much from the beginning. And if Nabal still doesn't regard your needs, I'll take a whip to him, because you deserve a husband as good as your Uncle Joel is to me!"

I laughed at the thought of my small, quiet Aunt Martha taking a whip after a big tall man she doesn't even know yet, and I hugged her for her understanding and support of me.

That was the closest encounter of any with the aunts and uncles.

I was thankful that Grandma Susanna and Grandpa Esau were last to leave. Mother's thoughtfulness came to her through her mother. I hugged Grandma Susanna to thank her for my favorite birthday present, the beautiful silk dress. She said, "Abigail, you deserve the best, for you are the best grand-daughter I could have. Your sweetness is my greatest comfort after losing my Sarah. Always stay so sweet. Let nothing make you bitter, though life may throw bitter things your way."

I cried as I extended my hug with her as long as I could before they had to leave. In the back of my mind there is a shiver now as I remember her almost prophetic tones. I wonder what is ahead, if there is more of bitter things for me to bear than any other life.

Well, I have to get into my day.

Lord, I do bless you for Mary in my life. In my earliest memories and up to this moment, and looking forward to her comforting presence in my married life, Mary is just what I need: help without ever letting me grow helpless, counsel when I'm confused, sheltering arms when I'm sorrowing, a boost when I'm burdened. Servant, yet friend, older and wiser, yet not condescending, the nearest I have to a mother, all this is what You've given me in Mary.

These days, she's not only helping me to assemble my wardrobe for the marriage feast and married life, but she's calming my fears. She says, "Not that I know by my own experience, but from my Mama and Daddy and my married sisters, I can relay to you these bits of wisdom: Keep the kitchen staff on their toes bringing good meals on time, and keep the bedroom and yourself as beautiful as you can, and ready for lovemaking. And then, if you make every effort that he know his work is valuable and his presence is desired, you shouldn't have a worry about how your marriage will go."

That not only sounds like something I can do, it sounds exciting and wonderful. Why do I still feel it's going to be bigger than I can do? It all comes down to this: who is this Nabal?

Well, anyway, You know who he is and what he needs from me, and You'll be there--and Mary, too.

Lord, all is in readiness. All my clothes are prepared and packed, all my girlfriends are ready to assemble at a moment's notice when he comes. The next time I write in this journal, I could be at his father's house amidst the feasting, celebration, and crowds.

I am so excited, my sleeping and eating are just in bits and at odd moments. Father is still eating and sleeping as usual, but he is a bit edgy with the new bookkeeper not catching on as fast as needed and my departure so near. I really must come over here often to audit the books and instruct this fellow in Father's and my accounting, or Father's business will suffer. At least now, all the shepherds are working together and submitted to Father's authority, the staff squabbles of a few months ago being all smoothed over. In that aspect, everything is ready for me to move on.

And I am ready, despite my heart's hesitations. Bring on the future and I'll meet it with my head up and my eyes and ears open to You and what You show me about this new world I enter. You are Lord in it, as in the one I've always known.

And if Nabal's nervous, or if he's not, Lord, rule over him and his ways with me--and others in his life. It will soon be "our" life.

I commit our life into Your hands.

Here we are, almost at the end of the wedding feast days, when all the crowds will leave and Nabal will take me into the marriage chamber and we become one in body and I hope in spirit as well. But he hasn't paid me much attention yet. It's been different from what I expected.

All the dancing and music, eating and drinking and merrymaking have been the total occupation of the guests, and I have had my share. But I have also been watching Nabal. I have to know what he is like. He'll be the one always here with me after the neighbors and relatives and my girlfriends have all gone home and gone on to their own lives. The girls and I have danced the women's dances and laughed and talked and enjoyed more time together than we've ever before had all at once. Underneath the comraderie and hilarity has been the keen awareness that when we meet again, things will be different with us. Our various experiences in marriage and life will take us on different journeys, away from our girlish bonds. And if bonds of friendship continue with some of these girls, it will be new, not the same. We've left the valley we've known and are going over a mountaintop divide into a new homeland. But we're not there yet, just looking across the landscape at a distant overview to see what may be alike, and what different, from life as we've known it before. Oh, bless all the girls, Lord.

But back to Nabal. To my eye, it appears he drinks more than a bridegroom would for only celebration. Is it for forgetfulness? What does he have to forget? And there have been a couple of moments when he barely controlled his temper, with some help from his brothers and friends rushing in to hold his arms to keep him from striking one of them. Whether any of the girls, or anyone else, have noticed, but Hannah, I am not certain; but Father looks at me so thoughtfully and even spoke softly into my ear, "Abbie-pet, I hope he is good to you. Tell me if you ever need anything I can do." I looked my gratefulness to him.

I don't know what he could do. He will not be here, but You will, Lord, and my Mary. Speak to me through her, and speak to my heart, when I need Your wisdom. It may be quite often. But I don't want to bring trouble on by expecting it, either. He may be under greater pressure than I am to begin his new married state. He may merely need me to be a burden-lifter in his world. I am glad I know the business of sheep--maybe it is more than he can handle alone. So I ask You to help me be the wife he needs and see his needs, the man inside, within the outer man that others may see. Let others see only what's on the outside, let the wife look into her husband's heart.

A wife is in a special position, and the duties have even a sacredness about them. So sanctify me for this calling, Lord.

Lord, many times I have come to this journal and lifted my stylus to write, and have sat here staring, and finally laid the stylus down with a sigh, to sit, unable to move or act, until duty calls me to go on about my business. How to make sense of what is happening.... I don't know.

Does my face mirror the mournful thoughtfulness of Mary's as she brushes and arranges my hair? Oh, I hope not. I am keeping a brave heart and I hope, a brave and cheerful face, though I let down my guard when she and I are alone.

If Nabal has something he is trying to forget, I have not found it out, nor am I likely to, unless something changes. At least, Nabal and his father built us a house before the marriage so that I am mistress in the household, and having a mother-in-law is not an immediate and constant presence in my home. That might be one pressure too many.

I have made friends with the cook, Zillah, and her assistant Phoebe. They were well-chosen for their jobs, and seem grateful for my administration, both claiming their lot to be bettered from their previous situations. Zillah is an excellent cook and has been eager to try some new recipes I brought with me. She makes the best sheep's tail I have ever eaten, and can cook for few or many, with little advance notice, and supervises the butcher shop well.

Phoebe works harmoniously with Zillah, and accomplishes all I list for her marketing and kitchen tasks. They keep a spotless kitchen. It has taken me and Phoebe both some time to catch on to Zillah's humor. She has a way of acting fierce and saying the opposite of the truth, just for fun, and holding off her own laughter till we catch on and grump back at her, all in sport. Phoebe was in tears a time or two before she saw Zillah was in jest. Now they carry on together and often can be heard laughing, all through the house.

They quiet down when Nabal comes in. He has nothing to complain about in his meals. But he does. Something is cooked too often or too seldom. Something is too tough, too hot or too cold. He seems to need them to be fearful of his coming. I would not say that they are truly fearful, but they give him the appearance of fear that he demands. "Yes, sir, sorry, sir," etc.

Salome, the cleaning lady and laundress, does not live here with the servants, but comes and goes back to her own family. She stays to herself and keeps quiet, but she has seemed grateful for my queries into the well-being of her children, and my praise of the thoroughness of her work. I believe her reserve is crumbling before my concern. There is a less wary look in her eyes now, and she glows when telling of her children's growth and funny spontaneous sayings. I don't think any other employer asked her about her own life, before. Mother's ways with her staff may be as exceptional as Father's ways with me, though I took them as normal and average, and learned them by observing her.

My new seamstress, Bernice, is expert with spinning and weaving and dyeing, as well as styling and assembling garments for the household. From the shearing of the sheep to the fitting of the clothes, she knows every step and can train others. She is also able to comb the lovely goats' hair and spin it and knit beautiful warm wraps from it. She's one who sings while she works. About the only time she's not singing is when Nabal is about. If I don't hear him stamping or shouting, I know he's near by the ceasing of her song.

That's the household staff, and now I have some household duties to attend to, but, Lord, now that I have begun to release here some of my new life's experiences, I know this will be a way for me to search for understanding and Your viewpoint on what I am now living, so I will be back here. You are somehow in this, as in all my life up to this. Clear my confusion. Oh, would that life were laid out in a tidy plan, like business records, and the truth of a human heart as easy to discern as the sale price of a roll of sheep's wool.

Lord, I must set some thoughts down. I've just come from a "conference" (I guess that's what it was) in the lambing shed. Bernice had taken me out this breezy spring morning to see the outbuildings, the servants' quarters, the spinning and weaving hut, where she works, and the goat pens, the sheepfold, and the lambing shed. Nabal was in town, trading, and all the shepherds were in at the same time for the upcoming shearing. Some were so far gone in a dispute that one had quit and already left, and two others would have been fighting with their fists had we women not appeared when we did.

As it was, we startled them, and they backed off from each other, bowing to us as Bernice introduced me as Nabal's new wife, and them to me as Laban and Shobab. >From rough and violent, their demeanor had changed in a twinkling to gentlemanly. I could not help smiling in amusement, but I quickly turned the smile into welcoming and friendliness. After a nod to each as I spoke his name, I began by kneeling and fondling some of the sheep, and even picking up a lamb. They were obviously amazed that I was not squeamish with the lamb, as many women would be, or all concerned to keep my clothes from being touched by animals. After exchanging astonished glances with each other, they began naming individual sheep for me from their two flocks, and talked at length about each one's problems and personalities. The more they could see I was truly involved in all these details, and knowledgeable, they more they talked, until finally it was as natural as birth for me to inquire as to the nature of the dispute; and they were not at all hesitant to reveal their grievances.

It seems that Nabal changes his orders, confuses what he has told one with what he has told another, until they end up with too many flocks in one place and each shepherd convinced that the others are the ones out of place. I kept asking questions of them until I learned a great deal about the nearby grazing lands with sheepfolds, and the hazardous features of the terrain to reach these places, and good watering sites--all the details related to the sheep's needs. From that basis we worked out a plan which they both accepted willingly.

And also, Laban knew a young boy, Amal, who would be a good replacement for the shepherd who quit today. Bernice brought Phoebe, who was dispatched to fetch the boy. We were all still talking sheep when Amal arrived and the two took him off to learn his flock, after we ascertained his experience.

In the midst of the conferring, Laban and Shobab let slip some comments about Nabal's having been drunk as he gave some of his orders. At first, they were aghast at having spoken thus before his wife, but when they saw that I was aware and not shocked, but only thinking it over, they relaxed completely, and we left in mutual understanding and esteem. I had learned just how extensive is Nabal's wealth, more vast than Father's. But it will take management to keep it.

I have no idea what Nabal's reaction will be to my involvement in the business that is now supporting me as well as him, but I do know we have a contented staff with clear directions, and thus a more stable business than we did a few hours ago. And I have staunch friends and supporters in Laban and Shobab--IF Nabal will listen to them.

Though it is painful, I would unburden my heart to write now of Nabal, but I must go to the kitchen to confer with Zillah and Phoebe regarding the dinner, which will be a large one tonight.

Meanwhile, Lord, please work in Nabal to receive my help as the good it is meant to be, as FOR him and not at all against him. With all my heart I desire in some way to touch his heart.

My Lord and my God, Nabal raged at me for butting into his business. Never in my life have I experienced such a barrage, not anything close to the noise and fury. He did not strike me. Only once did he touch me, only to grip my upper arms in his hands until they are bruised and to jerk me until my neck is sore. He has left me to myself, as if I would spend my time alone pining for his company. I never could have foreseen I would rather be alone than with my husband. I am not afraid of him, and I thank You for that. But he has done nothing to endear himself to me. That is an extreme statement and I can hardly believe it myself, except that I have lived through it.

When we have been alone, he has been rough and distant and not willing to take time for tenderness or sweetness. He has come in every night, and, on the nights he is more sober, has wanted me. No, not really me, he has wanted his own satisfaction, gotten it and dropped off to sleep. Other nights he's already been too drunk even for that much. Either way, I'm alone. I've tried to keep myself attractive for him, but if he's noticed, he's not let me know. It is Mary's beloved round face beaming into my own that tells me, "You're looking lovely, my sweet. When God made you, He made one luscious beauty."

And then, Lord, You speak Your love for me in Your still way, in my heart.

As it is now, I don't see how Nabal and I would ever have a child, and anyway, I hardly can bear to think of bringing one into a home where the poor little thing would have to live with such a father.

Days, he is off on business. At meals, he delivers a soliloquy in two-part harmony. One part is in complaints about the food and household help, and the other part is on his business and the poor help he has to put up with there. The town merchants and traders are dishonest and greedy; the shepherds are as stupid as the sheep. And so it goes. If I try to put in a good word for someone on the staff, he turns on me.

Why is he so angry? I have found no key to understanding. Lord, show me his heart, that I might help heal it. Only two months married and it seems like years.

Thank You that Mary is here to assure me that the fault is not in me. But she has no more idea than I do what actions I might take, or avoid, to make things better. I pray to get along with my husband, even half as well as with the other people in my life. I'm grateful there's no other disharmony. But I'm lonely. If there's anything more I could do, show me, Lord. If there's nothing I could do, help me to accept the fact and find peace and contentment somehow.

The shearing celebration brought many people together for great fun and rejoicing. And I am grateful for a bountiful year and so much wool for the market. Most of all, I'm grateful to be at Father's once a week lately, where his esteem is such a balm to my spirit, though it is a strain to keep a chipper tone in my voice and not to refer to my loneliness, but only to speak of our prosperity and my pleasure in the servants, shepherds, and sheep. Father is burdened enough these days with his own loneliness without having to bear knowing of mine.

Tomorrow, I have a visit to Hannah, just before her marriage feast days. Toward this visit I have mixed feelings. I can never conceal my true state from her, as sensitive as she is to what is going on in me, and I need any comfort and wisdom she might have for me, need her friendship; but I don't want to put any cloud over her own time of rejoicing in her bridegroom.

Lord, guide my words and actions with her, and grant her all her heart's desires in her marriage with Reuben.

Lord, for the birdsong, flower bloom, breeze caress and sun kiss, and for my forever friendship with Hannah, my heart was light and singing as I rode over to meet with her. I thank You that You give wings to my spirit to fly above the woes that weigh upon my soul. All is well, I shouted to the glorious day and my faithful horse Dapple. When Hannah saw me coming and ran to me, I know my face glowed with a joy of living that matched hers, and we whirled around with hands clasped like young children as she said, "You old married lady, you! You are looking good!"

"You blushing bride, you!" I responded, "You never looked better!"

And we laughed, as always. It was a good beginning. And to keep it good, I immediately started in asking her about her preparations for her own nuptials. She showed me her new clothes and chattered on at length before turning to me and my situation.

Though she sobered as I talked, and cried for me, her own inner exuberance buoyed her up and carried me along as well. And I told her the good news about our prosperous shearing and the harmony I enjoy with the household and business staff--and the sheep. She's always loved the way I can describe a sheep's personality. "Oh, Abbie, you're a character!" she said. "You make them sound like people."

"They ARE like people!" I retorted. So lightness was restored.

And at the end, which came all too soon, Hannah prayed with me, that I find the key to Nabal's heart, and in the meantime don't let him pull me down. I prayed that all her dreams come true...

As I rode away, she waved to me for a long time and I looked back to wave to her and to lock in my memory the picture she made, the sun bringing out her most beautiful feature, that dark auburn hair, thick and full over her shoulders.

Altogether the visit, the friendship, the very weather itself, ministered to my heart, and I give the glory to You, Lord, for You provide all good, all we need.

I SHALL keep joy in my life, by Your grace.

Tonight, Nabal met in town, with some men from synagogue, and Elishua showed up to go over the books, not realizing Nabal would be gone. I visited with him a bit about his family, and then mentioned that I had kept my father's books, almost alone, and would be happy to look at Nabal's with him, if he would permit. He could not conceal his shock at my suggestion, but after some stammering and shaking of his gray head, followed by a thoughtful staring at my face, said finally, "Why not? My wife has a good head for business and I judge you to be very like her, Miss Abigail." His eyes spoke a birth of possible confidence in my abilities.

As I had feared, there are some trends that are of real concern, if Nabal's--and my--prosperity is to go on. After Elishua had made some suggestions and showed me the way he keeps the records of the sheep, goats, other livestock, wool and hide accounts, shepherds' and servants' wages, and occasional sales of milk, meat, and fruit, and proved to his satisfaction that I did know bookkeeping, he leaned back with a sigh, and actually asked me, "Now, Missy, what do you say we ought to do next?"

He listened to my suggestions. I had a strong sense of being guided beyond my knowledge and experience, and the look in his eyes confirmed that hunch. We worked for two hours.

He left with an understated assurance, "Miss Abigail, Nabal shall be none the wiser as to our changes, but he'll have to notice the results. I'll let him take the credit."

Nothing could have been more to my liking. I need no more rampages, and Nabal obviously needs some boosts.

Lord, You are at work. Prepare Nabal's heart for a greater work.

My Lord and my God, we've just returned home from the wedding feast for Hannah and Reuben, and You have revealed to me in no uncertain terms what I already knew in vague form, just from what You allowed me to see of Reuben's ways with Hannah, though they were in public. No matter that there were crowds of relatives and friends around, no matter that Reuben wanted to (and did) have fun with his lifelong buddies at his nuptial feast, he was attentive to Hannah in ways to fulfill any girl's virgin longings as she anticipated having a husband.

Reuben often stood at Hannah's side, his arm about her waist, hugging her to him as he offered up still another toast to her beauties, inner, too, not just outer beauties. He was often talking quietly with her, and listened with total attention when she played her harp, as she insisted on doing, though musicians had of course been hired. And when he would stand facing her, I often watched from beside her, how his eyes gazed over her in rapt absorption of every detail of her hair, forehead, eyes, nose, cheeks, lips, chin, as if he could never have enough of nearness to her--all this, despite the loud jibes of his male friends (long-extended whistles, catcalls, shouts--"Reuben, wait till you get her in the chamber!"). It was as if he were deaf to them, and blind to the eyes that took in his concentrated adoration, almost worship, of Hannah. The only thing that was in HIS world was himself and his bride, all else was shut out.

I could watch him with her only so long before I had to drop my eyes and move away, my very organs rolling over inside me with the rolling of my emotions. If he could adore her so in public, what WOULD it be like for her to be with him in private?

Oh, I know nothing of marriage.

I am glad for Hannah. I love her too well, and have cared for her too long, to let anything like jealousy into my heart and mind. Only, I am so lonely.

I remember she prayed my marriage be as blessed as hers. She prayed and I know the depth and power of her prayers. But Your answer is simply, No. My marriage is no marriage at all. There is nothing in it that You made to be in a marriage.

Only You. You are with me, Lord. If You are all I have, then You will be all I need, as well, even to being my supernatural Husband; and my soul will find satisfaction in You.

Bless Hannah and Reuben with even more love with each passing year than already obviously flows between them.

And, oh, Lord, help me.

Lord, the rains were so heavy this last year, all October through January, that now we have a bountiful harvest. The planting done shortly after our marriage in February has borne fruit so that we are enjoying fresh vegetables and fruits at meals, and preserving our apricots in honey, and our grapes by drying into raisins and fermenting into wine. I've never heard such singing as the treaders this year, downright raucous with exuberance to be treading such a bumper crop.

I have been busy with Zillah and Phoebe in the kitchen, several hours a day. For the harvest, I am grateful. Gardens and orchards are part of our wealth, part of Your provisions for our needs, though Nabal shows no gratitude. I thank You on his behalf; he is not able, for reasons You alone know, Lord.

Father has remarried, a widow with grown children, Damaris. I wholeheartedly approve of her character and see the change in Father, for the better. Whereas before, his loneliness kept his attention from focussing on my own loneliness, now his bliss is a similar shield for me, so that I need not fear revealing too much to him. I am often with Damaris in the kitchen and gardens when I visit there, and for the rest, I'm helping on his business records, both with him, and alone or with his new bookkeeper, Caleb. Damaris has no head for business, or interest in sheep, only in Father and his well-being. It is enough for him and so for me, too. In fact, I would feel too displaced from his life if she were a businesswoman as well as companion and cook. I leave there each week with a lighter heart, knowing Father is no longer lonely.

Hot days are upon us. Things are still blooming now, but will begin to wither, as always, as the dry season marches on.

Salome now brings her oldest daughter, Sharon, with her to learn the cleaning and laundry and to assist her at her tasks. Sharon will soon be old enough to work out and help the family income. I'm enjoying the visits with her. At twelve, she is nearest in age to me of all the servants, though I am past fifteen and a half now. To her I am an old married lady, but still able to have some fun. I even taught her the Binkums game and she took it home for her younger brothers and sisters.

Change is all around, but in Nabal. I have no clue into his heart. Whether he has any satisfaction from our marriage bed, or more often, passes out in drunken stupor too early, I lie unsatisfied and alone on my side of the bed, praying my way to sleep, listening to his snoring and the gecko's wail that floats down from where it clings to the ceiling or wall overhead, matching the wail my heart would release if I let it. I do not let it. I turn toward the listing of Your blessings--the provision of our material wealth, and the relationships of Father, Damaris, my old girlfriends, and all the servants and shepherds, the people around me. If I have no husband with whom to share my soul, I share bits of my soul with many, and all with You, my Lord. The ledger of my life then balances, as business records must. And rest comes.

Samuel has died. All our nation is in mourning. Father and Nabal travelled to Ramah, along with many other men, while I met with Hannah. We prayed for our nation more than for any personal needs. It seemed the dry season was upon us in our spirits with the departing of this great old prophet, as it is upon our land with the ceasing of the rains.

Yet, Hannah's new state, expectant motherhood, is a sign that life does renew itself, dry times do pass. She is radiant, and I soaked up the peace that saturates her, and their whole household. Just being in her house, there is a feeling of peace strong enough to reach out and grasp.

She said, "Oh, Abbie, if I could, I would give you from the abundance that is Reuben's and mine. It seems we have enough for you and Nabal, too. But I know that if Nabal were able to receive, you'd have no need for any overflow from us. I know you, and if your husband were a match for you, how rich your marriage would be. Abbie, there is something coming for you. I know it.

What it may be, I do not know, but something good is coming your way. Keep heart, my dear friend."

So, Lord, while You are taking care of the needs of our nation, remember your Abbie-pet, though I am but such a small part of all Israel, and You have so much more on Your mind than the lonely heart of one young girl in this, Your nation and people. Yet I dare to think that You care for me, too. Even Nabal, too.

Dry season is over. Rains are coming upon the land. No rain for Nabal, however. If anything his explosions are more frequent. Now, almost weekly some servant or other, or some shepherd or other, comes to me with hurt feelings, or resentment, an argument, a threat to walk off and never come back, a need for supplies that should have been met before it became an emergency (Bernice had requested of Nabal that two worn shuttles be replaced weeks before coming to me, and Laban and Shobab had waited all through dry season for Nabal to carry out roof repairs on the lambing sheds, without action until the rains began and they came to me with the roof leaking, and Nabal still putting them off.), tools needing repair or a mix-up in orders (Bernice needed a loom repaired and the butcher shop needs knives sharpened.)--all traced to Nabal, and his absence of leadership, contradictory commands, or drunken state.

My gratitude to You, my Lord, that in each case, the situations are met and handled, by Your giving me just the soothing word, the person who can be contacted to make the repair or supply the lack, or the solution the disputing parties can agree to. It seems a miracle that no one has resigned since that one young shepherd months ago, before I had met any of them.

How I am blessed to see these instances of brokenness made whole again. Without the seeming disasters, I'd never have seen Your hand working in such mighty ways.

Surely You will work upon Nabal's heart, too, one day. Oh, let it be, Lord.

Today You revealed another way You are working to protect the provisions You've supplied to Nabal and me. Laban and Shobab have told me before that the Philistines from time to time sweep in and raid some local flock of sheep. Thus the vigilance of our shepherds has been extended beyond watch against wild predators such as bears, lions, or jackals, to watching for a human enemy. But lately, they report that David and his band of some 600 men has been encamped in the area; and while the men have to be fed every day, David has managed them so that they are fed by solicited donations, never by raids. In fact, since they've been nearby, the Philistines have ceased their raiding flocks all around our area. Our shepherds rest easily, compared to the tension when Philistines ravished local flocks unimpeded.

Meanwhile, we are having good rains, and though there is flooding along the streams in low-lying areas, we are so glad for the prospect of good planting and reaping that we do not complain over some flood destruction on the way to the harvest for next May.

The time for our first wedding anniversary is drawing near, and then the shearing and harvest of wool from our flocks. Aside from the failure of my marriage, I have much for which to be thankful. Time after time I have seen Your hand of protection upon our wealth and that of our staff, as well as upon the concord among all of us, excepting Nabal. How this little community can be in accord, with the leader out of sorts with all of us, is a wonder beyond any explanation that I have. The regard given to me by all of them has been a balm to the wounds of my spirit from the disregard of my husband, and the loneliness at the core of my life.

For all these mercies, I thank You, Lord.

Dear Lord, I must still my soul and reflect upon the strange, horrific and wondrous things that have swirled in upon us in a mighty whirlwind the past several hours. I must clear the fog that has been stirred up around me as so many things happened so quickly, one after another, that the beginning of this day seems as the beginning of an era. We are not at all where we were as this day began--or where we might have been if things had gone as they started to (Oh, I shudder to think of it.), and we will never again return to the routines to which we had become accustomed.

Where were we as the day began? We were in the midst of shearing. Of course, that meant many more people around than usual, and thus much activity from before dawn in the kitchen, preparing for large meals. Zillah had been making loaves of bread and her special spicy barley-fig cakes with almonds, for days. We'd been making our lists of supplies to bring from storage--honey and honey-preserved fruits, spices, wines, grain--lists of things to do each day to have all in readiness for the first day of shearing feasts, and lists of what Phoebe will bring from market. Meanwhile, the butcher shop was bustling to prepare all the meat we will need--mutton, kid, and even a buck that Nabal brought from hunting.

In the midst of this hubbub, Laban came breathlessly to the kitchen and asked for me to step outside, panic all over his face, and gasping for breath from his haste. In bits he gave me this information: David sent some of his men to Nabal and begged a share for all of them in the shearing feast, with blessings on our household; and Nabal insulted him before his men, claiming not to know who David is! He knows David. All Israel knows David. I believe, with many others, that, as You have anointed David to be king, he SHALL be king, but Nabal sees only what is now, not what You are bringing about. By present appearances, David is only a hopeless fugitive, not safe in any one place for any length of time. Oh, Nabal, Nabal.

Laban reminded me of the wall of protection that David's men have given to all our shepherds and flocks, and the friendly communication between them all this recent time. And of course, Laban feared for the very lives of all the male staff of our household, including his own life, and for the women perhaps a fate worse than death--slavery and forced unions with strange men.

He ended his message with a question to me of what I would do to stop the attack, leaving it to me because he is not able to get anything across to Nabal--that "son of Belial" he called him--not without reason, especially after this display of foolishness today.

I could see that we were all doomed if it were left to Nabal in his drunken stupor, and that I must act very quickly. Praise Your Name, the food was ready and had only to be packed on mules for delivery.

Zillah, Phoebe, and I flew around and, praying all the way for Your anointing upon me and my words, I left at the head of a mule train bearing 200 loaves of bread, two large wineskins full of our own finest wine, five full sheep cooked into savory cuts, including Zillah's matchless sheep's tails, five measures of parched grain, a hundred raisin clusters, and 200 fig cakes. Maybe they could smell us coming by the time we met, definitely soon after.

As I rounded a small valley, and came out on a hillside, there were David and his men, thundering up before me. I immediately lighted from the mule and fell to the ground in obeisance to our future king. And as soon as the men were still, I began to speak, begging him to place all blame upon me and to hear my words. I am not sure what all I actually said, because You spoke through me, but I would say that the words are burned upon David's mind and heart and he can re-create them, especially as the men nearest him heard also. Among them, they would remember every phrase, I have no doubt.

Speaking softly, I asked him to forebear placing emphasis on what a poor drunken fool has to say, who is not able to speak other than foolishness. If I had heard his men's appeal, they would not have heard such talk. I swore by Your very life, Oh Lord, that You were protecting David from taking his own vengeance, as he has always refrained from doing in the case of Saul's aggression against him. And I gestured to the feast I offered to him and his men and begged him to receive it and forgive any earlier trespass. I gave him assurance that You are surely bringing to pass his kingdom rule because they are Your battles he has always fought, and fought honorably up to this point, and that one mere man seeking his soul cannot stop Your protection of his soul; and Your vengeance on his enemies will be sure and his kingdom established over Israel without his ever having to blemish his record by taking vengeance upon himself to accomplish. And I ended by asking him to remember me, his servant.

I can never, never forget David's face at this encounter. At the first, his eyes were narrowed and his face contorted as his mouth spewed forth his mission of destruction on all that pertains to Nabal. At the sight of me, all that suddenly ceased.

I could not see his face as I knelt, but arising to speak, I fastened my gaze upon him. Oh, it was wondrous.

The intensity of this man's soul was focussed equally on two things that were in essence one, my person and my message (ultimately Your message spoken through me). His eyes rounded, and swiftly, swiftly, covered my face and then my figure, and returned to my face, blazing with what I can only say was exactly the way I saw Reuben looking at Hannah, with a hunger and an appreciation amounting to adoration. Your words coming through my mouth were anointed to his ears, but more. I am convinced my very person was aglow with Your Spirit in a way I never was before. The message and the messenger burned with truth and light. You did that. I did nothing but allow You to flow through.

David stood in an awe of silence in the light of the moment. Truly time stood still before it moved forward again.

His first words acknowledged that it was You, Lord, preventing him from bloodshed, by sending me that day. He blessed You, then me and my advice, and admitted the crime he had been about to commit. He accepted the gift of food needed for his men.

I made as if to do obeisance again, but he took my hands and lifted me to my feet and, looking into my eyes with his whole soul in his eyes, bid me go to my house in peace and assurance that he had hearkened to my words and accepted my person.

I led the mule train back empty, and found Nabal far gone in drink, feasting with the shepherds and shearers and other staff and some neighbor men, heedless both of my absence from the dinner and of the danger that all that assembly had narrowly escaped. There was no talking to him in that state. Tomorrow is soon enough for him to know.

I go to bed, perhaps to sleep, later, after wondering over all that has happened. Oh, Lord, once in every woman's life, she ought to know a man's gaze such as David gave to me this day. That look can carry me through many a lonely day and night to come. Your acceptance of me, as I am, was expressed by that look from David's eyes.

He is my king, Nabal is my husband, You are my God. All is well.

Lord, I arose early so as to be sure that Nabal would not leave on business before I could speak with him. Seeing me, he turned his back on me and strode away, but I ran after him and tugged on his sleeve as I pleaded with him, "Nabal, you must hear me--an emergency!" He turned and glared down through blood-shot eyes, hazy with hangover. As I spoke rapidly and softly, using as few words as I could, understanding slowly dawned upon his befogged brain, and he perceived just how deadly was the danger I had diverted from him--how near he came to losing not only his entire holdings but his very life as well. He groaned loudly and staggered and fell to thc floor. I knelt beside him in shock and finally recovered enough to pray.

There was no response from him, though he still breathed.

Finally, I rose, running and calling for help. We women knew we could not carry him, so Phoebe ran to the shearing shed and back with some shearers behind her. They carried him to his office and laid him on the couch there. They hollered to him, pinched his cheeks, did whatever they could think of that might rouse him to consciousness. After he still showed no response, they took off his belt and purse and outer garments and made him comfortable in the bed. Stepping outside with me, they listened with grave attention as I described what had happened yesterday afternoon and evening.

From them, the news quickly spread so that all our people knew of their escape.

All day, one after another, the shepherds, shearers, all the household staff, everyone in our community, has come to me with a holy hush, to communicate more by touch and expressions on their faces than by their few words, that they stand by me, and hurt for Nabal. Though he caused them all trouble, they can see he has been the most troubled of any. There's no desire for revenge among them. Most blessed state of things.

But not for Nabal. He is alive, but only barely. There is no movement. Mornings, afternoons, evenings I sit by him and remind him that our high priest offers the lamb to cover all our sins, his too. At times he opens his eyes. Under the general appearance of haze, I can discern a terror in his expression. So far, I see no release of terror, though on the third day I told him his father was taking a lamb to offer a sacrifice--a sin offering--for any sins of Nabal, travelling to Shiloh, that our high priest might accept the blood of the perfect lamb. Still no flicker in Nabal's eyes.

But I sit by the side of his couch, touch his hand, his forehead, sing and pray aloud, and remind him of the blood of the sacrificial lamb that covers the sins of all Israel. And day flows into night, might into day, no change.

Lord, now on this, the tenth day after Nabal's collapse, You have taken him from this earth. How I weep before You, before all, not able to stop my tears from flowing. Oh, that his life is over and I never saw his heart, never knew why he was so angry, nor what I might have done to help set him free.

Can there be a greater loss than that someone dies without having lived? Oh, Nabal.

Lord, I know You have purpose in all You do. It is our human weakness that we cannot see as You do. It is too late for Nabal, but there are others for whom it is not too late. I know that I will not always weep. But for now, I need to. In some ways, I am a lost lamb. Shepherd, find me.

Lord, in these days of mourning, there have been moments of peace that came from You. I know they did not come from me, or my surroundings. There are no words yet in which I can form what this peace means or is about, and then the waves of grief and sorrow come rolling over my soul like a storm on the Sea of Galilee, and there is nothing in my world but weeping. I eat, sometimes, in between, but I am doing nothing. Like an unmanned boat, I float in the peaceful times and toss and roll on waves of weeping, surprised each time they subside that I am not capsized. But I am still alive.

Lost boat, lost lamb, lost girl. But I am still alive. My captain, my shepherd, my Lord, You know where my life is going.

Now that the burial is accomplished, the storm season has ended. Now I know why we have periods for mourning and the finality of the burial--not that all mourning is over, but the intensity will never return to threaten to engulf. I can feel it from deep within me.

I am beginning to function. I see, truly see, the other people around me, Mary first, the most constant person in my life. It is she who is there to give the hugs, to assist me to take up again my usual care for my person and my garments, and of course my tasks toward the others. They have carried on beautifully what had to be done, but now they welcome me back to my place.

My place. No! As a widow, I have no place now. A great change must come, and what it is to be, I do not see. I cannot go to Father and Damaris, please, Lord. Where am I to go? They will ask me, I know. But grant, Lord, that I need not impose upon their new household. They see me as grieving the loss of the love of a husband. May they never know the true nature of my grief. May they be blessed in the love they share in their mature years, and not be burdened with trying to find another husband for me, a widow now. Lord, will you take me up and establish me somewhere, in some station?

Why I am not afraid, I cannot say, but despite the facts of my case, I am at rest underneath the layer of unrest, the murmurs and questions of household staff, even as Nabal's father takes over his herds and shepherds, all his business. I have said my goodbyes to Laban and Shobab and the other shepherds, with a peace that passes understanding.

I may not understand, but I accept gladly. You're my Lord and I'm still your Abbie-pet.

Lord! You are amazing! From the depths to the heights! I who am a widow, yet who was never really a wife, am now to become a true wife. I have not yet taken in the new reality, the new position that I am yet preparing to embark upon.

Wife of DAVID. Oh, can it be? The anointing of my Lord upon me in that one meeting with David has been the spark that has started a flame of love in his heart--and mine. Oh the sweetness of his words in the messages he sent by his men, asking for my hand in marriage. It is so sudden, in one sense, yet so right. I wonder that I never thought of it until the men rode up and bowed and handed me the first message. I could only cry yet again, but in a new way, and ask them to stay for dinner. After instructing Zillah and Phoebe, I left the meal preparation to them and retired to my chamber to reread the message and lay it before You, Lord, and fall before Your throne in an awe such as I have never known before. You have a plan beyond all my possible imagining. David is to be Kind of Israel, one day. I know there is still a time of testing and uncertainties, even deadly dangers, but I also know he is the king you have chosen for our people. Am I then to be a queen? Oh, I dismiss it. It is too huge a thought.

More to my capacity is the thought that I am to be wife of this man who can be so touched to have been stopped from a wrong act that would have been the only blemish upon his record as he waits out the time before he is crowned, this man who has shown himself true in waiting upon Your time to place him upon the throne by Your acts, not his. What a man!

And what he saw in me, to appeal to him, was Your use of me, my being Your vessel. Oh, from such a beginning, all in You, surely this is to be that marriage that Hannah's prayers were all about, a marriage as blessed as hers and Reuben's.

This one insignificant young girl of Israel is just one big song of praise to my mighty Lord, God of all Israel, Who alone can take someone like me out of oblivion into history.

Wife of David, sweet prince.

Oh, as I find out all that is in him, I will at the same time be learning all that is in You, Lord. That's the wonder of this coming union. It's to be a union of a man and a woman, yes, but more, a union in Your Spirit, ordained by You, for all time and eternity, a flowing between time and eternity, earth and heaven, all that You meant a marriage to be.

All is well,
All is well,
All is well.

Messengers to dispatch to Father and Damaris (and they can tell all the family) and to Hannah (and she can spread the word to all our bunch of friends). And sleep to come, if I am able to sleep for wondering. And then tomorrow a new life to begin.

My heavenly King on the throne of the universe will establish my earthly king on the throne of Israel, my husband, my David. Truth beyond belief. I love You, Lord, I love my life.

Excerpts from Abigail's Prayer Journal
Part II: Abigail and David

My Lord, You gave me a wedding to treasure. As Mary helped me dress, after arranging and rearranging my hair till she was satisfied with it, I wondered whether she were not almost as excited as I was for my nuptial night with David. Yet she spoke very little. She knew that David would speak all I needed to hear.

As she surveyed the final result, she finished with a quick hug, squeezing my shoulders and whispering, "Now, you have the husband you deserve, my sweet Abigail. I am so glad." And she was gone.

I dabbed a last bit of perfume behind my ears and danced around the tent on my toes, enjoying the flow of my gown and the anticipation of David's coming to me. Despite the suddenness of all of this, I was more excited than fearful.

It began with his entry, as he gazed at me the same way he had as I first came to him to intercept his fury, when Your heavenly anointing was upon all our words, and he had come into his right mind again, and had seen me as Your agent in his life, protecting his kingship by protecting his record of refusing to turn aggressor. Now, as then, his eyes feasted upon me, my face first and longest, as if I were an angel, then all of me as if he had been starving for so long and had come into a banquet to end all hunger from now on.

He held me as if he would never let go and he whispered bass into my ears such sweetnesses. He sees in me more than I am. But I rise to be all that I hear him calling me. My heart soars, my mind, my spirit, my body, on wings above all that is common in life. He is so intense, but he did not rush, as if what is sweetest and best deserves a taking of time to admit its timelessness. It was one night, but it was eternity.

And many nights to follow have been as sweet, only each is something different.

I am learning to know him, though he is so complex no one will ever know him well. He has spoken of all his anguish over Saul's turning against him so completely, of his hanging onto the Lord's promise of his kingship back when he was hardly grown, and his wondering how it can be, as so much time has passed without fulfillment. He has told me of his being overwhelmed by Saul's making him the king's son-in-law and by Michal's love of him, and then her removal when he was running and helpless to do anything, his loneliness and missing of her and marriage, and then his realization when he heard of her remarriage that that part of his life was lost forever. He told how his rage over Nabal's insult was the release of this other rage and helplessness, and then how, when I appeared so unexpectedly as he rushed, blind with rage, to take action where he thought he finally could, to avenge all the wrongs against him, and how the suddenness of the presence of God had come upon him to halt, correct, and redirect him to his former trust. In that moment, once again he could wait upon God to take care of all his enemies, if Saul, then surely Nabal; and then, when Nabal died, God's voice assured him of divine intervention on his behalf, that would never cease. And, in the same moment, God told him to take me to wife, as the helpmeet of God's own choosing, because of my love for God.

For David, for me, everything is coming together, as David and I come together, stronger in union every day.

David says, "Oh, Abigail, I am so grateful," and he refers to many things. And I say, "Oh, David, and Oh, Lord, I too am so grateful."

Every day, David is out with his men, and in the afternoon sometime comes back to the tent his servants prepared for me--our marriage chamber. How can he be so urgent and intense in his need for me, yet at the same time never rough or rushing, but tender, taking time for me, wooing and bringing me with him, honoring my person, my wishes, my needs, my likes and dislikes, all that I am, fulfilling my every dream for what a husband might be. And he is refreshed, as I am. I think that I could stare into his eyes, or lie by his side, forever.

For this union that is in You and of You, I bless You, Lord.

That I am here at all is a miracle. Then everything that happens here is another miracle.

Dear Lord, for the beauty of this earth, I bless You. For the days I spent as shepherd of my father's sheep, out in the open air, for green pastures and still waters, blue sky and blue flowers in the fields, and flocks of sheep grazing, for valleys and rushing brooks, hills and distant mountain peaks, and for the capacity to see and soak in and enjoy all these, I thank You. And now, for giving me a husband who has also learned in the same school of shepherding. These days now, being just after the later rains and before the drought time has taken hold, David and I walk   hand in hand over the land near the encampment. Each of us knowing You in the beauty around us in Your creation, wedded with knowing our mutual loss of loneliness and gain of a kindred spirit with whom to share the created beauty that means so much to each of us--oh, I could walk with David forever. If David and I together, watching over some sheep, were all there were in life, it would be enough.

Everything is good.

"All is well." Yes, truly.

Lord, this man is not only lover and shepherd, he is poet and singer. He has his harp here in the tent, and in the evenings he sings. Whatever he does, he is pouring forth all that is in him, and that is a great deal--more than I will ever know. Such a depth of feeling, awareness, understanding. He has been singing, caressing his harp as he caresses me, with his whole soul, aware of nothing but the song he sings to You, as in loving me, he is aware of nothing else.

He has been singing:

>How long wilt thou forget me, O Lord? for ever?
>How long wilt thou hide
>thy face from me? How long shall I take counsel
>in my soul, having sorrow
>in my heart daily? How long shall mine enemy
>be exalted over me?
>Consider and hear me, O Lord my God: lighten
>mine eyes, lest I sleep the
>sleep of death. Lest mine enemy say, I have
>prevailed against him; and those that

> trouble me rejoice when I am moved.
> But I have trusted in thy mercy; my heart shall
> rejoice in thy salvation. I will
> sing unto the Lord, because he hath dealt
> bountifully with me."

I am writing these words because the anguish he feels for Saul's opposition is a representation of all the anguish of every human soul because our destinies are never worked out without opposition. And as he turns to You in all his anguish, trusting and looking forward to Your outworking of Your promises to him, so must we all--our only hope is in You. And a million people, each going through a unique trouble in life, can sing these words to You, and they'll be as fresh as they are now.

What I record of David's songs will last long, long after the business records I have kept are all lost in oblivion. This is what I am here for.

Oh, I am so glad to be here.

By Your grace, I am here for this part to play in history.

Oh, I praise You, Lord.

Lord, still another facet of David's character that You're revealing to me is that of commander of his men. He does all things well, this too. Each day when they are out, they are either drilling for battle, chasing Philistine marauders, or communicating with local herders, farmers, orchard and vineyard keepers, who are all supporting this small army of 600 with foodstuffs to keep us all alive-- more to the point, keeping our future king until he comes into his reign. David simply loves these people You are giving him to lead and guide, as he loves You, Lord, the Giver.

At some time almost every evening, I will ask David questions about the encounters of the day, the men he leads, the people of the countryside that he meets and how they supply us, and he will talk. His closest companions, now that Jonathon is no longer able to contact him, are the ones he calls The Thirty. These are the nucleus, the ones who've been with him from the beginning, the leaders of the others, the ones with whom he shares strategies, the ones whom he trusts for dangerous but necessary assignments, the ones whose loyalty is proven. I am coming to know these men so that when David speaks of one, a face now comes to mind to connect with the information.

Every Sabbath Abiathar, the priest Daved shelters, leads the men in worship. Those families that have accompanied the men also attend. After Abiathar's message, David sings a short psalm of praise, repeating until we all can sing together. Or David invents new lines and sings them, one after another, and we all sing a response, "For His love endures forever." Once David led the men in a dance of praise, at a moment when he was so in Your presence he was transported beyond words, and only with his whole body involved could he continue Your worship. His Thirty are able to follow David in worship as in battle. Sabbath is a blessed time.

Oh, in spite of the uncertainties and dangers, this is altogether a blessed time.

Yesterday the Sabbath was the most precious of all. After a wonderful worship time, when all the men and families were dismissed to their tents, David took me by the hand, and, picking up a basket of food packed yesterday at his request by Zillah, a surprise for me, he led me toward one of our favorite destinations for our walks, a brook with a grove and thicket of oleander. A few last blossoms remained on the tall stems, though the wet season was some weeks past by now. Nearby was a huge, tall old plane tree, under whose shade we had often rested during a walk. It was "our" tree, though it probably filled that place in many lives besides ours alone. But today was our day for our tree. No one else was around.

With shade so dense, with a refreshing breeze, and with the stream bubbling and splashing close in sight and sound, we had a respite from the heat of the day. A subtle fragrance came on the breeze from a solitary terebinth tree up the hillside from the valley of the brook. As David opened the basket, the strong fragrance of the excellently prepared meat and fruit and pastries aroused our hunger.

Eating quietly, with no need for words to add to our delight in the day, we let all the stresses of our times and situation fall aside for those few hours of balm and blessing. Talk and thought we have had before and will again, by necessity. For just this time, the greater need was to dismiss cares and retreat to a distance in soul and spirit from trials and sorrows and uncertainties. Everything was sweet--the scents, the breeze's gentle touch, the brook's steady babbling murmur, the trills of birds in the branches overhead, the sky so blue above, the earth green beneath, and each other, near and tender and caring. And time to look into each other's eys and memorize features and expressions. Time without interruption to touch and hold, run fingers through each other's hair, wade and splash in the brook and laugh over nothing.

Oh, I will carry the memory of this afternoon in my heart forever. Whatever comes cannot overcome this that has been. A love that is better in reality than all the dreams I dreamed has been mine, ours. And let it be recorded here in this journal: I know what it is to be a woman loved.

Bless You, Lord.

Lord, this altogether blessed time is the honeymoon I dreamed of, only much more. Strange that it could be so...though we live in a tent, not a house---though we have no wealth, or even daily provision until the day is upon us, and then only by the gifts of the people---though we cannot plan for our future---though it is a second marriage for each of us and we come out of great disappointment---though our families never knew each other, and there was no betrothal or marriage celebration---though nothing about this marriage started as things should be for a marriage in Israel---

Yet, David and I are one.

How You do redeem what was stolen and transform what was empty.

Lord! I see that this is the fulfillment of Hannah's prayers for my marriage! It took a long way around, but the answer has arrived. Lord, you have provided beyond all I asked.

This tent that David's servants prepared for me is very spacious with even rugs, two tables with lamps, some chairs and as fine a bed as I have known, with beautiful linen covers. For tent living, nothing could be improved upon, though I don't know what it will be like when the rains come. It is truly fit for a king--a king on bivouac.

My five maids share a tent nearby. They have not as many duties as they have had and will have when this time of exile is over and David has a house for us to live in. Mary is here at my side to attend to any personal needs I have. (But now she need not be the one to tell me I am beautiful.) When I came, Salome stayed behind with her family, but allowed her daughter Sharon to come with me. Sharon goes to the stream to do laundry, dusts and sweeps in the tent, and keeps the lamps trimmed and supplied with oil. Zillah and Phoebe assist in the meal preparations with the cooks that have served David's men all along, working in the open air these sunny days. Bernice would have the least occupation of the five, but has made herself available to mend the soldiers' garments, so it appears there will be no lack of work for her, for the time being. It is not as diverse or interesting-- or creative--as her tasks have been, but she is not one to complain, is still singing, in fact. I am blessed to have my familiar staff to carry over into my new life--just one of the ways David shows consideration.

In walking about the compound, I have met some of the other men's wives. Most of the men have left their families behind (if they had a family), of course, but among The Thirty, several wives have come to stay with their husbands, bringing servants and children; and others are said to be arriving over the weeks to come. These are the women who are willing to accept some lack of the comforts of home for the sake of being close to their husbands--also women of some means that enable them to keep their houses staffed in their home towns, while away from home.

For example, I am getting acquainted with Myra the wife of Ira of Tekoa. As we chatted, her two boys, Thomas and Timothy, were at play in the dirt before their tent, making paths with their hands and using blocks of wood for animals. As they took up sticks and began a battle with each other, she watched for awhile, then as the play grew rowdier, she called to them to stop before one was hurt. They threw the sticks aside with only a small complaint by the older one. I commented, "You manage these boys very well."

"Oh!" she responded, "You would not know them for the same two boys if you had met them two months ago when we arrived here. They led their mother a merry chase, I can tell you, when their father was only a dim memory and not an everyday presence. Now that he comes in every evening asking for a report on the boys that day, they find they don't have to do all the mischief they think of. For this, I can stand living in a tent for awhile. Who knows? By the time their father can come home to stay, they might have been great grown boys and their mischief turned to far worse things, with only a mother to keep track of them!"

Then she smiled at me and added softly, "But I missed him for myself, not just for the boys' sake. Still, I am glad that Ira is loyal to David. Your husband is a man worthy of the devotion of these soldiers, and destined to be a great king--as he is already a great warrior for Israel. And every one of them would gladly give his life if it would hasten the day David becomes king! And as for yourself, you are fit for a queen." As I shook my head, she rushed on, "We all know how you prevented a massacre that would have been a blot on David's kingship--or even the loss of it. The Almighty would not have held him guiltless for taking vengeance upon himself and shedding innocent blood, no matter the provocation. For this alone, I'm glad to have you for Queen of Israel; and now here you come, visiting the families of your husband's soldiers, same as he does. God will bless a nation with such a king and queen."

Lord, as I ponder her words, I can not make it real to me. I can only live this moment now and tuck her words aside until such time as they come true. The changes that have come are great enough. And the joy that I have now, to be finally, truly, a wife, will never be surpassed. I know it.

You are good to me, Lord.

Things have settled into a routine here, but it is interrupted, as it had to be. It was never a way of life that could last. The Ziphites have told Saul that we are here. David has sent spies who came back saying that 3,000 of Saul's soldiers are marching after David. He has left with most of his men, leaving some here with the baggage and us wives and the children, so that Saul's forces will follow the main body of David's men.

And so we wait.

For the first time, fear is coming to try to claim my abdomen, where such peace has reigned that I have felt a fullness there every since first yielding to David's touch-- almost a constant sensation of such warmth and such fullness of peace as I had before known only in rare moments of worship. My union with David is so much a part of my worship of You, or should I say You, Lord, are so much a part of my union with David, that is is no wonder that rare worship sensation is an everyday experience now.

And I have just confirmed that there is another aspect to the fullness. I am with child. The fruit of the union will soon be filling me out in a physical sense that all can see rather than just myself being able to feel it. Oh, it is a wonder, to know a new person, a new generation, the fruit of a blessed union, is being formed within my body.

It is an uncertain world into which this child shall be born, a father still on the run, though promised a kingship. What will we go through on the way to the promise? This pursuit of Saul, renewed yet again, threatens to make the promise seem unsure. But underneath this threat, this fear, this seeming, I know that Your promise is sure. One day, one way or another, all this confusion and chaos, this misplaced aggression of Saul's, will be past. Saul--all Israel--has an enemy all right, but it is not David. And his pursuit of David keeps David from pursuing the real enemy, the Philistines.

David knows. He left knowing his child is on the way, also knowing that, in my heart, I am positive that this child will be a girl. I don't know how I know, I only know that I am certain. She won't figure in the genealogies, only sons. Only sons can be king and warrior and carry on the father's line and dynasty. But she will be special to us, a friend of my heart, and a part of David always with me, whether he goes to battle or is someday off on kingly conferences and seldom by my side. She will always be there. Even when she is grown and married, our hearts will be united in the kinship of soul-friends. As David has approved, I will name her Hannah, after my other dearest woman friend. And we will be one in spirit from the start.

Oh, God, protect David from Saul. Bring him safely through.

Waiting, waiting. Most of the time I am quite sure I have no desire to be a man and go through all the threats and labors and trials of a man, particularly David's. But this waiting in inaction when all my being cries out to do something for the cause--this makes it very hard indeed to be a woman just now. Of course, I would not risk our daughter by any foolhardy action, mistakenly thinking I could do anything to stop Saul or aid David. So I send my prayers to You, Lord, to bring down the enemies of Your will and ways. Exalt Yourself, Your plan, and Your man.

Bring Your promise to pass, but in Your time and Your way. All else is folly and futility, as fruitless as a first-year walnut tree.

Lord, protect David.

Finally, David is back. He filled me in on all that has happened. First, he and Abishai went alone down to

Saul's camp. All the men were asleep--ALL. That had to be a sleep from You, Lord! Always some men are awake and on guard! As it was, the two of them were able to walk in to the center of the camp, to the very side of Saul himself. Abishai asked David to let him kill Saul. David refused. "Saul is the Lord's anointed," he told me. "The Lord can kill him, or let him die of old age, or in battle. But I did take his spear and his cruse of water, and with them we climbed the hill where my voice would carry over the valley of their camp, and I shouted to Saul's men, Abner in particular, for not keeping watch over his master, the Lord's anointed."

"Then," David continued, "Saul himself recognized my voice and called my name, and I hollered, asking him why he still pursued me. It has to be either the Lord or men around him that stir him up against me. If it is men, they should be accursed for driving me out from the inheritance of the Lord toward other gods. I asked Saul not to kill me. Saul broke down and confessed his sin, even called me Son, and asked me to return and he would not harm me, because I did not harm him. He said, 'I have played the fool, and have erred exceedingly.' "

I gasped, "He said that?"

"Yes, and then I told him to send a man to me for his spear, and I asked the Lord to render to every man his righteousness and his faithfulness, since I did not strike my hand against the Lord's anointed, though the Lord gave Saul into my hands. As I respected Saul's life, I prayed aloud, let my life be respected, and may the Lord deliver me out of tribulation!"

"What did Saul say to that?"

"He blessed me and again called me his son, and said I would do great things and would prevail."

"Do you think you are safe now?"

"NO! I have seen his madness return too many times to trust one moment of clear thinking. He realized the truth in one flash, but his mind is too far gone to hang onto that truth. Or maybe he has gone too far now to change his course and save face."

"So, what will you do now?"

"I must think and pray and then I will consult with my Thirty and announce our plans."

"David, will you come back and tell me what the plans are?"

"Yes, Abigail, you shall know as soon as I know. For now, continue to pray."

"Oh, yes, David, always."

We held to each other for a long moment as if we could stop the march of time. But then he was gone.

Lord, guide the deliberations and the decision to come from them. Let Your will be done in our lives.

I have taken a few moments from all the confusion of packing of tents and supplies to come to our plane tree and try to record the most horrible news of my life so far-- worse than my own mother's death when I was a child.

In the midst of the packing, Mary took me aside. Her face has been so happy ever since I came to David and found my own happiness. I could not imagine the cause of so much distress on her face now. It had to be more than our uprooting, which of course had to come sooner or later, things being the way they are for David these days. It was more, all right, much more.

She wrung her hands and began to sob as she said she hardly knew where to start or how to tell me. She overheard some of David's servants saying they had to prepare another tent as fine as mine, for David has taken another wife.

Another wife! How can it be?

I folded over as if stabbed in my stomach. I moaned and tried to walk, but could barely stand. Mary brought me outside the tent, away from the hubbub of packing, and supported me by my shoulders as I staggered in circles, drawing me further away from others, until I lost my breakfast in the dirt, and then she guided me to a rock to sit down on and sat beside me enfolding me near to her in a long hug.

I do not know how long we were there, motionless except for my shaking with sobs, until she said, "My sweet, I must be helping to pack, but I will bring your journal and you go down by the brook until I come to get you, when it is time to be on the move."

Here I am now, left with my journal and You, Lord. Out from the scroll peeks the poem of Hannah to me two short years ago, ending, how well I know it, with "All is well," repeated and repeated again.

God, only You can make it all well now.

We are heading into the land of the enemy, where David figures Saul will, first, not dare to look for him, then perhaps forget about him and the pursuit of him. There is enough to be afraid of in all that. And now I stand alone, without David's love. Oh, I know I am never alone, that You are always there. It's just that David's love had seemed to be one of the ways You brought Your love to me.

Well, You have other ways. Here is baby Hannah on the way, for one. I must not let sadness rule my mind or she will absorb sadness through my body. But, Oh, God, how can I ever be happy again?"

Maybe it will just be a different sort, or quality, or level, of happiness...

Oh, thank You, for faithful Mary, who's always been at my side, a comfort from Your hand, through many losses and sorrows as well as the happiness of recent weeks.

Lord, just don't let me ever have to see this Ahinoam of Jezreel. I can't bear that.

And help me to think rightly of this wrong. There is still nothing that can take away what I have known just lately. I don't have to rewrite my history, or change the meaning of the love I have known in the past, no matter how it changes in the future.

There is a record, in all matters of this life. And to erase it is always falsehood and deceit. Let it stand.

I know what it is to be loved as a woman.

In the Philistine city of Gath, David met with Achish the king. After several days of waiting for David's conference with Achish to be over, we heard the settlement. Achish gave David the town of Ziklag, near to the border with Judah.. For now, Ziklag is home, the same tent and furnishings now being set up here as I first knew with David as my new husband.

I need to know how I will receive him if and when he comes to this, our marriage chamber, from his other wife. Forearm me, Lord, and heal my heart, and give me Your wisdom and words to say, and how to act and respond. Whatever will he be like, or say to me, now?

Perhaps it is true that a high-powered man of many facets and talents, and great intensity of soul, can never be satisfied with only one woman. Or perhaps that is just an excuse. The Mosaic law makes it clear by forbidding adultery that You esteem the marriage bed and would have it unique to the one man and one woman who unite there. Maybe it is politics, as with all kings all through time, though David is not yet a king (marrying the daughter of some wealthy herdsman or vineyard owner of the fertile valley of Jezreel in exchange for ongoing supplies?). Maybe he feels that if his marriage to Michal was severed, one more severance is no matter. Maybe he just succumbed to a momentary surge of passion. Who can know the heart of a man?

Whatever it is to him, it is a death to me. Something I thought was settled now appears to have been temporary. Well, Lord, I was there to be used by You at a crucial moment and kept him from displeasing You by taking vengeance. But no one was there to keep him from displeasing You in the matter of marriage.

Things are too complex. I am trying to make them as simple as keeping business records. Maybe life should be that simple. But I see that it is not. No place in my ledger for this Ahinoam. Poor woman. I can pity her for the marriage she might have had for life, except for David, whose orders changed all that for her forever. I can pity her, but that is all. Let me never see her, not once, not ever. Facing David is more than I can manage, already. That I have to do. God, don't ask more. Help me, Lord.

For the third time this morning, I had vomitted, with the pregnancy sickness, when David came rushing in and took both my hands in his and said, "Abigail, pray for me." His eyes were not focussed on me, though I knew his need for my prayers was real to him. His focus was on the internal workings of his mind, which were complicated by many serious considerations. I listed them for my later remembrance as he continued. "I have the governing of this city to do. I need discernment as to which of the former leaders will obey and which may be involved in some sort of insurrection. Achish has been here to address the people and to enjoin them to allegiance to me. But I cannot be sure how it will set with the leaders--not to mention all the citizens, having a one-time enemy for their king. Achish I convinced, that I could serve him in exchange for the safekeeping of living in this city. It was God moving Achish to give me Ziklag." His voice and his face were full of awe, as if it had been too good to be true. "A whole city as a base for my operations. And they are not to be in his interests, but my own--and all Israel's. You see, Abigail," he said, while looking at me without actually seeing me. (I know I looked as sick and weak as I felt, and had he seen me, he would have been alarmed, but he went on, thinking as he spoke.) "The hand of God has provided a way for me to wipe out many Philistine towns, while staying safe from Saul, and appearing to Achish as his ally."

At this point, David began to walk around the tent, pacing to bring out his thoughts and plans. "In order to conceal the true nature of my activity from Achish, I must wipe out all life from every town we attack. Don't you see? If even one soul remained alive, word would go through to Achish. But I have to do it, if not now, later, so it had best be now. The Philistines have set themselves against the God of Israel. They have made themselves our enemies. I have to do it. I have to tell Achish that I'm attacking Judah, but it will be his own people--not just fighting men--women,....   children,....   even babies,.... servants,.... old people."

His voice had grown more and more hoarse and distraught. Finally, he almost staggered to the bed and sat on it with his face in his hands, leaning over, wailing at first in his low bass voice, and then rising in pitch, a horrible, unforgettable sound. And the picture he made, also unforgettable--a strong man made weak as water spilled out. I wept to see him so, and waited on him, oh, I don't know how long.

Finally, he raised his head and reached out his arms to me, "Oh, Abigail, I need you to pray for me."

I rushed into his arms and leaned into him, half kneeling before him, my own tears falling as his fell.

I don't know how long we held onto each other.

But in that time, I knew I could love him. The hollow place inside, left by the news of his taking another wife, had been filled, mostly by pity. Pity, and the assurance that he would need me still. And just loving regard for who he is.

There was a healing in both of us. For me, it was almost regaining my place as his wife, wedded to him in Your Spirit. For him, who am I to say what it meant, only, I saw him rise with resolution again after I had prayed. What I said, God, You alone could be sure. But I know I asked Your favor and anointing on him, and Your keeping of his soul through Your use of him as instrument of Your vengeance on a people set against You, and then mercy on their souls. They know not what they do. And they know not the cost they are about to pay for what they do.

After some moments of nothing but silence--no sound or movement, David rose, went to the basin and splashed his face, dried himself, and rearranged his clothing. He took in a deep breath of resolution and let it out again, and came back over to me.

He held me close and said softly, "Abigail, you're an anchor for me. Thank you!"

Only then did he look at me, and alarm took hold on him. "Abbie! You're not well!"

"It is only the pregnancy," I murmured.

"Yes." He sighed in relief. "Yes, of course, the child, the little girl," he was almost smiling, "who is on the way. You're a vessel of new life in many ways. You're a treasure."

He kissed me, sweetly.

Then again, he was the soldier, the ruler of Ziklag, the man of burdens and responsibilities, straightening his belt, speaking tersely, "As soon as I can secure this city, we will leave for our first attack." He ceased from arranging his clothes as if calling himself between worlds, "But tonight," again he softened for a moment only, "I will see you."

"I will be waiting for you," I whispered, and looked into his eyes as long as he could sustain it, in his hastening on to his duties.

One more sweet, longer kiss, and he was gone.

Oh, little Hannah-on-the-way, for many reasons your father may not be able to give you the father-love my father gave me. But, he is quite a man, excellent in many ways. And I hope that something of him is in your make-up. And I hope that you look like him. And I hope that his heart is full of love for you. Even if you're not a son to carry on his name and dynasty, you're the first offspring. May he treasure you, always.

God grant it.

The pattern for these days seems to be that David comes to me almost every evening that's leading up to a new attack upon a town or village of Gath. The attacks may last for days, and then there is always business awaiting David when he returns to Ziklag. When he returns to me, he always says, "I came as soon as I could." He is generally somewhat abstracted from me on his arrival, but I feel a unity between us before he leaves again for another military campaign.

During the days between battles, he has city business and army drills. Whether he is in town or out, there is much to occupy me, preparing for the baby, walking in the countryside nearby, and visiting among the military wives. Myra and I talk at least some almost every day, and she is lending me some clothes for the soon-coming days when mine won't stretch over my ever-enlarging girth. Lord, I thank You for her and the other wives I am coming to know, for their caring and their offered bits of mother-wisdom, their humor, and the music some of them make together, reminding me of my dear friend Hannah and young Esther when they played for us girls, in another life. Bless all the girls, wherever they are now.

And always, my thanks goes up for Mary. Her girth grows too, with age, not with child. And if anything, her caring for me has grown. She is so blessed that my union with David was not ruptured completely, and so excited for the baby's arrival. Another generation will enjoy her tender ministrations. She wants Hannah to look just like me. I say, "No, Mary, she must look like David."

"Well," she concedes, "some of him, maybe, but more of you, especially your nature."

"Mary, are you saying anything against David's nature?" I accuse her, only half in jest.

"Now, Abigail, did I say one word about David?" she remonstrates with me. "I just know no girl could be sweeter than you were--and still are."

So You see, Lord, I am spoiled by having heard such talk all my life. And, glory to You, I hear some of it from this husband, too. He's not only not repulsed by my growing out of shape, he keeps coming and often he calls me "a vessel of new life," and he's not talking only of the baby.

I am blessed. Shall I add, "All is well"? And I'm not forgetting how well this tent stands up to the rains!

Actually, I cannot say that "all is well", except in the limited sense that maybe life always requires. Is it ever true that everything is well in anyone's life? These days, sometimes I realize that on some of the days, and nights, David is away from me, he is almost surely with his other wife. I could almost begin to loathe myself for accepting this arrangement. So I push the awareness far back in my mind, although I hate playing games with truth. The record should be all out in the open. And really, I am not so much playing games with truth as I am leaving the complexity of the truth in Your hands. So many times, the horror of being betrayed as a wife tries to take over and I find myself singing as David sang to you:

> How long shall I take counsel in my soul, having sorrow in my heart
> daily? how long shall mine enemy be exalted over me? (In a sense, Ahinoam
> is my enemy, but only in one sense.)
> Consider and hear me, O Lord my God: lighten mine eyes, lest I sleep
> the sleep of death; lest mine enemy say, I have prevailed against him; and those
> that trouble me rejoice when I am moved.
> But I have trusted in thy mercy; my heart shall rejoice in thy salvation.
> I will sing unto the Lord, because He hath dealt bountifully with me.

And then again I remember when David sang:

> A father of the fatherless, and a judge of the widows, is God in his
> holy habitation.
> And again, I remember and sing for myself:
> Like as a father pitieth his children, so the Lord pitieth them that fear him.

I do fear You, Lord and I do remember Your provision at every point of need in my life.   You are as a father to me.

What helps sustain my balance is knowing that it is David, and not myself, who must answer to You for what sort of husband he is. And it is I alone who must answer to You for what sort of wife I am. I took the vows in good faith and I will keep them as long as they are required of me. Another bit of knowledge that I keep pushed far back in my mind, along with Ahinoam, is that my role as wife is probably gradually coming to an end. Now I know why I never could imagine myself as queen. Meantime, I do my duty--and receive the joy and favor that goes with it--as his wife, with a willing heart, knowing this much is in Your will for me. Help me in this, and then the time beyond.

I'm thankful Myra is a mid-wife, and knows another one, among the servants of another army wife, who can come with her, when I call, because my time is coming. Myra assures me I will not only survive the pain, but will forget all about it when she places the baby in my arms. I'm sure of the joy to follow, but I'm pretty scared of what has to happen to me first. Some of the stories I'm hearing in great detail are too much to take in.

But, Lord, I leave this in Your hands, too. So far, You've done all things well, even through my losses, and I trust You to bring me through this. Maybe my story one day can ease and comfort another expectant mother, it'll be such an easy birth. A few are like that.

And Lord, while You are at it, could You bring David in as soon as she's here?--so he sees her new and tiny, fresh from heaven!

She's here. And David was here, too, for two days and nights before leaving again. Thank You, Lord. And he was fully absorbed in her tiny perfection, examining every toe and finger, her dark curls and her little round nose and cheeks. I know she has looked into our eyes, his and mine, though she's not supposed to be able to do that yet.

"New life," David said, looking at her. And he did not forget me, but his gaze into my eyes was as a re-enactment of his first gazing on me some 16 months ago, when our love was born. I let my heart fill up with joy, without reservation. In these moments, I could not have asked for a more attentive husband and father for our baby.

Now he is gone again, another city to take and destroy.

What would I do if I did not know You hold our lives in Your hands?

Tonight Hannah was six weeks old, and David was back. Hannah slept and I lay holding her in the crook of my arm, gazing from her to David and back again, as David sang with his harp this evening. He sang his psalm about being knit together in his mother's womb, changing the pronouns so that it was Hannah's creation rather than his own that he contemplated this time.

> Thou has covered her in her mother's womb. I will praise thee;
> for she is fearfully and wonderfully made: marvelous are thy works;

and that my soul knoweth right well.
Her substance was not hid from thee
when she was made in secret
and curiously wrought in the lower parts of the
earth.
Thine eyes did see her substance, yet being
unperfect;
and in thy book all her members were written,
even the days that were ordained for her,
when as yet there was none of them.
How precious also are thy thoughts unto her, O
God!
how great is the sum of them.
If I could count them,
they are more in number than the sand:
when she awakes, she is still with thee....

David ceased singing, but played on, his fingers running all over the strings of his harp, as heavenly chords flowed twinkling in the air. Pure peace.

Finally, he stopped, leaned over his harp for a moment, set it down and came to lie down beside me. I fell asleep in the midst of my family.

Hannah's cries awoke me. She nuzzled for my breast and I set her in place. David aroused, raised himself on one elbow, and glanced quizzically at me. I apologized for my uncustomary behavior. "I know, David. I just couldn't resist her the first time she sought nourishment. The wet nurse could not believe she was not hungry for her, yet contented, as if she'd already fed. Then she caught on that I was doing it myself. She said that was a first for her, but as I am mistress, I may do as I choose. But she agreed to keep my secret. Mary knows, and now you.   Do   you   mind?"

"Abigail, I've said you are a vessel of life. The wet nurse is right. You are mistress and may do as you choose."

"It does not repulse you?"

"Nothing you could ever do would repulse me," David assured me. "You're an amazing woman. This picture I prefer to the stereotype of a lady handing her baby over to someone else all the time."

He watched us awhile. Then, playfully, "Do you change   her,   too?"

I laughed. "Even that. Am I still a lady?"

"Still a lady," he declared without hesitation, "always a lady."

"Of course, sometimes Mary insists on changing her, even Sharon has, too, and the wet nurse."

"You can't do all their work for them."

"No. Delegation. Just as with your soldiers."

He stiffened and I was sorry to have brought it up. With a will, he stretched and relaxed. "Well, for now, it's just us. Is she about ready to go to her own bed awhile? Are you, uh, healed?"

"Yes, I'm ready."

And already, this soon, another daughter is on the way. I knew in my spirit almost immediately. Likewise, David knew. Sometimes, You speak to our hearts, as clearly as on those tablets of stone, even something so particular.

She shall be named Zeruiah, after David's sister, who was almost like a second mother to David, as baby of the family. He grew up with her three sons and has made them officers in his army. She was always partial to him, over all their brothers. Now he'll have two little girls partial to him, almost like twins, only eleven months apart. Oh, I am glad.

For now it is our secret, Yours, mine, and David's. Time enough for Mary and others to know, when it can no longer be hidden.

Though Hannah is only a tiny baby, I pack her in a sling and carry her as I wander the places near here that I've come to love, and I show her the wildflowers that have bloomed with the rains, naming them and setting her little eyes and nose near to them as if she were old enough to smell and memorize the colors and forms that are dear to me. I repeat the melodious names of the flowers as if she could understand the words and repeat after me. She babbles. I can tell she loves the out-of-doors. She never remembers anything to cry about until we are indoors again, her senses all filled with too much information to tune in to her bodily requirements.

Today we came upon one of the sheep-grazing places and I introduced her to sheep, leaning so that I could place her hand deep into the wool and over the sheep's ear. She smiled and wiggled her fingers and exerted all her force into loud and enthusiastic babblings of delight in discovery.

A little shepherdess in the making.

I showed her a butterfly on a flower, and she focussed her gaze on it and startled as it flew. When a bird sings, I say, "Listen," with an insistent whisper in her ear, and then I hum after the birdsong, as near as I can duplicate such unhuman music.

When David came, as he held her, I told him of her zest in learning; and after I hummed some melodies of birdsong, he handed her back to me with a few nuzzled kisses behind her ears and over the back of her neck, picked up his harp and played after what I had hummed. It was nearer to the birds' own melodies than I could sing, but in a class all its own, haunting and sweet. Hannah reached and cried out for him and the harp. He held her and put her hand on the strings with his, causing her fingers to pluck strings. Her eyes glowed and widened. In that moment, our musician was born in Hannah's soul. We both could sense it and exchanged a long look of satisfaction in this little morsel of humanity that is part him and part me.

Oh, Lord, You bind us together with cords of love even as forces gather to draw us apart. But I will remember ever after these moments of light, brighter than any sun.

Lord, as I am beginning to walk funny with this pregnancy, Hannah is beginning to crawl, and that's funny, too, one knee bent up in the air to her side, and the other on the ground with her hands. She can scoot along pretty fast that way and brings out a laugh from everyone who sees her.

She always goes to David, no qualms. Even after his absences for warfare, she's known him and never whimpered for me when in his arms, or stretched away to be set down for action, though once down, she's all action. It's as if she has found her place, when he holds her, and chooses it above anything else. She traces her little fingers over his face, and obviously melts his heart. He laughs with her baby giggles when he tickles her ribs.

I, too, am choosing above anything else. I choose to focus on this family and to push far back in my mind the overheard news that his other wife is about to bear David a child as well. As when I heard he had taken her to wife, my body and emotions reacted together in vomitting, before I could gather my scattered soul and pray to find Your peace. I cannot do anything about it, cannot begin to understand it. But this family I can do something about. And I will, as long as I can. Only You know how long that is to be. Only You can instruct me, carry me, comfort me.

Here I am, only a few short weeks from another birth, and things are stirring. Achish is amassing a large Philistine army for an attack on Israel. Thinking that David has made himself odious in his own country by attacks on Judah, not knowing it is his own cities David has destroyed, Achish calls for this "loyal ally" to join him in his assault.

David is overwhelmed. He knows only You can deliver him from this dilemma. He came in completely preoccupied and distraught. We knelt and cried and prayed. After a time, he turned to his harp, played and sang:

> Hear my cry, O God; attend unto my prayer.
> From the end of the earth will I cry unto thee,
> when my heart is overwhelmed:
> Lead me to the rock that is higher than I.
> For thou hast been a shelter for me,

and a strong tower from the enemy.
I will abide in the shadow of thy tabernacle for
ever:
 I will trust in the covert of thy wings. Selah.
 For thou, O God, hast heard my vows:
thou hast given me the heritage of those that fear
thy name.
Thou wilt prolong the king's life:
and his years as many generations.
He shall abide before God for ever:
O prepare mercy and truth, which may preserve
him.
So will I sing praise unto thy name for ever,
that I may daily perform my vows.

As he sang, as so many times before, I not only prayed with him, I wrote his words to pray again for him after he is gone with Achish, and to keep them always.

Mary and Sharon had taken Hannah outdoors as soon as David had arrived, so that we could be alone. As David ended his song, he set aside the harp, a changed man from when he had entered. The presence of our Lord had come as we prayed and had assured him of his promised destiny and of Your everlasting Father-care and protection. All shall be well. How, we do not know. But we know You.

As we embraced over our coming child, Your everlasting arms wrapped us in Your embrace.

"Praise to God Most High," David said and I repeated, and he left to meet Achish.

Oh, Lord, You are mighty to deliver and to defeat the enemy! What a trial we have been through! And now we are safe. We are in makeshift housing, but we are full of praise to be alive and safe, when so short a time ago, we almost despaired of life itself. Shortly after David left, the Amalekites swarmed over Ziklag and herded all us women and children, those native to Ziklag, and we of David's army, away from the city, which they then set on fire behind us as we were taken captive and marched further into enemy territory. They prodded and poked at us, screamed and swore, and the lewd remarks flew, the more as the younger girls and women gave vent to their terror in shrieks and wails. Bless them, Mary and my other servants hastily retrieved our most valuable and necessary possessions in the first tumult--David's harp, my scrolls, the baby's things, a few items of clothing for us all.

All the horrors of remembered tales of the fate of captive women played over in my mind, trying for ascendancy over my emotions. But even then, Lord, a song of David's came into my memory and Your peace took control. I was able to speak words of comfort to Myra and other women as we were bunched like sheep or cattle and driven along. Pregnant women and women with infants were allowed on donkeys. And a distinction was made for wives of David. I did not know whether this boded for good or evil as to our destiny in enemy hands. But I was forced close to Ahinoam for the first time. All possible hatred or even fear of her was banished in a wave of pity as I saw not only her terror of slavery and possible death, but her deep maternity in clutching her infant daughter to her breast. And, even more, I sensed in her demeanor that she considered herself my inferior, and myself First Wife. How pitiful. How very degrading is her position. Never could I have foreseen my bowels of compassion rising strong on behalf on one I had thought had robbed me. Oh, we are both robbed, of course. And in all that tumult and threat, I came to love her as a sister. How very strange. Sad that we are placed in such unnatural, such hard-to-endure, roles, of sharing a husband. But, as is so often Your way, Lord, in the midst of the sadness of bizarre sin, something wonderful blooms. Two who are hurting can overcome the natural heart to hurt each other.

As I rode my donkey over near to hers, and placed my hand on her shoulder, she burst into tears. After a moment, to recover herself, she reached to touch my hand with her free hand, then the curly hair of Hannah, who sat before me, then my swollen abdomen, then her own small baby, and began to weep again, more quietly, tears flowing down her cheeks. As she looked timidly into my eyes and away again, my tears streamed, too.

Mary, Zillah, Bernice, Phoebe, and Sharon stayed close with me, as all the servants did with their mistresses. For three days we were kept marching, allowed to stop only for the night. Being kept on the move was horrible, exhausting, but nothing to the terror of the night, when the Amalekite soldiers took the young girls and women and used them, though they wept and begged. But it was no use to them to struggle. Indeed, it brought only painful blows. They could only succumb in numb silence. Mothers wept for their daughters' violation and loss. I held a crying baby close to me and wept for Sharon, as an Amalekite soldier roughly dragged her away, her eyes beseeching me, though she knew I was as powerless as she. She stumbled back to collapse beside me, some two or three hours later, and curled herself into a ball, falling into an exhausted sleep.

Sleep for any of us was hardly possible, and never for long at a time. The men's loud shouts in their sensual triumphs hardly let up until the last few hours before dawn, when the march began again.

Then, lo! On the third day, at twilight, just after we had stopped and eaten, our rescue came. We had had no idea David was anywhere near, thinking him still with the army of Achish, marching in the opposite direction from our march. Later David told me that the men of the army had seen farther than Achish, and had persuaded him there was no trusting the leader of Israel to stay on the side of Achish as he battled Israel. You had released David from the trap, Almighty God, and led him to these poor women and children. Not one of us was killed, except for the spirits of the molested ones. Where there is life, there can be hope of healing. Meantime we huddled and prayed and held the children, as David's army battled furiously the next 24 hours to kill all our enemy but a few who escaped on camels.

When David found me beside Ahinoam, I looked long into his eyes, but she only dropped her head. We held his children. He did not embrace, but said, "Praise the Lord," and rode on his business.

After a night's rest, David led us back to Ziklag, soldier husbands riding alongside their wives and children, except for the 200 who had stayed behind by their supplies. All the spoil of war was carried or herded with us, flocks of sheep and cattle, and other goods.

Such a reunion it all was, the husbands from the army of David with their wives and children, begun when the enemy was defeated, and continued into Ziklag. The women of the original town had no homes to return to, and husbands still gone with Achish, but were rejoicing to be "home", such as it was.

David sent men around the area to ask for additional tents and supplies, and began the job of sheltering and feeding us all again. The Amalekite flocks and herds taken in spoil are the meat of our meals. Because of his work, I have not seen David yet, but I am in a tent, and have been able to gain much-needed sleep.

David has come. He came straight to me and wrapped his arms around me and held me as close as my very pregnant condition allows. Mary again quickly disappeared with Hannah before she could set up a fuss for her papa.

David held me for a long time in silence. When finally he released me, he looked into my eyes, still without speaking. He walked me slowly to the bed, set me down tenderly but firmly, and strode across the room purposefully to take up his harp and sing. He sang:

> For thou hast been a shelter for me,
>   and a strong tower from the enemy,

several times over, and then just played the harp in new melodies, somber and majestic, rising in glory and crescendo until he stopped at a high pitch of the song's emotion and bowed over his harp, worshipping.

Such peace, gratitude, and joy I felt.

Our shelter is basic, our situation still precarious, but oh our rescue so splendid, supernatural. Grateful hearts make this present peace great indeed. You have provided, You will provide: all glory to our God.

Once again, tumult. But tumult of a most different sort. David's kingship is to begin. We are soon heading to Hebron, in Judah.

We had two nights of peace in our new tent in Ziklag, and on the third evening a messenger came to report to David that Saul and three of his sons--Jonathan, Abinadab, and Melchishua--had been killed at Mt. Gilboa. If he had thought David would rejoice to be made king by the death of Saul, he was mistaken. David began to wail, wail and stagger about, crying out, "Oh, Saul and Jonathan!...How are the mighty fallen!...Oh Saul...Saul and Jonathan were not divided in life or in death...Oh, daughter of Israel, weep over Saul...Oh, Jonathan, your love to me surpassed the love of women....Oh Saul, Jonathan, how are the mighty fallen!"

David is honorable. David is deep. David is made to lead, is noble through and through. His heart is wrenched in pain for the loss of all that Saul could have been, should have been, Saul AND Jonathan.

I admire him, admire his genuine grief, admire his leadership in mourning, admire the depth of the brother-love he and Jonathan knew. But, oh, David, Jonathan's love to you surpassed the love of women because women is plural to you. To know a woman's love, you'd have had to have one single woman, for life. I am sorry for you, David.

David will soon be king. My days to be wife are numbered. Our Zeruiah will be born in Hebron, some sort of palace. Where are we going from here, Lord, this little family You placed these two solitary people in, this David and this Abigail? I ask as I pack, what we have left to pack just now. We go to Hebron to make David king. You are there, too, in our future as in our past. Forgive this flood of tears. I will not always cry.

Lord, we are in temporary housing in Hebron, but it is much superior to the tent in externals, though I foresee that in family life, the tent will hold my best memories.

David was not here to see our new daughter until she was a week old. Hannah is now toddling about. She ran wobbily to him and clasped her small arms about his leg as he knelt beside the bed where I lay with Zeruiah. With one hand on Hannah's back, he stroked Zeruiah's head with its fuzzy auburn covering. She has his hair.

Turning to Hannah, David said, "Were you ever that little, Cherub? It seems hard to believe now."

Hannah said, "Papa, papa," and held out her arms for him to pick her up. He held her close to her baby sister and me, and leaned his face over mine for a kiss, our four heads very near to one another. "Abigail, you have done well again.   There'll never be a better woman." He stroked my hair and we looked into each other, as we have been able to do all along. I saw depth, but also restlessness and yearning. I think he saw peace.

He finally spoke again, "I'll be back tonight, and we can talk. So much is going on. I'll need your prayers, as always."

His attention was turned to Hannah, who wiggled in his arms.   The baby began to fuss as David tickled

Hannah and she laughed. So my attention was taken with Zeruiah. After a few tosses of a squealing Hannah into the air, he set her down, saying, "Papa has work to do, Cherub. Hannah's a good girl," and patting her on the seat, he came to touch my shoulder, wink at me with approval and a promise to be back, and strode out, once more soldier and king.

Lord, I do pray for David. I ask You to subdue his enemies within Israel, as well as the Philistines. I pray You to keep him safe as You always have. I feel assurance that he will not die in battle, but live to a long old age, and be a great king, and that he will be king over all the tribes, not just Judah, as now. I pray You to bring down the last diehards who cling to the house of Saul, and his remaining son Ishbosheth, seated precariously upon a throne for which he has no capacity. Unite our torn country once again, with the least possible number of deaths. Oh, Lord, it is a sad thing when countrymen kill one another. We need to unite to fight our common enemy. Let it be so. Let it be soon.

Give David all the wisdom he needs, for diplomacy, for battle if necessary, and for reading the true character of his friends and enemies and knowing the difference. And make his enemies in Israel over into his friends and supporters--Abner, son of the captain of Saul's army, and all with him.

Lord, keep David close to You. Above all else, keep him close to You, now and always. Protect him from sin, willful or unknowing. May the girls always be able to be proud of their Papa. Bring shame upon his enemies, and far from David. May he be honored as Your man for king for this hour and all this people of Israel.

And Lord, be near to me, whatever comes.

Hannah is 17 months old now, and Zeruiah six months old. Mary tells me that court gossip has it that Ahinoam is showing with another pregnancy. Her daughter is now about eight months old. And I am with child, only just barely. It is time for David to have sons. Many things I do not know, but You have given me to have sure intuition regarding coming babies, in the case of my own two girls, and now these two coming sons. So the first son, and the one in line for the throne after David, will not be ours, but theirs. It is just as well. Just as I could never imagine, at any point in time, myself as queen, so I can not envision myself as mother of a king, or my son as a king. I will never permit him to imagine himself such.

Let there be unity in David's house, not intrigue, insofar as it is in my power to prevent it. May this son of ours take on all that is noble in David's character, except the spirit of a ruler of this nation. He will rule in his sphere, without desire of a larger sphere. And let that other son be the king we need, after David.

God grant these petitions of my heart and teach me to do my small part in making them come true, for the sake of Your people, and Your honor. Let the nations see Your glory in the conduct of Your nation.

David, David, can it be that only last Friday night, we had such sweet communion? I can see you still, playing with the girls before sending them off with Mary and Sharon, and her little one born of the Amalekite. I play over in my memory our united prayers for the peace of our nation and an end to Philistine attacks, for your wisdom to be God's man. I can hear the sound of your sweet singing and the pure and holy notes of your harp carrying me to a spiritual rapture. I can feel the other rapture of our physical union, and the satisfied rest in your arms until you left at dawn for your duties.

All this is so fresh to me. And yet, I hear now that you have taken a third wife, a daughter of Talmai, the king of Geshur (a new ally?), Maacah by name. This time the blow was not as dramatic in its impact upon me physically. I was only nauseous for hours, and rested, sending the girls off with Mary and Sharon. This pregnancy is not making this nausea, only the news. David, how I have prayed for your wisdom as king, and I see and hear evidence that the prayers are answered, but in the matter of women. You can never know what the love of a wife could have meant to you, David, less with each wife you add. Every new one diminishes every other one; and you, too, are diminished. You will always have my prayers. Oh, Lord, I vow before You, I will always pray for David's rule and for him, himself. But there's no retrieving what we had and could have had. God, I see what You meant marriage to be, and I thank You for the time we had. But I mourn for what is lost, as well.

I reread the notes of the last psalm David sang here:

O God, thou art my God; early will I seek thee:

my soul thirsteth for thee, my flesh longeth for
thee
in a dry and thirsty land, where no water is;
To see thy power and thy glory,
so as I have seen thee in the sanctuary.
Because thy lovingkindness is better than life,
my lips shall praise thee.
Thus will I bless thee while I live:
I will lift up my hands in Thy name.
My soul shall be satisfied as with marrow and
fatness;
and my mouth shall praise thee with joyful lips:
When I remember thee upon my bed,
and meditate upon thee in the night watches.
Because thou hast been my help,
therefore, in the shadow of thy wings will I
rejoice.
My soul followeth hard after thee:
thy right hand upholdeth me.
But those that seek my soul, to destroy it,
shall go into the lower parts of the earth.
They shall fall by the sword:
they shall be a portion for foxes.
But the king shall rejoice in God;
every one that sweareth by him shall glory:
but the mouth of them that speak lies shall be
stopped.

As David sets his will to rejoice in You, so do I, my
Lord.... regardless of what is happening. Regardless.

Dear Lord, the civil war goes on. So tragic. In one way, I see the national situation pictured in the domestic realm, with wives and children being multiplied. If this doesn't make for civil war, what could? Amnon, number one son, has been born to Ahinoam, and joins his sister in that household; my own Daniel Chileab rests in my arms, while Hannah and Zeruiah are growing and developing day by day (the joy of my life, these three precious babies); and Maacah has borne Absalom to David. David is reported to be partial to Absalom, who is most like his father in appearance; yet David has taken another wife, Haggith. The taking of wives seems as a plague to me: it spreads, it destroys, and it appears nothing can stop it.

David has placed my household in a large and commodious residence. My servants have never had it this fine. Yet Mary pities the loss of husband and father. When we moved into this house, David's harp did not come with us. For the first time, my bedroom has no harp in it, no hope of heavenly music. I miss the music. I miss David more. But I knew it was coming, and I have my three children to bring up to know joy in living. If I desire them to have a sense of purpose and I do, of course, then I have no choice but to find a purpose in my own life. More than ever, I lean upon You, Lord.

When I saw that the harp was gone, and came to terms with the loss of David and his music, I copied the psalms I had written down and gave them to Asaph, for the nation to know.

Hannah is old enough to ask after her Papa. The other two will grow up knowing him only as a distant figure. I explain to Hannah that her Papa is king over many people now, and that some people don't want him to be king over them yet, but God does, and so Papa has to fight, with

God, to bring God's own promise to pass, that Papa will be king over ALL Israel, all twelve tribes. I'm trying to explain tribes by explaining cousins. She will understand it all, soon enough. This one was born to understand much, and ask more. Before long, I will approach David about a harp for Hannah, and lessons.

Zeruiah, on the other hand, is the merciful one, sometimes even crying, herself, just for hearing her baby brother cry. She goes to comfort anyone who appears in any distress. Everywhere she goes, she carries a doll that Bernice made for her, mothering it with steady tenderness, cooing lullabies to it in baby-talk.

With Daniel Chileab, it is too early to tell much, but he is forceful in making his needs known. I will need more wisdom than my own in dealing with him. For some time, he will live in a house of women--myself, my five servants, his nurse, and his two sisters. But there will be training with the other sons of the king, probably sooner than I am ready for it. So I have resolved to enjoy every moment, and to instill into him, in every way I can think of, all that I think a man should be. Lord, help me.

Sharon needs even more help. Her little son, Adam, half-Amalekite, between Zeruiah and Daniel in age, is even more strong-minded than Daniel, and has not the prospect of the training in manly arts that Daniel has. However, with Daniel and Adam growing up in the same household, I doubt not that Daniel will be only too glad to be teacher and coach of Adam.

Adam is the focus of Sharon's life. He became so as soon as he was born, though not until. Her pregnancy was a heavy trial for her, beginning, as it did, with a rape. It took all the rest of us to keep her spirits from plunging into an abyss of no return. The birth was one of the hardest the midwife ever saw, but from the moment the newborn boy was placed into Sharon's arms, she was overcome with love for him. His name came to her in that moment. All of us women breathed huge sighs of relief, and laughter and song burst forth that we hadn't known we had left behind in our hurting for Sharon.

And so this completes our household. It is all that we shall have and so it is enough. What You ordain is what we all need, whether we see it or not. I don't see it, but I see You, always with me, through it all.

Excerpts from Abigail's Prayer Journal
Part III: Abigail and Children

We are packing. David is to be crowned king over the other eleven tribes. Supreme irony, the incident that brought Abner's support from Ishbosheth to David: Abner's taking to himself of one of Saul's concubines, Rizpah, and Ishbosheth's attempt to control and punish Abner for this breach. Ishbosheth did not have the authority over Abner that his father had had. Because of this, he is doomed to die, and David's reign is inaugurated. Abner has been meeting with all the elders of the tribes of Israel, reminding them of David's early exploits on behalf of them and Saul. Daily, even almost hourly, the court is buzzing with the news of still another tribe declaring allegiance.

Six royal households are packing. In David's seven and a half years' reign in Hebron, six legitimate royal sons and as many royal daughters have been born to six wives. In addition to Ahinoam's Amnon, and my Daniel Chileab, Maacah bore Absalom, Haggith bore Adonijah, Abital bore Shephatiah, and Eglah died bearing Ithream, named "remnant of the people" by the mid-wives, in honor of Eglah's passing. Some daughters as well have been born to David with some of these wives. Other sons and daughters have been born to concubines in the last few years. The concubines have small cottages and few servants. We wives have more and better. All are packing. All go where David goes.

Hannah is now eight and a half, well-versed in the stories Moses recorded in his five books, and in the lore of wildflowers, birds, butterflies, trees, and animals. She plays her harp with feeling and accuracy, even if not with the skill she will have one day. It is a balm to me to hear her melodies and chords, in the calm of evening, when the family gathers.

Zeruiah is seven and a half now. Bernice has taught her to sew, and she does fine needlework as Hannah makes music. She has a quiet, accepting nature, and lacks the inquisitive alertness of her sister, but keeps her sweetness and caring.

Often in the evenings, Daniel, just six, and Adam, almost seven, play long games on a checkered board, moving colored stones about with great deliberation. Both are adept in strategy, and the silent and studious competition is broken now and then by loud sounds of victory or defeat, before they break out into running about the room, tackling each other, or rolling like puppies on the floor.

Adam is a good deterrent to Daniel's desire to pull his rank. Adam won't stand for it, asserting his natural skills against Daniel's without a trace of cowering. Whether it's physical strength or mental prowess, Adam is a match for Daniel. I, too, have my ways of making sure that Daniel is not overly taken with being son of the king. I want him to learn to rule, but I'll permit no dreaming of his ever being king. I have told him, from as soon as he could understand, that God has ordained Amnon to be in line for the kingdom, and that he must be content with whatever realm or province is given to him to rule. And he must study and train harder than other boys who will never rule over more than their households and servants and jobs.

When he says, "Adam, you must do as I say, because my father is king and I'm destined to rule over you," and

Adam responds with high spirit, "You must treat me fairly or I'll not have you to rule over me, not for a minute," I smile and say to Daniel, right in front of Adam, "You see how it is, Daniel. One who rules must be wise and good to keep his rule." And Daniel comes down from his posturing and throws an arm around Adam's neck, wrestling and giggling with him, as equals.

And so the lessons in justice and mercy proceed as a matter of fact, in the midst of childhood and family life. Daniel will be all right. It won't be he who tries to usurp the throne some day. He'll be content with the realm he is given to rule. And the people he rules will be content with him. He won't be famous or written up, but he'll be loved and successful where he is planted.

And I'm also planting the seeds that, as a simple government official, he'll be content with one wife; and his children will know him. This is important to me. God grant it, that I might see happy, united households for all my children. It is not hard to make him want to be a father whose children know him, for he longs for such a father himself. At the same time, I never forget to build up David's strong points for Daniel to emulate.

All the court is in shock and mourning. Abner is dead, killed by assassination so soon after bringing the support of the eleven tribes over to David. David's own nephews and army officers, Joab and Abishai, are the guilty ones. Joab evidently thought Abner had come only to deceive David, but a greater motive for his deed was revenge. Abner had killed their brother Asahel. Regardless of all the motives, if Joab thought David would uphold him in this action, he was mistaken. David has ordered Joab and all the kingdom to mourn the death of Abner, and declared himself innocent of any part in it. He went further. He put a curse upon the house of Joab, a curse of ill health upon all the men of Joab's house. He has wept and fasted and prayed the Lord to avenge Abner's death. The people are impressed with David... all the tribes.

But David did not go so far as he could have, as king, in the punishing of Joab--or so far as he has already done in the case of those who killed Saul. This time the murderer is one of David's own, his nephew, son of his beloved sister, and his close companion since childhood, not to mention a most efficient and worthy leader of David's army. If you are valuable enough, and closely connected enough, you can get away with murder.

Will the violence go on and on? Again, the court is in shock, before we could recover from the murder of Abner. Now we hear that Ishbosheth was murdered. Two brothers, Rechab and Baanah, brought his head to David, whereupon David immediately ordered his men to kill them, cut off their hands and feet and hang the bodies over the pool in Hebron, in plain sight of all the people going about town. Ishbosheth's head was buried in the sepulchre of Abner here in Hebron. All this is a king's prerogative, but in stark contrast to his leniency toward Joab and Abishai so recently.

This is a city I shall be glad to leave, a city and a time in history. Surely we are due for a time of peace, once the Philistine opposition is quenched by a united kingdom's force, by Your grace, O Lord. Let it be.

Even as David's forces fight the Philistines, David has ordered the training of his sons to begin. From age six and up, they must be learning the Hebrew, the Books of Moses, marksmanship with bow and arrow, swordplay, horsemanship, and games of athletic skill and mental strategy--all with experts. So far, Amnon, my Daniel, and Absalom have begun, but it will seem no time until Adonijah and Shephatiah join them, followed by Ithream, and others as they come of age. There are also some sons of the concubines nearing six.

Each son brings a servant to be armor-bearer, fetch the arrows for reuse, and other necessary tasks. Daniel has been allowed to retain Adam as his attendant, for which we are all grateful, and Sharon is proud. It is doubtful whether the other royal sons have so much time for practise in the martial arts as Daniel and Adam, who are together constantly.

And in the evenings, I gather our household for discussion of Moses' writings so that the boys must express what they have absorbed and present it clearly to Hannah and Zeruiah. Daniel must be able to understand and apply wisdom from our sacred writings if he is to lead others, and he must be able to instruct others if he would be a good leader. I ask questions to provoke reasoning and application to life and relationships. And I encourage the girls to ask questions and interact with the boys. I do all this for the sake of the staff and myself as well. I would that all this household walk in the faith of our fathers, Abraham, Isaac, and Jacob.

We close our evenings with psalm-singing to Hannah's harp, and prayer. I open the prayer, and then any others who desire pray aloud as we all pray silently. Daniel loves this. Adam is not to be outdone by Daniel in any endeavor, and can pray aloud with as much ease and sincerity as Daniel. The girls, too, are fluent in prayer, though Zeruiah speaks so softly, we cannot always catch all her words. All the servants pray at one time or another, not every evening. Dear, precious Mary, when she prays, can have all us women almost in tears, she is so soft and perceptive toward the heart needs of every one of us--and does more than anyone else to forward unity in this household.

Here is what I remember from Daniel's prayer tonight:

God bless my father, the king. He needs courage and wisdom, and Your might behind his army as he finishes off the Philistine enemies, so thanks for that sighing in the mulberry trees that brought Your force in and made us win this last battle. And then he has stuff to take care of at home while he's off at war, so keep the messengers safe going back and forth with news and orders and keep everybody faithful to him. And thanks for Hannah getting better and better on her harp so she's easier to listen to and sing along with, and help Zeruiah to speak up so we can hear her, and thanks for the good food we get from Zillah and Phoebe, especially that pastry tonight, whatever they called it, it sure was good, and thanks for Sharon and Bernice keeping us all in clean clothes and help me to be less messy for them to pick up after, and take care of my mother and Adam's mother because they don't have any husbands and You know how women need husbands and so please do whatever they need done, because they're always doing stuff for us boys, and please, I would like to make more bull's-eyes tomorrow, and don't let any of my arrows go too far where Adam can't find them. And give me a good answer when that twirp Absalom acts too big for the rest of us. Amen.

Lord, may he ever speak so plainly and openly with You--and listen and obey.

Lord, our first house in Jerusalem was fine enough for me, but now we are moving to a bigger house. We will require more servants. While I don't need more house and servants, I am greatly comforted by having larger grounds, gardens, and an orchard; and Zillah and Phoebe are eager for fruit to preserve once again, gluttons for work. They want to see us well-fed with fresh produce and their own personally preserved fruits. I want to teach the children how to care for plants, how to organize servants, and--the girls--how to process foods; and I want to see them all engaged in more outdoor play than they have had before. It will be busy, interviewing servants, presiding over their tasks and disputes, and having some outdoor work myself; but I am eager for the challenge, more to do in the line of what I was brought up doing.

Mary, on the other hand, is not so eager for more going on, and a larger household. I'll never ask more of her than she can do, and she can still care for my needs as ever, but her step is slower and sometimes painful. She doesn't speak of it, only sometimes an involuntary cry escapes her as she rises or sits. She always follows it with a smile or chuckle. She'd never talk of her own woes. She listens as I speak of my plans for flowers, fruit and nut trees, and says only, "I'm glad for you, Abigail. You deserve all the joys that come your way."

Mary's been attending the girls, too; but one day before too long, I'll see about interviewing girls to choose an attendant for each of them. Not too soon, for Mary dotes on them, so I don't want her to feel displaced. And they love her as I always have. How could they not love someone so devoted to them and complimentary of them? Hannah plays her harp and Mary rhapsodizes that she hears the music of the angels. Zeruiah finishes a needlework project and Mary vows it should be framed and hung in the king's palace where all who come to court can see its perfection. She calls them to come to her by singing out, "Come, my beauties, Mary NEEDS you!" One of them twirls around the room or garden, or performs an act of kindness to one of the servants, and Mary purrs, "What a little princess!"

Mary praises Daniel in a like manner, but his biggest supporters are Sharon and Adam. Sharon fancies Adam almost a prince himself as he is in proximity to Daniel, sharing the same education and sports, as Daniel's attendant, as well as the same household. She builds Adam's character by telling him he does something as well as Master Daniel, realizing full well that she is also building Daniel's character, causing him to see himself as an example, and thus to set himself a high standard for his conduct. And she knows, too, that she is helping to build a bond between the two of them like unto David's with Jonathan. I expect one day to hear that they've actually cut a blood covenant and exchanged garments and weapons and vows of lifetime fidelity to each other and all their descendants. Many things of adult import and consequences are thus forged in childhood. And all that we can do in the process, we pray to know and do.

Sharon and I pray alone together once a week for our two sons and all their destiny. I think I am to her what my Daniel is to her Adam, and I do not take it lightly, but pray to be a woman worth her emulation. My being without David draws her to me, husbandless as she is, in a way that could not have happened had my domestic bliss gone on as it began.

Such entanglements of human hearts, Lord, You are using to enable me to live beyond my loss and sorrow, into joy and peace. I am grateful.

We've just come from the great celebration on the occasion of the bringing of the ark of the covenant to Jerusalem after its sojourn in Gibeah, where Saul had his palace. David tried to bring it three months ago, but left it at the house of Obed-edom the Gittite, after a man was killed trying to steady the ark as the cart carrying it swayed over a pothole. The ark is not to be carried on a cart, only on men's shoulders. Today no one died. All was in order, as prescribed by law.

Obed-edom will miss the ark, as all sorts of blessings are reported upon his household in its three months with them. But all Jerusalem is wild with joy today. I sat in my stand with my household servants (the households of the other royal wives each in a nearby stand), as my children passed with others of royal blood in the parade following the ark, the girls dancing in the multi-colored robes of king's daughters and wearing flower garlands in their hair, and Daniel wearing his colorful robe signifying a royal son, and carrying his child-sized sword with its safety tip, Adam with him in his best clothes with his own similar sword with which he and Daniel practise swordplay. Daniel already bears himself with dignity and authority, though I must say that Adam could pass for royalty himself. He absorbs all the instruction, posture, stance, and gait, as well as the academics and sports. It makes me wonder who his father is, Amalekite nobility perhaps, whose good eye recognized that Sharon is a beauty, though lowborn. Well, I cannot dwell on that useless path of thought. Doors will be open to Daniel and not to Adam, regardless of his abilities or even his unproven blood line.

I saw Jehiel, who's in charge of the royal sons' education and who's their hero and arbiter of all their thinking, marching with the boys, modelling noble bearing, and his father Hashmoni the Wise being borne in a palanquin, his white head nodding to the crowds along the street.

David passed first in the parade, immediately after the ark, dancing like a madman to the triumphant music of untold numbers of cornets, trumpets, cymbals, psalteries and harps, and singers, each group in matching uniforms of splendid color and design. A fortune must have gone into this event, and much practise.

As in whatever he does, David dances with his whole self, without reserve. This he is doing today is his worship of the most devout sort, in the exuberant mode. I've seen the silent, motionless mode of devoutness as well. In his exuberance, he cares not a fig for who is watching, or how he exposes himself. His audience is the Lord God Almighty. And his gratitude knows no bounds-

-after all that the Father has brought him through. So why should his movements have bounds?

I feel all the same love for him and wish that bounds could have been set around that love too, for him, as they were for me. I can love no other, even if it were granted me to have that option, while he cannot stop loving ever more women. I pray, God, that You set bounds upon our son You have not seen fit to set upon his father.

But let me not dwell upon this line of thinking either, but return to rejoicing over all that the ark of the covenant means to our city and our nation--the presence of the One True God in our midst.

Tonight we will read of the ark as our household gathers. Daniel--we all--must know what it means. What a fitting culmination of a day of celebrating with all that is fine--with parades and feasting and glorious music--that which is best in all the world, the God of the covenant, with us, Emmanuel.

I wish Hannah and Zeruiah and Daniel to know the nature of their father's worship. I wish to extol worship before them and to have some glimpse of worship in their conduct. I will bring one of David's psalms for us to sing together. May everything about this day be sealed in their memories all their lives long.

We have heard the report that Nathan, the prophet, brought word, Lord, that David may not fulfill his dream of building You a temple. This is a boundary You have set for David. My heart hurts for the hurt I know he is feeling now. But he will transfer his dream to his son to finish, Amnon by rights, or perhaps Absalom by his father's favor. David will not cease from worshipping You, Lord, no matter what dream you say No to. I know his heart, and it is all gratitude. They say the supplies are being laid by in great quantity, all of the highest quality, to make a temple, fit for Almighty God, Lord Most High, Maker of heaven and earth, Who sets up kings and brings down kings and has sworn not to bring down David and his line. I know it will take years and years to assemble all that is required. May I live to see the temple, and worship at Your House.

As Hannah is turning thirteen, I have sent to David to appeal for a betrothal for her among my own people. David has kindly arranged a meeting of his emissaries with my father to find which of my cousins is eligible for such a match, and to pursue the negotiations. She will have two more years here at home with me before going to make her own home among my kinsmen, in the area of my old home. I feel a strange mixture of peace and exultation to think of her being near to Father and Damaris. Surely I may be permitted to travel to visit them often, with a daughter and grandchildren to visit as well. Father does not care to travel any more, and travel has not been safe during most of the years since I left, with the various battles occurring in the civil war and against the Philistines.

As if that were not enough warfare, we now have the Ammonites risen up against all Israel, with hired mercenaries from Syria, Maacah, and Ishtob, a mighty host of warriors. Daniel, now ten and a half, brings us the news of current events as he learns of them daily from

Jehiel, who insures that all the king's sons stay abreast of the political and military situations such as they will one day be involved in first-hand. God grant that there is peace before Daniel's day of maturity comes, though I am proud that he is eager to be a soldier for his country and king, and his God, if he is called. Of course, he thinks it all glorious and has no concept of the death and devastation, as he rattles off statistics of casualties as if he were merely doing math. He is proud to be son of the mighty warrior, King David, and of David's latest victories, among many all through the years. He knows all the history. From his identification with David in refusing to take revenge on Saul during years of being pursued and being placed in opportunities for revenge, I believe with all my heart that Daniel is developing character traits of David's that are most admirable.

All three of my children please me. Mary says I deserve it, but she's always been partial. I myself feel it's a gift I've been given, apart from any deserving, largely due to You, Lord, becoming their Father when they have not known their earthly father in their home, only from afar. It's a strange way to grow up, as I of all people should know, who had an earthly father very present all through my childhood, making it easy for me to transfer affection to my heavenly Father when I was taken far from my old home place. Without that foundation, the three of them have come to Father God, and I give You glory, Lord.

Now I pray to Your father-heart to make the right betrothal for Hannah and in another year or so for Zeruiah, men who will be at home with wife and children and love them day by day. Then in a few more years, may Daniel, too, receive such a home. I'll know You did it, but I do not forget David's consideration in making the arrangements as I requested. He didn't have to do that.

Never shall I forget the anguish on his face as Daniel came home from school today, and walked silently, woodenly to his bedroom, keeping military posture and clenched jaws and fists, in an effort to be manly, without a word to anyone, without even Adam, who vanished like a wraith to his own room. I knew that Daniel had had a shock that had touched the core of his young soul, and that I must go to him. But I had no idea how deeply he was affected. As I entered, he sat on his bed, bent over, his head in his hands. I sat beside him and he jerked up to lay his head in my lap and sob in convulsive heaves and cling to my knees with his arms. I stroked his hair, his back, his forehead, and waited. He was a small boy again, training cast aside in trauma too great for his age. I do not know how long we were there together in this way before his sobs subsided. I prayed for him as I waited for some revelation as to what had happened to shatter him. For he was shattered.

As he quieted, "Can you tell me what it is, Daniel?" finally I felt free to ask him.

"Mama," he choked out, "I don't want you to have to know, but you will find out. Better from me than..." He sobbed again. It's been some time since he called me Mama. He's decided he must call me Mother. But today he needs me in a way he has not for a long time.

"Mama," he sat up and looked at me and took my hands in his, for all the world like a father comforting or counselling a young daughter, and his eyes held a depth beyond the eyes of eleven-year-old boys, rather like his father's, I could not help realizing. Then he proceeded with haste, as if once having decided to tell, it must be over quickly.

"Mama, prepare yourself. I know you've been through a lot already with Father's other wives, being left alone and having others share the place that should belong to one woman alone. But now--Jehiel told us to spare us hearing it in court gossip--it is even worse. Father has had one of his Thirty killed to cover up that Uriah's wife is pregnant by Father, while Uriah has been in the battle and Father stayed here. And Uriah refused when Father called him home and told him to go to his wife so it would look like he's the father. Uriah wouldn't enjoy his wife while his men were in war, far from home and wives. Nathan has already confronted Father with what he has done. Oh, it is the worst of all. Why did he have to take another man's wife when he has so many already? And then he had one of his most faithful warriors killed, who's been with him all through fighting Saul's army, the eleven tribes, the Philistines, the Ammonites and Syrians. Mama, I don't want to be a king's son. I just want a mother and father together, like other boys. Why was I born?"

He cried again, more quietly than before, hugging me, and swaying with me. Later I would think of poor, lovely Bathsheba, and of Uriah's death. But now, I must think of my son. It was a critical moment in his life. I prayed as he swayed in my arms.

We stayed together through the dinner-hour and into dusk and twilight. I waited for him to go limp and still in body and voice before speaking.

"Daniel, one thing I feel I can assure you of, regarding your father, is that he will be affected, probably is right at this moment, in much the same way you are." Daniel sat upright and stared into my eyes for a long moment, taking in this unexpected utterance and mulling it over, searching for understanding, hoping he could forgive his father, but far from able to believe it yet, and certain that his father could never again be a hero to him, even for all the battles. So much I could read in his eyes, without his saying a word.

"Do you think God could forgive him for this wrong, if he were hurting for having done it as badly as you are hurting for his having done it?"

I could tell Daniel would have to think about that question, that it was alien to anything he ever thought of before. He countered, "Mama, how can you have mercy on him after what he did to you, and all these other wives and children, and now murder to cover up taking another man's wife, and not just any man, his close, personal friend and faithful soldier for many YEARS?" He spoke in a low monotone until he got to the last word and it came out with force as he hit the bed with both fists and fell face down on it, the first time he'd taken his eyes off my face. He had to. It was all he was ready for hearing, just now. I knew his mind was whirling as he lay there motionless.

I waited. I prayed as I waited for him to process his thoughts, his feelings. I prayed for Your father-touch, Lord, for a boy in such need of that, and not able to find it anywhere else but through You.

Finally, he sat up, "Can you answer me, Mama?"

I sighed. "Daniel, I need God's mercy, too." And instantly he had grabbed my shoulders and squeezed them fiercely, "No, Mama, not you. You DON'T. You're GOOD. You don't have any such black sin on yourself. You're the opposite of ....HIM." He said it with rejection and repulsion, but also sadness and regret. He didn't want to be repulsed by his own father, but what David had done WAS repulsive, and I knew it was repulsive to himself as well.

"Daniel, the Law asks us to be holy as God is holy. I may be good, in your eyes, but I am certainly not holy. Therefore, I need God's mercy."

His eyes widened. "Yes, I see that. No one is holy, as God is holy." His eyes narrowed now, "Then is that how you are able to have mercy on Father?" He asked it with an urgency to know the quality of mercy, as if his life depended on it. And it did. He had said he wished he'd never been born, and now to recover his gladness to be alive, he had to forgive the man who begot him, and whose likeness he bears in so many ways, the man of whom he is a part, even if he lives apart from him. He cannot hate the man, his father (though he hates the deed done), or he must hate himself.

"Yes, Daniel, that's how I am able to have mercy upon your father."

I let him think about that some more before I said, "Daniel, you see what your father took from me, but I would so hope that you see what he gave me--yourself, your sisters, and some of the best moments of my whole life. He did love me, very much so, when we were together; and our union, which is why you are here with me now, was good all that time. I do not understand why a man pursues more than one woman. But I know what we had, and I know what I have now besides my memories; and Daniel, I love you so much. Your life is of greatest value to me, to God, and will be to many who come to know you--your wife and children some day."

He grasped my upper arms with firmness. "Mother, I swear to you I will love that wife and those children and I'll never, never leave them for any others. I hate it when all the boys in school talk about all their mothers and how their father is a king and he loves THEIR mothers better than some other boys' mothers, and which one is favorite and who will be king some day. I hate it, and I won't do it to anyone else. I swear to God."

"Daniel, that is so important, so important. I believe you, and I know you'll do as you vow. But, believe me when I say, you'll be a better man and a better father to your children if you forgive your father from your heart, and admit, and follow, his good qualities."

Again, he had to think it over. "I can see that, Mother, and I swear I will set that as a goal. But IT WILL TAKE SOME WORK. ...If I can do the work we have to do in school, I can do that, too."

We stood. He put his head on my shoulder. He is tall enough to do that easily. I held him and kissed his forehead. "My son, I am proud of you. God bless you."

"Mama, what would I do without you?"

I began saying the shepherd psalm and Daniel joined me, as we have done so many times before. As we ended, there was a reverent silence before I spoke again.

"Good night, sweet boy, and God bless. You came a long way toward becoming a man tonight."

I left him, in a much better state than the one I found him in. And he is only one of the three who will be most hurt by this news. I must be prepared for Hannah's and Zeruiah's own emotions as they absorb the shock, each in her turn, and her own personal way.

As I prepare Hannah, just fifteen, for her wedding, I remember my preparations for marrying David, though the celebrations she and my cousin Judah will have are more like the ones I had when marrying Nabal, the traditions all being fulfilled in the Judean way. Little Cousin Judah, who was only a toddler at my fifteenth birthday party, is now taking Hannah to wife. May their marriage be as blessed for life as mine and David's was for a season.

Hannah's new servant, Rhoda, is in the place of Mary now, and, after a year and a half, is very in tune with Hannah, and as good to her as Mary has been to me. Hannah is calm and ready, not fearful of being married. She says, "Mama, you knew him when he was little. It may not make sense, but that makes him seem familiar to me and not strange. And then, Rhoda goes with me. And of course, my grandpa and Damaris will be near, and lots more cousins to meet, and I just know I'll be friends with the daughter of your dear old friend that I'm named after. Mama, even more, I know in my spirit that I am to have a good marriage, the same way you always said your friend Hannah knew before she married her Reuben. I have this blessing from the Lord on my life, that my marriage will be good. I remember you said your aunt told you if you knew how to make other people happy, you could make your husband happy. Well, I've watched you with the servants and learned for myself--and your forgiving of our father! I even think I remember some of when he was with you, and me, when I was very little and how he loved us and called me Cherub, and, Mama--believe this or not--I have a foreknowledge that Judah is going to call me Cherub."   She scrunched up her shoulders and squeezed her fists against her chin for joy as she grinned widely and her eyes misted.

"If he does, I will tell him right then and there, all of this; and then when I have treasured it awhile, I will tell you, Mama, for you to treasure, too. You know how some things you just KNOW even though there's no way you could possibly know?--the way you knew Zeruiah and I were going to be born girls, and Daniel and Amnon were going to be born boys--and the way your friend Hannah knew something good was on its way to you when you were married to Nabal and feeling all alone."

Hannah had finished talking and was organizing her clothes with Rhoda, when Sharon came in to clean, with the secret smile gracing her face that has been there ever since Zephaniah, the gardener, finally persuaded her that a man could be gentle and could really love her for herself and consider her needs. She was a long time releasing all her fears and reservations. But he was kind and patient, also winning Adam with his attentions to the boy's needs and his obvious good effects upon Adam's character. Adam has become much more at peace with himself and his confidence has more calmness about it than the old aura of tension and pressure to measure up to everything Daniel did. Zephaniah also has given something of that fatherhood to Daniel, though he makes it known that Adam is the apple of his eye. And now there'll soon be a little one belonging to Zephaniah and Sharon together.

Back here in Jerusalem after the wedding festivities of Hannah and Judah, it seems so quiet around here without the harp music we've enjoyed all these years--and just the presence of Hannah in our home. Presently the nuptials of Zeruiah and my cousin John will be upon us, the way time is flying, and then both the girls will be settled in the midst of my relatives. Being in the old neighborhoods of my childhood, I felt a pull in my spirit to make my home there again. Jerusalem is not home to me. As the sons of David approach manhood, he will be assigning them to govern in various provinces. An idea is forming in my mind. Perhaps Daniel's jurisdiction could be the Judean hill country. Whether I speak of this, and if so, when and how, to David or to Daniel himself, or leave it only a matter between You and me, Father God, I commit to Your guidance. If the idea comes from You, it will be fulfilled, in due time. Show me my part.

Lord, Daniel has dressed and left for a royal event. All this day, servants prepared his best garments and his personal mule, with its own festive ornamentation-- headdress with the star of David atop, ribbons trimmed with Daniel's colors and gold thread, its fur brushed and hoofs reshod. When Daniel came in for my inspection and farewell, I could read a troubled look in the depth of his eyes, though he strove to exhibit only manly assurance, as he's been trained to do these past years. He could have passed for 21, instead of his 17 years, but to my mother's perception, tonight he seemed more boy than man. Instinctively, I dismissed Mary and other servants who'd been dressing my hair and arranging new flowers and incense in my room.   At the same time, Daniel dismissed his personal attendant.

When we two were alone, he stood before me, tall and elegant. I motioned for him to sit. He pulled up a stool and sat facing me, taking my hands in his as I sat on my divan.

"Mother, there's something about this evening that bothers me. Absalom has called a feast for all the king's sons.   It'll be the older sons; the ones of Father and Bathsheba are too young.   Father's not attending. Absalom has asked that Amnon be sure to be there. You know he's been brooding over what Amnon did to Tamar two years ago. In all this time, there's been no justice. Father was angry, but that was the end of it. I know how I'd feel if it had been Hannah or Zeruiah that Amnon raped. I'd not have waited this long for justice. But I'd have been to Father himself demanding it. I believe Amnon thought it ought to have been taken care of without his having to beg for it. Of course, that's true." He paused, thinking. "And, then, Mother, Absalom's been used to being favorite son, and now it seems Solomon and Nathan and the baby, Shobab, are the favored sons.   Absalom not only never got justice rendered to Amnon, but he is not held in the same place in Father's attention as he had become accustomed to. I fear for what may transpire in this evening's festivities. I fear there's a darker purpose behind Absalom's invitation than just a gala event, brotherhood and comradeship, friendly competition, and all that."

I looked into his eyes as I took in this revelation of his concerns. Some of them I'd been aware of all along, but I'd not connected them all together in regard to this evening's event.

"Well, Daniel," I sighed, "I will be here praying for you all this evening, for you and for all your brothers, Absalom, too, and of course, Amnon. May God's will be done. May it not take a tragedy to open your father's eyes to trouble brewing among his offspring."

"Yes, that's just it, Mother. It is a simpler matter to manage a kingdom than to manage so many children living in different households, when Father doesn't live in any of these households himself now. How could he keep up with all of us? I'm just glad you are the one who is my mother--and none of the others. I don't like what I hear of other mothers. You don't even want me to be king, and I'm so glad. If you wanted it, I'd probably want it, too, and it's not the good life it appears to be, to some mothers and sons."

"Bless you, Daniel, you have wisdom beyond your years. I'm glad you've told me. Now, go in peace, and rest assured nothing will keep you from God's destiny for you. You are not afraid for your own safety, are you?"

"Not any more," he smiled for the first time; and the release from the troubled look restored the manly aspect to his face. He rose, gave me a hug, adjusted his sword, and strode from the room, in command of himself, stabbing me with his resemblance to David, years ago.

I will await his return with eagerness, but, all glory to You, no fear.

It was very late, and I'd fallen asleep, against my resolve, still on my divan, in my sitting room, by the time Daniel came in.

He'd been through the gamut of emotions, and it showed on his face. He wept again, telling me of Amnon's murder and Absalom's fleeing, and the assembly of the remaining sons with King David to assure him none of the others were murdered, as it had been reported to him first that all his sons were dead.

As with David, Daniel paced as he thought aloud.

"Mother, we all were weeping and wailing and shaking, and talking all at once, telling what we each heard and saw. Father wailed, too. He had been already distraught, thinking us all dead, and had torn his garments. With us all there, he was crying for relief that some were still alive, and for grief over Amnon dead and Absalom fled. Mother, he had to be crying, too, for the prophecy and his part in bringing a sword of violence to his house. For all he is a majestic man, he is a pitiful man, too. I could never hate or reject him, but oh, I would not be him for all the world. Mighty king, brilliant general, sweet singer of Israel, and all the rest--it is not worth the suffering I saw him going through tonight. He's responsible. Responsibility in such a wide sphere. The intertwining of history and personal life! The complex web he has woven and been caught up in! And people envy him. They do not know, they do not know.

"If they had seen what I saw tonight, no one would wish to be a king. The cold rage on Absalom's face as he ordered his servants to kill Amnon, the rush to obey him, the sight of Amnon's terror as he saw what was happening, and so soon, the shedding of his blood and him lying in a heap, then the panic that hit the rest of us. Were we to be killed, too? Why not? Everything was crazy. How were we to know how far Absalom's revenge would go--or his ambition!!!   Did he want us all out of his way? I hope I am never that scared again. It has to be worse than war--murder in your own family. We've all been together, nearly every day, for years now, training and studying. Yet Absalom could throw it all over and watch Amnon being killed at his own orders, cold and unaffected.

"There'll be no schooling for some time, and then what will it be like?--for those of us who are left." He shuddered and dropped down onto a stool he swung over, to face me on my divan.

He sat quietly for some time and I did not speak either. There was nothing to be said.

Finally, he took a deep breath in and let it out slowly. "Mother, it is almost dawn. I think I will just sit here until Zeruiah is up and talk with her so she hears it from me personally. It will be hardest of all for the girls, all the sisters of all of us. Then, may we order horses and mules and provisions and go to see Hannah and Judah and tell them ourselves, stay with them a few days, and get out of Jerusalem awhile?"

It is exactly what I would wish. And so we go.

As ever, it is not so simple. As soon as we can do our part in the mourning and burial, and organize supplies, we go. Meantime, I spend as much time as I can in the garden and orchard, seeking peace and direction. Apples, apricots, almonds, figs, flowers, birds and bees--all these hatch no plots, betray no confidences or alliances, reminding me, Lord, of your steadfast presence behind the turmoil. And our evening gatherings still refresh with the unity and loyalty of our household. Still, the background of it is mourning, whenever any two people meet. We all need to go away.

Here in the hills of my childhood is another world, so different from the heavy spirit that is in Jerusalem and the court. Here the horrors we have so recently faced fade like a nightmare upon the rising of the sun for a new day.

I need a new day.

Coming in from walking where once I herded sheep, back to Father's house, where we are staying and shall eat together this evening, I found all my children talking together, Hannah great with child sitting close to Judah, her sister Zeruiah at her other side, and Daniel facing them, talking earnestly until Hannah saw me entering. The talk ceased and Hannah lifted herself and came to me for a hug. I have missed her. My eyes misted over and no one spoke.

Then Hannah said, "Mother, we have been talking. We have an idea for you to think over. Don't say anything until you have let it soak in." A quick sigh and she continued, looking into my eyes thoughtfully. "We'd like you to think about moving your household back here near to us, and applying to Father for Daniel to be assigned this province to govern. Wait! Don't talk yet!"

I was sinking and reaching for someplace to sit. Daniel guided me to his chair. Hannah rushed on. "We think, Daniel thinks, he would like to live here forever, make his home here, marry here, govern these people, never live in the city again."

"It's true, Mother," Daniel stated firmly. "What do you think?"

Crying, I told them it had been my fondest hope for a long time. Then the girls both cried, and even Daniel and Judah became teary-eyed. Daniel spoke huskily, "I think Father will not turn us down. It may take a couple more years or so of training--or else!" His eyes lit up with hope and he rushed on, "He could send me here with a counsellor to help guide my judgments the first few years!"

To seal the hope, Hannah brought her harp and played a dance, which brought Father and Damaris to join us. The men linked their arms and sang a joyous psalm as their feet moved them around the room.

Thou hast turned my mourning into dancing.

O Lord, my God, I will give thanks unto Thee forever!

Thus it was begun, a process for homecoming.

We are given one year in which to make all the arrangements and complete Daniel's schooling here. Then, in Maon, there is a year for Daniel to be under tutelage among the government officials of Judea, with a court-appointed counsellor to advise all his decisions. Then Daniel will govern that province. David is arranging a purchase of real estate and a palace to be built for Daniel's household, with a wing for me and my servants. This year shall also see the marriage of Zeruiah and John.

Already, the news from court brings less impact to my heart when I know we shall be out of Jerusalem soon. Daniel will always serve the king, of course, and can be called at any time to return for any reason. But he will live his life away from here. May the sword over the house of David never reach as far from Jerusalem as we shall be.

But, Lord, I feel Your firm yet gentle reminder that I am always, always to pray for my king and country. Yes, I will.

As we left Jerusalem for the last time, I looked back at the city set on a hill, and prayed for peace there, peace in David's heart, and an end to Absalom's banishment and to intrigue. I memorized the sky line and prayed for the day when it shall be dominated by the temple that is to come, with all the people gathered in unity.

Then, I set my face toward Maon and the future of my family there, where it all began.

O Lord, hold me, for my grief is great.

The move was too much for precious Mary. She held herself together to see us all safely home, by strength of will, and soon after we were moved in, died peacefully in her sleep, as I sat next to her bed, holding her hand in mine. She stirred at the end, and gave a faint squeeze to my hand, whispering, "I'm going home, Abigail. I'll see you later."

I smiled through flowing tears, remembering this faithful servant. She had seen my growing up, that of my children, and had blessed my grandchildren that have been born to Hannah and Judah so far: Jeremiah, just learning to walk and talk, and Nathaniel, newborn, named after Father. Mary wanted to live to see John and Zeruiah's first baby, but she missed it by a few months. Zeruiah cried and cried.

"I thought Mary would never leave," she choked out. "I wanted my children to know her, too. Oh, it's the end of an era. Why do people have to grow old and die? Remember the last time she prayed for me, Mama? Just last week... She was remembering things I'd forgotten about when I was little, and praying my little girls would be like me, always kind to servants and a princess in my heart, not in my clothes and looks. That's what she said. Mama, if I am all that, it is you and Mary who made me that. Oh, she was a queen in her heart, and I hope I keep her memory alive for my children, and I hope I can pass on the wisdom she gave us, and love half as well as she did. Mama, I'm so glad you're still here."

Even granted Zeruiah's emotions being tipsy with pregnancy, this was an unexpected eruption from her. Always so quiet and contained, she probably never knew, herself, how much Mary meant until she was gone. Having your first child can bring a new perspective on your childhood heritage, too.

It's a new world and I'm grateful beyond explaining that I can be close to see my grandchildren come and grow. And Mary lived to see me back home again, and my children grown.

Forty years old! Can it be? We girls who gathered for my 15th birthday party are all coming to celebrate my dear friend Hannah's fortieth birthday, the first reunion to which I've been able to come.   All our children and grandchildren are invited, and of course, husbands. Husbands. Yes.

It will be interesting to see something of how life has treated all the girls, how each one has settled into her circumstances and families, how their children are turning out, and whether we can be friends again, after twenty-five years of experiences taking us on different paths. And to see what remains of all us girls inside the women we've become.

What shall I wear?

O Lord, where to begin...? So many impressions out of one evening.....

Hannah, first and foremost. We, at least, of all the girls, can be true friends again. I had hoped so, and believed so, and I see that it is so. It's as if we were taking up a conversation of yesterday. Intuition, more than words, or rather behind our words to each other, enables us to feel what the other means and stands for. She and Reuben have aged handsomely, and that's the first impression she had of me, as well, she told me after the others had all left.

One time I saw a look Reuben gave to Hannah as she laid down her harp after playing for us late in the evening, a look like the one he gave her at their nuptial feast, full of adoration, only deepened with years of getting along together and sharing everything life has brought their way. Most of the time, they'd each been making sure their guests were comfortable and well-served, drawn into the conversations and listened to, he with the men and she with the women.

Reuben retired after the others had left, graciously giving Hannah time with me so that we could share confidences freely. She was tired after the events of the day and all the visiting with the others, as was I, but we gained a second wind, inspired by our first chance for a lengthy talk since my settling into my new home in Daniel's royal residence some miles away. After this, we will ride to visit each other, regularly.

Hannah had her sixth child just four years ago. She thinks he will be her last child. Her first grandchild is two now, born to her daughter Abbie, with whom my Hannah has begun a steady friendship, to the delight of both our hearts since it was our dream as girls that our children grow up friends. The dream is late in coming true, but perhaps is all the sweeter for the delay, which threatened to render the dream dead for all time. She named her second daughter after me, when I was far away, and not likely to be back in her life.

All her children, though different from each other, are a delight to her and Reuben, though the third son left once and was gone two years, with no word, brought back by their prayers, and reinstated in his inheritance, to everyone's satisfaction. I loved hearing about each of hers and rejoiced that she is close in various ways to each of her children.

She knows my Hannah herself, and asked questions which I was happy to answer in regard to Zeruiah and Daniel. We had both noticed that Daniel and Elizabeth, a daughter of our old friend Esther, were attracted to each other this evening. This is a match that David can endorse, since Esther married a well-known older man of substance, though he died a few years ago, leaving her a wealthy widow. Elizabeth took up the harp, after her mother, and shows more skill in music than either her mother or my daughter Hannah, we heard for ourselves when my friend Hannah invited her to play tonight. She played like an angel and looked like an angel, with inner poise and depth coming out in her demeanor as in her music.

Hannah shared my pleasure in Daniel's interest in a girl we know from her background will be able to build a solid, lasting marriage with him. We spoke of Hannah's prayer years ago for me to have such a marriage and marvelled at the odd way the Lord chose to answer. But, as I told Hannah, I have much that I treasure of my memories with David and of course, the three children given to our union. Daniel could never deny his paternity, he is so like David. And now, as I may tell only Hannah and You, Lord, I have a satisfaction in a strange way to see that David has (after all the wives and concubines) settled into a marriage with Bathsheba, that must be the sort Hannah and Reuben share, the sort Hannah prayed I would have. I desire David's happiness, contentment with his lot, and a bond that will last, even if it is not with me. And I am all right in myself, as Bathsheba never could have been.

It is a strange world, but seeing Your hand behind things, Lord, it comes into a focus I'd never see on my own, and, as Hannah wrote to me so long ago, "All is well." At least, it's the longest David has ever stayed with one. And I foresee it lasting to his death.

I need sleep before I write of our other friends.

Because only Esther and I came without a husband, we spent more time visiting together than I had with any of the others, up to my late visit with Hannah. Esther has been a widow for six years. Whatever grief her loss gave her at the time, she has not let it stick with her. She radiated joy. "I had to recover quickly--for the children," she smiled as she told me. "They keep me going." Indeed, she smiled as she spoke and as she listened, all evening. She had wanted lots of babies, and now she is surrounded with six grown and half-grown children, and her first grandchildren. Elizabeth, at seventeen the oldest of the four who came with Esther, directed her younger sisters in making music for us, and led some in their games in the garden. Frequently, each of the girls dashed up to Esther to lean upon her in affection and repose, and half-listen to our adult visiting, absently twiddling with Esther's hair and at a pause whispering some brief report of their play, before taking their leave, usually after bestowing a hug upon their mother and kissing her cheek as they danced off with spirit, but no undue noise. Esther was the heart of her family, it was plain to see. Each of the girls radiated joy, too, only in individual styles, Elizabeth being the one who most resembled Esther. Every added tidbit I observed from seeing this family gave me added joy to think of the home Elizabeth would make for Daniel. My prayers for a wife for him could find no sweeter answer. There was no coyness in her, but she innocently revealed in her eyes and her blushes how glad she was of Daniel's interest, as I could see across the way when he spoke with her. There was no question of their needing a chaperone, with the three younger sisters close. Daniel had a taste of being a big brother, while being a suitor. Earlier in the evening, he'd spent time with the older boys in archery and footraces. It was after he stopped for more food and drink that he noticed Elizabeth and sought her out.

Later, back at home, when Daniel came by to talk, I determined to hold back any comments I had to make about Elizabeth and just to listen to him. It was not hard.

"That's the girl for me, Mother; I need no more looking around," he said, with his usual resolve. "Whatever time is needed for negotiations and a courtship period, I'll take the time. But I don't need any time for myself. I am ready. I realize Father will expect me to continue my tutelage in the governing of this province, until I have proved I can do it. You may be sure that is uppermost in my attention, and always will be. The people need leadership. But I need a wife, too, and Elizabeth is to be the one. I'll leave it to you, Mother, to decide the time and method of approaching Father to begin the process. I'll not rush you, but the sooner the better. I don't need to ask whether you are with me. I saw you looking at Elizabeth, just as you saw me, and we both know it is right. I prayed that God would show me as soon as I saw the one for me. And He did."

"Yes, Daniel, it is right." Finally, he smiled, then whooped and leaped into the air, and came down doing one of the men's dances, with his own voice his accompaniment.

It was David all over again.

But I say that without any pain or sense of loss.

Well, I have work to do.

Lord, this evening looking over the notes of yesterday, how I wandered from talking of my friends to talking of Daniel! But it is all tied together. Esther and I will see each other often, all through the years, as Daniel and Elizabeth marry and have children. Esther and I will have to make up in grandmothering what the children will lack in not having a grandfather. We will be able to share not only grandchildren, but gardening and the managing of a large estate. She, too, has recently buried her long-time attendant and is breaking in a new one. It is a blessing that Esther and I can be congenial, as of course I am able to be with the in-laws of my girls, having grown up knowing these relatives who raised my two sons-in-law.

As with Esther, with Hannah, too, we'll see each other often, though her first priority will be her husband. But we'll speak together more deeply and widely than I can with Esther, and pray together for our families and our nation, as we did at the end of our visit the other night.

Less frequently, we'll have the larger gatherings such as at this birthday party. I enjoy them, as always, but none of the other of our set of girls has grown into a woman I can feel close to. Mariah spent the entire evening with a full plate in front of her, though she is already much too heavy. She ate and talked, ate and talked, and her talk was all of possessions obtained and desired. Jedidiah made no attempt to cover his weariness with her and her chatter, or to attend to their children, who disdained to participate much with the other young people, except one son of about 10-12 who had the others laughing, mostly by mimicking various personality types.

Mariah has gained much of what she desired, but it has not contented her. We did not visit long. And she is not back in our area often, either.

Lydia and I visited mostly about flowers we are growing or want to try growing. That is as close as she comes to poetry or beauty. Her relationship with her husband Ethan, ten years her senior, seems fairly solid, but lacking in romance of any sort, more a business partnership in the raising of children than a meeting of minds and hearts. The children were well in hand, hardly noticed, functioning as followers with the others, except that one daughter of about ten led some other youngsters in dramatizing an old folk tale for the younger children for part of the evening. Where she inherited her flights of fancy, it is hard to say. Lydia does not know what is to become of one who is so little connected with everyday tasks, whereas she is the only one of their children I found appealing. They seemed a mediocre mass otherwise, solid as a rock, but not interesting.

Kettie's and Simon's children were at the opposite extreme, boisterous and much noticed, full of life, energy, and ideas, getting up a game, and more than once, a ruckus. They were good-hearted, just rowdy. Kettie and Simon kidded with each other and the children in the same manner. They'll always be young at heart this way. They livened up the evening and brought us to laughter several times, and thus refreshed us; but I would tire of her company before a day was out, though I could spend whole days easily with Hannah or Esther.

Miriam completes our old group. Though Jonah, her husband, is Kettie's older brother, and laughed at the antics of his sister and brother-in-law, along with everyone else, he has a serious side. He and Hannah's husband Reuben spent a large portion of the evening in close conversation as if they enjoy frequent visits and give each other ideas. Their oldest children are married to each other, so it is good that they see eye to eye. Hannah and Miriam are often together as well, and the two couples get along. So I will surely see Miriam fairly often.

Altogether I am thankful to be back in communication with these old friends. I will not lack for company as I grow older. I am here where I can care for Father and Damaris as they age, I can have a close personal contact with my grandchildren as they are born and grow, and I can roam the beloved hills of home. It is all so much more to my true nature than the court life of Jerusalem. God, I praise You for the deliverance and restoration, and for giving me a heart of gratitude for the relationships of my life that can sustain me into my declining years until I go to You. You have been my source and sustenance through the losses and disappointments.

You have been my shepherd, preparing a feast for me in the presence of my enemies, anointing my head with oil when I was ailing, filling my cup to overflowing when it had been tipped over and spilled, and here and hereafter, I know I will dwell in Your house forever.

Thank You for this life, O Lord.

Excerpts from Bathsheba's Prayer Journal
Part I: Bathsheba and Uriah

Dear Father God, here begins my diary with You. I am trying to grow up. Meemaw tells me I have to accept "the way things are", or I will use all my energy fighting reality. She says reality is just another word for Your plan, that if You are God, and of course You are, then it follows that You have things Your way, and a very good reason for it, too. Well, when it comes to my recent complaint, she ought to know, because she was exactly where I am when she was twelve, and she says Mama was, too. I can believe her, because the evidence is right there in front of us, and so I must also believe her when she says that eventually I will be glad over what I am now sad over. She is. Mama is. Even Meemaw's Mama, long gone now, got the gladness before she was twenty. Will I ever get to twenty?

What is sad now is that I want a true girl friend. ANY one of the girls would do--Jerioth, Orpah, Shuah, Zibiah. A true, close, special friend--besides my own sister, Jael. But no girl wants to be true friends with someone who, as Orpah puts it, "may be twelve, but could pass for twenty." They are partly jealous, and partly they see me as being a flirt, when they do and say the same things, but just don't get the same response from the boys. I don't think I'm a flirt. I'm not near as playful with boys as Zibiah, but they treat her like another one of them and they bother me-- drive me crazy--with their silly "love notes" and hanging around, and blowing kisses, just all-around foolish and disgusting behavior that I don't want or need, but don't know how to get rid of.

The most horrible example was just yesterday, and that is why Meemaw had her words of wisdom for me when I went to her bawling my eyes out. It was at the nuptial feast of Shuah's older brother and his bride. A bunch of the boys a bit older than we five girls had had a bit to drink and were laughing loudly and looking over at me, punching on one of the boys and finally shoving him in our direction. Here he came, the worst of the lot, Obadiah, swaggering over to me and right up into my face, but looking only and directly at my breasts. He acted a stumble and fell into me, spilling his drink on the front of my dress, and, still staring, smirked a fake apology. I tried to keep my dignity, but I spit out, "Does your mother know where you are?", just as icy as I could be. I fled, with the girls nervously gasping and giggling and the boys in raucous laughter. Mama covered me with her shawl and we left.

See, that's what I mean. My body is defining me, and I don't like it. But Meemaw says not only that I have to learn to like the way I'm made, but that one day I'll be so glad. Today I just want to be as skinny as Jerioth, and never be noticed by the boys, just be another one of the girls, accepted by them, taken into their confidences, all that they enjoy while wishing they looked like me.

If it wasn't for a sister like Jael, I'd be almost all alone in life. Oh, of course there's Mama and Meemaw, and my little sister, Iscah; but Jael is the one who really understands, because she's in it with me.

So, thanks for giving Jael to me, anyhow, and thanks for listening to my cries. I guess someday I'll be able to thank You for how I'm put together.

Oh, and I need help to curb my tongue. Meemaw said I'd always be glad if I controlled my words and almost always sorry for the times I don't. I'm trying to decide whether I'm sorry for this one, but I'm too humiliated by what happened to me to feel for Obadiah. Meemaw said he'd be ashamed sooner or later, and I just hope it's sooner. Why should I be the one feeling ashamed, when I wasn't the one acting shamefully?

Father is home! Oh, joy! He'll be here for a fortnight, then back to the war. He looks so splendid in uniform, but so much more approachable after he's changed into civilian clothes. Big as I am, he still takes me upon his lap, me on one knee and Jael on the other--after he's hugged Mama and swung around little Iscah, and knocked about with the boys. Once all the fuss over his arrival is past, he'll hear me out, wonderful man that he is. Father is one of the main reasons I know I'm more than the shape that holds me. Maybe I'd be flattered by foolish boys' foolish attentions if I didn't have Father's wise attention. Tonight, once he tucked Iscah into bed, he retired with Mama for the evening. But sometime tomorrow he'll have his visits with Jael and me. She'll want hers in the courtyard, but I'll want to wander out into the hills, up the Mount of Olives, as we always have, in the late afternoon, after he's taken Boaz, Dara, and Eliah hunting in the morning, and we've all had lunch, and Jael's had her turn.

Tonight, she's writing, too, but when I start playing on my pipe, she'll bring out her lyre to make music with me. It'll be light and happy, because everything's right when

Father's home. Thank You for bringing him through so many battles to so many happy homecomings. He's here and he's whole, and that can't be said for every soldier.

Almighty God, what a wonderful time, walking with my father. I never want to forget a single detail of this day. I was so proud to be his daughter and to walk beside this brawny man, so obviously a soldier, though he wore no uniform. His gait, requiring me to skip to keep up with him, his stance, towering above me, the very set of his jaw--all spoke unmistakably of soldiering. As we walked through Jerusalem, we were stopped by people greeting Father and asking how the battles are going, whether their relatives' cities will be next reclaimed from the Philistines so that they can return home. Some have had extra people in their households for years, exiles waiting for the army to do its job. Father listened patiently every time, knowing how hopes are tied to home. I shared his pride in what he does. His broad shoulders carry the burden for all the people his work is restoring to their rightful inheritance.

Sometimes there were bright-eyed, laughing children of all sizes running about, with whom I could play as he talked. Otherwise, I stood by listening as he conversed. Once a man noticed me and exclaimed how like my mother I am growing to be and surely I must be the oldest daughter, not the second, already so grown up. My heart sang to be likened to Mama, though I could feel a blush overtaking my face, as Father hugged me to his side and claimed me. "Yes, this is Bathsheba. She IS quite grown-up now, and no better woman to be like than my darling Leah!"

As we left the city, Father spoke thoughtfully, "You see how grateful the people are to King David. It's nothing less than miraculous how he is overthrowing the Philistine invaders. Some of our cities they've held for years. But Bathsheba, I believe I will live to see the day that all Israel and Judah dwells in peace." He had stopped walking and looked me in the eyes as he spoke, until I knew how much this meant to him. Before walking on, he said, "Sometimes it takes a man of war--and his army-- to bring peace. That's when an enemy has taken what is yours from you. I've been privileged to be a part of history, and to see this man develop from the first promise, through the years of running, when not everyone believed he could be king, up to being crowned over part of the nation, waging a dreadful civil war, uniting the nation, and now, piece by piece, taking back lost land. I'm proven right in placing my confidence in David." He paused and spoke slowly and softly, "I wouldn't take anything for the life I've had, serving him."

After he'd made sure I knew his heart, he placed his hands on my arms and switched his concentration, "Now, my pet, let us talk about you. Enough about this old guy. You're the one with your life all waiting for you up ahead. The rest of this afternoon is yours."

After that, it was all lightness for a long, luscious time, just soaking up the sun, relishing the breeze, so gentle and kind this special day, as if it knew this was no time for force. Father matched his pace to mine. Most of the time it was no hindrance to him, since I was full of the joy of life, expressed by running and skipping. But I had to stop at moments, for gathering wildflowers. I like a bouquet of all colors. One was so tiny and exquisitely formed, I moaned with delight, and bent over it, not to pick it; it was too tiny. Father, soldier or not, knelt beside me and studied its delicate, tiny white petals with the tiniest purple stripe in the center of each. I'll never forget what he said. "Bathsheba, there's a message in every bit of creation. What do you think this flower is saying to you?"

How could he have known to ask that? Instantly, I knew the answer, the true, the only answer. "It's telling me that our Creator is involved in the tiniest detail of all that He created." Then I burst into tears, and when he had calmed me with his hugs, kissing the top of my head as he asked what could be so worrying his young blossom, I told him all my loneliness and doubts and my fight against the way I am shaped.

He still held me after I was all finished talking until I was still all over. He said, "Your Meemaw is wise, Bathsheba. I love everything about your mother and wouldn't have her different in any detail. Someday you'll be loved this way," and, after a silence, he went on, "if there's anything I can do to make the right choice."

That moment, I could tell that he had something particular to tell me this day. First, he stood and stared off into the distance. He spoke, finally, very softly, "Do you see that tree, just on the horizon?"

I followed his gaze and saw a silhouette of perfect proportions and graceful, drooping branches, at the highest point on the horizon and standing alone, no other trees for some distance down the slope. "In a moment, we'll walk over to look at the tree more closely. I see it as being like you, my darling daughter, standing alone, a bit away from the others, high and able to withstand the storms that always hit the higher places hardest, because the roots go deep. No matter what the other girls may think or say, certainly no matter what rude and childish boys may do to you, you are shaped as perfectly as the tree. You are not yet as full-grown or fruitful, but once that tree was not grown to its present stature, either. I see you in years to come, with a character like your mother's, as mature as your body has already developed to be, sweet and wise at the same time."

He turned back to look into my eyes again, this time to see me as he'd wanted me to see him, earlier. I returned his gaze. I trust my father completely. "You're an uncommon girl, Bathsheba," he said, "and you must have an uncommon husband."

He looked off again, toward the tree. "Your cousin Araunah has asked for your hand in marriage." He looked at me with the corner of his eyes only, judging my reaction. I gasped.

Araunah is kind, far removed from Obadiah and his gang, and well-formed, but so young for his age, and, even more, so mild and indecisive, for being eight years older than I. From all I'd ever seen of him, I had no desire for him. I gave a weak, one-sided smile to Father. "And what do you say to that?" I asked him.

"I say, 'Thank God he's not the only one who's asked!'" he exclaimed. He was looking at me full-face as I shrieked, "WHO?"

"A colleague of mine, another of David's Thirty, like myself, one I know to be a real man, a true man, loyal to David for years, though not a native Israelite. He's become one by choice, so I know his heart is Israelite."

"A man like you, Father? Oh, Father," I hugged him around his neck and he lifted me off the ground and swung me around.

"Let me finish the arrangements and I'll tell you as soon as it's done. I had to see how you felt about Araunah first. He will be disappointed. So will his parents. They've dreamed of this for years. Everything will have to be settled before I leave again. They have waited long enough. I had to be sure of you first."

He picked up a rock and threw it toward the tree. "Let's walk up close to the tree," he said.

Under the tree, the breeze rustled the leaves with a soothing swishing. Seed pods hung among the leaves. The sun shone through the vibrant green as we looked out from under the tree, but where we stood was a refreshing shade shielding us from any glare, as we sat down to rest and eat our snack. Overhead a couple of birds sang in soft twitters to each other. Below, looking back down into the Valley of Jehoshaphat, which we had climbed out of to reach the tree, and looking over the city of Jerusalem, we could see the lowering sun of early evening, my favorite time of day, this and on into dusk and twilight.

Looking off the other way from the summit, we could see the Jordan emptying into the Dead Sea. These views east and west are worth the climb. Either way I looked, loveliness awaited my gaze. I sighed with satisfaction.

"Your Meemaw was right, too, in saying it wasn't ladylike of you to talk back in kind to Obadiah's rudeness" Though he spoke sternly, he smiled, a small one at first, but growing more broad each second, "However, I am glad you were not just allowing yourself to be a victim." He let that soak in with a long penetrating look, then sobered almost to anger. "What I'd more likely be wanting to know is: where is that boy's father?--allowing behavior no man should ever show to any woman. If I ever heard of any of your brothers treating any girl so, you can be sure it'd be the last time they ever did it. I know they never would!"

He shook it off, "Well, anyway, looking forward, I feel confident you will be treated with only respect when I think of this man for your husband. And I'm blessed that you see the value in a soldier's character." He paused. "You must know it's not easy being married to a soldier."

I did know it was hard each time Father left, and I did know the risk that he could be injured or killed. But he never had, he always came home, and home was so good when he was there. I thought I was ready to be a soldier's wife. It's all I'd ever known.

"Only just let me have a few months to prepare for... everything," I whispered. He laughed his hearty laugh and jumped up. "I'll race you down the hill!" he yelled.

Anyone who saw us would have said, not "There's a young woman," but "There's a young hooligan," as I hurtled myself, running and squealing with all my might, down the hill with Father. My ankle bracelets jangled, and my headband fell with the curls falling out of my hairdo.

After we slowed to a walk, catching our breath, and my wild giggles had settled into softer tones, Father said, "You know, of course, that Jael will be married first, in a few months, after she turns fourteen. When that is settled, it's your turn."

"She hasn't told me!" I spouted, half in amazement, half irked with her.

"She hasn't had time. Talk to her tonight. I'm sure she'll be ready by then."

"Who is it?" I asked, then quickly, "No, don't tell me; she will. I'll let her."

Our walk ended in companionable silence, and we arrived home just at dinnertime. I hurried off to arrange my hair before I appeared before the family, trying to act calm and ordinary when I wanted to laugh and shout.

Now, bedtime, and I speak to my shining face in the glass: "I'm to be not only the daughter of one of the Thirty, but wife of another." Glorious. Oh, God. Is it true?

The tiny flower and I, the tiny flower and I--all details in Your control. Yes.

My Creator, my Father, glorious in holiness, I would be good; I would be holy; I would be wise, as I am surrounded by those who are, my dear family. Tonight Grandpa and Grandma came. If I become foolish, it is not for lack of counsel. After dinner, dear Ruth took Elial and Iscah off to bedtime, as she once took us all; but we older children were allowed to stay, Dara for the first time, since he is 10 now. Elial had some mild protest and a downcast countenance, but Father cheered him up with reminder of the hunt tomorrow morning. Iscah clung to every one of us in turn in her bedtime hugs, but went, peacefully smiling, being tired, and an obedient child, too--and satisfied with the attention given the baby of the family, not yet out of the cute stage, but nearly.

Then followed the best time. Grandpa Ahithophel, fresh from King David's court, brought intimate insights into royalty. He made sure that all of us women realized that in most households we would not have been allowed to stay visiting with the men, but all their talk would have taken place after we left for a woman time elsewhere. Husbands would talk things over with their wives in private later, if they chose.

I think I had known before that our family is different, but tonight I know it better, and just what the difference is. Call it education, class, breeding; as Grandpa said, there's some of all that involved, but more to the point, he says, is a revelation from God Himself. Grandpa spends enough time alone with You, Lord, and the sacred writings of Moses, to have some revelation. He didn't get to be King David's privy counsellor without the qualifications. A king recognizes the resources in his people. That's just part of the job of being a king.

I was just about breathless with the privilege of my position. For one who wants to learn, always--that I should be given such a grandfather! I know the value of the gift.

I listened spellbound as Grandpa told of how he sits with the king over battle maps, and counsels him in the best ways for the army to proceed, the tactics of the enemy to be overcome, the timing, the arousal of support from potential soldiers, even among civilians, capitalizing on a man's inborn protectiveness over his territory, nowadays territory he's dying to regain. Grandpa even advises the king over promotions or demotions of military officers!

Then, too, Grandpa sits with the king as he plots the education and training of his sons, and finds the best tutors in every area, from martial arts to sacred scripture to math. He interviews the candidates to narrow down the field, saving the king for the final decisions--and making recommendations and observations all along.

In all areas where King David needs officers, Grandpa is in on the process: the workers over the livestock, the gardens and vineyards, orchards and fields, wine-making and butchery, kitchens and garment shops, the governing of the provinces near and far, the judging of inter-tribal and other issues, more than I ever dreamed of.

"Oh, it's a lonely job David has," said Grandpa, and I started up in my spirit at the thought--a king? lonely? like me? Ever since, that thought has been brewing in my spirit. Of course, he is lonely. Ultimately, all the decisions are his alone, and as for vulnerability! Oh, my! The king is not only prime target for the enemy, but also target for those who would gain and use power for their own ends, if they could. Grandpa is not one of these, I know in my bones. He serves only the ends and aims of David. That's how he has come to rise so high, that, and, of course, the wisdom of his counsel, proven in how well the kingdom is being managed.

I could have sat in the midst of this talk for hours, just listening.

Grandpa's eyes shone as he extolled David. "He's in prayer every day, from early in the morning. He has never forgotten the Lord for sustaining him in exile. He's writing the most beautiful songs. I'll sing some to you before we leave, and I'll leave the words behind for you to sing yourselves. People will be singing these songs for all time!"

Grandpa paused for a puff on his pipe. Of all things, Boaz, soon to go for a soldier in King David's army, broke into the silence with the oddest observation.

"Surely no man is perfect.   What's his weakness, Grandpa? Every man has one."

Grandpa fixed his piercing look on Boaz, but my brave brother did not squirm, but looked steadily back. Grandpa's eyes took on the faraway and thoughtful look that I am sure is on his face often, with daily deliberations on mighty issues involving influence over many lives.

"Yes, my young grandson, you may well ask, as you embark on service for this commander-in-chief. If you think long, you will realize. But it will not, in all likelihood, endanger you as a soldier." He caught himself up short, "It could. It could mean a battle that never had to be fought."   In the stillness of people entranced, Grandpa sat and thought. Finally he sighed, "Yes, it may come to even a battle. I am referring to David's actions in the area of women. Concerning women, my counsel is never sought, nor would it be heeded if sought. He's a king, and kings can have any woman they want, or all the women they want, however they want. It's the one area in which he misuses his power, though I have to say that for a king to have only one area of misuse of power is indeed exceptional. He is still an exceptional man, most worthy of your loyalty."

But Grandpa didn't stop there. "This is a military family, and I am sure you are all aware of the reputation of soldiers in regard to women." At this, Mama said only, "Eliam, the girls..." softly aside to Father.

Father did not act or speak immediately, and somehow, before I knew what had happened, I had spoken, "Father, I wish to be wise, like you and Grandpa. I have to know things. I would beg to be allowed to stay."

Jael, barely above a whisper, said, "Sir, may I be excused. I do not wish to stay."

I tried to hide my surprise at her reaction. It will take some thinking time to understand her. But for now, I have plenty else to think over.

Father nodded to her. "You may be excused," and to me, "You may stay." Mother's eyes flashed as she rose with Grandma and Jael, and left me there with the men. I will have to talk with her later, too.

Grandpa resumed when they had left, turning to Father. "Eliam, I know you've spoken with your boys before, but I would add my words, based on what I've seen, as briefly as possible. And you, Bathsheba, have before you a man, your father, who stands alone in the privilege he has offered a daughter. You realize that, I am sure. I would only say that none of this evening's discussion is to go beyond this family. I trust you. This is the only place where I can speak as I have here this evening."

He leaned back and reflected a moment. "Wherever soldiers go, there are women who will allow themselves to be used, and make themselves abundantly available and attractive. Boys, your father has never been interested. Your mother is the one and only woman for him, as your grandmother is for me. We thus spare these wonderful women much anguish--and ourselves as well. Some men can forget, and others cannot, casual and fleeting liaisons. We are among the more sensitive, and that's a part of wisdom, in my opinion."

As Grandpa sat thinking, Father said, "You have more opportunity even than soldiers, moving in the circles of the king's court every day."

Grandpa took a sip of his wine and responded to Father, but looked at Boaz and Dara. "That is true. Any man in the king's inner circle could have a woman just about any time he wanted--only not from the harem. Those women belong to the king alone."

"All their lives?" I asked, shocked.

"Yes, sadly, once they enter, some at your age, Bathsheba, they never leave."

I turned to Father, and he said, "This is one reason I must complete your betrothal arrangements, yours and Jael's, very soon."

Boaz cried out, "How can any father let his girl go to the harem? I feel like throwing up!" I knew Boaz was thinking of more than sisters. He was thinking of his secret sweetheart, Orpah.

Father answered, "There is no choice. If a girl is summoned to the harem, the king's command must be obeyed. There are advantages to the family: money and favors."

"Yes, but at the cost of the girl's life!" Boaz exclaimed.

Grandpa spoke, "I tell you, we are an unusual family. Most families think of the advantages, not the girl's life."

"If they took Jael or Bathsheba, would we ever see them again?" I'd never have thought that Boaz would care about seeing me again, before. Now, it occurred to me, maybe he WAS thinking of Jael and me, and not just Orpah. I know I cared what happened to my brothers.

"Oh, the family may see the girl. But she can never consider any other man, nor can any man consider her, though the king may see her for only one night. She's his."

Grandpa turned to Father. "Even though in the court, I may have more access to more women more often, I have an advantage over a soldier. I say to myself, 'Yes, there's a beautiful, willing woman, but I have a beautiful, willing woman at home.' While you may not see women often, once out of bivouac and into battle, when you do, it must be a worse temptation for you, because Leah is far away in time and space."

Father agreed. "Yes, and then there's the battle fear, the fear that I may never get home to her again, anyway. This drives many a man to the nearest woman. I have to remember my resolve and cling to that, and to any reminder of Leah. That's why I carry a lock of her hair, her perfumed handkerchief, and a note from her in this small box in my pocket." He produced the box and showed us. I recognized her scent as he lifted the handkerchief out. Tears came to my eyes, and Boaz and Dara stared solemnly.

"Getting back to the king, here's another aspect of the problems for David," Grandpa went on. "There is internal strife ever breaking out afresh among all the king's sons of many mothers. I leave that to your imagination. You know how mothers are about their sons." The boys nodded with raised eyebrows to each other. "It's a constant problem, and an obvious prevention of it would have been simply monogamy. But David is not a simple man. What man could stay simple with all the power of a king? At least, neither of you will ever be king, but you'll know some power in your positions. Your challenge, boys, is to gain and develop a complexity in accomplishments without losing the simplicity of wisdom. You'll have a wife, each of you, to help. And Bathsheba, you'll be a wife."

He rose, sighed, and stretched. "I've given you all enough to think about, and I'll hush up. My excess, of course, is in words. It's an occupational hazard, for a counsellor." Grandpa grinned. "In the family, I can let down my guard a bit."

Later, when the songs were over, I had to have my moment to hug Grandpa and to thank him for his excess of words. Last, I hugged Father and thanked him for regarding me as worthy of hearing all the words, to the end--and worth protecting. A harem sounds so horrible.

Oh, God, make me wise, sweet, and simple. Guide my meditations. And my actions. May I be the wife Uriah needs. I know Father thinks he's the man I need.

Jael is to marry our cousin Jesse. She's all starry-eyed. She's liked him ever since we were little, when he, along with other boys, pestered her. But with him she responded by chasing off after him to retrieve what he'd run off with, whereas the other boys she ignored as much as possible. Sometimes, since her wedding date has been set, she and I have had such fun times, trying on our clothes and jewelry, and experimenting with perfumes and hairdo's. And just talking and laughing. We've always loved to laugh, and we make each other laugh.

Other times, she's turned away. "Not now, Bathsheba. I want to be alone." But, never mind, I feel the same at moments myself. Sometimes I want to be with my sister, and sometimes I want to be alone with my thoughts of marrying Uriah and having my own household and servants and gardens. So much to dream toward. Uriah and Bathsheba may not have the same ring as Jesse and

Jael, but it sounds right to me. And Uriah is certainly more of a man than Jesse! I like Jesse all right, but he can be juvenile. That's all very well and good when it comes to playing, and I hope that Uriah has not forgotten how to play--like Father racing me down the hill the other day. Father and Mama have their playful times; sometimes lots of laughter and shrieking comes out of their bedroom. But when it comes to taking up the man's duties, I can't picture Jesse measuring up. After all, he's only 20. Uriah is 27, really a man. All my life, he's been fighting with King David, waiting for me. It seems almost too good to be true.

Just seeing him when Father signed the nuptial covenant, my heart left me and went to him. Our eyes met and we spoke so much, without a word, before I dropped my eyes, so as not to appear unladylike, but more because I couldn't have stood staring in that way any longer. I'd have folded up onto the floor. It was too glorious. I'm sure my veil was waving with my breath, I was so excited.

Later, I watched him as he was leaving. Oh, such form. Such beautiful, thick, wavy hair, such a countenance of experience gone through in triumph, such muscles, and decisive movements. And his voice!--so deep and strong.

Oh, God, already I am starting to be glad for the way You made me, all of me. I am ready to be a grown-up. Soon, I'll be thirteen, and then by fourteen, married to the most wonderful man my Father could have found for me. That young woman I see in the glass belongs to be with that man.

Lord God, revelations keep coming.

Today, I went down the hall to have a visit with Mama, now that Father has left again (all the army has gone back, and Uriah has gone to make a place for us, given time off now that we are betrothed).

As I knocked on Mama's door, I heard a sob. If I'd heard it a second earlier, I'd not have bothered her. But I was glad I had already knocked. I'd have died of curiosity as to what in the world Mama had to cry over.

She came to the door almost composed, enough so that if I'd not have heard the sob, I'd not have noticed anything different from her usual appearance. "Mama? Is everything OK?"

She looked into my eyes, deciding whether to pass it off, or level with me. I refused to lose composure in any way, but looked right back at her with equal thoughtfulness, woman to woman. I won. I knew, the way she invited me in and shut the door, that she'd tell me her heart. I had to have that confidence from her. Jael, Mama, and Meemaw are all my girl friends from now on, and I'm not looking back.

We sat side by side on the edge of her bed, and she took my hand in both of hers. "Bathsheba, it's quite a time in my life, with both you and Jael soon to be married, and you marrying a soldier, after all. I'd thought for several years, it'd be Araunah for you." She looked away. "Your father knows you better than I do."

I started to protest, but she hushed me with her fingertips at my lips. "Yes, we've been close, 'Sheba, all along. But I had not realized how you felt about Araunah, nor how you were modelling your ideas of a husband so closely after your father."

She let go of my hand and rose to walk over to her dressing table. She leaned over it, looked into her glass, and again sobbed. I rushed over to her and put my arm around her. "What is it, Mama?"

Quickly, she composed herself again, and I was amazed at the transformation in her appearance, and even more at how she could be so fast at collecting herself. She smiled, even gave a little laugh.

"Silly me," she said, "I had hoped none of you girls would be married to a soldier."

I gasped, shocked. I never knew how she felt.

"Oh, he's a wonderful man in every way, and I treasure the time we've been together. But it is not much time, out of all the years since we've been married. He's gone for so long at a time." She spoke this last very, very softly, losing awareness that I was even there, for just that moment.

She shook herself and turned to face me and study my face, then proceeded. "My dear child, I don't want to cast any cloud over your hopes. You have inner resources, both bred into you, and given you by God, and you'll do fine, contenting yourself with the joys when Uriah is home, and bearing yourself as a soldier's wife must, each time he leaves. You know how to be happy, in yourself, even more than I do. And I don't do too badly. These moments of weakness are not frequent. If they were, you'd not be so shocked to see and hear me thus." She smiled one-sidedly.

"Mama, I love you. I hope I am all you see in me, you and Father. I want to be, with all my heart."

I hugged her and she held me long and hard.

On an inspiration, I said, "Mama, do you know Father carries momentoes of you with him when he goes with the army? He showed us the other night."

She released me and turned away. I thought I had said the wrong thing. "Yes, I know," she finally spoke. "He is a good man, and I know he loves me faithfully. I know he's done his best to choose a good man for you, and I'm sure Uriah will love you faithfully, or your father would have read otherwise into his character and rejected his suit. It's just very hard for me to believe another soldier could have the character your father does. I've not seen anything from Uriah to make me doubt him personally. I just know your father is one in a million."

She picked up her brush and stroked it down through her hair. "And then, I've already told you I've seen the strain soldiering puts on marriages in many ways. You may be sure my prayers will go up for you and Uriah."

After we hugged each other again, I left, different from ever before, a sober side to my joy in my position that I'd never known up to now, but that will be with me, whether I like it or not, from now on.

God, I will need You more than I ever have. You have a lot of work to do in me over the next year. I should say 'years'.

Well, God, now Jael is married and gone. When I see her again, I wonder what will be different and what will be the same, between us. It's quiet around here now, and I treasure the times we had together these last few months. We've spent a lot of time in the kitchen, observing and even helping, so that we'll be ready to manage our own kitchens. Mama even had us go to market with Eglah so that we'd be familiar with cuts of meat, quality of produce, and the ins and outs of bargaining. "Every bit of knowledge you have of everyday functions will make you a better mistress," she says to us, "better at managing your servants AND your husband's money."

She had us spend time in our orchard and gardens with Hilkiah, our gardener, on many occasions. I've always loved being out in the gardens and Hilkiah has always had a soft spot in his heart for me; but I had not before thought of the complexities of his work, fertilizing and pruning, studying the needs of each variety of fruits, vegetables, and flowers. I loved every minute of it.

As mistress, Mama says, we have the choice of any area we want to be more involved in, but we don't have any choice about having some involvement in every area of a large household. Now, I will spend much more time in the orchards and gardens than in the kitchen, but Jael takes to cooking like a bird to the air. I don't mind knowing about cooking, but I'll mostly leave the servants to that mess. Jael thinks the garden work's mess is worse, but my hands yearn to be working the soil and making plants grow.

We have always spent time around the animals, too, but now Mama has insisted that we learn from our stock-keepers as well. Both Jael and I love the animals and can ride well, but we've learned a lot more these last months. Mama says both of us need to know what the stock-keepers do, to make sure things are going right, especially me when Uriah's off with the army.

I think we'll both be able to carry on, as Mama has, and pass along to our daughters the art and science of estate management and hostessing that we've seen in her without thinking about it, up until lately. Now, I can see how much she's taught us all along without calling attention to the fact that we were being taught.

Maybe the best times were the evenings Jael and I spent alone together. I think I can see why she wanted to leave the man-talk that one night when Grandpa was here, but I never made her understand why I had to stay. She wants to be sheltered from harsh realities. She'll find that shelter, with Jesse, seeking it as she does. It'll never be too much for me, between being able to call on You, God, and being able to laugh and have a wild downhill run every so often, and such as that. I can always pipe beauty back into my life, making music on my pipe, dance it back, or just soak it back into my being by the presence of the sun, breeze, birds, flowers, animals--all Your vast and varied creatures. I don't want to miss one single part of it, good or bad. There's more good than bad, and the good is stronger.

That little flower, the tiny white blossom with the even tinier purple stripe down the center of each petal--I think I'll put a whole plant of that in the midst of my bridal bouquet, though I'll be the only one who knows it's there--besides You, God.

At my first faint hearing of the music that preceded the arrival of Uriah and his friends, I was the most excited of my life. I had seen Jael transported out of herself and now I knew for myself that level of joy. In one way, I was aware of the girls around me, arranging my clothes, hair, shoes, and jewelry, flowers and perfume, their laughing and mine ringing in my ears as the music increased in volume until it entered our house. As I had never been truly one of them, now I was even more separate and apart, for all that it must have appeared otherwise as they hovered around me, and we all laughed and laughed.

The instant the music reached its highest pitch, they parted from me in a holy hush. I emerged, as I'd once seen a butterfly emerge; only, unlike the butterfly, I needed no time to pump up my wings. I must have had wings, for I floated, or flew, not aware of using my feet or of anything ordinary or earthly. And there was Uriah.

Everything else, everyone else, faded from my sight. Out of the crowd, I saw only him, and though the music went on, for us there was no crowd, no sound, no sight, but each other. He was close, he restrained himself, bearing himself as a soldier, and he looked down into my eyes, in a way that I knew he was aware of all of me, my body and my spirit at the same time.

Finally, alone in the swirl, he spoke directly to me for the first time, his deep voice thrilling me as much as his words. "Bathsheba, you are more beautiful than ever," he began. "You've grown lovelier than my memories. In all my work to prepare our house and grounds, I carried the picture of you as our betrothal was sealed; and when I went back to the army, I closed my eyes and saw you; and I could not believe I was the man your father chose to be your husband. From your birth, he's spoken of your understanding and unusual perceptions. I'd not have thought such a girl willing to marry an old soldier who's never understood much but following orders. But I'm glad."

I felt myself blushing all over with his ardor, but I could match his with mine.

"And I am glad," I told him. "I've always dreamed I'd marry a man like Father. I knew it was right as soon as he first told me about your asking. And then, when I saw you, I knew so much more that it is our destiny. I am ready to be all yours."

I had been speaking in a strong voice, not loud, just for his ears alone, but fervent and slow. Now I spoke more softly, more quickly, studying his face for his reaction, "But I have to tell you, you may have to help me finish growing up. I've been working on that, especially ever since I knew we were truly betrothed. And I'm ready to take on whatever comes up in the household, or in our life." I searched his eyes. I trusted him. "In a lot of ways, I've been grown up for a long time." He was looking at me in such a way that I could speak no more. As we stared into each other, I placed my hands upon my loins to calm the fire that burned there. Uriah reached for one of my hands.

At that moment, a spirit of mischief overtook me. "But I intend always to play, every chance I get, too! See if you can find me," and I slipped away from him among the people. I couldn't have stood there in such intensity another moment, or he'd have been picking me up off the floor.

I darted between clusters of people in conversation, ending at the refreshment table, where I picked up a drink to cool myself. I was so warm, almost hot, ready for Uriah to take me to the bridal chamber, and there are seven days of feasting before that can be, the most intensive socializing of my life, and I'm expected to be present for it all. Jael had been a natural when it had been her task. But I knew I was going to need all the resources I can summon, and then some. If I could not leave with Uriah right then, I would choose to be alone with my pipe, the music I can make--some of those psalms Grandpa brought us, as well as my own melodies--or wandering in the orchard. I need to be quiet.

I sipped the wine and imagined I was sipping from the Spirit at the same time, supernatural strength and wisdom, as I surveyed the crowd over the wine glass. They are all people I've known, neighbors, relatives, my lifetime girlfriends, Father's fellow soldiers, and their families; I have talked to them all many, many times. But I was never a bride before. Now, everything is different. In spite of all my dreams, I don't really know how it is going to be, to be a wife, mistress of a household. I cannot speak of it, for I do not know it. What I know, I am leaving: being a girl, a daughter, a sister. In a sudden insight, I resolved to ask questions, get others to talking, and deflect any questions they ask me, with still another question for them. At that point, I knew I'd be all right for seven days, and I thank You, Lord. I know where wisdom comes from.

And it has been working. People like to talk, and furthermore, I like to listen.   There's nothing so fascinating as a person's life. Until I can uncover the life of the one person I'm most interested to know about, I am content hearing details from the lives of many. Only one day of the seven is gone now, and I've expanded on the art of asking questions, layers of questions, one flowing into another until I have people telling me all sorts of things. God, this is wisdom! This absorbing of the ways people are living--I love it. All the pressure is off me. I wonder if this is how Jael seemed to float through her feast. I'll ask her. I even think it's what Mother always did when there were people over to see us.

Going to bed last night after the first night of feasting, I heard Iscah crying in her bed, and I crept up to her. At first, she turned her back to me, then flung herself around, threw her arms around me, and wet my neck with her tears. Her little body was shaking with her sobs.

"Sweetie, what is it?" I crooned over and over to her, to soothe and settle her so that she could tell me.

"I don't want you to go away and get married. I'll be left here with only boys if you and Jael are both gone!" Her sobs renewed.

"Oh, Iscah, bless your heart, I've been selfish, thinking only of my own desires. Listen, I have an idea. You'll come over to see me, say, once a week. How about Fridays? I think Friday afternoons would be good for you. I'll send a servant to fetch you, and you and I can have all afternoon to do whatever we want. I'll fix your hair for you, and we'll have snacks and play in the garden and orchard, make bouquets and garlands with the flowers, even cook if you want. And, Iscah, what about this? Would you want me to teach you to play the pipe?"

As the recital of promises grew longer, she gradually sat upright, and now her eyes sparkled behind her tear-dewy eyelashes. "Oh, Bathsheba, I love you," and she hugged me hard for a long time.

"Before I go to bed, I also want to remind you, Iscah, that Mama is a girl, too; and she'll be needing you even more with Jael and me both leaving in the same year.

Promise me that you'll go to Mama with everything. She wants you to do that, I know. She's a good Mama."

"I promise. I know she's good. If I ask her, do you think she'll play games with me?"

"I know she would. She just needs you to ask for what you need."

Iscah nodded and lay down on her pillow. I patted her back until she was asleep again.

God bless her, and make me remember my promise to her.

Oh, Lord, seven days is a long time to wait. So much happens. My head is swimming.

Today, second day of feasting, Uriah found me and indicated that he wanted to find a private spot. I led him quickly to the garden and down the path into the far corner near the tool shed, where there is a bench for working with soil and fertilizer and seeds.

Instead of liquid love, the gaze he turned on me was rather hurt, hurting and stern at the same time, it seemed to me. He said, "Bathsheba, you must not run and hide from me. You told me you wanted me to help you grow up. Hide-and-seek is a child's game."

"Oh, Uriah," I impulsively reached for his hand and he let me hold it. Somehow, I could focus on what I had to say, though holding his huge, strong hand filled me with sensations that would not be dismissed. "Uriah, that's not what I was talking about when I asked you to help me grow up. I meant helping me to manage everything, especially since you're in the army and I'll have to keep track of so much. Oh, hide-and-seek can be a lovers' game as well as a child's game. It is fun to run after each other. Mama and Father do that, and you know Father's no child. Sometimes we have to play just to face the things that are hard, like letting you go back to war after I've grown used to being loved. Oh, I have to play."

His look showed that this was all new to him, and he was not sure of any of it.

I felt in some way that I was the more grown-up, and had things to teach him, if he'd let me.

After he looked at me quizzically for awhile, processing what I'd said, he took my two hands that had been holding and stroking his one hand, and carried them to his lips and kissed my fingers.

"I don't know," he said, just as if he did not understand at all, "If your father does it, it would not be childish."

" 'Child-like' is the word," I told him.

"Ah, yes, there would be a difference," he murmured, turning it over as he was also turning over my right hand in both his. With only this light touch, I was next to overcome with feelings for him and desire for more. I wanted to, believed I could, kiss the bewilderment from his eyes, stroke his hair until he understood. But it is still too soon. Our day is coming. For now, it was with the eyes that I strove to speak to his soul. I know there must be play still there, though he has been such a serious soldier for so long, no girl to take away his cares. I'm the one for the job, I willed my eyes to tell him.

"Yes, we must go back," he shuddered as if to draw himself back to duty. "We must give no cause for any criticism that we are violating our time. But I hope you won't disappear so completely any more. I didn't understand. And I didn't see you for a long time. I don't know women. You will have to teach me, too."

I nodded and slipped down the garden path just in front of him, greeting people along the way as we neared the house.

Oh, Lord, this is going to be some adventure, getting to know this one.

The time has passed. The time I thought would never end has ended. The time I thought would never come is here. An epoch is over, and another has begun, since I last took up this journal. It is good that we have a year to focus on nothing but being married, before Uriah has to go off to the army again, for it will take that much time, at least. I thought it would all just happen, but I am waiting for something, and wondering what part I have in bringing it to pass. I cannot bring myself to believe that there is no play in Uriah. There is the boy remaining in every man, and the girl in every woman. Maybe Uriah never was a boy. But he had to be. Didn't he? Doesn't everyone?

About his life, Uriah is very reluctant to speak. He does not remember his mother. Somehow, she was gone before he was old enough to know her. So he never saw his father and mother together, as far as he can remember. His father moved about with him, took him among men from an early age, and often left him for months at a time with relatives that took little notice of him, until at age ten or so, he joined with a band of boys and young men who attached themselves loosely to the Hittite army. Somehow, in the course of war, his group became separated from their army and met up with some soldiers of David. The Israelite soldiers took Uriah's group and kept them, taught them Hebrew, won them by kindness, food, and promises of a place they never had found before, with no families to tie them to a homeland. They seemed to belong to someone, for the first time in their lives.

Uriah was taken up with the spirit among David's soldiers, their assurance that they were on the Lord's side, and that the anointing of God was on their leader, who would one day rule over all the tribes of Israel, though at the time, he had no place even to call home, but went from cave to town to wilderness, never able to stay long anywhere, as they were pursued by the army of the then-king Saul. Uriah, being a natural-born soldier, and knowing the terrain and survival techniques, rose in David's notice until he became one of the Thirty, alongside my father, who became second to David in Uriah's esteem and loyalty.

Uriah noticed that my father did not go for women, as the other soldiers did. Often, he was left with Father, because he too could not stomach the temporary taking of a woman he'd never see again. With Uriah, it was instinctive, but not articulated. He was fascinated that Father had articulated his wartime celibacy in the context of his faithfulness to Mama. He hung on Father's counsel as he hung onto David's way with his men, as well as his way of worship. Now he hangs on my words. In this I see the boy in Uriah.

I've never had a copy of Moses' writings, but Father taught us the stories. I've never heard David sing and play nor watched him worship, but I have the psalms memorized that Grandpa taught us. And singing them brings me into worship. I've never done so much praying before as I have since we've been married. Uriah can spend lots of time as I retell the stories of the children of Israel. He has, as Father said, come into the camp and become a child of Israel in his heart. He is so touched by a Father who yearns over His children. Uriah can spend a lot of time as I pipe and then sing the psalms. He even has begun to sing the psalms as I play, singing now loudly enough for me to hear. He remembers more psalms and after long patience and tender coaxing, I have persuaded him to sing them so that I may learn to pipe them for him. He can spend much time praying. I prayed aloud with him, at his insistence, though I never did that before; and now he prays aloud with me, simple, childlike words in his deep, strong voice. We have had much time indoors in the rainy season.

All this has developed in three months. And since the rains are letting up, we have been more often out among the animals, gardens, and orchards, of which he knew almost nothing. He listens to me and asks the simplest questions about all of this, plus the household matters. Households, too, have not figured in his experience before now.

He has time to take, time to give, to all these many areas of life. But in the bedroom, he is as swift as an animal. Animal mating is all he ever knew of, before. For him to be so sensitive in some areas and so obtuse in this, I can not reconcile. Nor can I seem to have any influence over him. This is part of what I am waiting for and wondering how I could bring about what I need from him, and what I believe he needs, too. I have a sense of shame that my husband will not linger with me, though I know that what is wrong is in him somehow, not in me. What can I do, Lord?

There's one other matter. I know he has tenderness and high regard for me, and even that it is growing. But his heart is not truly here. I know soldiering from having grown up with Father. I knew Father had a need to be off, after some time at home. But I also knew Father's heart was with Mama, and with all of us, and his home itself. All that home meant was dear to Father. This devotion is missing from Uriah, no, not missing, placed elsewhere. He's never had a home before, and he doesn't know what to do with it now.

Lord, help me to help him see what a home can mean to him. Thank you for giving us this year.

Lord, is the gift to be snatched away? Are we not to have our year? I am shaking so that I can hardly write, though for an hour already I've sat here, willing myself to stop shaking.

Uriah says he must go back. He says David needs him. War is resuming after the winter's rains, and he is one of the Thirty.

"Uriah," I pleaded with him, "you were given a year, every soldier is given a year, to spend with your bride. You're not expected back."

"Yes," he said, "but I have a duty I cannot ignore."

"You have a duty here, too. I need you, too. You're my husband."

"It is different, Bathsheba. You can do very well. I have seen your competence. I have full trust in your ability to manage everything."

"Uriah, David has a whole army. I have one husband. They give you a year so that you can be home for the birth of your first child before you have to go back to war."

His eyes opened wide, "Are you telling me you are with child, Bathsheba?"

I wondered if it would make a difference to him. I could not tell. How sad that I did not even know whether he'd want to be here to see his first child born. "Well, not yet, not that I know of, but I could be at any moment."

"Well," he hesitated, thinking and weighing, "if you are, you can send me word and I'll see about coming back."

I was aghast, almost staggering from the blow, as if it had been a physical blow as well as an emotional one. "Uriah, I need you," I made one last attempt to reach his heart with mine.

"Not as much as you think you do," he said, "not as much as you think you do." He turned and walked away without holding me, though I was all but sinking onto the floor, and so bereft I could not move to go after him, nor utter one more cry, though my heart cried out for him to stay.

God, help me. He is really leaving.

Uriah is gone. Not even four months married, and I'm already having to draw upon those resources Mama spoke of. Those resources would have been so much greater with a firm foundation of a whole year of unity with Uriah. If I'd known the satisfaction that I know can come in a marriage, I could draw on that, and know it would be back when he came back.

And then, to top that off, if I had a child of his to hold and care for and raise, to complete the family. Well, maybe I still will have that much, though a child would mean so much more if I were truly one with its father.

What if I am pregnant? Maybe he would come back. Maybe he would see me in a new way, be anchored to his home if his own child were here, too, waiting for him, besides just me. Oh God, grant that I may be pregnant. God grant this, then to be what Uriah needs to be as devoted to home and to me as he is to David and the army. Let it be.

It is not. I am not expecting any child. I am not even quite fifteen yet, married but not feeling it, alone more than I ever dreamed when I thought I was alone as a girl, among girls who couldn't take me in. I said then that Jael, Mama, and Meemaw would be my girlfriends. But where are they? They are in their own households and I can see them at most once a week, usually not that often. Iscah is too little. I fill needs of hers, and of course I love her and feel our sisterhood, but not in a way that addresses the void in my heart of hearts. God send me someone. To whom can my heart be opened, but to You? I know that should be enough, but I need a person.

God, here is a person, right in front of me. My personal maid, who began with me when I left home, Miriam, is your gift to me. I know I must keep the boundaries between mistress and maid. Help me to do that. But she is my age, and sweet, and undertstanding. And she is HERE! Here, here, here, not away at some battlefield, like Uriah, or off in her own household, like Jael, Mama, and Meemaw. This is her household. Since Uriah has been gone, she's responded to my requests and has spent more time with me than just what is necessary to aid in my grooming. The time Uriah spent with me in music and outdoors, she can now spend with me. She is delighted to do that. The stories of the children of Israel, and the prayer time, no, she is not with me. And, of course, I sleep alone. But then, I was more alone than not, even with Uriah sleeping beside me. Oh, but I did love seeing him in sleep, when he was vulnerable to my tender touches that he could not take time for when awake. I could run my fingers through his hair, just after he fell asleep, when his sleep was soundest, or over his chest, arms, legs, all that I loved about him. Dear, funny Uriah, when will you take time for being with me without a story or prayer or anything else?--just you and I together. Will you ever? I once asked him silently, as I lay next to him, smelling him and pretending he took the time to touch me, too, as I needed him to, as he slept on, unaware.

No, being with Miriam cannot make up for my missing Uriah. She cannot fill the emptiness. Though he didn't, either, I always hoped the day would come, sometime in our years. At least she is a friend, and it fills some of the time. It is better than not having a companion at all. And it is what I do have just now.

It's been a long time--months--since I sat with pen in hand, many days of sameness, sameness and work. Iscah comes each week, and I exert all my efforts to give her a good time and keep my personal life from her. Jael comes about once a month. I talked with her at the beginning. Now I do not bring up my life, but ask her questions and listen about her life. She is supremely happy, and soon to be a mother. Mama knows everything, mostly without my speaking. We stay on safe subjects: our servants, our gardens, our kitchens.

Lately, Miriam and I have taken to going up on the roof to enjoy the peace of the evening breeze and the sunsets. It reminds me of seeing the sunsets from the Mount of Olives, with Father, when we would take our walks, when he came home on leaves. There's not the wide panorama, but the same sun sets with the same colors on display; and it's a touch with old times. Maybe Uriah will come to the roof with me when he is home. I wonder whether he ever sees the sunset where he is. Probably not. He'll be too busy performing some duty, if I know him. Maybe we could make a bed up here, when he comes home. He sleeps out a lot, soldiering. Maybe he'd like it here better than in the house. Maybe my daydreams are taking me over, and I'll end up living in them instead of the reality I do have. Or maybe daydreams are what I need just now.

Miriam interrupted my reveries tonight by banging up the stairs with my bathtub. I hadn't even noticed that she'd slipped away, I was so far gone in my imaginary world.

Miriam banged the tub down and said, "I'm going to get Haggith and Reba to help me carry up some hot water buckets, and we're going to fill your tub, and you can have a nice bath out here under the sky as the sun sets and the stars come out. It's a glorious, still night and you need to do something different and treat yourself. You've worked too hard too long. All work and no play is not good for you. Some pampering is what you need. Do I sound like a mother or a friend?" She laughed and I laughed.

"Both, you dear girl!" I assured her.

I caught up her hands and we danced around in a moment of playful exuberance, ending on our tiptoes, our four feet together as one pivot around which we whirled as fast as we could spin, leaning back so our hair flung as our skirts flew out around us, and laughing the whole time with abandon. It was a precious and much-needed moment, my cares dropping off by our momentum, as leaves drop off the trees in a fall wind.

What a jewel she is, I thought as she ran off, and how nearly she matches my own thinking. I'd thought of everything but a bath on the roof, and it fitted my other ideas. I settled myself to be pampered indeed and not to allow one sad or even wistful thought to enter my world, just for one evening. I picked up my pipe and improvised a dance tune, then flung it down on the settee and danced the dance, humming the turn to accompany my movements all over the roof. I was quite out of breath by the time Miriam returned with Haggith and Reba, all three carrying two buckets apiece filled with hot water.

I burst into laughter and it was contagious. All three of them laughed with me as the tub was filled, and Miriam began my undressing. As she helped me remove articles of clothing, Haggith and Reba sobered, bowed, and floated off down the stairs to their other duties. Miriam draped a towel over me and pointed out the perfumes and oils, promising to come back as soon as I called for her. I impulsively placed my hands on her arms, leaned to her, and whispered, "Thank you," and she, too, whisked away, after an understanding look into my eyes, and disappeared down the stairs.

I decided to pretend Uriah was watching my bath, taking time just to be with me and love me, as if he'd never had a duty to go to, as if he let his cares go for once, as I was letting mine go. Why not? I was alone under the sky, and the night was falling, and I was young and lonely, and full of need for him, but not in the usual heavy way, instead hopeful that this place would indeed be the scene of a new awakening in Uriah, which would surely be coming, one of these days. After all, he was my husband, he was still alive, and one day he would find it out, bless his dear shriveled heart. My prayers and my patience would win him. He'd be here in person and not just in my imagination, in person as never before.

I danced slowly about on the roof with my towel, covering myself, uncovering and waving the towel.

In my mind, Uriah was sitting on the settee. So, every so often, I danced or glided or flung myself or swayed over by the settee and leaned over him for a kiss or caress before I slipped away from him again.

I let down my hair. I shimmied my shoulders and swiveled my hips. I swayed, I spun, I slunk, now humming, now moaning, now silent, bending, arching my back, enjoying the feel of moving freely in the evening air, unhampered by clothes as by cares.

Finally, I entered the bath and sank into the warmth with a moan of delight. I lay there relaxing, finally reaching for the soap and slowly, slowly raised first one leg, then the other out of the water as I lathered and rinsed. Never have I luxuriated over a bath as this one.

Miriam called softly up the stairs, "Bathsheba, are you ready for my help yet?"

"No, I'm just enjoying myself, Miriam. In fact, you just go ahead on your way. I'll finish up myself, tonight."

"I'll see you in the morning," she called, and all was silent again.

Rising from the tub, enjoying the feel of water receding from my body, I stretched and sighed. I dried slowly. Then I lay on the settee and oiled my legs, arms, body, dabbed the perfume, shook my hair out and brushed it, and began putting on my clean things, all slowly.

Gradually, I began to have a sense that Uriah was watching me, really allowing himself to take the time, as never before, that he was very near and real. "Wherever you are, I love you," I whispered.

When I was clothed, I lay on the settee staring up at the stars, taking a moment out of time, pretending Uriah lay beside me, prolonging the waiting to make the coming together more special. As the darkness deepened, I picked up my pipe and played a slow and haunting new melody, pierced through with passion and longing.

Suddenly, I laid the pipe down and began to cry, for the dream that had not come true. It had seemed so near and suddenly it was completely gone. My crying, like all the rest of this evening, was the most profound of my life. I shook with sobs. I was more alone than ever. I should never have imagined and pretended. I only made myself hurt more. I cried all the tears I'd held back for so long. Like everything tonight, the crying was deep, slow, and slowly subsided.

As suddenly as the dream had come and gone, a peace came, from I know not where, and enveloped me. My grief dissipated. As I had received the bath, the dream, and the crying, I now received this strange sense of peace. Truly, Lord, I knew Your presence as I never have before, knew You to be in control, regulating every detail. Once again, I thought of the tiny flower. I rose from the settee and fell to my knees, bowing my face to the ground for a silence of worship. I lifted my head and arms high to honor You, and to receive whatever life You gave me. I knew You were working in my life, and I would face whatever came, armed with this new assurance.

A psalm came to me. I played it on the pipe, then laid the pipe aside and sang:

> "I will extol thee, my God, O king;
> and I will bless thy name for ever and ever.
> Every day I will bless thee;
> and I will praise thy name for ever and ever."

Once, twice, and again, I sang the simple thought, then another psalm and another. I don't know how long. There was no time, only eternity.

Everything was all right, or would be. I knew it beyond all imagining.

I fell asleep on the settee and slept all night.

I awoke early and felt an urgency to record what I had come through.

The dawn is beautiful. I never before watched a new day come.

Some few hours later:

This morning, a summons has come.   The king requests my appearance. Tonight.

But, the king is off to war.

No, it seems the king is not off to war.

I am, on one level, overcome and full of doubts and questions. On another level, I know the same assurance I knew as I fell asleep last night. All is well. All my life is in Your hands.

I go to answer this strange summons, quieting any inner turmoil and encouraging myself in You.

Excerpts from Bathsheba's Prayer Journal
Part II: Bathsheba and David

Oh, God, You tell me what in the world has happened here. All the time I thought I was so alone on the roof, I was open and vulnerable, watched, as I felt myself watched, only not by my imaginary Uriah, but by my very real David. It's not possible, yet it is true, he is mine. And I am his. It cannot be. How can the thing that must never happen be all accomplished?--and no pangs of conscience! I did not seek any of this. God, it came upon me. And I know the truth of your absolute sovereignty. David is a king, but an earthly king, and ruling only by Your ordination, You Who are the real King.

God, it was terrible, it was wonderful. From the moment I knelt before him, and he came from his throne to take my hand and lift me to stand next to him, dismissing all his attendants with a nod, there was a fire between us. It flamed in my hand and all through me, as his hand held mine, and even when he let go. We spoke of many things. He'd seen my body and my soul naked, last night on the roof. I had thought myself naked before You alone. You had arranged another to be in the audience.

After I stood next to him, he did not touch me again, through all our long time of talking. But in all our words, the fire travelled beween us, and in our looking at each other's faces. Though I scarcely dared to look, and glanced up only infrequently, I knew him to be watching me every moment, watching intensely, seeing everything.

How had I known his psalms? I told him of my Grandpa Ahithophel and Uriah teaching them to me. I hardly recognized my own voice. Indeed, it seemed as if another were speaking, and I was watching and listening to myself. Part of my mind was full of the warnings of Grandpa, and the revulsion I felt toward a man who would have so many women. But this part grew foggier and more distant, the more David talked to me, drew out my responses and listened to them.

Who was my family? I told him all. He knows everything. I told him even about the tiny white flower with the tiny purple stripe, and my aloneness, and what I'd known of Your provision in all things, up to last night. He saw and knew all about last night. No need to talk of that.

After, it seemed, I'd told him all my life, and had heard many things about his life as well, and the fire between us had built in intensity beyond anything being able to stop it, he touched me again, to draw me close to him. My whole being responded, body and soul. Yet-- note this, my God--I did draw back to ask him, "Doesn't the king always have to have a virgin? I am not a virgin."

"You are," he said, "You have never been claimed until this moment."

There was truth in that, along with the untruth. Before I submitted, I had one last thing to say, "I'll not be just one of a harem."

"No, you'll not," he vowed.

I accepted that.

It was a long and beautiful time. I'd not have thought it could be. But it was beautiful, beautiful, beautiful.

Now, today, the complications, even the horror of it, wash upon me from time to time. But always they are overcome by the beauty of what happened. This is the love of a lifetime.

God, You are my witness: I did not ask for this, in any way. If You permitted it all, then God, fix the mess it has made, please. I am swinging between the greatest joy, even ecstacy, and the greatest despair, each greater than I'd ever have dreamed possible.

What is to become of me?

What is to become of Uriah?

And, if, as I feel I am, I should be with child, what is to become of the child?

No matter how it may turn out, I will never be able to regret these last two nights, not one bit of it; nor would I recall it and go back to the world as it was before. The same assurance that all is well, and all is in Your hands, is with me and is greater than my fears.

I hear David's voice saying, "You have the most beautiful body and the most beautiful soul I have ever seen." How can I be afraid?

I await the outcome.

Two weeks have gone by. I have gone through my duties, have supervised the kitchen and the gardens and have conducted the necessary conversations with servants. For myself, it has seemed as if I were operating in a trance, but none of them seemed to pick up on anything different--except Miriam. Miriam knows. I know that she knows. And she can tell that I am aware of her knowing. But we maintain the mistress/servant roles the same as always, almost the same.

Iscah has come and has relieved my mind with her childlike innocence and her faith in my goodness. I AM good, to her. It is with her that things are most nearly as they always were. She is learning to pipe, and Mama has plans to buy a pipe for Iscah soon. Mama has someone in mind for Iscah to marry, not a soldier.

With Mama, we have practice in not talking about tender matters. Still, sometimes she looked into my eyes until I turned away from her to tend to anything I could think of. Mama is thinking. But she doesn't know.

Jael and the baby came, and that was easy. We focused on the baby and the plans for his life, on his sweetness and the sharpness of his growing awareness, all his preciousness. I am thinking babies. But Jael doesn't know.

Three weeks. I know now. I called Miriam and gave her a message, sealed, to be taken to the king by a reliable messenger. Miriam gazed into my eyes, but I would not turn away. I am her mistress. She turned away, with a small bow and a "Yes, Bathsheba, I know a reliable messenger."

This is an emergency. I am newly with child and my soldier-husband has been gone to war for many months. I should be in a state of alarm. But I walk in assurance. Even beyond that, I walk in hope and joyous anticipation for the child of a great love. He shall be a great person. I do not know how this is to happen.

I await the outcome.

David sends word, "All is well. Do not fear. I shall attend to everything. Uriah will return for a special assignment and a week at home."

Ice took over my mind and my body. Fear, the greatest I've ever known or imagined clutches at me. Whose am I?

If Uriah comes, the child will be known as his, unless his looks reveal the truth. Am I to be lower than a member of the harem? Oh, God, that assurance I've grown to think of as a permanent part of me, that You are making all things right regardless of how they seem-- where is it now?

I must keep going. No one must learn my true state of mind. The state of my body will be all too apparent before too long, but, God, I must be calm and serene. I cannot. Give me the peace again. I must be at peace for the people around me. Most of all, the baby must dwell in peace within me.

Uriah has come and gone from Jerusalem and I NEVER SAW HIM. Am I to be abandoned by both? What is this? David arranged for Uriah's visit to cover up the fatherhood issue, for appearance's sake. Uriah would not come to me. Why?

I have wondered for days, but now I know. His duty was to be with the other men, separated from their wives, not to have what others may not. Duty, always duty, Uriah's only thought, overwhelming any other thought or purpose in his life. Oh, his nobility is beyond human. It is so cold, I think it lessens his humanity. It is too much, this cold nobility that has no room for the needs of love and those who love him. He cannot be personal, but so devoted in a public sense, he gives up all that is personal, sacrifices himself, and me, for his duty. May God reward this excess of duty. But Uriah is as dead to me. How can I ever come alive to one who will not come to me?

God save me and my baby. Does anyone have a duty to me?

A messenger has come. Uriah is dead, killed in battle, in the very forefront, along with many others. Other women who weep this day have known the love and devotion of their husbands, surely most of them. No one knows I never had that of Uriah. I wear black to show my mourning. And I do mourn. I regret the death before he knew of life, the life that comes in loving. I weep for what could have been. My child could have been his child. Life could have been simple.

But it is complicated. What will David do now? Does he have any idea that Uriah was more committed to him than to me?

Now, as I am beginning to be swollen with child, I have received another summons. The king requests my appearance. Tonight. After dark. He will send his men to accompany me. I am past feelings.

How can this baby grow right, in a mother whose emotions are being torn apart? No matter how great the promise for this child, at the conception, this turmoil can only have harmful effects on his development. I am sorry, baby, so sorry. I love you, and I always will, but I don't know the world you'll have to grow up in.

God help us all.

David has married me. I cannot get past the wonder.

As soon as the men deposited me in David's chamber, not daring in his presence the knowing looks they allowed at times with me alone, they were dismissed. They bowed, and one dared to look at me as he rose, a look of compassion, even respect, beyond the knowing. I never let my head hang. Why should I?

David had allowed five minutes to hold me and tell me that I was to be his wife, not only his wife, but his queen. After the despair I had been in, the shock was almost too much. He held me as I began to sink, and revived me with his kisses, kissing my hair, my eyes, my cheeks, my lips, my neck and my lips again, until I knew he was devoted; and I could return the kiss.

"Forever," he said, and ushered me out to the room where a priest waited to perform our wedding. I knew it was forever. To describe how that can be communicated in a few words, kisses and caresses is beyond possibility. But the assurance is no less for being ineffable.

All the assurance came back, with more added, not only Yours, but his. This is a man to be believed. I do not know about the other women; maybe he doesn't know either. But this we know: we are husband and wife. Forever.

Living in peace and harmony, I had begun to think that this baby could grow well inside me, and all the growth during the turmoil be repaired. Then came the visit from Nathan the prophet. I heard every word, behind the curtain, as he told David that God was not pleased with his taking another man's wife, and another man's life. It was surely God, the way he told him, by a story of another, whom David condemned with angry passion, only to be told in prophetic tones, "You are the man."

David knew, and I knew, that he WAS the man. He took me when I belonged to Uriah, then arranged for Uriah's death in battle.

All the horror of what he had done flooded over me as it flooded over him. For a long time David knelt and wept before You, Lord, and I the same, separated from him by the curtain, until I knew that we each had completed our transaction with You, repenting after acknowledging that You are right, and we are wrong. At that moment of catharsis, I crept to him and we held each other and wept before You for all the sin of our hearts and lives, for being human and not holy, as You are.

Afterward, we agreed we were glad Nathan had come and we could begin from this moment forward to live in forgiveness and newness. It had to be brought forward, the whole truth, and expurgated from us.

Now, God, a new start. Only You could do the cleansing and renewal. Our mighty and merciful God, we do adore You. Oh, bless the child, and give the cleansing and renewal to his formation.

We agreed to name him Nathan, after the prophet who brought us Your word, in boldness to dare to correct a king--who needed to be corrected. We desire never to forget--that You are holy God and we unholy people, that You forgive and renew, that You turn our mourning into dancing, that your Father-heart cares too much to let us go uncorrected, or remain in guilt and fear, that You love us and bless our love for each other.

Today, David said, "My queen, what do you wish, now that you are queen. You shall have your heart's desire."

I replied, "David, what I wish most of all is to have a copy of the writings of Moses and to learn to read, that I might read his very words for myself and not have to hear the stories from another."

Such a look of wonder came over his face. He gazed at me as if it took a long moment of realization before he could believe such a request. As his mind took it all in, his eyes settled into understanding and then filled with tears and gazed over my face in love and devotion. He held me a long time close to him before speaking.

"I should have known already your first request would be spiritual and not material. You could have asked for anything, and you want the writings of Moses and the work of learning to read. Of course, you shall have it. The best Hebrew tutor in the land shall be at your disposal, what?--twice a week?"

"Oh, can it not be every day?"

Amazement again flooded his face. "My dear, precious girl, yes, every day." Again he held me for a long time. "Now, surely there is some material thing your heart desires. Think, woman."

"A harp," I said, "I don't have to think, I know. I want to be able to play and sing at the same time. I have to lay my pipe down before I can sing your psalms. And I want to know every psalm, every last word you ever penned. I want to sing them all."

This time he wept until I began to fear for him. It was I who clasped him to myself this time, and crooned, "David, David, why do you weep?"

"For love of your soul, my own wife, for the beauty of your spirit, for your love for God, and your love for me."

When he was quieted, he said, as in solemn vow, "You shall have the finest harpist in the realm for your music tutor--myself, your own husband."

Again, a long tender hug, and he added, "I'm not going to ask you to give any more requests just now. You've about broken the resources of the wealth of this kingdom with your extravagant desires. I will need to amass more gold to make you happy."

"You're silly, David," I stroked his hair as I whispered it; and all the fire took over us again, and we were one. We always will be.

Out of the exhaustion after birth, I perceived, as in a fog of my spirit, voices deep with concern. Panic took over the peace. The baby, Nathan, was not well. God, I cried in my heart, is the tiny baby to pay the price for a sin not in any way his own? Like a sacrificial lamb, shall he be made to pay the ultimate price in his innocence? It is too much! No, Sir, Lord over all, the Holy One of Israel, it is not. It is only fitting that a great sin require a great sacrifice. Oh, but I shall ask and hope for his healing as long as there is breath in his tiny body. I think You would not forbid it, Lord.

And so David came, to pray with me in like manner: Spare the child, if there is any way; if there is not, we bow before Your holiness and know that Your mercy exceeds Your judgment.

The entire royal household walks on tiptoe. David prays and does not eat. All else is set aside, that he may spend his time waiting upon You in solitude. When he comes to me, his solitude is not broken. Or mine. All the air is full of the holy hush, and You are as real to us as if a third person were in the room with us. The communion is palpable, though not a word is spoken. You, he, and I kneel beside the cradle. I hold the tiny, perfect body of our baby, and he is anointed with my tears and David's. There are no words. Not in the air, not even in my mind. Your Spirit, David's spirit, my spirit and the baby's--these fill us.

And the baby's spirit grows weaker.

Yes, the son is gone to You. It is just. It is all right. Yet, I weep and weep. My heart has been ripped out of me, but I am not diminished. Another heart is being placed within me. It's a heart for You alone.

The first thing David said, after all the weeks of wordless sorrow, was that You'd ripped his heart out of him and given him a new heart, clean before You.

"Only God can do that, Bathsheba," he said. And he picked up his harp. "Listen to what came while our son lay dying."

To the most mournful tune I have ever heard, David sang and sang.

O Lord, rebuke me not in thy wrath:
neither chasten me in thy hot displeasure.
For thine arrows stick fast in me
and thy hand presseth me sore.
There is no soundness in my flesh because of thine anger;
neither is there any rest in my bones because of my sin.
For mine iniquities are gone over my head:
as an heavy burden they are too heavy for me.
I am troubled; I am bowed down greatly;
I go mourning all the day long.
For my loins are filled with a loathsome disease
and there is no soundness in my flesh.
I am feeble and sore broken:
I have roared by reason of the disquietness of my heart.
Lord, all my desire is before thee;
and my groaning is not hid from thee.
My heart panteth, my strength faileth me:
as for the light of mine eyes it is also gone from me.
My lovers and my friends stand aloof from my sore;
and my kinsmen stand afar off.
They also that seek after my life lay snares for me:
and they that seek my hurt speak mischievous things,
and imagine deceits all the day long.
But I, as a deaf man, heard not;

and I was as a dumb man that openeth not his
mouth.
Thus I was as a man that heareth not,
and in whose mouth are no reproofs.
For, in thee, O Lord, do I hope:
thou wilt hear, O Lord my God.
For I said, Hear me, lest otherwise they should
rejoice over me:
when my foot slippeth, they magnify themselves
against me.
For I am ready to halt, and my sorrow is
continually before me.
For I will declare mine iniquity; I will be sorry for
my sin.
But mine enemies are lively and strong:
and they that hate me wrongfully are multiplied.
They also that render evil for good are mine
adversaries;
because I follow the thing that good is.
Forsake me not, O Lord: O my God, be not far
from me.
Make haste to help me, O Lord, my salvation.

At this point, David leaned over his harp and mutely
played some of the same strains he had just sung, then
continued the song:

I said, I will take heed to my ways, that I sin not
with my tongue:
I will keep my mouth with a bridle, while the
wicked is before me.
I was dumb with silence, I held my peace, even
from good,
and my sorrow was stirred.

My heart was hot within me, while I was musing
the fire burned:
then spake I with my tongue,
Lord, make me to know mine end,
and the measure of my days, what it is;
that I may know how frail I am.
Behold, thou hast made my days as an
handbreadth;
and mine age is as nothing before thee:
verily every man at his best state is altogether
vanity. Selah.
Surely every man walketh in a vain show:
surely they are disquieted in vain:
he heapeth up riches, and knoweth not who shall
gather them.
And now, Lord, what wait I for? My hope is in
thee.
Deliver me from all my transgressions:
make me not the reproach of the foolish.
I was dumb, I opened not my mouth; because thou
didst it.
Remove thy stroke away from me:
I am consumed by the blow of thine hand.
When thou with rebukes dost correct a man for
iniquity,
thou makest his beauty to consume away like a
moth:
surely every man is vanity. Selah.
Hear my prayer, O Lord and give ear to my cry;
hold not thy peace at my tears: for I am a stranger
with thee,
and a sojourner, as all my fathers were.
 O spare me, that I may recover strength,

before I go hence, and be no more.

David sighed and took his hand from his harp for a long moment. When he replaced it, the music changed to fit more hopeful words and feelings.

> I waited patiently for the Lord; and he inclined unto me, and heard my cry.
> He brought me up also out of an horrible pit, out of the miry clay,
> and set my feet upon a rock, and established my goings.
> And he hath put a new song in my mouth, even praise unto our God:
> many shall see it, and fear, and trust in the Lord.
> Blessed is that man that maketh the Lord his trust, and respecteth not the proud, nor such as turn aside to lies.
> Many, O Lord my God, are thy wonderful works which thou has done,
> and thy thoughts which are to usward:
> they cannot be reckoned up in order unto thee:
> if I would declare and speak of them, they are more than can be numbered.

My own weeping continued calmly all through his first song. My wonder grew as he finished with the peaceful song. He was spent and, laying aside his harp, came silently to me. We lay beside each other for the first time since the birth, but did not touch, only went peacefully to sleep, like babies.

Tonight, David said, "The Lord will give us sons that live, and daughters. As only He can, He has made right what began wrong. He knows our hearts, Bathsheba, and a son of ours shall be next king. Only from this union can an heir to the throne proceed. I bring His comfort and mine to you, and promise you that you shall never know a loss as this again."

"God has restored your strength, David," my assurance came softly to him from deep within me, or high above me, some commonly inaccessible place of wisdom and peace.

If I'd thought there was fire before, this one was greater, as when the fiery furnace was made seven times hotter and the children of Israel survived it. We are one in every way.

Afterward, we wept softly, for the joy and the peace, the freedom and forgiveness, and the new life that was on the way, from this night. His name shall be Solomon, for the peace.

But there shall be a Nathan of ours. Solomon shall have a brother Nathan who does not die, until old age, and other brothers and sisters. We have only, and truly, begun.

Lord, can it be true? Like a man who's finally found a home, every evening David comes. All his business he finishes in the days, and comes to me every evening. What about the other wives?--and the concubines? I dare not wonder. He hears my reading. I am really reading for myself, the books of Moses. Oh, what a wonder. Then he teaches me how to play my new harp. He has infinite patience, and skill in explaining. He says I have a gift for music and that I am a joy to teach.

It has been thus for a month without one evening's break. In the days, while he has his meetings, I am organizing my new household and garden. We had some dismissals among the servants, but now all are honoring, obedient and hard-working.

In my heart, there is a depth to the joy that would never have come to be in me, but for the sin, the pain and loss, and the reception of Your great mercy in forgiving us and elevating our union as You have, Lord. It is as the chant and response that take place in the synagogue: a new expression of Your infinity and the ageless answer repeated, for His mercy endureth forever. Each repetition goes deeper because of the new revelation that preceded it.

Among the ageless aspects, always in my character, is the playfulness. For a long time, I did not play. But for David, it must have been decades since he played, if he ever did. His boyhood was spent so much in solitude, with only sheep for company, and You, Your creation in all its splendor. But now, once again I play, and David is discovering he can, too. I hide from him. He must hunt and find me. When he does, I run from him; he must chase and catch me. I am laughing without reserve, as I did when I was a girl; and he is amazed to hear himself laugh as he never did.

Only, the play is balanced by and freshened by Your great, great mercy to usward.

A joy in simple things fills my belly with peace, even as I begin to swell with child, a child of peace. Then, Lord, tonight there came an abrupt announcement from

David: I am to appear by his side as queen at a state dinner, before my confinement is upon me. I say it is abrupt, but we knew it had to come. Our private commitment must of necessity be acknowledged, because of David's position. He refuses to allow entrance to any tension over this, into his heart or mine, or our union.

He said to me, "Bathsheba, regardless of what has gone before, make no mistake, YOU are my queen, and the sooner it is made clear to the court, the better. In women, maybe I never knew my mind before, but I do now; and I will, by the power that is mine as king, come against all opposition to your place at my side. All the officials shall be here for this banquet. I know you know what to do, how to be, as queen, for you are the only queenly woman I have known, no matter the rank any have had by accident of birth. None can compare to you, and this shall be seen, acknowledged and honored throughout this court, before this week is out."

As he went on to detail the arrangements he has ordered, I was able to attend with my whole mind. I am not afraid. I do know what to do, by Your grace, O Lord. May our standing before You foreshadow our standing in the eyes of the people, starting with the court. Amen.

I know what I shall wear, that will not show my condition this early. By another week or two, nothing will hide the fact.

Father Lord, how I do praise You for the ovation and reception given to me after David's introduction. I shall always treasure this night. My heart went out to each person, one after another, who came to bow and greet me.

Father, I sensed no rejection among those there by the time I had conversed with each one, even if upon approaching me there'd been a hint of hesitation or suspicion. The only exception was my own Grandpa Ahithophel. His eyes bore hard into mine, his lips were clenched and white before he spoke, and he saw the tears that swam in my eyes before I could blink them away, as he said, "This is wrong, Bathsheba, and nothing can make it right. I thought I'd taught you so that you'd never come to this."

I was able to control myself, because of what I know, and I begged, "Grandpa," as I looked peace into his eyes, "Please come to speak with me, and you shall know how it all came about and how it is now and my profound innocence of wrongdoing. God has forgiven us, and you can, too. Have you never known God to turn evil into good?"

Grandpa only stared and moved on through the reception line, without a word, only a "humpf" of disdain and refusal. But there were tears in his eyes as well as mine before he broke eye contact with me. I know he has always loved me.

All evening, I felt his stare upon me, but no storm he felt could affect the fair weather surrounding me or take the peace filling me.

I stand not alone, but with You, Almighty God, and King David, and all our sons and daughters to come, as well as most of the court. If any who absented themselves are against David because of me, God, You are able to war against opposition to Your will and plan. Solomon, our son, shall be king after David. Only, I pray that David rules for years before that, a united kingdom. And I pray Grandpa joins the unity You're making.

Father, in my confinement, I am comforted by Your presence, always David here every evening, and the child growing within me, as well as the memories of that grand dinner and the acceptance of so many. Though Grandpa has not come to see me, David says he counsels the same as always, attends every meeting where his advice is desired, and seems the same toward David, almost. He seems to be weighing David's character afresh, but unable to find any complaint in that regard. Once only, he made a reference to David's first-born son, perhaps as if to indicate that he will not support one of mine as successor to the throne. But David carried on as if he had not heard, and the comment has not been repeated.

This is a blessed life. So much comfort and company, after the many months of as great loneliness. Every possible dream of my life is now reality. I am 18 years old. I am where I belong, I am who I belong to be, and David is the man I always dreamed of, and more.

The first son of our family is on the way. The future beckons.

Our new son, Solomon, the very picture of health, lay sleeping in his little bed. Solomon is all David could want for a son born to be next king. You can see royalty already in every feature. As I admired my baby, his father came and picked him up without disturbing his rest. Slowly, Solomon opened his eyes, eyes already so like David's, intense and intelligent.

David held Solomon, only two days old, in his arms and blessed him, speaking of his future as a man of God, a wise king, a king in peace, all his enemies subdued before his reign, speaking over him every blessing he could summon, so eloquently, I half expected him to begin singing the words; but he kept to simple speech, his tones familiar, as if his only audience were Solomon and You, Lord.

I stood nearby, listening, praying and willing all the blessings to be so, now and always, and drew near for an embrace, when David motioned me to join them. David's eyes glowed with approval, taking in all of Solomon and all of me with that gaze of husband and father that's like no other. I had to bow my head to ease the thickness in my throat and the tears in my eyes at the sweetness of that look. But I had to look up again quickly, so as not to miss any more of it. How I bless You, Lord, as the Source of this mixture of rapture and peaceful contentment.

Oh, my God, You are good. You have redeemed our lives, buried our transgressions, and blessed us. And we bless You, Lord.

My cup runneth over. I had no sooner said that to myself than David began to sing his Shepherd Psalm as he danced with Solomon around the room. They say it isn't possible, but Solomon watched his father, and smiled, too. David swung around the room in his father-dance with his son, then drew me with one arm and cradled our baby in his other as we all three finished the dance.

By then, I was ready for a rest, and he tucked me in, after laying Solomon back into his bed, and tenderly bade me not to exert myself any more today. He lingered a long moment, and I shut my eyes to sleep.

I heard him softly giving instructions to Solomon's nurse, and leaving, going, I knew, to meet with his council, having put me--us--before business.

Tomorrow there'll be the ceremony, with David on the throne and the priests, Zadok and Abiathar, formally presenting his new son to the king, but tonight the family without ceremony. The king arranges it to his liking. He is father first. I slept until he came again.

Solomon is only three months old. But things are changing.

Father, tonight after a great tumult of stamping boots and shouted orders in the halls outside, I sat in stunned silence behind the curtain between our sitting room and the bedroom, where I had been having my hair arranged, as messengers of Joab stormed into the sitting room, where David sat playing his harp. From their entry, I sat motionless before my looking glass as I heard first their bowing and murmurs of "Your majesty," all showing due respect, then their words which, while spoken calmly enough, left no mistaking that Joab was ordering his monarch, and leaving David no choice but to go with these men if he wanted to stay as commander-in-chief of his army. Joab had had all he could take of David's absence, the messengers made very clear. If David did not appear, by the time Rabbah, the Ammonite capital city, fell, which would be very soon, he, Joab, would claim the city's crown for himself, since he'd been the one fighting all this while.

David, quick to recover kingship, ordered the messengers out of his chamber, promising them that he would be ready to leave with them within three hours, after he had arranged matters with his privy council for the kingdom in his absence.

It was no matter that my hair was not done, I rushed to David as soon as the men cleared the room, knowing that his momentary paralysis would soon give way to his customary purpose of action. I had only a moment before he became not husband but king and commander. He needed me as I needed him. His departure would be suddenly executed, as it had been suddenly demanded. The kingdom possesses him, in a sense.

All this I knew as I knelt before him and laid my head and arms in his lap, "Oh, David, God go with you."

"Yes, He will as He always has," he answered softly, stroking my hair, my arms, my shoulders, "only I am getting rather too old and weary for soldiering. It has taken its toll on me. Joab knows. But he is right. I must go. He's felt the pulse of the army and found they've taken all of my absence that they can, if they are to keep allegiance to me. I didn't win their hearts by keeping to the castle while they fought my wars."

He spoke this in a tone of quiet revery, then shook himself. I stood as he stood. We embraced. "Bathsheba, you came almost too late. But before, I couldn't have received or entered in. Funny how things work out. You a young girl, me an old man. Shh," he said as I pulled away to protest. He drew me near again. "I'm not old when I'm with you, it's true. You have given more back to me than you'll ever receive. Shh," he said again as I wailed, "No."

"Yes, it's true. I know what I know. You are God's gift to me, and our son Solomon is God's gift to the nation. You must help me to teach him wisdom, more than I had when I was young. It's you, and it's knowing we have this work to do with him and our other children to come, that assures me I'll return safe from this battle. I'm protected, as always, only more so. To God be the glory. Praise His Name."

He looked into my eyes long and hard, kissed me and held me as if never to let me go. Only, he did, and left, saying, "Your prayers, my precious, I'll need them."

"You have them," I answered.

"Thank you," he said, so fervently, as he left with one last look at our sleeping son.

I wept quietly on my couch, I don't know how long, loving and aching more than I ever knew was possible. Part of me has been torn away. Oh, God, You will bring him back?

David has returned! Joy, joy, joy! He came here first, crossing the room to me with great strides as I ran to him and threw my arms around his neck for a swing around the room. Round and round he spun me, as full of joy as I. Laughing with me, he first set me at arm's length while he put the crown of Rabbah on his head, then kissed me. That done, we went to Solomon's bed, where David bent to lift him out and to lay the crown in Solomon's place. Again, they danced the father-son dance, and then we had our family dance.

And our family is now set to grow again, next one: Nathan, in nine months!

Father Lord, my twenty-second birthday is here. Solomon is four, Nathan is two, and Leah, my newborn, first daughter, lies in the little bed where her two, three really, brothers slept before her. A girl, a little princess, not as important to the kingdom, but to me very precious, indeed. To David, too. To my mother, of course, her namesake is the best in all ways.

David's third father-dance. After the mother-father dance with the newborn, this time the family dance followed, with Solomon holding to one of David's legs and Nathan holding to my skirt, and the solemnity quickly dissolving to laughter of all four of us, and startled cries coming from Leah, who then called forth all David's skill in soothing as I hustled the boys to their bedtimes, laughing with them as we exited.

As in Solomon I've always seen a wisdom beyond what any infant ever could possess, and in Nathan I see already the devotion to God and godliness that his namesake possesses, in tiny Leah I see a droll look, as if she laughs at her own joke. Just a few weeks old though she is, yet I experience, coming from her, a charm we must be sure to guide well to keep from turning to foolishness and even manipulation.

Oh, it is all the challenge any human life could ask, to raise up a godly seed for Your glory. Is it any greater to rule a kingdom than to order a household of growing souls? I think not. And David bends his will to the task even as I do, every evening reading to us a bit of Moses' writings and singing psalms before the boys' bedtime. Did ever two toddlers know so many songs?--or sing with greater gusto? Then there's a romp ritual before or after the reading and singing.

After they are in bed, often David and I discuss their tutors and the content of their education. Solomon is to be the wisest king who ever ruled, and Nathan is to have his province to rule over. Of course they are handsome, wealthy, and will rule over many subjects, but they must have character. God's kingdom of Israel must be led by the wisest of earthly rulers, bowing his knee and receiving his directions from You, and being served by his brothers in their provinces, ruling as wisely and well, without envying Solomon's place. David and I pray for Your wisdom and guidance as we guide these children into their destinies, playing, singing, laughing, and loving as we go. And it is all by Your grace.

Oh, God, it is as Mama and Meemaw told me those ten long years ago: I am so very glad You formed me as You did. As silly as it seems in one way, I'd not be where I am today, right where You planned and where I'm most blessed and most used, if I were not in the very physical shape You made me to be. That shape that brought me so much grief at twelve now brings me so much good at twenty-two. How I now glory in having such a body as this, once my shame. I told Mama and she only smiled in total understanding. God, You are so wise and good. You do all things well.

As if I could ever forget it, I am ever reminded by the tiny white flower with the purple stripe. David has dug one up from the hillside above Kidron Valley and transplanted it into the orchard here at the base of an apple tree that bears our favorite fruit. Leah knows the flower already. I held her over it and pointed to it and her eyes took it in as she wiggled all over and gurgled. She will know it well and be told the story every spring of her life. When she's twelve, she'll not be distressed by her shapeliness, nor overly taken with herself either. That's my prayer.

Father Lord, all the court is torn by Tamar's tragedy. She had made a public display, and rightly so, of her grief over her shameful rape by Amnon, her half-brother. He revealed his character, despicable. But something of David's character has been revealed in this matter, too; and as proud and thankful as I am of his efforts with our family, I am much saddened by the absence of effort in his earlier families. Here we have the fruit of the neglect. If he wasn't there before when Amnon needed him, that is one thing. He could do something now. Yet, he does not step in with a judgment fitting the offense. Perhaps he feels he cannot, because of his taking me in the way that he did. Perhaps he receives this as part of the fulfillment of the prophecy over his house. But lack of justice now may bring worse to come. I have nothing to say about any of this. I only pray: Lord, please do not let this rip apart the kingdom, Your chosen people. So much is at stake in the rearing of royalty. If commoners knew, they would never envy.

Poor Tamar. Poor Absalom, her brother with whom she has been, they say, inseparable since she was born. They say he broods. Father Lord, brood over this injured pair, and let no lasting harm come, let no ripples of evil from a horrible offense become a wave to engulf a kingdom, Your kingdom, David's kingdom, one day Solomon's kingdom. Most of all, the kingdom from which Messiah will come.

I say that I won't think about the other families, but the past comes into the present unexpectedy and, in the case of a king, powerfully. The servants bring the talk of the court into my hearing. Absalom is spoiled, and is spoiling for revenge. A word from David, of punishment for Amnon's great offense against Tamar, of comfort for her and Absalom, not to mention her mother, Maacah the Geshurite, could save the day. Yet he goes on as if nothing happened, after his initial anger over Amnon's brutal act. God only knows what is being brewed up among the three--mother, daughter, son, in the privacy of their own household; but I feel it with my whole soul that no good can come of David's inaction. Instead, a storm able to destroy everything in its path is forming on the horizon. And we are in its path.

It is as Nathan the prophet spoke when David had first brought me here to him, the sword in David's house, never to depart. Thus, a dread lies alongside the joys of our household, and of my new pregnancy. David ignores, but I cannot. I fear for him, for us, but I am not the one to reach him on the subject of one of his previous marital alliances and the offspring from it. It is not my business. David made that clear to me when I once, at first hearing about Tamar, asked him about a punishment for Amnon. "THIS is your family, Madam," he emphatically reprimanded me, waving his arms toward our children after tapping his own chest. Fire was in his eyes then, and it was not the fire of his passion for me. I never want to see his anger again turned my way.

Even as I acknowledge the justice of any repercussion from David's sin involving myself and Uriah, I ask, Lord, for the sake of Your people, let this bitter cup be spilled before David has to drink it, if it be possible. But God, all Your ways are holy and right. And Your blessings toward us are many and deep, despite our lack of deserving. You are present in all things. All things.

Another son is born to David and me, Shobab, "returning", for my prayer that we, and he, are ever returning to You if we ever wander in any way, and that all that is due to these sons of ours is ever returning to them, by Your mighty hand, if there's any threat to come against what is their due. Prayer is my defense against the destructive forces at work under the appearance of calm in the kingdom. It is not the calm of conflict resolved, but of unresolved conflict having gone underground and waiting to erupt in greater damage.

With David, I live in the pretense he has chosen, that this family and its peace is all that's needed for things to go right for the kingdom. At times I almost believe it. After all, Absalom has not been heard from. Amnon, they say, is going about his life as always. Tamar is no longer visible. Has it all blown over? Something in my spirit says No. Mostly, the source of my background unease is vague, almost mystical. Yet, at rare intervals, I come upon the abrupt ending of a conversation among the servants at my appearance. "You mark my words, he's not forgotten, no matter how long he's been...Oh, mistress, would you be needing anything?"

Then it is evening again. I pick up Shobab, and at once my peace is returning to me, holding him close, small and soft and squirming, healthy and beautiful, as we gather with David and Solomon, now nearly six years old, Nathan, soon to be four, both handsome and so like David--and little Leah, now toddling about to plant a kiss on Shobab's cheek. The Word heard, the psalms sung, the boys' lively chattering and tumbling--surely we are as any other family, only more blessed, more surrounded by love, more beautiful and right, totally within Your favor, Lord. That is all I receive from David. Nothing about him, words or actions, with the family, with me alone, with You as well, when he and I pray--in no way does David give a clue that there is any concern beyond loving and raising this family to be rulers over Your kingdom in a time to come. I think he wishes all the other, before us, into oblivion. It's as if he believes that the people he brought into the world before these four somehow went into the depth of the sea along with Your remembrance of his sins.

Would that it could be so. But I fear they are all too real and present.

Oh God, Absalom has called a banquet for all the kings' sons, excepting ours, who are still too young. David has refused to go. All this I learned from Miriam, my personal maid still after all these years. She hesitated before deciding to tell me. I urged her. She knows my lifelong love of the truth, no matter how painful it may be. Ignorance of it is more painful, too often for me to prefer to ignore. God, what difference could it make in what transpires this night if David would go to join his other sons? His absence will mean the absence of all restraint, I fear. The storm will burst. These other sons have not known, as my sons do, the steady presence of a father. Even now, at this portentous event, not to have the presence of their father!

Lord, I spread it all before You, thanking You that my sons are protected, but fearing what may come to all the other sons and the kingdom and king that I love with my being. God withhold evil in this, Your kingdom.

Oh, Lord, horrible news has come, that all the kings' sons are killed. David cries out in loud, heartrending wails. Help us all.

Time stands still and there is no sound but David wailing, calling to You. There's no approaching him in his present state. So far the children are still sleeping. God, I appeal to You to right these wrongs. As You are ever present with us, do not desert us now. Help David to make some sense of the loss and give him some direction. God, comfort him. It sounds as if he'll never be sane again.

But wait, a messenger is arriving. It's David's nephew Jonadab, close friend of Amnon, almost unable to speak for his own cries of lamentation, finally blubbering that it is only Amnon slain by Absalom, that Absalom has been plotting it ever since Amnon forced Tamar. David grabs his shoulders, pleading, "Is it true? Is it true? All are safe but Amnon?"

Now all the sons are here. Such a tumult of lamentation, and each one telling David his own experience of the evening's bloody events. He's surrounded by all these sons, so many who look like him, all the ones before me, but Absalom and Amnon. All their differences and feuds--and they've been many--are forgotten as they hug one another all around, trying to purge from memory the sights they've witnessed this night of hate and violence and death to one of their number. The poor boys.

The children awoke, and I've spent time with them. They are back to sleep for now. This emotional outburst outlasts my endurance. I feel as if I've been here for hours, and indeed it has been a long time. Still they are carrying on, David and his sons of many wives. How will the horrors of this night affect all these and all they are connected with--the various mothers, their sisters, even my own family. From this moment on, things will never be again as they were. The lives of all whom David has touched will never forget when murder and mayhem broke out in their midst. How they do cling to one another, overcome by fear and grief.

Will this bond of grieving enable them to trust again, or will they live with a wondering of who might be plotting treachery against them?

Soon, tomorrow, our boys will have to know what is behind this tumult that awakened them. Tonight I only wept with them and soothed them back to sleep, a fitful sleep with the lamentation ebbing and flowing in David's hall below them. I myself will keep vigil the rest of the night, mourning the death of Amnon and the guilt of Absalom, and recovering from the shock that gripped my soul when we thought all the sons were dead but ours. David and his sons keep vigil, too.

Today the sun was high in the sky before I awoke. David slept on. I arose to relieve and refresh myself, eat an orange and check on the children, and bathe quickly. I lay back down beside David and he roused, drew me near, and held me closely without words, a long time.

Finally, he drew back to look into my eyes. So much love and so much grief all in the same look. "It's all so complicated," he admitted, "too much for any one man to understand--or cope with. God will have to straighten the mess, repair the damage." He gave a small snort, then, "Too late for Amnon, though..." A long pause, then, "perhaps too late for Absalom, too. Where was I all the years they were growing up? I know where I was. I was in battle. I was in conference. I was taking more wives, making more alliances, ever and always conquering, conquering, conquering, never stopping. I never stopped running, even after there was no need to run from Saul any more, until you came. I fought the fight to gain the kingdom and come into my rightful, God-given kingship. Then I fought the fight to keep the kingdom from the attack of the enemy, the Philistines. I've been fighting them since I was a boy, Goliath, you know, right after the fight against the enemies of the sheep. Now, here are the sheep of my own little flock, fighting."

He sat up and turned his head to look at me as I sat up beside him. "When you came along, I quit fighting. I thought to make a family, with you, as if there'd been no families before." He reached out to touch my temple with his forefinger and ease back a loose strand of my hair, his eyes going tender and then deepening into revery again. "There really were no families before. But here are all these sons. And daughters, too. Who are they all? I don't know. I never found out. I left all that to their mothers and their tutors. And now what do I do?"

He wept again, falling in a fold over his legs. I fell onto his back and held him, and wept with him.

Presently, we rose to a sitting position again, and he prayed. I prayed as he spoke, right along with him. Everything he prays, I pray.

He went for his harp and sang and sang. Well into the afternoon, he finally went for his bath and meal, and called for his privy council to come to his chamber downstairs instead of meeting at the usual place. I think he wanted me to hear, and talk with him afterwards.

God, we need you as never before, and that's a lot.

Father God, of course it is time for David to order pursuit and punishment of Absalom, but still he does nothing.   Miriam brings me the talk of the court. Everyone knows where Absalom has fled--to his maternal grandparents in Geshur. Still, David does nothing.

I heard with my own ears Grandfather Ahithophel telling David that his first-born is now no more, and his second-born is an incompetent, and his third-born is a murderer and a fugitive from justice. He should name Adonijah to succeed to the throne. He is old enough himself that the kingdom is at risk if he does not. David did not tell him that he has promised the throne to Solomon. I think he fears my grandfather. As do I. He is a man of power as well as wisdom, and has had his counsel taken into action, to great success, all these years. He contained his rage. He is not an emotional sort at all, too wise for that. But a coldness was in his tones.

Oh, Grandfather, I shudder to see you and David parting company in the matter of the accession to the throne. David is king. He will have his way. If you could only have looked beyond the externals, as bad as everything appeared, to the work God has done in me and in David, if only you could, even at this late date, work your way into forgiveness--oh, I fear for you, if you cannot.

Lord, dare I approach my grandfather? I think You would have me only to pray for him. And I shall. Oh, how I shall pray for my dear, wise, good grandfather. So much of what I am--what I pass on to my children--came from you, Grandfather.

Lord Almighty, the months are passing and David still grieves for Absalom. Occasionally now, he will speak to me about him, how promising his studies always were, how charming and well-liked among the sons and staff he always was, how David had wanted to name Absalom his successor to the throne, until he saw me that night on the roof and all his affections were engaged as never before.

"He was my pet for so long," David admitted, "though I saw him but seldom, as you know, and his mother never again after Tamar was conceived. There was another allliance, marital and political." He looked at me for the first time in this revery. "How pointless it all is, making marriages to gain allies. What we have together is the only basis for a marriage. The only basis."

He was glad to leave all the complexities for a time apart with me. It was as always. Almost as always.

The complexities just do not go away. He pours himself all the more into the evenings with Solomon. I say with Solomon, though all the children are there for quite some time before he sends the younger ones off to bed to make extra time with Solomon and the two of us. He engages Solomon so wondrously well, I wonder that he never did so with any of the other sons, even his former favorite, Absalom. I realize afresh there's never been a union for him like ours--for him as well as for me. He never wanted to spend evening after evening with a wife before. He never even knew what it could be. It wasn't just the wars, either. It was the wives.

Oh God, how grateful I am. To top it off, another new life is stirring within me. He shall be named Shammua, "famous". Poor boy, in the light of Solomon's glory, his name will surely be his closest claim to fame. Yet, I know that all these sons will be of good repute among the people under their protection.

No one, not even Grandfather, will ever be able to say that one of our sons is an incompetent. Or a murderer. Or a rapist. Grandfather, your blood flows through them, and the blood of the king you served and believed in for almost all your life. Oh, come around. Open your eyes and your heart. God, open his eyes and his heart.

I would that my children know and love him as I did. He's never seen them. They don't know him at all.

Anyway, Mama and Father do. They think these are the world's most extraordinary children. Father said, watching them all play, "Bathsheba, it's not just that 'blood will tell'; there's a blessing of God upon your children, flowing from the blessing upon you and David."

I treasure these words among my greatest treasures.

Absalom has returned. His long exile is past. Much has happened here since he's been gone. Our family is complete with the birth of our last, our daughter Jael, named after my sister. Such a virile man, David would no doubt have fathered children up to the day he died, but for the harsh life he was forced to live as warrior against the Philistines, and the desert time fleeing the forces of Saul. It wore him down. As it is, he is man enough for all that is required of him as king, very much so. But Absalom is preening and preparing a base of support for an early bid in his own prime-of-life strength, knowing he has no chance of being proclaimed successor by his father. His only hope is to take the throne by force.

I shudder to imagine how this will all be played out, though in my depths I have no doubt that Solomon will be king after David. It is the mind of God. At eleven, Solomon stands on the threshold of his entry into manhood, even as David stands near to the portals of life everlasting. Each draws strength from the other, as both look to You, Lord.

If Solomon were our only offspring, my heart would be filled to bursting. Then, here are these others, each so fine in his own way--the girls, too, though Solomon is like no one before or since. For wisdom, for grace, for beauty, for intelligence, for strength and agility--by every standard Solomon excels. Absalom knows he has to act soon, and has to bring down these sons of ours, not just David, not even David and Solomon together, but all: Nathan, Shobab and Shammua, too.

But David for too long made no attempt to receive or even contact Absalom, leaving him to his own devices. If

I have heard the reports from Miriam, through the servants' grapevine of news, I know that David has heard, through the advisors in his privy council and their many contacts around the kingdom. After the initial order for Absalom to return to Jerusalem, which was precipitated by Joab, David only lately received Absalom here in the palace, kissed him, and sent him on his way again, with no settlement of the issues. His entire concentration is on grooming Solomon to be his wise and strong successor, and the others for lesser but still important posts. A drama is being played out here, all-absorbing to David. I myself cannot help wondering what is the extent of the drama being played out in Absalom's world, so removed from ours, but not, I fear, far enough. David chooses to ignore all the rest. To build upon what we have here is, in his mind, as far as I can tell, all that is needed to secure this kingdom to Solomon.

God, I've prayed Your wisdom into David, so I have to trust that it is Your wisdom that's driving his decisions. I just still wonder at how it will all happen, and at what cost to us.

Father Lord, when the call came to evacuate the palace, to flee for our lives before the forces of Absalom, I was strangely calm, while all around me was a flurry such as I've not seen since the night I moved to David's house. Miriam oversaw the packing of all the things I will need. The children's nurse packed for them. Solomon stood beside me, sixteen, but, as ever, acting older than his years, manfully taking David's place, his arm often placed around my shoulders, and as often placed around the shoulders of the younger ones. Leah, now twelve (wasn't it only yesterday that I was twelve, only less contented with the fact than she is?), mothers Jael, eight, as she would mother the younger boys, Shobab and Shammua, now eleven and ten, if they'd let her. They prefer to stick with Solomon and Nathan, fourteen, the two younger imitating the older boys' deep voices and an air of assurance. I can see in their eyes that they are afraid, but unwilling to be ruled by fear. I know they are remembering, "What time I am afraid, I will put my trust in You," as they've been taught so well as they listened wide-eyed while their father told them how he managed to keep his courage when the Philistines took him in Gath. They will themselves to be the man he is.

"I am so proud of you all," I spoke in their hearing in the final moments before the guards surrounded us for our escort to the waiting royal mules. We've not been free of guards ever since.

Aside from the clopping of hooves, all we could hear across Jerusalem, as on all our journey, was the loud wailing of the people. Supper smells floated on the air. Some women leaned out of windows to wave brightly colored cloths, rocking as they cried out, tears streaming down their faces. I lifted my eyes and smiled at them, nodding slightly, but did not wave or speak. David still has his supporters, I was heartened to see, though I never truly doubted it.

The previous wives, with their servants, preceded us. All their offspring are grown now. Only our children were in the royal evacuation, except for some children of servants in the other households.

After crossing the brook Kidron, where the blood of the sacrificial lambs flows at Passover, we ascended the hill where Father and I used to walk. I was shocked to see the ark being borne back toward the city. Zadok and his son Ahimaaz led, and Abiathar and his son Jonathon followed the men who carried it. As they passed, Abiathar leaned to say, "David shall return to Jerusalem, as he finds favor with the Lord. He and his men ascend Olivet crying, but they shall return rejoicing. He is the man after God's own heart. God reigns above! David reigns below!"

Tears of gratitude filled my eyes so that I could not see but could smell them as the breeze brought the scent of spring wildflowers above that strong one of horses, mules, and leather. Gradually, my eyes cleared. Our family stayed riding as closely together as we could with guards all around us, the girls sharing one mule just beside mine, and Solomon to our right, riding slightly ahead and looking back often, meeting my eyes in wordless encouragement, the younger boys riding close behind.

The birds still sang, the life of spring going on as if nothing were amiss. Conies darted their heads out of their colonies in the rocks, curious and alert, retreating again for security. I hazarded a smile in Jael's direction, which she saw and returned as quickly. Any other time she'd have wanted to stop to try to make friends with a cony, see whether she could pet one at last. Not today. Ordinary life is suspended. Solomon, her resource on animal lore, turned back to wink at her and say, "I'll tell you all about conies one of these days, Jael." She blew him a kiss.

All afternoon we descended and traversed Jordan Valley. By the time we crossed Jordan, it was dark. We dismounted for the ferry ride. On board, the children crowded around me and we helped support one another as the ferry lurched on the waters. Solomon quoted, "When I cry unto thee, then shall mine enemies turn back: this I know, for God is for me. In God will I praise his word: in the Lord will I praise his word. In God have I put my trust; I will not be afraid what man can do unto me," with assurance, looking into the eyes of each of his brothers and sisters in the moonlight. By the time he was half through, each of the others whispered the words along with him. I knew that they were hearing in their imaginations, even playing on their harps, the tune to which we had set the words and sung them, so many times. Before the passage was over, they all were singing softly. Tears sprang into my eyes, tears of pride in these heirs of the legacy of David, flesh of my flesh as well as his. Indeed, what can man do to us?

We rode until it seemed as if we had lived in the saddle. Now we rest our weary bodies on donated beds, wash in donated basins, eat donated food, so grateful to be so cared for. As they had not whimpered on the long ride, the children now utter not one word of dismay over their primitive conditions, though they've never lived this way before. They rise to the requirements upon us. They thank every person who brings succor of any kind. They express more concern for the mules and guards than for themselves.

Even now, as the battle rages, so near us, a cloud of calm surrounds this family. Our guards have taken note. I overheard one saying low to another, "This is royalty, all right, if Absalom did come first in the birth order."

I looked over at Solomon, as they did. He stood at alert, taut with the desire to enter battle himself, but restraining himself because of David's orders: he must live to ascend the throne, who knows how soon. No foolish risks are to be allowed, regardless of his eagerness to test his training, to prove himself a man and a warrior. "You are a man of peace," I can hear David admonishing him. "By the time you sit the throne, war will be past. War is far more wearisome than glorious. And your skills will meet greater tests in keeping the kingdom than in any number of battles."

Solomon felt my eyes on him and turned to look at me. "I remember," his lips formed without a sound. He smiled. I smiled. He looked back intently, no trace of a smile left, awaiting a messenger with news of how the battle was going.

Nathan, coming up to stand beside Solomon after finishing a game of chess with Shobab, with Shammua on the sidelines, leaned near and said, "You know the news will be good."

Solomon simply shook his head Yes, put an arm around Nathan's shoulders and asked, "How long do you say it'll be before the battle is over? I'll make you a bet. See who comes closest."

"Today before the sun sets," Nathan answered.

"Tomorrow by noon," Solomon declared.

It is as Nathan said. The battle is over today. Twenty thousand of the men who started the battle will never see the light of day again. So many lost. God mend the broken hearts of wives and children. God mend the kingdom. May all opposition be as poor Absalom. With all his manly glory, looks and talents, all his promise, risked to rob his own father, now lost for good. He had to know that his father, so partial to Absalom for his likeness to himself, would rather have done anything than to see Absalom killed, yet he forced David to the necessity. This can only be done out of hate of the darkest and coldest sort. How much he hated the father who so indulged him, yet ignored him in the midst of the indulgence!

Now they say David shames his soldiers after their hard-won victory in his behalf by wailing loudly in his chamber over the gate of the city of Bahurim. God bring him to his senses. And to a proper gratitude for Your intervention and for his soldiers' faithfulness in risking their all that he might retain his rule. Shameful, that's what it is.

Oh, but Lord, I love him. What he must be feeling!-- to be unaware for even a moment, at such a point in the nation's life, of his effect as king upon his people, his army. Oh, the depth of his sorrow over the effect he's had in the lives of his own sons. It overrules all his consciousness as king. He's only a broken man just now. How I wish I could fly to him, just to take on myself some of his sorrow, if I could. We've been through shame before. This time he bears it alone.

Only, he's never alone. You are there with him, as here with me.

And David and I shall be together again. In Jerusalem.

God, watch over him, comfort and hold him, while I am apart from him.

Another messenger. Joab scolded David at length and threatened the desertion that would surely follow if he did not collect himself and speak gratitude to his faithful followers. He did. He even has asked Amasa his nephew to be in place of Joab over the army, though Amasa was over Absalom's army in this battle. It will unite the remaining rebels under David. Everything David does now must serve to mend all rifts.

We are to return to Jerusalem, all glory to God.

Oh, God, seeing David for the first time since our forced exile from Jerusalem, I fell to pieces as he held me, cried and trembled all over--so unlike me. After the pent-up emotions were all released, I sat weakly beside him and said, "David, I'm so sorry, such unbecoming behavior." He held me closely as if to crush me.

"You are not alone," his voice came, choked and faint. I looked into his face for the first time and saw tears in his eyes, too.

"Yes," I said, "we, of all people, know the hand of God upon you and the will of God concerning you--and Solomon--and yet... and yet, oh, David, I am so glad it is over."

"All but the grieving. And the rebuilding." We sat in silence a long while, just to realize that we were both safely through such a trial, and here together again. Then he sighed and spoke softly. "I'll be much in meetings, my precious one, here and around the kingdom, before I can be with you, with our family, as we would have it. But that day shall come. Until I can, spend much time with the children."

We spoke of the children. He was hungry to hear their reactions during the crisis and blessed by my descriptions. We spoke of Ahithophel, the factions to be reconciled, even the battle, but not of Absalom. The omission was conscious to both of us.

It was good to talk.

Afterward, he said, "Now it is time for the two of us." And what a time!

Oh, blessings without end. That such a love is mine!

Lord, in the tumult of the return to Jerusalem, crossing the Jordan again, bowing to the crowds cheering along the way, receiving shocking news of Grandfather's suicide after Absalom's death, settling back into home, reuniting with David, I had not time to notice Solomon--or any of the others. As each day, I spend some time alone with each child, I met today with Solomon first, after our noon meal, in Jerusalem's quiet time during the heat of the day, planning to visit a few minutes and see each of the others in turn. As it turned out, I spent two hours with him and did not see the others today.

Weeping has long been disciplined right out of the boys by their training as royal sons, but Solomon wept today, not loudly as is the custom, as we did at Grandpa's memorial service, but with a flowing of tears instead of voice, off and on as he opened himself, talking as a means of release as well as reflection, seeking always to understand, as we've urged him to, night after night, over the Books of Moses--to understand the ways of God and the ways of men. He'd been, along with David, a rock for me to lean on in my own grief over the end of the wisest man I've known yet, my Grandfather Ahithophel. Now it was my turn to be something of a rock to him, mostly to point him to the true Rock, our Lord and Father above.

He spoke as out of a cavern. "Mother, before this, in all my training and in all yours and Dad's counsel, as I approached the day I rule this land, I did not know the cost. I march to the throne in blood. Dad has always taught me I'm to be a man of peace. I pray to God this is the last of the blood to be shed. I AM a man of peace. I have not the stomach."

He paused to draw forth out of his depths. I only waited to listen when he was ready.

"It's not only what I saw on the battlefield, the bodies of many that I never knew--except that they are my people, Israelites every one, no matter what tribe. It's thinking that before Dad saw you, Absalom would have gone to the throne, once Amnon was dead. Absalom. He is my half-brother, even if I never was around him, so much older than I. His education was almost over by the time mine began. But people say he looked the most like Dad, before I came along."

He had been walking, stopped now to sit beside me without acknowledging me, and to cry without sobs. I wanted to touch him, hold him as when he was only a boy. But it would not have done at all. He was a man, sorting out a man's issues, issues far too complex for anyone to be thrust into, but nevertheless his own milieu, and not to be avoided for one with so much responsibility soon to be carried for the rest of his life.

"And Jehiel, in sessions with me, preparing me, as I insist and I know Dad does, too, for all the undercurrents of court life which I will navigate to my dying day..." He paused and stared at his hands and then out across the room. "Jehiel told me that Absalom was like Dad in many ways besides looks, was the smartest one in classes until I came along. I can only think that his counsellors informed him. He was scared, that's part of it. He was scared he'd have no place in life, no place big enough for his abilities, just as he had no real place in Dad's life."

Solomon got up and paced again. "But I know now for the first time, from the reports, how large a place Absalom held in Dad's heart, the way he almost lost his army mourning over this son's death--my half-brother, after all." He stood at the window and stared out. I prayed for him to have at his disposal all Your wisdom, Lord, to sort things through to his own peace of mind. I waited. I pictured the scene before his eyes, as I've stared out that window, the quiet street as people rested indoors until the heat of the day begins to subside, the rooftops with their abandoned couches, where the people, his people, would gather for the evening in a few hours.

"He had to have some clue from Dad as to how dear he was. But I try to imagine how I'd know Dad's heart if he weren't with us in the evenings. Would I have come to hate my own father, as Absalom did, if I'd not had him by my side all the days? I could never, never wish Dad out of my way for the sake of taking his throne. It is the heart of evil, such hatred of one's father."

Finally, for the first time, he acknowledged me as more than his listener. He came to me, took my hands, and placed both of them between his own, and said, "It's because of you, Mother, and all you are." He shushed my quick moan of protest. I did, too. I knew the truth of what he was saying. "It's the reason all of your children have their father in a sense that none of his other children ever did. It's you." He smiled through his tears, and walked again.

"Absalom came of a rejected mother. All the other mothers were rejected, dropped, one after another. Dad never knew what home means, before you. And I see why, more than I ever did as I heard the both of you say, night after night, all those years, why I'd be counselled to love the wife of my youth."

He stopped at the table and drank a long drink of water. He dismissed the servant who knocked at the door to see if I was ready to see Nathan. "She will be here with me until I come out." It was a king ruling his household.

When the servant's footsteps had gone out of hearing, Solomon walked the room and talked again. "I just pray that the wife of my youth will be the love of my life. I don't want a repeat of all this bloodshed for the throne after me. I don't want to be crying out someday for a son of mine, dead of his own hate and ambition, 'Oh, Absalom, my son, my son'." He sighed. "Jacob and Esau, Isaac and Ishmael, Solomon and Absalom..." Stopping abruptly, he raised his face and one clenched fist and shouted, "Let it come to an end in my generation!"

As in shock from his passion, he was silent a long moment. Then, "I don't ever want the succession of wives, always searching for one to settle my soul."

He looked at me from across the room. "Mother, pray for me. I know you do. No one but you and Dad know just how much I need it, the help of God to live all the good counsel you've poured into my soul." He paced to the window and around the walls.

"And there's the grandfather you've loved all your life, and I never knew, but through your tales of times with him as you grew up. I loved him because you loved him, and I always cherished a hope I'd know him for myself some day. Some day before it was too late, and the chance was gone forever." Another silence settled down.

"There's something I've learned by his death, after knowing his life only second-hand. That is that unforgiveness cost him too much. He never had the opportunity for direct input into the lives of his grand-children. He lost the times with you that could have blessed him and you. He lost the bond with his king and earthly master that he had with Dad before, for so many years. And now he's lost his very life. I even think he lost his wisdom, backing Absalom and not discerning that hate could never have built a wise throne, only a foolish and cruel, blinded ruler. Oh God, I wish it had gone differently for Grandpa Ahithophel."

By now we were both crying with voices as well as tears, and I rose to run to him as he ran to me. We clung together, united in our grief, a mother and son in an accord made in heaven and sealed in so many encounters over his lifetime.

How can one man negotiate his way as ruler of a vast people unless You speak with him, oh Lord? He needs wisdom in women, wisdom in knowing his counsellors, their character and their counsel--and their changes, wisdom in judging disputes among his own people, wisdom in dealing with other kings and nations. It is endless. Endless demands, endless challenges and endless temptations await him. Yet I have a confidence in him because I have confidence in You and Your working in him.

As he composed himself to leave, I felt weak with an admiration and gratitude. Did ever such a mother have such a son, of such a father? Such good looks, grace, and intelligence, such promise. It was a high moment of my life, not to be exceeded, I fancy, even by the moment of his coronation. As that moment will be clouded by the decline and approaching death of my beloved David, so this is clouded by the deaths of Absalom and Grandfather, and the many young soldiers. But, thank You for the glory that balances the grief. Earth's moments of glory are glimpses of eternal glory in Your presence. Knowing that makes them even sweeter.

But I have three other sons as well, and my girls, too. Meeting with each of the other three boys is so different. Nathan is much less articulate than Solomon, more solid and silent, unmoved by the moving of events, so far as I can see. He brought his harp, as usual, and played for me his latest composition, three movements: one slow and pensive, haunting; one intricate with quick runs and trills and flights as of birds' song; and the last inspiring me to rise and dance and end up laughing and breathless. He only smiled at me, his calm in all his aspect but his twinkling dark eyes. They danced.

When I had caught my breath, he asked me to hear a portion of the Exodus story which he had just memorized, the part in which the children of Israel have come forth out of Egypt and are approaching Sinai.

"What if the people had said to Moses, 'We can never do all those commandments' instead of being so confident that they could? What if they'd thrown themselves upon

God's mercy, knowing His holiness and His commands were not something they could accomplish in human strength? Then would God have prohibited them from approaching His glory on the mount? Did He allow only Moses and Aaron to go up because only they stood in proper awe of Him? Did He really want people to approach? Was He warning them not to, only because that's the only way He could arouse them to know His truly awesome glory? If they'd opened their minds and hearts to admit He is holy and we are not, then could more of them have come closer to Him?"

I only smiled thoughtfully at his earnest questions, not knowing how to answer for a moment. Then I asked, "Do you want to come closer to Him, Nathan?"

"He IS holy," he said quietly, "but, yes, I do want to be one of the ones He calls to come closer, higher up the mount with Him. But not all the time. Sometimes I feel He WOULD break out upon me, and I'd better keep my distance."

He picked up his harp and sang in reverence, "Holy, holy, holy, is our God, Lord of hosts, mighty in battle."

He laid his harp down and said, "The Lord won the battle because Solomon is to be king."

Nathan, the prophet.

Leah, the princess...   When I meet with Leah, we often do our handwork together as we visit, then end with some music. She, like me, plays both pipe and harp. I'm spending extra time with each child in the aftermath of the turmoil. She and I must have had an hour to ourselves today.

"Mama," she asked me as she bent over her embroidery, "were you scared when we had to flee the city and cross Jordan in the night? Did you think we could all have been killed?" She did not look up, but kept her fingers busy and focused her eyes on them. I knew her thoughts were all with me and my answer. She showed no impatience as I pondered how to answer.

"Leah, it's Yes and No. We cannot deny that the intent of Absalom had to include removing our entire family so as to secure himself on the throne. So, yes, I was tense and sensitive to the threat. We didn't have multiplied guards for no reason. But, as you well know, one cannot act out every fear that comes to one's mind, or fear takes control. I had to act fearless for the sake of all you children, for the sake of the guards, for the sake of your father's honor, for the honor of our Lord. If we say we believe in Him, shame upon us if we act as if He were not able in our extreme danger to deliver us, one way or another."

She looked up, met my eyes, nodded solemnly and returned to her handwork. "Yes, Mama."

There was a silence as we both worked away. Then Leah spoke again, "I sang to myself Father's psalms; and it was as if Almighty God were speaking to me a peace that made no sense. But it was good. I wasn't afraid, Mama, truly."

"I believe you," I assured her. "I was so proud of all of you. Our Lord has given those psalms to your father for just such times in life. I am so blessed as a mother to see you children living the truth. I have no fear for your future, Leah."

"Me neither, Mama. Our Father God has all details in His hands, right, Mama?" She sat up straight to show her mature figure and shimmied her shoulders impishly, reminding us both of my stories told to her about my emotions at her exact same age. She winked as a conspirator, "And my father and mother know the one to choose for me just as Father's the right one for you." She took a deep breath for dramatic effect. "I wouldn't cry if it were one of Aunt Leah's sons, say the oldest one..." She turned her grinning gaze from me to her working hands with a mischievous roll of her eyes, and began to blush.

"You're not taking me by surprise, you little imp. I'm not blind. I see you and Gibea at our family events. I can assure you, you'll be the first, or at least the second, to know when your father and I are ready to announce your betrothal. And your wishes are of paramount consideration with us, you know that."

After handwork, we made music.

When Leah laid down her pipe and broke into dance, I continued with my hands on my harp, but my eyes and my heart were with her movements. My little girl is becoming a young woman. My own blossoming is still so vivid and near in memories. How the time does hasten away. Lord keep her, my little girl.

Shobab is the naturalist. It's as if each of the other three boys has concentrated in his personality one of the many facets of David's, and Solomon's, complex nature.

Giving Shobab extra time with me means one thing, riding out on horses into the hillsides.

We rode exuberantly, notwithstanding that his bodyguard and mine accompanied us at a discreet distance. We are able to function as if they were not there, from long habit. And they make it easy to do so, from long training.

He reined in his horse and I followed his lead. We tethered the horses under a tree that a moment's flash of memory told me could well have been the same one my father and I spoke under, so many years ago. It was grown larger, but the view all around struck me as the same--Jerusalem to the west, Jordan Valley to the east, a magnificent vista.

After standing beside me to take in the views in all directions without any comment but a long, satisfied sigh, Shobab pulled scrolls out of his saddle bag and motioned me to sit down beside him, leaning against the tree. For an hour, it must have been, he unrolled each scroll in turn, showing me his sketches of trees and bushes and their leaves and blossoms, birds and their nests, wildflowers in their settings, and small mammals with their young beside their dens, naming and describing each in turn with animation in his dark eyes and in his voice, which becomes deeper by the month, often stopping to exclaim "Isn't it amazing how....", filling in some fact of the creature's activities or attributes. Once he jerked to attention, naming a bird whose song he had just heard. I'd not heard the song until he told me what to listen for, and I cannot remember the bird's name. "It's migrating through," he said.

It is astounding, the breadth of his knowledge. He is by no means one-dimensional, being a musician and marksman and mathematician, as they all are; but this is clearly his first love, knowing the created world in detail. Most of the creations he's drawing are those with which he's come personally into contact right around Judea, but some were specimens brought to court from Africa and Asia.

As he rolled up the last scroll, he confided, "I'm not done. There are more to sketch and learn about. It's endless. I'm always discovering something new about some creature as I watch them. Mother, when I'm grown, I hope to have many of these animals and birds on my own estate, living as nearly as possible in their native habitat and habits. And then my gardens will have every known variety of plants that can survive our climate. I'll have special occasions for the people under my rule to come to the gardens, so that any boy like me, who couldn't otherwise learn, will be able to. Anyone who wants to should have the opportunity to learn the creation of our awesome Creator in all its fullness. And artists can come to sketch. And my children will learn to care for the plants and animals, just as part of their growing up. I want them to have the broadest possible education, just as you and Dad have provided for me--the best teachers, everything." He had been talking faster and louder as he went along, and waving his arms and pacing about, absorbed in his dreams completely.

"May all your dreams come true, Shobab," I blessed him with my eyes on his face and my hands on his shoulders. He is as tall as I, but heavier. "God bless you, my son. You inspire me to see God in every small part of all He's made, as my father did when I was growing up."

"Well, you inspired me in the beginning, or I wouldn't be doing all this today!" Suddenly, he picked me up and swung me around as my father used to do.

As he set me down, I was a bit dizzier than I had been then, and he was panting more than my father had done.

It was almost more than he could do to lift me. But I know he was proud he could.

We were laughing as we mounted the horses for the ride home, myself and my naturalist son.

I am blessed.

Now, Shammua is more soldier and athlete than anything else. "Watch me do this, Mother," he says many times over. Then, with intense concentration, he aims and fires off an arrow, or enters into a sword play with his attendant, or races off on a sprint to circle back by me for my approval. I remember the stage from the other boys having preceded him. My appreciation of their accomplishments is a part of the sequence. They grow out of the need for it gradually until they stand as a man, as Solomon is now, and Nathan is almost, as a man secure in himself that he has worth and abilities. I love seeing the proceeding. I love having sons.

Now, with Shammua, I say, "How many times is it now to hit the mark, Shammua, ten out of twelve?" and "That was five seconds faster than the last run," and other incentives to his efforts.

After the sword play, he came panting to sit beside me once he'd dismissed his attendant and sprinted boisterously in place, saying as he sat, "Lemuel is a worthy match for my skill level, keeps me growing and challenged, wins some, doesn't always lose to me. If he ever came to that, I'd have to find another, much as I'd hate to do that to him. He's been with me all my life, and I care for him as a brother. Maybe he'll keep on improving as I do. If not, I'll have to ease him from the role gently and substitute another role for him to perform, equal in importance. Dad says to keep every friend and ally, and always to respect the loyalty and devotion of every single servant and counsellor. It's the way he's kept his great army."

Shammua sighed, turned and picked off a piece of grass to chew on as he continued in deeper thought than his active life usually allows him. Speaking in a low tone, he went on, "I don't know what good it's going to be to me, to be such a skillful soldier, when the enemies are all defeated now, and Solomon will reign in peace, just as his name says." He turned to look directly at me. "What place is there for an army, if there are no enemies left?" He had an almost plaintive note in his query, and I knew how important it was to him to have an army to command some day. No point in bringing in anything about the horrors of war. Some other time, maybe.

I reached to clasp his shoulder as I contemplated how best to answer him. "Well, Shammua, you never know when some king, even a distant one, will suddenly turn aggressive and cast a greedy eye on your land. Having a strong army ready for action is definitely a deterrent to such a warrior-king. I'd say you'd best keep your young men in the best of training, even in peace time."

Relief spread over his features, joy and energy filled his expression, as he said, "Mother, you don't know what a load you've lifted off my mind. I didn't want to bring this up with any of the men--Dad, Jehiel, my other counsellors, even my martial arts tutor, at such a time as this, when a war within our own kingdom has just been concluded and everyone wants to move past it. I'm not a war monger, really!"

"I believe you," I said, "You just love the competition. I'm sure many other men and boys do, too; and you'll never have to give it up for more sedentary tasks. Have no fear."

Again, the exchange of smiles and the sense of oneness with one of my sons. I breathed a sigh of deepest satisfaction--and gratitude to You, my Lord, as my soldier-son and I walked back home. Shammua picked up rocks one after another and threw them as far as he could as we walked along.

Every good and perfect gift comes from You--such as my four sons here with me and my one gone ahead to heaven, the one I'll not know until eternity.

And my daughters. Jael in my mind I have styled The Little Mother. How often I see her mothering some little creature or some doll she has fashioned to play the part of a baby. She's heard Leah speak of the days when Shobab and Shammua were babies and toddlers and has had a bit of a time accepting that she herself will have no baby brother or sister. Today, she arranged a fabric-swathed "baby" in her lap as she sat on the swing in the jacaranda tree before giving a push and swinging, still cradling her small charge, talking equally to me and to the "baby".

"Do you like going so high?" spoken to the baby.

"She likes it, but she wants me to stop when she says, 'Stop'," spoken to me. "Did I like to swing high when I was little?"

"Yes, you did, and I held you just the way you are holding your baby, until you were big enough to hold on yourself."

"I feel as if I'd always loved to swing high. It feels so, I don't know, like flying or something, like being a bird. Oh, you're ready to stop now? Can you hold her, Mama, because I want to swing some more."

I held the "baby" carefully, after Leah had arranged her in my arms, wrapping her little blanket snugly around her.

"There, you stay with Grandma while Mama swings some more. I'll be right here if you cry." She kissed the baby, smiled at me, and pumped the swing as high as it would go. She was silent for several moments, swinging with all her might. I watched her, thinking of how lovely she looked, and wondering which of the children would make me an actual grandmother first, and how near that might be. In some ways, it seemed so recent that I was a child in a swing myself, never dreaming I would be where I am today. And where will Jael be, when she is my age? Thirty-six years old, come my next birthday. I used to think that sounded so old. Yet, I have a notion to come out and swing, myself, later, when no one is around.

As she began to allow the swing to slow, Jael leaned back and looked up a long time, enjoying the slow end of the swinging. "The leaves look like lace against the sky, Mama. Isn't it a beautiful day? And look!--the flowers are the same color as my dress, bluer than the sky. I want to pick some. I'll wear one and put the others in some water on my bedside table."

I laid her baby on the bench where I had sat watching her and joined her in picking the flowers. "I'll put some on our bedside table, too," I told her.

Suddenly, she cried out, "Waaaaa," and ran to her baby. "Oooo, did you think everyone had left you?" She handed me all the flowers and patted her baby as we left the garden.

We went inside to arrange our bouquets and put her baby to sleep.

Jael, all too soon you will be a mother, but first you'll watch your big sister doing just that, and imagine what it is really like.

As if reading my mind, Jael asked, "How long will it be before Leah is married, Mama? I know the one she wants to marry. Have you seen the way she acts whenever Gibea is around? She doesn't even try to keep it a secret. Mama, whenever I'm grown up like Leah, nobody is going to be able to guess my affections." She whirled to me, "But I'll tell YOU, because you won't tell until it is time."

She laid down the panicle of jacaranda blossom she'd been arranging and gave me a hug. I hugged her back and hugged the memory to myself.

Quickly, she released me and spoke to the blossom, "Now, if you'll just cooperate and stand up until I get you in place here with the others, you can droop all you want to, you radiant blue beauty!" She was back firmly in the present, a good place for us to stay.

"I'm just glad to be home again. I like things quiet and simple. I hope all the news is good news for awhile. For always." Her hands kept arranging the flowers as she spoke.

"I do, too, sweetheart. I do, too."

"Is Dad about finished with all the meetings and business so he can be at our bedtime?"

"I'm expecting him this evening."

"Ooooo," she squealed and hugged me again, smiling as she wiped happy tears away.

"And I need to get the servants going on a special dinner for all of us, so I will leave you for now, and see you then."

I enjoyed one last smile exchange with her before rushing off with my blossoms, as eager as she is for David to be here.

David. Youth and age are doing battle in him. There will always be vigor and energy flowing out of him, but when he is out of the demanding situation, he sighs in a new way, deeper and longer. With all the children surrounding us, he was as much the man as he ever was. He gave something of himself to each one, starting with the whole group in our psalm-singing and scripture reading and discussion, drawing an insight out of each of them and ending with his own wisdom for this time in the kingdom.

"Your brother Solomon will be king after me, when that day comes. He'll rule over a land at peace. Peace is almost here for Israel. I do expect the Philistines to make one last attempt to overtake us, because they think we are in disarray after this uprising has had us momentarily split apart, and losing many soldiers at the hands of our own countrymen. I may be gone again for a while..." The children all kept composure and merely listened in due solemnity as he continued. "...but I don't expect it to last long. We are stronger than they think. God brought us back into unity, and He completes His purposes. I want you all to know that I am aware of your conduct under great trial, and you are a credit to your father and mother, worthy, and ready to take up whatever realms of responsibility are thrust upon you in times to come. You are an inspiration to me, you and your Mother..." He drew me near with his arm around my shoulders, "...second only to God Himself. Such a family!" Tears came to his eyes. "I am a blessed man. Much has been given to me. God has been my strength and song and has wrought great victories and redeemed great shortcomings. May you each walk with Him all your days."

They all gathered about for a round of hugs with him, me, and one another.

David took each one aside for a few moments, starting with the youngest, before sending each off to bed. He knows exactly how to listen and how to speak to the needs of each one of them.

At the end of the family time, it was only the two of us with Solomon. David regarded this one so like himself with pride and affection, as we shared some last few words regarding what has happened in the kingdom and where we are now headed, ending with particulars about the accumulating of supplies for the temple which is to be build by a man of peace, not war. He showed Solomon the plans.

"Not a sound will be heard in all the construction. Work that requires noise is all taking place elsewhere so that the peace of God and proper prayer and reverence are in the temple even as it is going up."

Solomon is as intense as David in temple talk. Two hearts beat as one when they bend over these plans. Even their posture is in symmetry. I store up in my memory the picture of them planning, and the words spoken.

Finally, Solomon retired, and David led me to our bedroom. After the intensity of his political meetings, and the great giving to our children, he was ready for quiet tenderness. I felt I was ministering to him that he might have a time totally away from the drain upon all his resources, and be refreshed in every way, by tomorrow, when it will all begin again.

There will be a time for us to talk together of all the tumult and changes the last few months have brought, but it is not yet. Let that tumult be farther in the past, and let us have more perspective, and perhaps more energy for the reflections that are needed. He's been through so much of that sort of thing with his council. He will inform me and hear my viewpoint another day. For this day, for him and for me, just to be united again was all we asked.

Now he sleeps as I sit here writing, to remember and never forget another blessed time to love my David, stopping to study him as he lies there in the abandon of sleep, appreciating all that he is and all that the Lord has brought us through, grateful and yet not able to ignore the physical changes I see, the aging, yes. Aging and waning of strength. I see the end approaching.

His peaceful breathing is the only sound I hear, but for a celestial chorus of hallellujahs for the glories God has sent our way. Far off in the heavenlies, the music waxes and wanes, while the king breathes in the best rest he has had for quite some time, or is likely to have again soon, until his final rest.

God restore him and carry him in strength through the duties remaining to him. It will be Solomon's turn, faster than I could wish, I fear. Let it not come before I am ready. I would cling to David as long as possible. But You know best. Make me ready for what comes next, my Father.

A Shunamite maiden, indeed! What ideas the council can have! David cannot stay warm. Is this the remedy? I believe I am still warm, though nearly forty, as this Shunamite maiden not yet twenty. Folly, nothing but folly.

Though David is not always in his full right mind, I could have hoped he would have commanded them to take her back to her home and whatever sweetheart is bereft of her forever, honoring me as his true queen before the council. My comfort is that he is growing senile. Sad sort of comfort that is. It is very hard to see one who has been so vibrant, vigorous, creative, productive, KINGLY, reduced to senility as any common man.

Now, when I am summoned to go to him, I am humiliated on the inside to see the maiden retreat before my entrance. No one can tell by looking at me. I've not had the discipline of all these years to end with tossing it all over. I am the queen. She is nothing. I have a pang sometimes, knowing just how much a nothing she is and is destined to remain, used, in a sense, by a king, and thus never permitted to belong to any other. But for my own place in life, my own peace, I must rejoice that I am queen and she is nothing, that I knew him in every way and she knows him in no way. I never look at her.

It is all happening faster than I could foresee.

But today, as I approached his bedside, he was present completely, in his right mind and remembering fully all we have known together as husband and wife. We spoke at length, slowly, it is true, but thoroughly, of many things. It was glorious.

Afterward, he asked that all the children be summoned also. I stood at the head of the bed, Solomon next to me, his depth of character and understanding reflected in his eyes and his bearing, as indeed it was in all this royal brood, Nathan next, Gibea and Leah, married already and expecting, Shobab and Shammua, and Jael at the foot of the bed, tears contained in her eyes. Too young to be deprived of their father, all of these, perhaps the youngest most of all, but facing this, as all that comes, bravely, depending upon the Father Who will not die and leave them. Only our family was present, and our Lord. No attendants.

David spoke to them all, reminding them that Solomon would be king and they would all serve him in various capacities of honor and usefulness. He gave a blessing to each in turn, asking each to come to stand between me and him, to hear and receive his words. Our right hands were on them as we blessed them.

After we left, the children gathered with me in David's and my bedroom. Then we cried. Again, no attendants were present, one of our rare times just to be a family, without protectors hovering nearby, though they were not far. They know when to be discreet, how to let us have privacy.

We stayed together for a couple of hours, prodding each other's memories, laughing and crying, scuffling and hugging, making another memory, leaving the future forgotten until it should intrude itself upon us forcefully.

As dusk descended with the setting sun, we called for a meal to be brought and lingered over it before going to the roof to view the end of day and the beginning of night, in the dark, before we came down in silence and went to our separate bedrooms, Gibea and Leah to their new home.

Jael was last to leave me, clinging wordlessly, then leaving with a determined smile and resolute step.

Nathan, the prophet, white-haired, his still-strong voice belying his ancient appearance, has fulfilled his last prophetic ministry to David in the fast-paced events of this historic day.

I take a deep breath, and try to remember it all in order, but I fear I am too close to sleep to fill in many details. It is just as well. The main points are the main things, after all.

As if Absalom's rebellion were not enough to break David's heart, Adonijah rose up to overthrow his father's will and have himself proclaimed king. Thank You, Lord, for revealing the plot to Nathan. He warned me, then sent me to warn David, and soon followed to corroborate my report. David, again thanks to You, Lord, was having one of his moments of lucidity and strength. He ordered all the arrangements in haste, for Solomon to ride the royal mule and be anointed king by Nathan and heralded through the city by the mighty men and all who remained faithful to David and were not called to Adonijah's invalid coronation.

Solomon is king. After Nathan placed the crown of gold upon his head, I placed the crown of laurels I had hastily woven as the royal mule was prepared for his greatest duty.

As the heaven resounded with Your approval, Lord, the solemn words were spoken and the deed done. King Solomon reigns.

As soon as we could, the family returned to the palace and gathered around David's deathbed. This last tumult, though it ended in a triumph against his enemies and completed his victorious reign, brought him a trial too great for his condition and hastened his departure from us.

He spoke his admonitions to Solomon, with long pauses, marshalling his strength until he completed this last duty, only his lips and eyes moving, powerful and expressive, true to his character. Then he sighed and closed his eyes.

Each of us touched a part of him as his earthly life left him and the angels bore him to heaven.

I am not the only one who heard the angels sing.

Excerpts from Bathsheba's Prayer Journal
Part III: Bathsheba and Solomon

David has been gone a fortnight. I am disoriented. I'd have thought I'd have grown accustomed, in his decline, to living as a single person. But the force of his personality came through even in his weakness, more at some shining moments than at others. I lived in the shine, even when it was eclipsed by the same senility as that to be expected by all mankind who do not die young. We were always one, and that unity drove my every thought. I did not realize it so much then as I do now.

In the midst of my vague unease, I love to draw up, and draw upon, the memory of his splendor as he sat up on his deathbed to give last instructions to our young new king, our son Solomon. If ever I wish to remember David as when I first met him and wed him, all I need do is to look at Solomon's face, hear Solomon's voice, see Solomon's walk and regal bearing, and ponder Solomon's nobility in all its aspects.

As David spoke to him of the long-due punishment to come to Joab and Shimei, my heart was rejoiced and stabbed at the same time, to focus between David's old, dying face and Solomon's resolute young face, the one seeing his eternal reward and the other seeing his earthly destiny and duty, and both on fire with one and the same divine appointment: to lead the people of God, to build the temple for their center of worship, to honor our God.

So many things David decided will now be carried out by Solomon: the placement of his brothers in strategic offices as they come of age, Nathan very soon; the placement of son-in-law Gibea with our Leah in a far corner to strengthen the kingdom; the marriage of Jael in just a few years to a neighboring prince, sending her also far from me; and, of course, the punishment of David's and thus Solomon's enemies; and, to crown every other task, the building of the temple.

One of the last decisions of David which is not part of the shining, which I would forget if I could, or, better yet, nullify completely, was the giving to Solomon of a princess of one of David's recent allies, Naamah the Ammonitess. She is no queen, far from it, a hopelessly foolish girl foolishly spoiling her toddler, Rehoboam. He is, of course, of necessity required to be considered Solomon's eldest son--but not to be his heir, never to be his heir. A real marriage must be undertaken in due course, when Solomon gets his feel as monarch and can arrange a suitable match. Fortunately, I do not have to grit my teeth to bear this reprehensible twosome, the mother and toddler, as they are kept out of my sight and presence, Solomon knowing my opinion on this, as on all things--because he asks. I would say nothing except as he asks. He has always valued my insights, as did his father before him, only obviously not quite enough in this one case. We have always had higher hopes for a royal consort and lifetime soulmate for our Solomon. They both, David and young Solomon, were able to separate this high hope from the indulgence with Naamah. I don't like it, but there it is. We shall see that nothing more comes of it.

One day before too many more years have gone by, a son shall be born to Solomon who will possess his attributes and abilities and will be worthy of the kingdom when his time comes.

Meanwhile, we all mourn the loss of David, in our own ways. Jael has been clinging to me after I have given to her what is in me to give. I am arranging some tutors in music, math, and handwork, beyond those she has had in the past, to finish her preparation. I enjoy her and arrange for her to be with me often, especially lately when I am organizing the servants. She must be able to organize her own, when the time comes. We will always have our special times as just mother and daughter, and special communications, but she must be able to leave me, and I to part with her in only three to four years. I am preparing both of us.

David and Solomon have arranged the last few years of training for Shobab and Shammua. I still see them separately and keep close communication with each of them. This I will do as long as I can, as long as they are living in my palace with me.

We are also still having our family gatherings in the evenings. It is good. It is precious. But it is here that David's absence is felt most keenly by all of them, I know; but they do not know, for I do not let them, how my own heart is but half a heart. I listen to them, and I do cry, but not as I do when I am alone after they have left for bed, and You, my Lord, are all my audience--sweet, succoring savior of my sanity.

Thank You, Lord, for giving me these children as comforters in my widowhood. I would be overly challenged to cope without them. But You are my comfort for always, in all ways, husbanding me in my spirit. And they will all leave.

Father Lord, what an honor and a blessing is mine, as Solomon has officially appointed and proclaimed me the

King's Mother. He had to know how it would lift me in my spirits as I mourn the loss of David and wonder where my life is to go from here on. It is a final vindication of David's proclaiming me queen so daringly after such a beginning as ours was. It is a public acknowledgement of my abilities as a wise counsellor to a king, my husband first and now my son. It is a personal tribute from a son to a mother that I receive personally, warmed by Solomon's high regard. It is a perpetual permission to enter the presence of his majesty. And it is the privilege to be seated on a small throne of my own, placed to the right of Solomon's throne, which will be large and ornate when it is finished, soon.

Above all, this appointment is a challenge that will keep me occupied in a task with meaning and purpose. I can not drift, or idle away my days. I must stay informed and involved, and seek Your wisdom, Lord, in all matters pertaining to the kingdom. I must stay fully alive. I must make David proud and honor his memory by showing the wisdom of his choice in a queen. Grandpa Ahithophel would be proud, too, if he had lived to see this. I know that Solomon has thought all that I have, and more, in making this appointment. What a son! I have great hopes for this nation at this time. I can hardly wait to see the temple.

Oh, David, David, there in the arms of God, enjoy the fruit of your life, and of our union. Rejoice with me. Oh, Father God, embrace David for me.

Heavenly Father, just when I was feeling wise enough, I found I had been so foolish. Thank You for giving

Solomon the instant wisdom to know that politics, not love or lust, was behind Adonijah's request, delivered to me alone in my chamber, that he be allowed to marry Abishag. He had seemed so contrite, so resigned to Solomon's reign, so humble and respectful and so enamored of Abishag, that I was taken in by the act. I see now that it was all an act. But for the moment he had me charmed.

Solomon jumped up from his throne and exploded in my face the moment I had spoken for Adonijah. Immediately, I saw this usurper for his true colors, not at all repentant or submissive to Solomon's reign, but wily and deceitful, and a tool for others who led him, or followed him, as the case may be, in his bid for the throne, others such as Abiathar.

In a flurry of commands, Solomon ordered Adonijah executed and Abiathar banished to his home town, Anathoth, allowed to live as a reward for his long service to David, and yet removed from any vicinity to the court, where he could potentially pose further threat to Solomon's reign.

After the soldiers had rushed off to carry out the commands of execution and banishment, and all other attendants had been dismissed, Solomon turned to me, still livid with his rage over Adonijah keeping his insurrection, after Solomon's grace in allowing him to live on condition of submission. But before he could say a word to me, I rose to face him, crying out, "Oh, Solomon, I see it now. I see it all. You must know how deceitfully charming and honoring and innocent Adonijah appeared when he came to me. I did not see it then. But I do now. You must forgive me, and I will never be so foolishly taken in again." I took hold of his arms, pleading, "But Solomon, do you see how the Lord has turned it all to good for you? Their plot has been exposed and squelched. It can never rise again. Your throne is secure."

Solomon never took his eyes from mine as I spoke, nor as I finished. In the silence, I saw him gather in all his fury by will power and receive a calm from above in its place. He had assessed my character. I had passed a test.

He was calm, but still in a state of action. He summoned other servants without any word to me, only a nod to indicate that I was to be seated on my throne. That nod spoke volumes. My heart began to settle into its normal rhythm gradually, as he gave orders for the execution of Joab for his cold-blooded murders of Abner and Amasa, leaders of the hosts of Judah and Israel, respectively. He ordered that Benaiah replace Joab over the army, and that Zadok replace Abiathar as priest. Then he ordered the house arrest of Shimei for his cursing of David. He sent couriers to notify the sons of Barzillai that they are to eat at Solomon's table always, for their kindness to David as he fled Absalom. In these few moments, Solomon had subdued his enemies, secured his throne, and rewarded his father's friends, and finished the hard business David had left for him.

Once again, he dismissed all attendants. He sighed deeply and sank back onto his throne, turning to me on his right for a long, silent stare, very kinglike. But when he spoke, it was as a son. "I can tell that you have learned much by this morning's drama. I understand how your womanly heart would have responded to Adonijah. I've seen him in operation before. Young as I am, it has been years since my faithful tutors have pointed out to me that I must watch, without appearing suspicious, the actions of those sons born before me, since they had rights ahead of mine, yet were doomed not to walk in those rights. I have watched them and have had them watched by those I trust. I have no worries about the others, but I just had more men assigned to trail Adonijah after my recent mercy to him. He showed himself sooner than I'd have guessed he would, as if he thought I'd not know the true import of such a request as marrying Abishag--how can romance be political? But this was no romance, just an edge into the rights of a king, to take the late king's concubine for his own to symbolize that he has kingly rights. Everyone knows that she's still a virgin, but he knows she's not legally one, nor legally free to marry. Well, he's out of the way now."

For the first time, Solomon smiled.

"Now, for the temple building," I said.

"Precisely!" he exclaimed, and after one of our blessed mother-son smiles, I left as he called for the temple plans to be brought to him.

God, I will turn to You for wisdom before I say one more word to this wise son, this new king of Judah. I've learned that lesson. Thank You for redeeming this situation. There'll not be another insurrection in my lifetime.

Lord, I am glad to be finally arrived in Egypt. Though the covered howdah gave me every known luxury for such a journey, it is an ordeal all the same, facing the desert, so dry, so dusty. So bumpy, so exhausting, riding that camel!

Here in Pharoah's court, every amenity I could imagine or ask for has been offered to me. I am duly grateful for the lotions, perfumes, clothing, and attendants Pharoah has provided for me, and for the sumptuous suite, as we prepare for the state wedding of his daughter to Solomon.

How I praise You that someone worthy of Solomon is becoming his bride. I was won over in the first half hour with her. As I entered her chamber for our meeting, I dropped into a bow, but she rushed to me and lifted me and bowed before me herself! She rose to smile and study my face, as I studied hers, so fresh and lovely, perfect in features and modest in make-up, innocent and sweet in demeanor.

She clapped her hands with delight, "Oh, may I be so beautiful as you when I have borne children and been queen so long. May I call you 'Mother'? Will you call me 'Ruth'? Come and sit."

As we were seated, she continued. "I know you would find it hard to pronounce my Egyptian name, but even more, I want to be Ruth. She, too, was a foreigner coming into the line of David. She, too, left the gods of her people to worship the One, true God. I want to be like her. I want to bless you as she blessed Naomi." With her hands clasped in child-like eagerness, her face appealed to me for acceptance.

My eyes brimmed with tears at the revelations and realizations that flooded my mind. Solomon's ambassadors had been well-chosen and well-instructed, and had carried out his wishes so exactly, it had to be Your hand guiding them as you guided Eliezer in finding Rebekah for Isaac, and as You guided Jacob in finding his Rachel. When I expressed this to her, her eyes lit with recognition. "Yes, yes, yes," she exclaimed, "Rebekah, Rachel, and Ruth. I will be Ruth. This will please you?" She wanted me to be pleased.

"I am blessed to call you 'Ruth', my daughter." As I said the word, 'daughter', another revelation lit in my spirit. She will be there with me in Jerusalem when Leah and Jael are far away! Oh, God, You think of everything. I could not tell her that just yet. We must have much more time together first. I must ponder it in my own heart for a season. My tears overflowed.

"You are weeping for joy, I hope?" she asked me.

"Oh, yes," I answered, "and I must ask you how you found our God in this land of many gods."

"Oh, God is able to preserve a remnant wherever one of his children has set his foot. Joseph left a legacy here in Egypt, and there is a remnant here of believers. It was an Egyptian princess, you know, who rescued and raised Moses. She was of the remnant. She kept the truth alive--and others followed her. And now you see me here today, a true child of God."

We spoke of our mutual prayers that brought us to this meeting here today. I felt I could speak to her of many things, almost anything, but not Naamah or Rehoboam-- although probably she has accepted the customs of kings of the East, having grown up in a king's court. I think she would not let Naamah have meaning in her life. Solomon has chosen her as his queen and will choose her son to be next after him. She knows this well. Naamah will fade away with her son to nothing. Solomon could never turn from this Ruth to one so inferior. I can dismiss that, and dwell on the glorious future before us, our family, all of Judah and Israel. Let Ruth become solid with Solomon and find out about Naamah much later, when the news will seem as nothing.

As Ruth played and sang for me, in Hebrew, which she has been studying the last several months, and on a Hebrew harp, I basked in the wonder of Your working, great God of our fathers. You do all things well.

I give thanks unto the Lord; for he is good--for His mercy endureth forever. Amen.

Oh, my Lord, this wedding was elegant. The Egyptian court went to extremes to display its wealth and beauty in the bridal party's costumes, in the accoutrements of decorations, table service, food (oh, the food!), servants wearing elaborate livery, attending our every need, music on the strange Egyptian instruments, which I find much to my liking. Ruth must bring some of these instruments with her. And the setting for the festivities! Egyptian architecture surely could be surpassed only by the temple and palaces that Solomon's crews are beginning even as we dally here in this opulence.

But, Lord, as impressive as are the sights, sounds, smells and tastes of this royal event, the underlying love of Solomon and Ruth, and their mutual devotion to You, brings it to a level of glory no one can know outside of You.

She is dazzling, witty, and talented, peppy and peppery, and Solomon is so in love. What more could a mother ask?

I am blessed beyond what any mortal deserves. And I bless You, Lord.

The journey back to Jerusalem seemed even more tedious and tiring than the journey to Egypt had. It was such a contrast to the ease and luxury of Pharoah's court. It seemed it would be a long while indeed before my skin would feel moist again after the desert heat and wind. But we are well settled in now. Ruth lives in my palace, awaiting her own palace, which will be built on the temple mount next to Solomon's House of the Forest of Lebanon. She and Solomon have their own suite.

Jael adores Ruth as I do, and they spend endless hours together when Solomon is working with the foremen of the temple construction and other business of running the nation. I am glad for the influence of Ruth upon Jael. Jael will be instructed in the ways and duties of wives of officials without having any idea that she is doing anything other than having one festive occasion after another. Ruth's presence is so captivating, it will be as hard for Jael to part with Ruth as with me, when her time comes to go to her own life and marriage. Ruth is a new sister for her, now that she's lost Leah. I see their hearts becoming as one.

Ruth has made many friends here. Everyone dotes on her, but she stays unspoiled, kind, and caring, ignoring those temptations that would make a snob out of a lesser girl. I feel as if she's always been with us. She and Jael play for our evening psalms before she retires with Solomon for the night. Family life is enriched by her presence but not changed any other way.

It is all so sweet, sweeter than honey and the honeycomb, as David used to sing. Ruth sings that same psalm of praise to the excellency of Your law. At times, in my spirit, I withdraw from them all, and David is singing it again to me, before any of them came along. And I am suddenly not singing with them at all, but with him. Then it is David and I, not Solomon and his bride, who retire together for the night.

But I cannot go into imagination and the past too often, or stay too long. I have a job still to do, today. By Your grace, I'll do it.

Today, Ruth, Jael, and I walked through the temple mount, where hundreds of workers are preparing the site and bringing in the first supplies for the building of the temple, some massive stones, lumber of several sorts of wood--beautiful and sweet-smelling. It is to be larger than any building any of us have seen before, and magnificent with gold, when done. As David requested, according to Your directions, no sound of a tool can be heard. The sky seems to absorb and make small the sound of workmen's talk. The silence penetrated our souls.

Where I supposed the Holy of Holies to be, from my study of the temple plans, we stopped to pray. All three of us were overcome with awe at Your glory that the temple will reflect as well as man ever can.

It was just at this time and place that Ruth chose to tell us that she is expecting. I leaped for joy and, with Jael, hugged Ruth as we all wiped tears away. I saw into the future. With such a mother and father, the little prince will turn out as fine as Solomon. Our nation is in good hands, a king in the line of David assured for generations to come. The three of us knelt again and held each other's hands and prayed aloud all our thanks to You for matters large and small. We wept some and laughed some and ended by singing as we circled in a dance of praise. Already the Presence of Your Holiness is real, almost overwhelming, at this place.

I imagined our prayers and praises rising as the smoke and scent of incense into the vast sky overhead, and You looking down with favor upon our offering.

Our lunch was being served as we came back into the palace, or we'd not have known how long we'd been gone, there's such a sense of timelessness already there. Imagine what it will be like when all is completed! We'll not be able to stand. Your glory will dwell there in a concentrated way, although you'll not be contained there, but manifest everywhere man can be. Yet, here is where we of Israel and Judah shall congregate and focus our worship, repenting and offering sacrifices for our sins, receiving forgiveness and restoration, building one another up in our faith, before returning to walk the daily walk with a deeper awareness of You there, too. Memories celestial shall be made in this place, by Your grace, for thousands of this chosen race of people, for centuries to come.

With such glorious thoughts filling my heart and mind, I expect any sleep tonight to be deep and refreshing.

David, do you see? It's all happening according to the plans you left. Your faithfulness to God's instructions lives after you, sweet singer of Israel, now singing around the heavenly throne. I can almost see you there.

Jael, my baby girl, is now married and gone, moved to a far eastern corner of the kingdom to help keep unity. As she and her new husband, Barnabus, rode away, I had the support of Solomon and my new Egyptian daughter, Ruth, standing beside me, their little daughter Taphath nearby in the arms of her nursemaid. When the nuptial caravan was out of sight, I reached for the baby and held her tightly, remembering when Jael was a baby, and all the dreams that were bound up in her tiny body, knowing I'd probably not see Jael's babies.

Solomon's arm was firmly around the waist of his beloved and they both looked their understanding of my emotions. The generations follow one another. Our last nights as a family before the departure of Jael, and soon Shobab and Shammua, had made clear to everyone how much we all had gained from this productive tradition started by David and me before any of the children were born, and continuing on past his departure from our midst. Nathan is no longer here, but far north, planted where his wisdom can help protect the kingdom. They are all going. David gone, Leah gone, Nathan gone, Jael gone, Shobab and Shammua soon to go. All that will be left of our original family is myself and Solomon. Yet a new generation is coming and the family is preserved. The faith is handed down, the same psalms sung; the prayers prayed are ever new, yet ever the same.

"Tapheth," I spoke into the baby's ears, my lips touching her soft black hair, "you are not the prince to follow your father on the throne, but he is coming. And you are special. One day you'll marry, like Jael, and take your part in keeping this kingdom of God's people. I pray blessings upon you. Grow straight and true, and when you leave and your mother feels all I'm feeling now, she'll have the same assurance I do that she'll see you again in heaven one day, even if earth's duties keep her from seeing you until then. You are my opportunity to be a grandmother, you and your brothers and sisters to come, since my other grandchildren will be too far away for them to come to me. You and I must do all we can together."

Tapheth had seemed to listen to all I had to say, and now that I was about to finish, she began to fuss. Ruth reached for her, comforting and cooing until it was apparent that she needed her nursemaid.

Our group broke apart and returned into the palace to go to our separate rooms, Solomon to his meetings.

God, go with Jael and Barnabus, and keep them true. He is a good man. David thought so, Solomon does, and I do. All that I've heard of him is good. I believe Jael will be happy in her marriage and in fulfilling her dreams of raising a family. But there are so many uncertainties in life. And I do not know the area in which she'll be living, nor what strange ideas and customs she'll face. I place her and her marriage and her future in Your hands--and my grandbabies that I'll never meet, this side of eternity.

Lord, one last journey by camel, but for a great purpose. Ruth, heavy with their second child, is not able to accompany Solomon, so I am travelling without her companionship. We go to Gibeon, to the high place, where the tabernacle is, where the ark of the covenant has been until lately, where David once left Asaph and his brothers to minister daily before the ark. David had the ark removed to Jerusalem before he died, but the brazen altar is still there. It is in honor of David's worship and offering there that Solomon has chosen Gibeon as the site for his great offering. The ceremonies will continue afterwards back in Jerusalem before the ark. This entourage is numerous, but the crowds at Jerusalem later will exceed even this. And then when the temple is completed, the spectacle will be so much greater as the temple surpasses the tabernacle in glory.

This is but the beginning. But as great as the prospects are, my weariness is overtaking me and I must try to sleep, in order to be ready for tomorrow. Grant Solomon rest, too.

Lord, it is but moments later, but sleep is far from my weary body. Solomon has come to see me, in much unrest of spirit. As he anticipates the offerings tomorrow, he has been overcome with feelings of inadequacy for the great job before him: leading the vast numbers of Your people, following in David's footsteps, wanting to do right, fearful of what could happen to this people should he make an unwise decision, altogether overwhelmed with the commission placed upon him.

His voice was breaking, his face was bleak. He fairly wilted upon the couch and leaned his head upon his hands, then flung it up to cry, "It's too much for me. I can't carry this load. But I have to."

I placed my hands on his shoulders, looked into his eyes, and these words came out of me: "Solomon, seek the Lord and His strength; seek His face continually." His face lit in realization and remembrance. These are David's words when HE offered at Gibeon. He quoted with me David's following words: "Remember his marvelous works that He has done, His wonders and the judgements of His mouth."   Then, I squeezed his shoulders and he left with bright eyes and light steps.

He has gone to pray where he can be alone with You. I must stay awake to pray here for him until I feel the release of assurance that he is at peace, walking in trust and confidence. Make Yourself known to him in all Your glory, Lord. Grant me to know when it is time for me to let go of praying and embrace sleep.

Lord, thank You for sending Solomon back to me. He was glowing. He had to tell someone. Ruth is not here. I know that he will tell her as soon as we return to Jerusalem. But, Lord, forgive me for being glad that I was the one available for him just now. Throughout the days to come, I will return to this moment in my memory--the sight of him, his words, his kingly authority--such a transformation from the perplexed youth who came but an hour before.

He paced up and down, raising his arms in praise, as he recounted all he'd heard from You, as much to seal it in his own mind as to communicate with his mother. "He granted me my heart's desire, Mother! Wisdom and knowledge to lead His people! That's the main thing. But His promises flowed on and on, to give me riches and wealth and honor--all that any man could want. Oh, that my God should speak thus to me, promise me so much. I will seek Him always, I will praise Him forever, I will lead His vast people to bow before Him. I will walk in this anointing from on high. I can do it. I can. Now I am glad it is mine to do. Now I rejoice to say: I must lead this Thy so great people!"

He was shouting. He stopped before me and said, much more quietly, "Mother, I will no more shrink from the calling placed on me." He took a deep breath and sighed, "Now, dearest Mother, get some sleep if you can. I can keep going now whether I sleep tonight or not, but you need sleep, I know."

I had no words, only laid my head upon his chest and rested a moment as his arms gently enfolded me. He kissed the top of my head and said, "Good night, sweet Mother."

As I look back to my dear David, the memories bring greater comfort than loss; and as I look forward, the hope grows fuller and sweeter. The King's Mother lays her weary head in gratitude upon her borrowed bed, with a peace that passes understanding.

If I thought that was a huge feast in Gibeon, this one in Jerusalem makes that seem small. I am not able to keep eating so much so many days, but ask to be served a smaller plate, day by day.

Here, I was interrupted by a messenger. Ruth has gone into labor. Now, I do not feel like eating at all. Solomon's heir is about to be born. How can I eat? I must go to prepare to help. I must be there to hold my grandson as soon as I am permitted by the mid-wives, after his birth and Ruth's turn and Solomon's turn. Her mother is so far away. Oh, God, what a day! I am off.

God, I have been many days in shock and near despair. What are You doing, God? I wish I could trace Your ways. I am fighting to come back to my old trust of You, but this seems too hard to bear. It would have been all right if it had been only that this child is no heir, but a girl. Basmath is as fair and sweet a baby as any could be. And there should be plenty of time for Ruth to bear sons. But then when she kept bleeding and her life was barely spared, the mid-wives say that she will never have another child. Oh, God, she must! There must be a son to Solomon--without his having to take more wives. Ruth was to be mother of his heir. It is unspeakable to imagine that the kingdom would fall to Rehoboam. And it is unfathomable that Solomon should fall into the old pattern of repeated marriages. But those appear to be the only possibilities.

God, You must undertake for the sake of this kingdom, Your kingdom. You must spare Solomon--and Ruth--the agonies of court intrigue and all the ugly politics and fighting that accompanies multiple royal marriages. We have already been through so much. Deliver us, O Lord.

Ruth is in such a state, now weeping for the son she'll never bear, now tenderly rejoicing over her second precious daughter. If anything can restore my equilibrium, it is her need. Hers and Tapheth's. Soon Basmath too, will suffer if we do not regain hope and trust. It must begin with me.

Then there's Solomon. He must be in almost as bad a state as I am, only he is so absorbed in the final preparations for the temple construction that he may postpone these considerations that so consume me: what about an heir?

Maybe he can begin to pour into Rehoboam. Oh, how the thought nauseates me. By now, his character has taken such form that instruction will be powerless to make any impact. You might as well put roses around a swine's neck.

Maybe I am wrong to want a better life for Solomon than David's was.

I must, really must, relinquish the future to You, Lord, and trust that You have a plan to come into place in an unpredictable way and time. May I live to see it. I do so love this land.

Solomon and Ruth are not dismayed, not at all. They are both young and healthy, they say, and loving the Lord and each other, trusting the Lord's promise of a son in the line of David to sit upon the throne through the generations. "What do mid-wives know?" they say, "Midwives deliver babies, but they are often full of superstitions and, at any rate, should not speak on matters outside their place. The Lord has spoken. We shall see a son of ours one day, wait and see. Oh, dear Mother, fret not, nor borrow trouble from the future. Listen to wiser heads than mid-wives."

I smiled as best I could, hugged them each, and the two little daughters, and left them to their dreams. I would not spoil those dreams for them. They do not need to know my heart in this matter. I pour it out to You instead.

You must help me, Lord, to fill my mind so with Your glory in all that You manifest before me, including these two precious little girls and the love, faith, and hope that dwell in Solomon and Ruth. I will myself to leave my fears with You and receive Your peace. Why should the same problems come upon Solomon, the man of peace, as upon David, the man of war? You are able to do a new thing. I spread my doubts before You alone. I vow they'll not know, not even by a look in my eyes, ever again, any attitude of mine that does not match their own faith and confidence. Oh, Lord, let them be right and me wrong. Make their dreams reality and seal their marriage unity for all their lives.

The building of the temple has actually begun. This is going to be a long, slow process, the final product is to be so vast. I would not have any idea how it would look from what I see happening, except that I have looked over the sketches and plans with Solomon as we meet from week to week.

We walk there each day, weather permitting, Ruth and I. Some days it is just the two of us; other days, but not often, Solomon walks along with us, explaining what is to come. More often, we take along Tapheth and Basmath and their nursemaids. Tapheth can walk some of the time. She finds such satisfaction in walking and running, and lasts longer than I thought she could, before needing to be carried again, her pride in her big new accomplishment giving way to a need to be small again. With four pairs of arms to share in the task, no one has more than she can manage as we take turns carrying the two little girls. The nursemaids are young and strong, Ruth young and nearly as strong, and I am stronger than most women my age. And the little girls are so appealing.

While I enjoy the children, and we are blessed to have Solomon's vision of the finished work described to us to enliven our observations, my favorite walks are those times when it is only Ruth and I. This girl surprises me time after time with her insights into life and matters of the heart. She is truly my daughter in spirit.

Today, she was saying, "Moses' instructions were so wise--to have priests living in each tribe to keep the people aware of the law and the history of God's dealings with His people. But just think what a boon to their job it will be to have this temple for the people to come to. Many will come each year for Passover and take the truth back to those who did not make the trip. What a deep impression will be made upon those who sacrifice their lambs for their sin with thousands of others, in the midst of the gold, the pageantry, the music and the feasting. There is no god like the one true God. His holiness is as far beyond our sinfulness as this magnificent golden temple will be beyond the everyday houses of the people who come here. Our royal hoses are elegant, but even ours cannot come close to what this will be."

I agreed, "Even now, walking here as they build, I sense an anointing from heaven on this place, even before there's a bit of gold applied, or even much built yet to which it will be applied."

"Yes," Ruth went on, "architecture is meant to serve God, as with all the arts, to turn people's thoughts higher than they would go otherwise, to blend with the heights of truth as to man's nature and God's nature. A people-- such as many of the countries around us, my own homeland of Egypt included--a people who do not know God may strive for heights of truth and beauty, but the sin problem is never taken care of without the blood sacrifices. Sin viewed too lightly is sin entrenched in the way of life. Our people can never view sin lightly when we witness the slaughter of the innocent lambs. It's striking enough to the mind and the senses when it's done at home, but here, on this grand scale, it will be indelible. It is just what is needed to keep us looking to God for our source of righteousness. We certainly don't find righteousness in man."

"No, never, except fleeting glimpses."

We were silent for a few minutes, our footsteps the only sound but the muffled talk of workers here and there. I was thinking of the many forms in which sin took hold of those in my life: my father's blindness to the nature of Uriah, Uriah's coldness and inability to form a bond, David's ordering of Uriah's death, David's use of women, the women's jealousies, the sons' anger and ambitions-- even to the point of rape, murder, plots against their own father and half-brothers; the willingness of tribe to fight against tribe, the unforgiveness of Grandpa Ahithophel and his shutting me and my children out of his heart. Oh, I have seen the sin of man against God, the shortcomings and failures.

And I have seen the sacrifices of the lambs. Nothing is so innocent as a lamb. Nor any meat so tender.

As if reading my thoughts, Ruth said, "It's not just that we see and smell the blood, as it is shed from the little lambs, and hear their pitiful cries, every bit as gripping as the cry of our own infants, but we smell the aroma of their cooking, and see the smoke rising high, and then we eat the meat of the lambs sacrificed for our sins, and their life becomes a part of our lives, giving us strength, and for the young, growth. The pictures are too vivid to forget. If only we teach our children what these pictures mean!"

At her mention of children, I thought first of the son she may well never have. What a mother she would be to raise the next king of Judah and Israel. God, You must work a miracle and allow her to conceive again, in spite of the predictions.

This time, she was not aware of the drift of my thought as she continued, "The music will drive it all home. The beautiful sounds of large numbers of musicians and vocalists will be wedded to the wonderful words lifting the soul to God, truth, and heaven. To think that you lived with the man who wrote so many of those songs, and the man who received from God the directions for this temple, Solomon's father! And now, I live with the man who is executing the plans. Oh, their hearts are true, though they be sinful men."

"Yes, we are two blessed women, among the most blessed of all time, I would say. I see your match in the same light as mine. No words can say what my life with David has meant to me--and still means to me."

Ruth blushed, "Nor can I speak adequately of what Solomon means to me." She paused, pondering before continuing, "And as you bore him and his brothers, may I bear to him a son, many sons! That's my fervent prayer."

"Mine, too, dearest daughter; mine, too," I answered softly. To myself, I added, *May my hope and trust rise as high as yours, Ruth.*

We prayed standing in the future Most Holy Place, where one day only the high priest shall enter, once a year. Soon we will not be allowed to walk there. None else but those with special permission, and the workers, are allowed there, even now.

You heard our prayers in the Holy of Holies, there on the temple mount, and in heaven.

Today, at our weekly meeting, Solomon went over with me the monthly reports: the tables of figures on revenue brought in from outlying nations now subservient to us, figures on the merchandise (exotic animals, spices, and woods) brought in by ships from trading, and figures on the trading with Hiram for the temple building, and lists of supplies being laid by for the building of Solomon's House of the Forest of Lebanon, his palace, and Ruth's palace. Then there were the records of the supplies sent in from our own tribes for our household use. All this is for my review. I will be thinking all week whether I have any suggestions for changes. Today, I simply absorbed, or tried to. And there was more.

We turned to expenditures for horses out of Egypt, and for chariots and the chariot cities where stalls for horses are being built. I reminded him of the passage from Moses' writing against accumulating horses. "I'm not going that far, Mother," he assured me. I wonder. May he hear You both directly and through my words.

Last, he showed me the records of the expenditures for the musicians and instruments. The imported Lebanese algum wood has proven to have use not only in the temple construction, but also in the making of harps, he told me.

"The harpists are all asking for harps made of algum wood, now that they've tried them. This wood brings out a truer tone than was possible with the previous harps. The craftsmen cannot keep the new harps coming out fast enough for the demand."

Now we were talking about something I understood well.   I have been to several rehearsals lately and appreciate the progress in the sound as more and more instruments and vocalists are added, and rehearsals continue. I had noticed the beauty of the algum wood on the newer harps. I was now curious to hear a single harp played, that I might compare the sound to that of my own.

As so often has happened, Solomon anticipated my desire before he'd even aroused it, and suddenly there was the first chair harpist coming in with one of the algum wood harps. He stopped and bowed a few feet in front of the steps that ascended to our thrones.

The wood was even more gorgeous at close view than from a distance. An attendant brought him a stool. He sat and settled into concentration before placing his fingers upon the strings. We likewise prepared ourselves to listen.

The performance was breathtaking, truly an entering into Your presence, Lord. Can any instrument surpass a harp in bringing down the glory? I was entranced. And I wanted one.

As the last tones lingered and faded into an awed silence, the harpist, Solomon, and I kept still for a long moment. Then in unison, Solomon and I arose and bowed to him. The harpist arose and bowed to us. We all sat again, still not speaking.

Finally, Solomon turned to me, "Well, Mother?" he asked.

"Oh, yes," I answered, "it is superior in tone."

"You shall have one!" Solomon exclaimed. "I was sure you would hear the difference. Thank you," he added to the harpist, "Would you mind if the King's Mother were to try your instrument?"

I gasped. The harpist spoke instantly and firmly, "I would be honored, King Solomon," bowed again, and brought the beautiful instrument up the six steps to me.

I arranged the harp, stroking the smooth wood as my gaze followed the grain and color of it. Then I bent over it and focussed my mind and my fingers. I played the best I ever have. He was better, but I was good. I sang the psalm as I played. When I had finished, they both kept a respectful silence until the harpist said, "You have the talent, your majesty. Excellent playing. You must have such an instrument."

Solomon thanked and dismissed him and turned to me with shining eyes and his special smile. "I am pleased to be able to give to you, Mother, who have given so much to   me.

This simple speech pleased me as much as the gift itself, which will be some time in coming. I can wait. I realize that workmanship takes time when the result is this special.

You have given me so much that is the best, dear Lord. How is it so, I cannot stop to wonder. I just bow before You and thank You.

Today, I've just returned from a walk through the temple area with Ruth and the girls, Tapheth now 8 and Basmath 6. I am pondering how the girls are growing, right along with the temple construction. Its progress is an important part of their childhood impressions, its beauty increasing as does theirs, and entering into their very souls in the strength of inspiration that comes from this place, surely unique on earth.

As is inevitable, given such a surrounding every day of their lives, these are uncommon girls. There is no frivolity in their actions. They are not just small adults, they are still children; but there is nothing silly or reprehensible in them. The servants all confirm this estimation of them, so that I am assured it is not just the grandmother's prejudice that proclaims them as unique as their environment. Would that either of them were able to ascend the throne after her father. For no son has followed them. Ruth is untroubled by the fact. Such faith she has! Solomon is still absorbed in the completion of the temple, which is probably only about a year off, as well he might be, for it is an absorbing task, so much is involved in organizing supplies and foremen, keeping up on details. Even though all are delegated, he wants to know everything that is happening, make sure it all comes together according to the vision and the plan.

I myself am quite caught up in this vision as well. I am so thankful to be living in these times, to live to see being done what David longed to do. He would be so pleased. I know he looks down from heaven and rejoices. He must be as proud of Solomon as I am. And as gratified by the marriage of Solomon and Ruth.

Meanwhile, Rehoboam is eleven and the only heir yet to the throne. Solomon has built and kept all the lands David conquered, and everything he does strengthens the extent and the solidarity of this kingdom. To whom will it all pass? I leave it to You, Lord. It is all I can do.

Oh, Father Lord, the moment is almost upon us, the moment I have dreamed of for so many years. Solomon is walking in a glory cloud, his every thought some detail of the preparation for the Dedication of the Temple. Except for our weekly meetings, I see him only at our psalms and prayers before the girls go to bed. Ruth does not see much more of him, but she is as ecstatic as he for the celebration. "What if God sends down His fire to consume the first offering on the great altar, just as he did in Moses' and Aaron's day?" she asked in wonder as she set the figure of the high priest into the court of the model temple she and Solomon have used to show the girls what is being built and what each part means.

The girls have caught the enthusiasm from their parents. It's not just the special dresses they will wear at the ceremonies. These girls know You, Lord, as much as their tender age allows, and more than many who are much older. I pray that half the people who come know half as much of the significance of what is happening here in Jerusalem these days.

Solomon has had classes for the priests of the outlying towns and villages in all twelve tribes, making sure they understand what they are to instruct the people. God, You require a people repentant over their sins as they offer their sacrificial lambs. But You've allowed for our human nature in the gathering together to repent in unison, as families, as tribes, and as a nation set apart by our having received the Law--not to mention the feasting, the music, and the glory of the gold all over the beautiful building that is our Temple. All our senses will confirm for us the message for our spirits. You are a great God and have greatly blessed us beyond our deserving. My anticipation builds and builds. All our hopes and dreams are in You. And our memories.

My memories, how precious they are to me. Could I ever forget Solomon bending to the girls' level, holding the priest figure over the Temple model, the girls rapt with attention to him and his words, following where he pointed, as he spoke with intensity, "The priest has twelve precious stones on his ephod here, one for each tribe. Here is the one for our tribe, Judah. Out of our tribe, girls, will come the promised Messiah, Lion of the tribe of Judah, Who will come as the Lamb of God."

Here Basmath giggled, and Tapheth asked, "How can a lion be a lamb, Daddy?"

"He is a lion because he rules, as a lion rules the jungle. He's a lamb because He'll be the sacrifice for our sins. He'll go to the altar, just as we'll put our lambs on the altar, after shedding His blood, just as we'll shed the blood of our lambs. 'The life is in the blood.' God should in justice take OUR lives for our sins against His holiness. But He made a way for justice to be done. The lamb is our substitute, taking our place, giving his life that ours may be spared. That's how Messiah will fulfill the altar."

Solomon kept his intensity and the girls' attention as he moved the priest figure out of the court and into the Holy Place, over to the Table of Showbread. "Here's a loaf for each tribe, offered to God to show that He gives us the bread we eat each day to keep us alive. Messiah will be our bread, spiritually our life."

He moved the priest figure to the Altar of Incense. "The incense rises to heaven in smoke and aroma to show that our prayers rise to God and are sweet-smelling to Him. Messiah is to be the way we may offer our prayers to a holy God out of our sinfulness, because He will satisfy God's justice and remove our guilt and shame as he removes our sins."

He moved the priest figure again. "The Golden Lampstand here has seven lights, one on each branch. The oil is to be kept refreshed each day to make sure the light never goes out. Messiah is our light, showing us truth and the way to live, never dimming.

"Why are there seven lamps, Daddy?"

"That's a good question. I know you girls like numbers. I'll tell you one part of it at least. Messiah combines earth and all it holds, including us, symbolized by the number four--for the four elements and the four directions--with heaven, symbolized by the number three for the Father, Son and Holy Spirit. Messiah will be both man and God."

He sighed. "Now, girls, what is beyond this curtain?" He pointed to the beautiful curtain of linen on the model, with its embroidery of red, blue, and gold.

They whispered in unison, "The Holy of Holies."

"Who   enters   here?"

"The high priest, Zadok."

"Is he a perfect man?" Solomon asked.

Again the girls giggled, stopping themselves quickly and regaining their wide-eyed composure. Zadok has been to dinner. "No, he's just a man like any other man."

"Why is he appointed to go into the Most Holy Place?"

"God appointed the sons of Aaron the Levite to be priests, and he is head of all of Aaron's descent."

"But I am king!" Solomon made a fake but dramatic protest.

"King and priest are separate offices, Daddy, you know that!" Tapheth responded vigorously. "YOU can't go into the Holy Place!" She was shocked, but seeing his face, she added, "I know you never would think of it. You're just saying that to make us think."

"Very good, young scholar! You are aware of the appointment and anointing of God for various offices. Messiah will fill them all. He will be our King, our Priest, and--what's the other office?"

"Prophet, like old Nathan and his son, Zabud, your counsellor, Daddy."

"We know his girls!" Tapheth piped up.

"Right again. Now, back to the high priest here. In the Temple here, Zadok's been overseeing the other priests as they offer sacrifices for the people's sins every day on the Altar of Burnt Offering, and as they light the incense each morning and evening, and replace the Showbread once a week, eating the stale loaves. He's made sure the oil never runs out in the Golden Lampstand and the light burns perpetually--all in the Holy Place. But he's going into the Most Holy Place only once a year, on the Day of Atonement. What's that, Basmath?"

"That's when all the sins of all the people for the whole year are to be placed on the scapegoat who goes off into the wilderness, and then a lamb is killed and Zadok takes that lamb's blood into the Holy of Holies to God, and God declares EVERYBODY clean to start a new year."

"Then how long is it before we start sinning again?"

Tapheth clapped her hands over her mouth and Basmath rolled her eyes and said, "About five minutes, maybe."

Softly Solomon asked, "We need a Savior, don't we?" Both girls shook their heads Yes, dark eyes solemn, and thick, dark curls bouncing.

"Yes, the Altar of Burnt Offering is always busy. 'Man is born to sin as the sparks fly upwards'. So, the Temple goes on until Messiah comes. But, back to the Day of Atonement. The high priest offers the blood upon the Ark of the Covenant with the golden cherubim bowing and spreading their wings over all, right on the Mercy Seat, the lid of the Ark." He pointed to the pure gold Ark in the model.

"And God has mercy," Tapheth spoke softly.

Solomon rose. "May all the children of Israel have as much understanding of all that the Temple is for," he spoke as a prayer and a blessing.

And to the girls he added, "Pray for Messiah to come, Tapheth, Basmath."

"We do, Daddy. And we pray Mommy is mother of Messiah."

Solomon was startled into silence, shared a long look with Ruth, and then motioned the girls to come to him. The hugs were exchanged without words, and the girls sent to bed with their attendants before anyone spoke again.

"Ruth, did you know of their prayers, for you to be mother of Messiah?"

She shook her head wonderingly and her eyes misted over. "No," she whispered. He went to her and held her close to him, as I slipped out.

Yes, my memories will stay with me forever.

Lord God Almighty, woe be to me, or any in Israel, if we can harbor any doubts after seeing Your fire come down from heaven, as in the distant day of Moses and

Aaron, fulfilling Ruth's prophetic hope. Oh, how the people fell to their knees as one. How strong was the aura of worship over the whole congregation. How silent the crowd, even little children and babies unable to speak after the first rush of sighing. Only the crackling of the holy fire, the sound of Your divine making, broke the stillness.

How long we were prostrate before You, I do not know. Then out of the stillness arose the magnificent music, today celestial, as the host of musicians and vocalists in their colorful uniforms brought to fruition their labor in rehearsals and received Your blessed touch upon their efforts. I thought of David and knew he was blessed that those appointed to make earth's best music to Your honor were rising surely almost to the level of the music he must be hearing--or making--in heaven.

And how David must have thrilled to hear the words of Solomon's prayer as Your anointing fell on him, too. I will never forget: "But will God indeed dwell on earth? behold the heaven and heaven of heavens cannot contain thee; how much less this house that I have builded.   ... thou, even thou only, knowest the hearts of all the children of men. ... there hath not failed one word of all his good promise, which he promised by the hand of Moses his servant."

You spoke to all our hearts through Solomon today.

Everything was joy and harmony, exuberance and concord all this livelong day. I know it will be so all the days of this feasting. Perhaps, just perhaps, going home again, changed by all that's been experienced here in Jerusalem, people will forget how to argue or misunderstand or hurt one another, and the goodness will be caught by those who stayed home. People cannot continue the same after experiencing the power of God.

It is my finest hour, the climax and culmination of my life's hopes, to have been a part of the construction and now the dedication of Your temple, to see Your people worshipping as one, repenting and adoring You amidst every form of splendor. If David could have lived to see it all, standing and falling prostate beside me--that would have been perfection. But I know that he saw from where he is; and more than once during the worship, especially when his psalms were sung, his presence was almost as real to me as if he had been physically beside me.

How grateful I am that my highest moment comes in my aging. How vulnerable must be those whose most glorious achievement comes in youth or early maturity. For Solomon I pray that he may keep the faith of this great hour, not necessarily to live on a pinnacle--that would be ridiculous, but to carry into the valley experience a new strength and discipline based on the reality within this pinnacle experience. You've promised him wisdom. He will need it, as life moves past this special time. Hard as it is to imagine just now, even the gold which covers this temple will shine less upon the people's imaginations as the years go by and its newness becomes sameness.

Before Messiah comes, the people's hearts may be dull, even with such a temple, such music, and the divine fire that will never be allowed to go out upon the Altar of Burnt Offering and the Altar of Incense. God, pierce our hearts if we begin to grow dull. Bring our Messiah before we grow beyond expecting Him.

One week has passed since the end of the celebrations. Today I met with Solomon as King's Mother to go over the records. I am amazed at the wealth that is being amassed, that is being spent on our household itself, let alone all around the kingdom, the chariot cities, everything. Increase seems endless.

Now, instead of the temple plans, we look over the plans for Solomon's palace, Ruth's palace, and the House of the Forest of Lebanon, where Solomon will hear cases in the Judgment Hall. I am glad there is still construction going on, to be superintended. He is so involved that I wonder what will happen when it is all built, no more construction plans to be studied, foremen to be supervised, details to oversee. Not that there will be no occupation, for there are always matters internal and international to be addressed by any monarch. But something always being constructed occupies his imagination in a way that other matters cannot. He is planning extensive gardens along with the buildings, loving the plants and animals of Your creation with such fervor as he does.

Always in my mind, but never expressed, behind any discussion with Solomon, lies the matter of the succession. As Tapheth and Basmath approach marriage age, the lack of a son to follow him comes into sharper focus. He is already speaking of the likely men to marry his daughters, leaders of high character and equally high standing. As David received Your promise of steadfast love to his offspring forever, I have no ultimate fear for any of my children or grandchildren, and so on through all generations. But Lord, is it not time for Solomon to be given an heir? A godly heir, a worthy heir, an heir after Your own heart?

Meanwhile, we speak of revenue and expenditures. And Solomon is as devoted to Ruth as ever. Bless their union with a son, Father Lord. I come boldly because of Your promise of a king in the line of David perpetually, even though my cup of blessings overflows beyond any poor deserving of mine. I think You would not forbid me so to entreat You. I think I ask according to Your will.

I'm stopping to take a deep breath after a very busy period of time.

Almost all the construction is completed now and Ruth is moving into her own palace, alone except for her servants. Basmath's wedding to Ahimaaz and move to Naphtali followed closely after Tapheth's marriage to Ben-Abinadab and move to Napheth-dor. The weddings and the move to her new palace have taken much planning and attention. When things settle down for Ruth, I expect it will also settle down upon her and Solomon that there is not another pregnancy. As I walk with Ruth daily and talk about what is in our hearts, as we always have, this subject is sure to come up soon, with her children gone to their adult situations now.

You certainly waited a long time to fulfill the promise to Abraham and Sarah. What faith and patience You worked into them before the child of promise arrived! May I, may Solomon and Ruth, likewise be purified, till we walk in trust. That is Your heart's desire for Your children, that we simply trust You.

Today, I sensed a tension in Solomon as I never have before in our weekly business meetings. There are no more construction plans to look over. After showing me the financial records, he rolled the last scroll and tapped it on the arm of his throne before stacking it with the others, frowning and sighing unconsciously as he did so.

"You may as well be told, Mother," he began without looking at me, but staring across the room and speaking woodenly, without expression in his voice or face. "My counsellors are bringing before me eligible maidens from the kingdoms we have conquered or entered into alliance with, seeing that Ruth has borne no son."

He did not pause as I stiffened, willing not to allow any of my shock to escape my control so as to be noticed by him.

"There is a princess of Ammon, there is a nobleman's daughter in Moab, there is a young Sidonian beauty whose father controls a fleet of merchant ships. Any or all of these could bear me a son, they say. No one is backing Rehoboam, as he has not the makings of a king in him--far from it. I would not speak to any of them what I speak now only to you, and not even to Ruth."

He now for the first time since the business talk was done, turned to face me. "I no longer believe the problem is with Ruth. For whatever reason, I believe that I am unable.." His voice broke only slightly and he quickly regained composure. "I don't believe I will ever be a father again."

He searched my eyes as he watched me absorb what he had said; and as shocked as I was, I noted that he himself was absorbing what he had said, seeking to grasp the enormity of its implications, as he watched me doing the same thing.

Finally he looked off again, staring across the room and out into infinity. "To the counsellors, I only said, 'Abraham and Sarah created great trouble, even to this day, by going ahead of God, to get an heir by human conniving.' " He spoke his last sentence one word at a time, emphasizing every word. " 'I do not wish to do that.' "

He stared for a long time. My heart stood still.

He turned to me again. "But, you can see that I am, in a great sense, but a tool in their hands, king or not. How long can I put them off? They will never believe that I cannot produce offspring, even if I told them that I believe such to be the case. I appear young and strong, still in the prime of life. But as I begin aging, they will keep insisting. And I have no one to support me in the conviction that I would have only Ruth for my wife. You, of course, are the exception, but not a strong enough force to counteract the unified counsel of all the others."

He stared off once more, saying finally, "It does not help that I had the Ammonitess before I became king. That was a mistake because it was wrong. I did not know then what I do now, after my union with Ruth. I neither need nor want any other. I would not, even if I knew I could still father another son. It will be Rehoboam, no matter how many wives they force upon me. For I know that they will prevail. You can see how they will. All is vanity."

He fell forward, wrapping his hands around his head as if it pained him. "I have cried before the Lord, but I am beyond tears now," he spoke hoarsely. "Even if Ruth would have me after I go in to other wives, I would not defile her in this way. I will lose her. Nothing can ever take the place of the love we have known, so special. God forgive me if He seems far from me now and not as strong as He ought to be."

I fell before his throne and wrapped my arms around his legs at the knees, and knelt there until a messenger came in and Solomon was instantly the self-contained ruler as I hurried to exit.

Today is the beginning of my dying. I know it. I cannot live to see what is to become of Solomon.

Today, Lord, I had determined to ask audience with Solomon again, when instead his servant appeared, summoning me to his side.

"Mother," he said, rising and descending the six steps with his hands toward me, taking my hands in his and ascending to the thrones with me, "Mother, I had to see you. I have been before the Lord all night. Let God be true and every man a liar, I will not leave it with you as I last spoke yesterday. God is altogether just. For one thing, His promise will be kept: Rehoboam is in the line of David, my father. It is my own sin--" he raised his hands emphatically to block my protest. "It is my own sin that resulted in Rehoboam's birth. Young as I was at the time I succumbed to the union with his mother, I was not too young to know. I had been well taught. I am aware that you have thought my father to be the one who arranged it all. But it was done before he knew, arranged by counsellors. Now I see that they were in the political opposition to my ascension to the throne, seeking to discredit me in my father's eyes that he might come into

Adonijah's cause against me. As soon as it was done, they informed him. I can still hear him saying, 'Better your mother think that I fell back into old habits and arranged this than to think that you did not heed what we taught.' He begged me with tears to leave off and never see her again. I complied, but it was too late. She was carrying Rehoboam, that quickly."

I sat sidewards in my throne, both hands gripping the armrest closest to his throne, filled with tension even though in one sense relieved. "Solomon, I am so glad you told me. It was a great wounding to my heart to think that your father approved or even proposed your liaison with the Ammonitess. But I have now to realize that it was you and that is as great, though a different, pain. We tried to teach you."

"Yes, and you DID teach me. But I did not learn what marriage can be, even with your marriage as my lifetime example, until I wed Ruth. Then I found what my father found when he wed you. Before Ruth, it was all abstraction to me, true, but not personal reality. I thought I'd found what God made marriage union to be very early on in my life. But it was not early enough."

He gave a great sigh. He'd been turned sidewards in his throne, too, facing me as I faced him. Now he shifted and sat square in the throne, looking ahead. And such a look as was in his eyes! Affliction, pain, depth, wisdom. Even courage.

He turned his head toward me. "God is just in all His ways. Whatever illness it was, He allowed it to affect my body. Rehoboam will be king because there will be no more children from this body. When I can no longer put off the counsel to take foreign wives, I will leave Ruth, the only wife of my heart, not because I want to, but because the meaning will be gone. Neither of us would have any respect for the other if I went back and forth from her to other wives. You know that. The unity will be gone. We would no longer be 'one flesh' as Moses says. I will be living a lie one day. God knows I've put them off already a long time, and I'll put them off as much longer as I can. Ruth must be told what is coming, but I cannot do that."

I knew what was next before he said it.

"Mother, will you prepare her? I think our last months, or years if that can be, will be the sweetest, despite the bitterness of the coming loss. Anyway, the girls were able to have their entire upbringing in such a union as I myself knew when I grew through boyhood to young manhood. They will know how to make such homes. I made sure of the character of their husbands by much investigation. They will be all right, and their children. They won't like hearing what I do, but it won't shape their character. And perhaps they will understand that I am a pawn in the hands of my council."

He shook himself as in waking from a reverie. "In any case, Mother, do you understand what I ask of you? Will you do it? Or will you require it of me to break the news to Ruth? I trust you to make clear to her my heart in all this, as a man, and my helplessness, as king."

"I can do it. I think I see why you would rather it be myself than you, for the sake of the time you have left with her being as a continuum with the way you've lived all along with her. I think I see, but I am not sure. I must take it to the Lord. I will ask audience again when I hear from Him."

"Yes, that is fair, only fitting and proper. You must be sure before you do something you would later regret."

"My dear Mother," he breathed out as we rose and he knelt before me for a hug as if he were my little boy once again. I stood and held him ever so long, thankful that he'd dismissed all attendants and asked that they not knock for any reason, until summoned again.

Here we were on the throne platform of the ruler of this vast land, wealthy and wise beyond any king before or to come, commanding and it is done, able to have anything it occurs to him to want. But cruelly at the mercy of lesser men who have no concept of the larger picture, cruelly and inevitably moved by others toward what is most unwelcome to him.

A sinner brought down by one slip.

His heart is pure now. Can he stay pure in heart, after doing what he will be doing one day? I hardly see how, but I leave that with You. My heart is breaking as it is, and I cannot begin to imagine Solomon's future, or I am dead before my destiny.

God, You know I do desire to live to fulfill all You planned for me, yet I would not be here to see Solomon's fall, if You can have mercy on me to go to You before it begins.

In the meantime, if You will, I will tell Ruth. May it be on one of our walks, and--YES--may we be right beside the Holy Place, or as near as we can get without being arrested by Temple Guards. I know one. He will arrange it, I am sure.

Wait! I not only know a Temple Guard, I know the King! Solomon will arrange that we may stand in the courtyard just outside the Most Holy Place for our communication.   He can even arrange for us to be escorted there by that guard and protected from discovery or dismissal, for this one time when we need to be near the Presence in every possible way.

Thank You, Lord. Now, help me. I throw myself on Your mercy. Myself and my dear Ruth.

God, it is done. Your Presence was there. What a precious daughter You have given me in my daughter-in-law. She heard me out, then, turning her tear-laden eyes toward me, with radiance glowing from her face, said softly, "I know, dear Mother. I have known that this was coming. Do you know, I saw even as a child, that my father, though the powerful pharoah of all Egypt, nevertheless was at times--not often, mind you, but at times--in the clutches of political forces that turned him against his will. My mother saw, and spoke to us children until we saw, too. She wanted no illusions in our heads as to what it means to be royalty, what it means to rule a mighty people. She rightly reasoned that if we knew the pressures, we would not be spoiled--or shocked, but grateful and wise, able to cope."

She leaned back against the wall, inside which was the Ark of the Covenant, with the gold cherubim over it and the tablets of stone inside, as if she would draw near the Presence. She lifted her lovely face toward the south, and the sun's rays set off her features to perfection, as well as her near-perfect figure.

Placing her hands on her abdomen, with her eyes closed and a gentle smile on her lips, she continued speaking, as to herself. She is always genuinely herself, but to me, and I am sure even more to Solomon, she reveals depths that are guarded from others. Sweetly, softly, she continued. "I thank God every day for my life, for Solomon and the girls, for you as a mother-in-law filling the place of my faraway mother, for being the wife of the wisest man who ever ruled a nation, wise and kind and good. I know him, I know his heart, I know what he would do if there were not awful pressures on him to produce a worthy heir and undo the damage of his youthful sin. Never doubt him, dear Bathsheba." She opened her eyes and looked into mine. "Shall I tell you what he is doing? Yes, I will."

She turned to lean against the wall facing me, and I leaned facing her.

"He is writing proverbs. Hundreds of them. Many of them are counsel to a young man to love the wife of his youth, to avoid the snares of seductive, loose women. One day, these will all be part of the literature of God's chosen people, and will guide the lives of young men and old, for generations."

Tears came to my eyes and hers responded with a like flow as our souls came nearer than we ever have.

"When he is gone, the good counsel of these days of his life with me will live on and do much good in many lives. For such a man, I will lay down my life. I will do everything I can to make his life sweeter and sweeter day by day, until the parting must come."

She sighed and fell quiet. In a few minutes she shook her head Yes several times with lips compressed in determination. "And when he is gone from me, I will pray for his soul. He's right, strange women lead a man to his own destruction. I will pray he is not destroyed."

"I, too. And I will pray YOU are not destroyed, dear Ruth," I promised her, "until my dying day."

"Oh, most blessed mother-in-law of mine, it is not for myself I am concerned, but for those poor young princesses who will not know a husband's love, who are to be used in a political scheme, without regard for their souls' needs and yearnings. They are the ones to be pitied. I have been rich in all that counts. Nothing that comes after can erase the record, not in history, not in my heart."

In one accord, we knelt and prayed of these matters so close to our hearts. We rose and hugged each other.

After our embrace, I summoned the guard, who had stood at a discreet distance as we had talked; and he escorted us back to the Women's Court and bid us a good day, with a bow and a salute.

We walked back to her palace, and she left me with a quick, light step, a smile and a wave.

I walked around for quite some time before coming back home, going over all that had happened, and praising You for making it possible: sweetness in the midst of pain, fellowship in the midst of aloneness.

Great God, I love You.

But I AM alone. Solomon and Ruth are making their union and their memories to sustain them when he must go the way he's being advised to go. My children have all made their places in life. My grandchildren are growing up far away from me, and soon there will be great-grandchildren. The generations keep coming, and it is time for mine to pass on.

There is no more advice needed. Solomon's wealth has grown until it is beyond what I could have ever guessed it would be. I have sat on his latest and finest throne-platform beside him and watched with the gold-plated lions sitting at each end of the six steps, as emissaries of many foreign kings brought their tribute. The ones I witnessed were but a fragment of all who came. The wealth I actually saw presented to him staggered my mind.

The latest of these monarchs is still here, giving homage to the wisdom and wealth of Solomon, the Queen of Sheba. Her own servant retinue was impressive enough, but his surpasses hers in number and in the elaborate and colorful liveries they wear when serving. Solomon answered her many questions in many fields of study. His breadth of knowledge exceeds hers, but it takes a mind as lively as hers to ask the questions and understand the answers, as she clearly does.

One session between the two of them was enough for me. I desire to see no more of this homage and adulation of Solomon. He is wise. He is wealthy. He is blessed of God in so many ways. But how long will he stay wise if he hears himself extolled so profusely, even if so far he gives the glory to God?

All things are conspiring to bring him down.

I have seen the fulfillment of my greatest dreams for my family and nation. I now see the seeds of decline being planted. Take me before the crop is harvested. God, take me as You take the glory from this king and kingdom. I want to be gone before Solomon acts foolishly. I am ready to go.

Old and full of years, Bathsheba died
peacefully in her sleep,
with Solomon and Ruth at her bedside
bidding her farewell and
hearing the angels' chorus as the flutter of
angels' wings
carried her home to her eternal felicity and
rest. Beside her
tomb, they planted a tiny wildflower which
still produces, each
season, its delicate bloom with the tiny purple
stripe, the color
of royalty.

By Ronda Scott Sherrill

www.ingramcontent.com/pod-product-compliance
Lightning Source LLC
Chambersburg PA
CBHW070801120726
47910CB00001B/256